AI MONSTERS ARE HERE

Thirteen Spooky Tales

Written by
AARON RAY BALLARD

Illustrated by Rusty Edwards

Copyright © 2022 Aaron Ray Ballard
All rights reserved
First Edition

PAGE PUBLISHING
Conneaut Lake, PA

First originally published by Page Publishing 2022

ISBN 978-1-6624-1941-6 (pbk)
ISBN 978-1-6624-1942-3 (digital)

Printed in the United States of America

To Mom,
the one and only

CONTENTS

Eden 1
Confession 107
Charlie 127
Hunter 153
Nomad 173
Unsub 203
Under the Influence 223
The Night Crew 247
A Vampire Walks into a Bar 259
I Suspect 283
Ghost Hunt 301
First Girl 325
Night of the Living 331
Acknowledgments 371

*Monsters are real,
and ghosts are real too.
They live inside us,
and sometimes, they win.*

—Stephen King

EDEN

On a remote island miles off the Texas coast, smoke began to rise and drift in the wind from a dense canopy of trees near its center.

Wave after wave of clear seawater bombarded the white sandy shore, each time creeping a little further toward the tree line and retreating in a spray of hissing white foam.

Adam, his legs moving as if they were filled with lead, staggered his way through the foliage while carrying a well-used machete. He lumbered across the sand until falling to his knees, exhausted, unable to walk any further.

His dingy white shirt was torn in places, and his face and arms were stained with blood. He stared down at the machete. It, too, was wet with gore. Not wanting to hold it any longer, he dropped it to the sand and wiped his face while keeping his eyes on the horizon.

As he eyed the deep rippling waters eternally coming in and going back, his thoughts drifted to another time and place. A half smile slowly formed on his face.

"Take a look at how beautiful the world is," he said.

He unfurled his legs and sat down on the sand with a series of grunts that belied his age.

He was twenty-six but looked much older. His face was weathered by the sun. His scruffy facial hair barely passing for a beard. His haunted, deep-set blue eyes filled to the brim with tears.

*****

Stan had predicted that a big storm was coming. But since his rudimentary weather predictions were hit-and-miss at best, no one paid him much mind at the time.

Four days later, everyone was scrambling around like chickens with their heads cut off.

We'd spent most of the day tying down everything that could possibly move. All in a last-ditch effort to make sure our shelters were stable enough to withstand the coming tempest.

As I walked across the beach with the sun past its high point, I saw Linda making a sandcastle with her four-year-old daughter, Eve. They were doing so in spite of the wind blowing sand in their faces and the increasing threat of the waves as they crashed to the shore.

Mother and daughter both glanced up at me as I walked by, and the smile Linda had for her daughter disappeared. Eve, however, smiled and waved at me like I was her best friend and yelled my name over the wind.

"Adam!"

I grinned and waved back at her, then saw her mother turning away from me.

Linda appeared angry, lost in thought, while constantly trying to keep her hair from blowing across her delicate face.

I knew what was going on in that head of hers. She wasn't the only one with those thoughts. I didn't blame her or the rest of them. Still, it was hard not to take it personally.

I turned away from Linda and Eve on the beach and entered a clearing in the tree line that led to our shelters.

As I strolled, I glanced up at the darkening sky, knowing the storm was only a few hours away.

Most of us were positive it was going to be a "doozy," which was a Stan word if there ever was one.

*****

For the islanders, storms have made for difficult times.

When they first arrived here almost five years ago, they made crude shelters built in equal parts haste and desperation.

At first, they only wanted them to be just enough to help them stay dry during the rains. But after their first island storm when Mother Nature had welcomed them to their new home with all her fury and might, she had taken everything they had built with her.

Learning from that mistake, their next set of living quarters were much better in construction but still not much to look at. But after the next storm came and went, it didn't leave much behind either. It took two years of failure on the island to get it right. So far as they knew. Their huts—structures made of bamboo and thick branches—were still not much to look at, but they were sturdy and safe, and that's all that counted.

This was all thanks to a happy discovery.

They'd found that if they peeled away long strips of palm tree husks, they could use this flexible material like rope to bind their bamboo and branches together.

Once they had effective shelter accomplished, they tried their best to make their island habitats as much like their former homes as they could. Or what those places represented.

Little touches of their past lives were evident, but only if one looked hard enough. They'd only had what few clothes and personal items they had the presence of mind to take with them during the chaos of their escape from the mainland. A photo here. Some jewelry there. What clothes they could carry. It wasn't much, but it had to do.

The majority of their time on the island was spent living day to day with nothing to do but ensure their continued survival. They fished. They collected coconuts and berries. They ate any island birds they could catch. They tended to all scrapes and cuts as best they could without medicine or even the most basic medical supplies, because infection out here meant certain death. They boiled the water from a running water source found inside a cave deep within the island. They even had a trusty flint rock to start fires that once belonged to a man who had saved them all but had lost his life in the process.

The only thing that made their situation tolerable was the knowledge they could never go back to where they came from. They were stranded here, and as far as they knew, there was no one else out there who could save them, and most likely, there was nothing to go back to.

Civilization, as they knew it, was gone. They figured they might be the only humans left. But even if there were more survivors out there somewhere, it's not as if the islanders could pick up and leave the island in search of them.

This island was their truth. It was their reality. They had accepted it when they crashed here.

All they could do now was survive. And that's all they were trying to do.

*****

As I approached the hut that housed the Duncan family, I could see husband and father Lloyd using flexible palm tree husks to secure their hut.

I paused and waited for him to register that I was there while standing out of sight behind him.

It took longer than I expected.

Since starting over on the island, we all had to learn to work and live together if we were going to stand any chance of staying alive. But it quickly became apparent to the rest of us that the Duncans preferred doing things on their own.

Despite this, we kept trying to include them in everything we did and offering our help to them whenever we could. We'd hoped against hope that they'd eventually realize the error of their ways and start to trust us and be kind in return. But that day never happened.

Their open distrust of others and their hostility and ungratefulness made them difficult to be around. And it hadn't taken long to realize this had more to do with Lloyd's wife than Lloyd himself. But he wasn't blameless. He'd played his part.

Lloyd was a man who never took chances because that meant opening himself up to failure. He always knew where he stood and never put himself into situations where he was unsure. He never wanted to appear foolish or admit he was wrong. He expected the people around him to feel and think the same way he did. He was a man who once had his life planned out to the millisecond and woe to anyone who made it go off the tracks even for just a brief moment.

But the cosmic joke was on him.

A lifetime ago, when I was a confused, angry, impressionable teenager, I was worried about taking my SATs. After all, this test was going to shape my future and perhaps even decide my path in life. My stomach was in knots, my brain was fried, and I couldn't keep a single thought in my head.

That was when my wise grandmother told me that if man wanted to make God laugh, all he had to do was make a plan.

After what had happened to our former lives, it was obvious that God still had his sense of humor.

When Lloyd finally saw my shadow, it caused him to hesitate. In that brief instant, his shoulders noticeably sagged. The weight of the world was too much for him, and he gave in. But before that hopeless feeling could settle in to fester and overstay its welcome, he shoved it away.

Lloyd straightened back up, and without turning to face me, he said, "It won't be much longer now."

He wasn't talking about the storm.

Inside the hut, his daughter, Amy, two months shy of her fifth birthday, was wasting away on her bed. A strange fever had come upon her less than a week before. Having no way to properly treat her, we could do nothing but pray, hope, and wait for her to pull out of her fever or succumb to it.

A couple of days before, we thought our prayers had worked, and the fever had broken. But sadly, that wasn't the case. Now, we all knew in our hearts that it was only a matter of time before Amy, as we knew her, would be gone.

As Lloyd headed toward his hut, a thought occurred to me, and I had to suppress a smile before he saw it and took offense or misconstrued it. I had remembered why I nicknamed the Duncan hut the Taj Mahal.

It was a running joke between the rest of us.

Their hut was the first stable structure we'd built on the island, once we'd figured out what we were doing. Its size dwarfed the rest of our shelters, which were barely big enough for two at most. But when it came time for the Duncans to return the favor and help the rest of us build our future homes, they refrained.

I shoved those thoughts away as Lloyd opened the rickety door to his home. Without even a glance back at me, he went inside, and I followed.

As my eyes adjusted to the darkness, I peered around the hut. I could make out Lloyd's wife, Nora. She was facing away from me while sitting in a corner with her back against the wall.

The atmosphere in the hut, like electric current reaching out to envelop me, told me that she'd been crying. Even though I couldn't see her facial features, I felt her harsh eyes judging me, holding me in contempt.

In all this time on the island, Nora and I were hardly what anyone would call friends. Our relationship had always been strained no matter how much effort I put into trying to find common ground between us.

I knew deep down in my heart this effort of mine was a lost cause because her ill feelings toward me had everything to do with what had happened the first time we'd met.

I had slapped her.

Our first day together only got worse from there.

All these years later, she still hadn't forgiven me.

I'm not proud of some of my actions that day, but I felt and still feel most of them had to be done. But Nora not only held on to her grudges, she fed them, watered them, and willed them to grow.

Despite her chilly behavior toward me, I didn't hate her. I was just confounded by her. I couldn't comprehend how someone could be that unforgiving, cold, and judgmental. It was beyond my scope of reason.

But now, as I stood there peering down at her, I now felt something new toward her.

Pity.

Because grief was something I did understand all too well. I reasoned that if I were in her shoes, I'd probably feel the same way toward me right now. It was the same way Linda felt about me on the beach. The same way Lloyd must have felt standing in the hut behind me. After all, I wasn't here to be there for them. I was here for Amy. Or rather, I was here for what had to happen after her eventual death.

Amy's sickness was not only devastating to her family; it was difficult for all of us. Amy was our special gift. The first child born on the island, which at the time gave us the hope we so desperately needed to continue moving forward. Because of this, we felt that, in some way, she belonged to all of us.

Every time I saw her kind, angelic face, looking just like a kinder, tiny version of her mother's, I couldn't come up with any reasons how or why she had grown up to become as sweet and selfless as she was.

With influences like her parents, it seemed like a goddamn miracle.

As I stood there, I didn't say anything to Nora. Couldn't, actually. What was the point? Even though my purpose here was justified, I felt miserable all the same. But to her, my presence here was most unwanted and uninvited.

Right there and then, I couldn't argue with her about that.

The only person in the hut who seemed to appreciate my being here at all was Justin. But that had everything to do with the fact I was here to take his place on watch.

Justin was barely in his twenties but looked ten years older. This was thanks in large part to the white streaks throughout the hair on his head and face, the latter of which still looked rather boyish.

Without saying a word, Justin handed me a stained, slightly rusted machete and took his leave. He hardly spoke to any of us anymore, with the exception of Linda and Eve. The former was not his girlfriend, and the latter may not have been his daughter, but he could almost always be found following them around like a shadow.

Justin was careful to avoid eye contact with anyone in the hut as he left. He also avoided making physical contact with Lloyd, who was blocking most of the path to the doorway. Justin moved around him like the point guard he once was, letting in a brief moment of sunlight as he walked out the door.

As I approached Amy's bed made up of piles of leaves, I could hear the little girl's labored breathing. I took her tiny hand in mine, and her skin felt hot to the touch. This moved me to tears, but I didn't make a sound. I quickly wiped them away and hoped no one noticed.

As I knelt by Amy's bed, I set the machete down by my side away from her parents. Out of sight and out of mind, I hoped.

It was then that Amy stirred and opened her large crystal-blue eyes, a trait that neither of her parents shared. When she saw me, she struggled yet managed to whisper my name.

That use of energy zapped her strength, but somehow she still managed to smile that sweet smile of hers.

It took everything in me not to weep.

Sensing that Amy was awake, Lloyd and Nora approached her, kneeling beside her opposite me.

In the light, I could finally see Nora's face as she gave me a brief sideways glance. In that quick moment, I saw hate and disgust in her eyes.

For the first time since I met her, I could finally understand her hatred for me. Because for the next four hours, if Amy's life happened to slip away on my watch, the most horrendous task imaginable would fall square on my shoulders. Because I would be the one to give her a second death.

In this day and age, that was our new normal. One that had been twisted and shaped by the most nightmarish circumstances imaginable.

It seemed like a lifetime ago when our lives inexplicably changed. When the world as we knew it ceased to be. When little Amy was still inside her mother's womb and had the promise of a long, normal life. When most of us lived in nice neighborhoods, in fine houses surrounded by mowed green grass and white picket fences. When most of us went to our jobs and eventually came home to do whatever it was normal people once did.

All the while, the world passed us by, day after day, hour after hour, minute after minute, as we absentmindedly waited for another day to spend the exact same way. It was a time when we took life for granted. A time we foolishly thought was always going to remain the way it was.

But then the unexpected happened, and we woke up in a nightmare that we haven't been able to wake up from since.

On that day, for reasons no one truly knows, the dead began to walk the earth.

The early news reports touched off a wave of panic like no one had ever seen. The dead were attacking the living. One bite was all it took to make you like them. Like a plague, it spread.

Before anyone could truly comprehend what was happening, it was a worldwide pandemic. Anyone listening to those fearful voices on the radio or the shocked faces and videos on television and social media before it all went dark had to know man's dominance over the earth was at an end.

If they didn't then, they would soon find out.

Through sheer circumstances that day—Judgment Day, as our group soon started calling it—the eight lives now on this island had come together. Although there had once been more of us.

At the time, even though we all lived in the same town, we didn't know one another. But in the midst of all the panic, we'd found each other. By working together for the most part, we'd found a way to escape the chaos around us and ended up here.

Our goal was simple. Get to this island.

Our own Eden.

*****

When the world's nightmare began, Nora was eight months pregnant with what she and Lloyd didn't know at the time was a sweet present named Amy.

Through some miracle, they had managed to drive through the war zone in the streets.

Lloyd, despite knowing full well it was best to keep the car moving, braked to a stop anyway and let it idle on the street.

He'd found what he'd been searching for.

About a hundred yards away, obscured by the thick, dark smoke of burning vehicles, he saw a convenience store with several gas pumps in its deserted parking lot.

Lloyd sat in the driver's seat wiping desperation and sweat off his face. He glanced down at the near-empty fuel gauge looming before him like a death sentence, then moved his eyes back toward the pumps which were either their salvation or their ruin.

He mentally hedged his bets, thinking, *Perhaps the smoke will be enough cover to get some gas in the tank. Then we can get the hell out of dodge.*

It's either that or run out of gas later on. Fleeing this kind of madness on foot is not an option. Not in Nora's condition.

He glanced up at the rearview mirror toward his pregnant wife. She was lying down on the back seat. Had been since she first climbed back there when this whole ordeal started a few hours ago. She'd been too scared to do anything but cry and retreat within herself.

Glancing forward at the gas pumps, Lloyd thought, *Maybe the smoke is the only advantage we'll get.*

He gave a firm nod to his reflection in the rearview. Then, having made his decision, he mashed his foot down on the gas pedal.

He soon brought the car to a stop next to a gas pump and swiveled his head around to check on Nora.

"Honey," Lloyd said as he gently rubbed her belly, "I'm gonna get some gas. Lock the doors and don't let anybody in, okay?"

Not getting an answer, Lloyd pressed further.

"Nora, can you hear me? Lock the doors and don't let anybody in."

Between sniffs and sobs, Nora nodded.

Lloyd took a good look around before opening the doors and venturing out into the open.

As soon as he exited the car, Nora made sure the doors were locked. At the same time, her wild eyes looked everywhere for signs of those people. Whatever they were now.

Lloyd pushed his way through the unlocked entry door of the station and ran behind the counter. As he searched for a button, switch, or anything that would turn on the gas pumps, his panic level rose. Time was of the essence, and he could feel the pressure tie a knot in his back between his shoulder blades.

Gaining goose bumps with every noise outside no matter how slight or familiar, he pushed every button and flipped every switch he could find. Somehow, without knowing how, he managed to turn on the lights over the pumps. With no time to celebrate, he hopped the counter and ran back out the doors.

With stuttering steps, he came to a stop before the back of his car. After fumbling with the gas nozzle a bit, he started filling the tank. All the while, he reassured his wife through the back-side passenger window that everything was going to be okay.

When the recently deceased Michael Dugger appeared out of nowhere, Nora saw him first and screamed. This alerted Lloyd, who saw the man reflected in the store window coming up fast behind him.

Lloyd ran to the other side of the car before what was once Michael could get to him, but Michael heard Nora screaming inside the car.

Now fixated on Nora, Michael tried to get to her through the side window but discovered that the window was rolled up. In the recesses of his brain, he somehow remembered the door had handles.

Awkwardly, he tried pulling up one to open the door but found them locked.

While Michael's attention was placed solely upon getting to Nora inside the car, he didn't notice Lloyd running up behind him with the gas nozzle held in his hand like a gun.

Lloyd sprayed Michael with the gas, soaking him. Lloyd then used his lighter to set the creature aflame.

Michael screamed an inhuman wail, then flailed and tried to run. His charred body soon fell to the ground in a smoking, writhing heap.

Lloyd recovered from the shock of that attack. But he failed to notice another recently deceased man, once named Jim Laughlin, running through the smoke wafting across the street and coming up fast behind him.

Lloyd was fortunate. Another man who was very much alive named William Blake had seen the creature. With a loud report, Jim was blown back a few feet, hitting the pavement with part of his head missing.

With a ringing in his ears, Lloyd saw their savior in camouflage survival gear complete with a Mossberg shotgun resting on his hip. The man was standing in the back of an old black Dodge Ram 3500 Laramie dually extended cab.

The first words Lloyd heard coming out of Blake's mouth were loud: "Looks like I saved your bacon!"

This was also the moment when Lloyd met Adam, who drove the truck while Blake shot the dead. The large smile on Blake's face suggested he was having a good time.

Sincere to the core, Adam shouted to the couple, "You okay?"

It took a while for Lloyd to come around. "My wife. She's pregnant."

Blake smiled as he reloaded his shotgun with a few buckshot taken from an ammunition belt hanging across his chest. In a booming voice, he shouted, "That's the best news I've heard all day!"

Then Blake saw more of the creatures approaching from across the street and yelled, "Get in the truck! More bad news coming!"

Without hesitation, Blake locked and loaded the shotgun and opened fire on the approaching mob of creatures. Body parts exploded, and blood spattered as Blake's weapon did its damage but not enough to stop the rest of the horde from charging.

In the rearview mirror, Adam saw the creatures continue their mindless approach from a distance. One had its lower leg blown off causing it to collapse onto the street. It then began to use its arms and remaining leg to crawl toward them.

Adam looked over and saw the bald man, Lloyd, yelling for his wife to unlock the car doors. But the woman was much too frightened to be reasoned with.

Adam took another peek in the rearview, gauged the distance, then got out and ran toward the Duncans' car with an AR15 in hand.

Lloyd was pleading by now. "Please, honey, unlock the door!"

Nora didn't respond. She was holding her belly and screaming for the life of her baby.

Adam, no longer having the patience for this sort of thing, shoved Lloyd out of the way and brought the stock of the weapon down upon the side window.

The window shattered, showering Nora with glass. She continued screaming and pleading for her baby's life, maybe thinking Adam was one of those creatures. But one slap from Adam brought her back to the present.

Lloyd glared hard at Adam but didn't have long to boil.

Adam yelled, "Get her in the truck! Now!"

At that moment, Adam joined Blake in shooting the creatures until their weapons were empty, then they reloaded them and fired again. Their spent ammunition continued to do damage, but more and more creatures kept coming.

When Lloyd saw no end to the monsters in sight, doing what he was told seemed wise. He grabbed his wife, who wanted no part of him, and lifted her out of the back seat. As she kicked and screamed, he carried her toward the truck.

Once Nora realized she was within an arm's length of the safety of the truck's cab, she stopped protesting her rescue and yanked the door open. With a slight struggle due to panic, she pulled herself inside and slammed the door closed behind her, leaving Lloyd standing awkwardly on the outside looking in.

Adam grabbed Lloyd by the shoulder, causing Lloyd to jump, startled, and yell in fright, thinking he was being attacked.

Even though Adam was only a couple of feet away, he shouted when he asked, "Can you drive a stick?"

Quickly over his panic, Lloyd peered over Adam's shoulder and caught another eyeful of the approaching creatures.

Adam shook him by the shoulder and shouted, "Can you drive a stick?"

Lloyd's eyes met Adam's, and he replied, "Yeah."

"Then get to it!"

As Adam joined Blake in the bed of his truck, Lloyd ran around to the driver's side and jumped up into the cab. With Nora screaming in his ear and pummeling his body with clenched fists like the day's horrific events were his fault, Lloyd shifted the manual gears, and the truck lurched. The engine fell silent.

During the loss of momentum as the truck stalled out, Adam lost his footing and fell backward. But Blake managed to maintain his balance. At the same time, he caught Adam by the front of his pants before he fell out of the truck bed. Blake then yanked him back to his feet.

Behind them, a creature reached the truck and was about to climb aboard. But Blake turned and unloaded a single buckshot into its face. The back of the creature's head exploded outward like a busted piñata at a child's birthday party.

As the body fell to the street, Lloyd started the truck back up, shifted gears, and stepped off the clutch. He drove the truck out onto the street with the rest of the creatures still in pursuit.

Blake and Adam, yelling and screaming, full of adrenaline, continued firing into the crowd of creatures.

When Lloyd reached second gear, he created more space between them and their undead pursuers. By third gear, they were safe and well on their way.

To where, Lloyd didn't know. He just cared that he and his wife were moving again.

*****

After being alone in the hut with Amy for almost an hour, I was finally feeling close to relaxed. Most of this had to do with Lloyd taking Nora out for a walk three hours into my shift.

When they left the hut, most of the tension had left with them. But not all.

The pressure I was putting on myself was almost as bad.

Amy had not opened her eyes again since the moment I first came in. Her breathing had become more labored. She was slowly drifting away right in front of me, and there was nothing I could do about it.

The door to the hut opened, and I was relieved to see Stan. It was time for his watch now.

I stood up, feeling my knees crackle and pop, and waited for the blood to return to my legs. But the discomfort I felt right then was nothing compared to the heartache I saw in Stan's eyes as he sat down next to Amy and gently touched her forehead.

I said to him, "If something happens, let me know."

Stan raised his hand to let me know that he heard me.

Satisfied, I turned to leave.

But Stan craned his head around and said, "Many years ago, when cancer took my son, me, being a man of God, convinced myself it was all part of God's plan."

I nodded but stayed quiet.

"You remember Justin's brother?"

"Chad," I replied, as horrible memories flashed through my mind.

"Chad reminded me of my son. It's why I liked him so much. He was a good person. He had a big heart. Always looked out for people. His reward for being a good person was being killed by one of those things. But before he died, right in my arms, he asked me if there was a heaven. But because of the way I felt at that moment, thinking about my wife and all those people who came back as something different from what they were, I couldn't tell him yes because… that would have been a lie."

Stan began to sob. Not holding anything back.

"I also couldn't tell him no because that felt like a betrayal. A betrayal of the values I tried to live by. But while I was playing tug-of-war with my soul, I ended up not saying anything to him. So, instead of comforting him in his last moments and giving him the peace he deserved, the one thing I was put on this earth to do, all I did was watch him die."

When Stan removed his glasses to wipe his face, I glanced away, on the verge of tears myself. All this after an afternoon of doing my best to hold them back.

"And now," Stan said, "while we wait for this little girl, this little angel, to pass on, I still feel the same way. Wondering if there is a heaven. Wondering if there is a God. Because what kinda God would allow any of what's happened to happen?

"What kind of plan is that?"

Stan was now glaring up at the roof of the hut. The veins in his neck protruding out so far that they looked like they were going to burst. His face reddened with anger. His teeth ground together.

"And right now, at this moment, it's occurred to me that the answer is simple. There is no plan because there is no God. So there is absolutely nothing I can do for this poor little girl except to kill her again after she dies.

"But if the joke's on me, and there really is a God up there in heaven, he can go to hell. He can go straight to hell."

As Stan broke down again, all I could do was give him a reassuring pat on the back.

By patting my hand with his, I knew he was grateful. That's just how Stan was.

*****

Around six in the morning, Stan Phillips awoke from a restless sleep and reached for the other side of the bed. When he found it empty, he sighed with disappointment but not surprise.

He had just been dreaming about his wife, Eleanor. In it, she'd been sleeping next to him as she had done in reality for over thirty-seven years. But a heart attack had taken her away from him just the day before.

It was a dream, he thought as he rolled over to go back to sleep. *Just a dream.*

As content as he was to go back to sleep, somewhere in the dark pit of his thoughts, something wasn't quite right. He felt it in his bones. As old as he felt, he trusted those bones more than anything else.

Moving through the dark house, wearing a robe over his pajamas, Stan moved past the empty wheelchair his wife had used the last few years of her life and descended the stairs.

When he reached the landing, he glanced toward the front door and stopped in his tracks. Alarmed, eyes wide open, he held his breath and made no sound. He swore that he had seen someone standing outside the door. As if someone were on the front porch looking in through the frosted glass. But now he saw nothing.

He kept watch from that spot in the dark but didn't see any more movement outside. After a few moments, he rationalized that his eyes must have been playing tricks on him. Or maybe he was still dreaming.

With hesitation in his movements, he approached the front door and reached out to place his hand on the knob. After a few deep breaths, he yanked the door wide open, looked out, and saw nothing.

Not knowing what he had expected to find, Stan relaxed and stepped onto the front porch.

As he peered around the neighborhood, there was nothing out of place. Everything looked the same as it always had. But just then, the wind picked up. Along with it came a familiar scent.

What is that? he thought. *I know that smell.*

That's when the answer hit him and made him smile.

It was Eleanor's perfume. The same perfume she wore for over twenty years. It was her favorite because it was his favorite.

Stan found himself calling out to her before he knew what he was doing. He quickly became angry at himself for being so foolish.

Stupid old man, he thought. *Go back to sleep.*

He shut the door behind him and went back upstairs to bed.

But as he did, a shadow passed over the door, and the knob started to turn.

Back up in bed, lying atop his covers in his robe, Stan stared up at the ceiling. So many thoughts and feelings were running through the recesses of his mind that he felt no more rest was coming for him that night. But he closed his eyes anyway.

He thought of Eleanor, and how they had lived in this house so long that they both knew all its sounds. The squeaky back door.

The faulty windowsill in the den that whistled when the wind blew. The loose board on the stairs four steps up that creaked when you stepped on it.

When he heard the familiar creak, Stan bolted upright in his bed. He was wide-awake now and had just noticed the sun was starting to come up.

He glanced at his clock on the nightstand and was surprised he'd been asleep for almost an hour. He swung his legs off the side of the bed, sat up slowly, and slipped his feet gently into his house shoes on the floor. He rose up and tiptoed toward his closet. He opened it slowly and saw his golf bag. From it, he retrieved the driver Eleanor had gotten him the previous Christmas.

Our last Christmas together, he thought.

He shoved the memory out of his head and held the driver by its shaft with his shaking hands. He approached the bedroom doorway and placed his hand on the knob. He yanked it open and peered out.

What he saw chilled him to the bone.

It was Eleanor, wearing her favorite blue pajamas. The clothes she had died in.

Stan began walking backward. The air having left his lungs. He stumbled and fell. His bed caught him.

Eleanor stood in place. Not moving. Not doing anything.

Stan stood up slowly and walked away from the bed while brandishing the driver before him.

"What are you doing here?" he asked. "This isn't natural."

Eleanor stood silently. Her mouth slowly opened and closed, as if she were doing it for the first time and was amazed by it.

"Eleanor?" Stan asked.

Eleanor began to growl. Low, like a dog. That warning they give you to let you know they mean business.

Stan barely had time to register this because she opened her mouth, bared her teeth, and ran toward him.

Stan stepped to the side just as she rushed past at him and fell to the floor.

Sprawling, Eleanor got to her feet.

"You're not my Eleanor," Stan said, sobbing, while backing out of the bedroom.

Eleanor charged her husband again, but Stan turned and ran for the stairs.

She lunged and grabbed him by the right ankle.

Stan screamed but remembered the driver he held in his hands.

He said, "I'm sorry, Eleanor," before bringing the driver's club down upon her back.

Eleanor growled in pain, and Stan started to weep, but he hit her again and again until she let him go.

He made it down the stairs as fast as his tired old legs could run. Then he bolted toward his open front door where predawn sunlight hit his face.

He sprinted across his yard and saw his neighbor across the street loading his station wagon with stuff from his house.

"Eddie!" Stan yelled. "It's my Eleanor! Something's wrong!"

"Everything's wrong, Pastor Phillips! Haven't you heard?"

"Heard what?" Stan asked as he reached the station wagon.

"The world. It's comin' to an end."

"What?"

"The dead. They're rising."

Before Stan had a moment for this to sink in, Eleanor barreled past him toward Eddie, who turned and screamed as he tried to escape. But Eddie had a bad leg and couldn't run very fast due to a limp.

All Stan could think about was how fast Eleanor was moving. He'd never seen her move like that before. Before he knew it, Eleanor had tackled Eddie to the ground.

Stan watched in horror as his late wife savagely bit into their neighbor's neck and tore away flesh. His blood gushed like a fountain and moistened the ground.

As steam rose from Eddie's wounds into the air, Stan glanced inside his neighbor's near-fully packed station wagon and saw the keys in the ignition.

With a pained look back at Eleanor, who was now feasting on Eddie like a wild animal, Stan ran around to the driver's side, threw his bent driver into the passenger seat, and climbed inside the vehicle.

He started the car and drove off.

Glancing in the driver's side mirror, Stan saw Eleanor's face in the glow of the taillights. She began chasing after him, snarling and snapping her bloodstained teeth.

Stan shifted his tear-filled eyes to his wife's reflection in the rear-view mirror until something caught her attention, and she veered out of his view.

He swung his head around and watched as Eleanor began chasing two women, one of whom was carrying a screaming baby in her arms. Stan forced himself to look away and continued driving.

He didn't know where to go at first. But then the obvious answer hit him.

My church, he thought. *The only other place besides home where I ever truly felt I belonged.*

But when he finally got there after driving through what seemed like hell on earth, he saw that the front glass door had been shattered.

Stan reached across the console and retrieved his now-crooked driver. Grasping it tight with one hand, he got out of the car and approached his church.

*****

As I left the Duncans' hut right before dusk, I heard thunder rumbling. At that moment, small raindrops began to pelt my skin. I looked up and saw swirling clouds lit up every now and then by soundless lightning.

It was going to be a huge storm. Maybe not the worst we'd seen so far but pretty bad.

I hoped everyone had their things tied down. But if they hadn't done it by now, it was too late. And it's not like Stan hadn't warned us.

As I ran to my hut, I thought of something I hadn't bothered to think about in a long time.

My family.

Over the past few years trapped on this island, I'd found that thinking of my family didn't do me any good. The loss and confusion were unbearable then, and those feelings hadn't subsided.

I was still angry and bitter, much like Stan, who on his worst day was still a better man than I could ever dream of being. I could never forgive or even begin to understand why events had happened the way they did. Over the years, I'd become quite adept at shutting out the memories altogether.

But tonight, between the Duncans mourning their daughter and Stan losing the last shreds of his faith, I couldn't help it. The memories were coming toward me at full force. Much like the coming storm.

When I realized I couldn't stop them, I resigned myself to their fate.

After I entered my hut and tied the door shut as best I could, I let those thoughts wash over me, allowing them to take me wherever they wanted me to go.

I could see myself at ten years old. From my bedroom, I could smell breakfast cooking as I woke up to go to school. I could remember how the night before I had been looking out the window hoping in vain that it would snow so I wouldn't have to go to math class.

I remembered the disappointment I had felt that morning when it hadn't snowed, and I would have to take that quiz I wasn't prepared for.

Then time moved forward. It was years later. I could see my family's faces as clear as day. My mother as she read her paper in the morning. I saw myself tormenting my sister's dolls while she begged me to stop hurting them.

More time passed. I watched my sister as she played tickle-fest with her children. My nieces. So young and precocious.

Finally, I saw the grinning face of my savior, William Blake, who was buried less than sixty feet away from where I now stood. A man whose strength, laugh, and enthusiasm were all dearly missed.

I thought of everyone I had lost and that terrible day.

*****

As Adam raced to his mother's house as fast as his Maxima, with its V-6 engine, could take him, he maneuvered through the vehicles burning on the road like he was on an obstacle course. But he soon made the decision to stop avoiding the creatures with his car and began plowing through and over any of them that got in his way.

This was doing a lot of damage to his car, but he didn't care. His mom's house would soon be in sight, and he would use her car from there if he had to.

When he turned onto her street, his heart leaped into his throat when he saw how many houses and vehicles were burning.

He repeated a quick prayer over and over again as he waited for her house to come into view.

When it did, he exhaled in relief. His mom's house was still standing and not on fire. Most importantly, there were no signs of any creatures nearby. Maybe she was safe.

But as he got closer, he noticed her front door was open. Not only open but forced open. At the sight of it, his nervous tension returned along with a sick feeling in his gut.

He pulled up in front of her house and parked in her yard. Leaving the engine running, he ran into the house.

It was dark inside and quiet. Too quiet. Not even a television was on, which was very odd for his mother. That was when he realized the power must have gone out.

The air was thick in the house, and something was very wrong.

He could now hear his heart beating in his ears.

He yelled for his mom but didn't get an answer.

He yelled several more times. Still no reply.

On the verge of tears, Adam heard it before he saw it.

Spinning around toward the noise, Adam saw a human shape standing in the darkness of the hallway leading into the kitchen. It loomed at just over six feet.

By the time Adam's eyes could make out anything else, the creature rushed toward him with an inhuman scream.

Adam fell backward out the front door. In no time at all, thanks to fear, and the adrenaline it provided, he flipped himself over and used his hands to get to his feet. Getting purchase on the grass, he started running, legs burning, toward his car.

He got into it just as the creature jumped onto the hood. Without shutting his door, Adam put his car in reverse and peeled out of the yard and onto the street.

As the creature desperately grasped at him through the open door, Adam stopped the car, causing the door to slam against its arm. It howled in pain and fury but continued to grab at him.

Adam shifted into drive and pressed on the accelerator. Within seconds, he was going forty-five. Then he slammed on the brakes again, and the creature went flying.

Moments after skidding to a stop on the street, the road-damaged creature began to move. It slowly started to pull itself back up to its feet.

With seething anger, Adam slammed on the gas pedal again.

The Maxima plowed into the creature. Most of its body fell under the car, and the wheels crushed it as it went over. But the creature's head separated from its body and rolled over the top of the car.

The head eventually came to a stop on the street. Its eyes watching the Maxima as it drove away. Its mouth moving.

As Adam drove through the city streets, he never stopped for signs or lights. He drove past deserted vehicles and around burning ones.

As he passed a supermarket, he saw dozens of frenzied creatures swarming through its doors and climbing through its broken-out windows.

Adam felt bad for the humans who had made the unfortunate mistake of thinking they were safe hiding in there.

And that was when he saw him.

A man was driving his black dually crew cab with one hand on the steering wheel and using the other to fire a rifle out an open window.

Adam began honking his horn to get his attention.

The man paid him no mind. He kept firing.

A creature was running up to the side of the man's truck just as he had stopped firing to reload his weapon.

Adam thought quickly and sped up.

Just as the creature was about to reach the man's driver's door, with a thump, it had cleared the top of Adam's car and landed in the street.

Unfortunately for Adam, his radiator was now finished. As steam shot out of his car, and hot water drained into a greenish pool beneath it, he realized his vehicle was useless.

The man in the truck jerked his vehicle to a stop and waved him forward.

Adam checked his side mirror and saw more creatures making their way toward him.

Adam was out of his car in a hurry and running for the man's truck. But just as he was within a few yards, the man stepped out of his truck and opened fire toward him.

Adam yelled and dropped to the street. Eyes closed, he heard the report of the weapon. When he opened his eyes, the man was still firing but at the creatures behind him.

The man shouted, "Hurry up! I can't do this all day!"

Adam got to his knees and then to his feet. Running low, he dashed for the truck and got inside.

The man shouted again, "Name's Blake! William Blake!"

Adam yelled his name back, then, "I'm glad you came along!"

When Blake got in behind the wheel, and the truck was going again, he gave Adam a once-over, then asked loudly, "You bit!"

"No," Adam said, looking out the windows to see more creatures. More destruction.

"You sure?"

"Yeah. Positive."

Blake summed it up. "Welcome to hell, my friend!"

After driving for a distance, Blake offered him a weapon much different from his own rifle.

"You know what that is, Adam?"

"Not really."

"What?" Blake shouted.

"No!"

"It's an AR15!" Blake shouted, holding up the assault rifle like a proud father. "I also have a Mossberg, a .270 Remington, an SKS, a Glock 45, and last but not least, this little blue chrome steel beauty!"

He reached between his legs and held up a .357 Magnum, brandishing it like he was a model on *The Price Is Right*. He couldn't take his eyes off the gun.

"This here is my Peacemaker!"

Then it was as if Blake remembered Adam was in the truck.

"But the AR should do you just fine for now!"

Blake dug in his pockets and extended a closed fist out to Adam. Adam put out his hand, and Blake put two earplugs in his palm.

"Put those in!"

As Adam put the earplugs in, his mind was spinning. The plugs made him talk louder. Just like Blake.

"I've…I've never fired a weapon before!"

"Now's the perfect time to start!"

With a quick grin, Blake fired out his window again. This time with his .357.

As Adam held the AR in his hands, he closed his eyes and thought of his mom, his sister, and her two kids. Tears tried to fall, but he wouldn't let them. Couldn't.

Hopefully, he thought, *there'll be a time to cry later.*

"First things first," he said low to himself. "Get out of this day alive."

With that, Adam fired a weapon for the first time in his life. He was surprised how much he liked it. A big smile broke out across his face.

"Damn, that felt good."

As he glanced over at William Blake, he thanked God he had come across him.

Adam was quick to surmise that in the old days, even yesterday, before anyone could even imagine the horrors to come, Blake was one of those people who were made fun of just for being prepared.

Adam knew because he was one of those people making the jokes. He'd read about survivalists, mostly gun nuts, preparing for the day that the government would decide to take away their precious Second Amendment. He shook his head at the thought of them stockpiling weapons, legal and not so legal, just in case any enemy, be they foreign or domestic, decided to attack.

At the time, Adam thought, *What kind of person spends their lives worrying about a day that will never come? What kind of man expects to go to war against his fellow countrymen?*

Well, that man was William Blake. And today, as Adam sat in Blake's truck with an AR15 in his hand, it turned out that people like him had been proven right.

Adam laughed. He couldn't help it. He found himself hoping there were more people like William Blake in the world.

*****

Stan had almost fallen asleep while on his watch, but Amy's body had begun to shake uncontrollably, and he was now wide-awake.

Lloyd immediately appeared at his daughter's side. With wide eyes, he watched in a panic as his daughter, tongue sticking out of her mouth, started to turn blue.

Stan leaned over her body and tried to pry her mouth open before she bit off her tongue.

As blood poured from the little girl's mouth, Stan yelled, "Go get Adam!"

Lloyd looked back and forth from Stan to his daughter.

Stan yelled again, "Go! Now!"

Lloyd, wanting to be with his daughter every second she had left, reluctantly left Amy's side and ran out of the hut.

Nora, still sitting with her back against the wall, seemed unusually calm. But Stan didn't have much time to think about that as he tried in vain to open Amy's mouth.

With sweat running down his face and into his eyes, he looked up to see Nora staring down at her belly.

"Nora, please help me," he pleaded. "Her tongue, Nora."

Stan noticed blood coming out of the corners of Amy's mouth. But her mother remained unmoved and quiet.

"Nora, she's biting her tongue off!"

Nora rubbed her belly with her hand and remembered a time. Months before the day it all ended. Back when she'd been happier than she'd ever been. When she had been with the man she loved.

She remembered his smell. The way she bit his lip as he came inside her. The surprised way his crystal-blue eyes had looked at her when he realized she'd drawn blood.

Spent and covered in sweat, he had rolled off her toward his side of the hotel bed when her phone began to buzz on the nightstand.

Without looking over at the phone, she grimaced, knowing who it was.

As her lover sat on the edge of the bed pulling on his socks, she ran her fingers down the length of his back with one hand. Then she began tracing the faint scratch marks she had put there.

He withdrew from her touch, stood up, and pulled on his briefs before turning around to face her.

As he checked his lip with the tip of his finger for signs of blood, he saw a smile form on her face, which made her beautiful in a stern kind of way.

"What?" he asked.

Her eyes gave him a once-over, then she replied, "Can I just admire you from a distance?"

He smiled and grabbed his pants that were hanging on the back of a chair. As he slipped them on, he heard her phone buzz once again.

He glanced at her as it vibrated on the wooden table. "You gonna answer that?"

"He can wait," she replied, coldness in her voice.

He shook his head as he buttoned his pants, then moved across the room to get his shirt that was lying flat on a table so it wouldn't get wrinkled.

"If you don't love him," he said while slipping on the shirt, "why don't you just leave him?"

"And go where?" she asked, raising up in the bed, exposing her breasts to him as she did.

He didn't answer her.

After taking in his silence with a poker face that told him nothing, Nora asked, "What makes you think I don't love him?"

"I don't know," he replied, shrugging. "The way you talk about him. The way you act when he calls."

He started buttoning the shirt.

"The fact you're with me in this hotel room instead of being with him."

She rolled her eyes. "You callin' me a whore?"

"No," he said, smiling. "Never."

He tucked his shirt under his pants, then fastened his belt.

"Because if you're a whore, then so am I," he added.

Nora swung her legs off the side of the bed and sat up facing away from him.

Now dressed, he grabbed his keys off a dresser along with his wallet and cell phone. He saw her sitting with her back to him and knew immediately she was upset.

"Look," he said, taking a deep breath while trying to find the right words. "It's just… You don't look happy."

"I'm happy when I'm with you," she replied, still looking away.

"But you know what this is," he said. "It's just us having a little fun. Nothing more, nothing less."

Nora picked up her phone and saw that Lloyd had left her three text messages in the past couple of hours.

The man crossed the room toward her and gave her a kiss on the cheek, then walked toward the door.

"Next week?" he asked. "Same time?"

Nora glanced up at him without a trace of a smile. "Text me."

He chuckled to himself as he opened the door and left.

As the door closed, the look on her face darkened as she stared once again at her phone.

When she looked up, it was another day in the hotel room with her lover standing before her. A troubled look on his face.

"Are you sure?" he asked.

Nora rolled her eyes. "Of course I'm sure."

"No," he said, glancing at her belly. "Are you sure it's mine?"

Nora was taken aback. "Did you really just ask me that?"

At a loss for words, he started to pace before her.

She knew what she had just told him was the last thing he wanted to hear.

"What now?" she asked.

He kept pacing and shaking his head. "Well, obviously we have to take care of it."

Her eyes widened in surprise. "Take care of it?"

He stopped pacing and stared directly at her. "I can't do this. You know I can't do this."

"Do what exactly?"

"This!" he exclaimed while gesturing at her belly. "I can't raise a baby. Not with you."

Nora took that in, then stood and glared at him.

He couldn't meet her gaze, so he stood there in silence staring at any place in the room other than her.

Nora's face hardened. Her eyes grew cold. But a smirk formed as she took him in. Seeing him for who he really was.

"And I thought my husband was weak," she said, watching as his eyes finally met hers.

With a dismissive shake of her head, she moved past him toward the door.

He made no effort at first to stop her, but as she opened the door, he turned and said, "I'll pay for the procedure. It's the least I could do."

Standing in the doorway without looking back at him, she replied, "You're right."

She faced him and sneered.

"That is the least you could do."

Then she walked out of the room and closed the door behind her.

Back in the hut, Nora, now with an angry look growing on her face, glanced up from her belly toward Stan, who was trying in vain to open Amy's mouth.

Her eyes shifted over to the machete at Stan's side.

"I can't let you," Nora said, too low for him to hear.

"What?" Stan asked.

He didn't realize until it was too late what she was about to do.

Nora crawled across her daughter's body and grasped for the machete.

Stan saw this, then panicked and let go of Amy. He sprung and took hold of Nora around the waist.

"I won't let you!" she screamed.

Nora's hands seized the machete blade, then she ran her hand across the length of it until she palmed the handle.

As Stan crawled onto her back and reached for the machete, Nora could feel his breath on the back of her neck. She reared her head back as hard as she could and smashed him in the face.

Blood shot out of Stan's nose, and tears sprang into his eyes as Nora rolled herself over and shoved him away from her.

As Stan recovered from the shock, he wiped his eyes and tried to clear his vision.

But Nora was now up on her knees. She held the machete above her head and brought it down upon Stan.

As blood splattered, Nora kept hacking away at his body. She had a fierce look on her face that didn't appear to be human at all. All the while, she kept yelling, "I won't let you!"

As Nora mindlessly chopped away at Stan, Amy, face speckled with blood, opened her eyes and took her last breath.

*****

"We're gonna be okay," Chad said, holding Linda's delicate face in his hands.

As he gazed upon her, he couldn't help but notice all the blood.

It was everywhere. All over him. All over her. But somehow they were fine. More than fine, really. They were alive, which was more than could be said for most at the moment.

His hands had done some awful things earlier that morning.

He reasoned with his conscience that he'd had no choice. But guilty thoughts kept creeping back into his brain.

All the awful things I did.

Now here they were hiding in the dark, him holding the porcelain skin of Linda's face as gently as he could.

Despite the blood spatter on her, he kissed her forehead, not thinking twice if he could get infected from it.

It did little to rouse her for she had been in a sort of catatonic state since she had witnessed him saving her from the monstrous thing that used to be her father.

The only body part moving on her now were her lips. They were silently repeating the same thing over and over again.

"All the monsters are here."

He could only nod and continue to hold her.

It just doesn't make any damn sense, he thought. *Just yesterday, her father gave me permission to marry her. This morning, all hell's breaking loose, and we get there just in time for me to save her from gettin' her throat ripped out.*

Maybe if we'd gotten there a little sooner, I coulda saved her mom and little sister, but with all the chaos, it just took us too damn long to get there.

He thought this as he peered across the assembly room toward his younger brother, Justin, who was fast asleep, slightly snoring, while curled up in a fetal position on the floor near the church dais.

Mom was right, Chad thought. *That boy can sleep through anything. Storms. Lawn mowers. Construction. Now this. Jesus.*

Justin was younger than him by two years. By all accounts, he was Chad's best friend. Chad had spent most of his life taking his little brother everywhere he went, even to places he shouldn't have.

Justin was with him when he met Linda at the mall. His little brother was standing three feet away when Chad first asked for her phone number.

He was even going to be the best man at Chad and Linda's upcoming wedding.

That memory returned to Chad like a punch to the gut.

What's gonna happen now? he thought.

He lowered one of his hands to her belly and gently touched it.

How am I gonna let this baby be born into a world like this without being saved? How will we ever get married now that the world has gone to hell in a handbasket?

Chad peered up and saw the stained glass windows lining the roof of the assembly room allowing multicolored rays of light to beam down onto the rows and rows of pews.

Hiding on the floor between the first row of pews and the dais where the preacher stood before his flock at his pulpit, Chad didn't know where else to go. He had reasoned that if they were going to die, it might as well be in a church. He figured if they died here, their baby would have a better chance of making it to heaven.

But just then, he heard a noise. Shoes crunching on glass.

Chad reached out with his leg and rousted Justin.

Justin slightly stirred but stayed asleep.

Chad kicked him.

Justin woke up, grunted, and said, "Why the hell did you kick me for?"

"Shh," Chad said, his finger to his lips. "Somebody's here."

"Who?" Justin asked, raising up.

"Shut up before they hear us."

Chad carefully laid Linda down on the floor while cradling her head. Then he turned toward his brother and pointed down at her.

"Stay with her."

Justin nodded as he crab-walked over beside her and stared down at her.

Linda's striking hazel eyes were now open in a vacant stare. Her lips still moving without making a sound. Her mind was millions of miles away.

To Justin, he'd never seen anyone so beautiful.

"Hey, you listenin'?" Chad said.

Justin glanced up and saw his brother peering over the rows of pews. Not seeing anything, he turned back to his brother.

"What?" Justin asked.

"I said if anything happens to me, you two run—"

"I'm not leaving you behind," Justin protested.

"You will because I told you to," Chad replied, a deadly serious tone in his voice. "Now promise you'll do it."

"Fuck you."

"Promise!"

"Fine. I promise."

"You better."

"I said I would," Justin barked back. "Now drop it."

They stared at one another in silence until a door opening across the room startled them.

They both turned and watched as the silhouette of a tall older man entered the room. He appeared to be wearing a robe and pajamas, of all things. He held out a bent golf club before him like a baseball bat.

As the older man stepped into the light, the boys finally saw his face.

Chad rose to his feet, smiling. His brother soon joined him.

"Pastor Phillips?" they said in unison.

Stan lowered the driver and shook his head. His brow creased as he gestured with his thumb, pointing it back over his shoulder.

"Did you boys break my door?"

*****

I'd been fast asleep when Lloyd, sounding terrified, woke me up by yelling, "It's Amy! Please hurry!"

It was now night. The rain was falling hard, and the wind was gusting. I tried my best to keep up with Lloyd, who ran at top speed back to his hut.

I'd never been much of a runner—not even when I was younger and in the best shape of my life—but I somehow managed to jog at a somewhat steady pace without keeling over.

Up ahead, I saw Lloyd reach his hut and run inside. Seconds later, I heard him yell in agony.

I picked up my pace and entered the hut soon after. But immediately upon entering, I slipped and fell to the dirt floor.

As I tried to get up, I glanced down around me and at my hands.

That's when I realized everything around me was covered in blood.

My heart clenched as I turned to see Lloyd wrestling the blood-soaked machete out of his wife's hands while Stan's bloody, mutilated body lay below them.

As Lloyd yelled obscenities at his wife, I saw the look on her face and knew she had snapped.

Resorting to her basic instincts, she screamed, "I won't let you!" over and over again to no one in particular.

With my adrenaline flowing, I ran over and twisted the machete out of her grasp without any care for her well-being. But when I glanced down at Stan's body, my anger swelled up inside me and took over. With all my fury, I slammed my fist as hard as I could into her face.

I heard a satisfying crack as her head snapped back, and she fell unconscious into her husband's arms. I didn't feel bad about hitting her. I wanted to do so much worse. And with the machete in my hand, I almost did.

But unbeknownst to me, Lloyd's eyes filled with hate. He looked down at his wife and gnashed his teeth. He then screamed and rushed me.

I had raised the machete by that point with my ire focused solely upon Nora. So when Lloyd tackled me, it took me by surprise.

But as I was going down, I took him with me by grabbing hold of him with one hand. In the other, I held the machete, and I wasn't about to let that go.

Lloyd now had me at a disadvantage. I found myself peering up at him from the ground in shock at how quickly he had moved.

The only thing I could do at that point was shield my head as best as I could with my free hand as Lloyd began swinging his arms like a madman, connecting more than a few times with my head and upper body.

During the one-sided scrum, he tired out quickly. I saw an opening and took it. I reached up, grabbed him by the throat, and began squeezing as hard as I could. My tactic worked as Lloyd stopped trying to hit me and pulled at my fingers that were now cutting off his oxygen.

Just then, I saw movement out of the corner of my eye.

Amy, despite her skin being cold and blue, rose to her feet. Blood covered the front of her dress. Before I knew it, she let out a feral scream, jumped onto her father's back, and bit into his shoulder.

Lloyd screamed as blood shot out of the wound like a geyser, spraying him, me, and his daughter. He tried to throw her off, but she held strong like a cowgirl riding a bull.

Amy bit down and tore a huge piece of flesh out of his back as if it were made of paper.

Terrified, I managed to crab-crawl backward away from them. I got to my knees and watched as Amy bit into him again. This time, it was his neck. As she twisted and ripped her head away, she severed his jugular.

Lloyd pressed his hand to his neck wound and tried to scream, but it sounded as if he were gargling. Then his eyes went unfocused.

Amy turned her head and saw me. She growled. Her father's blood dripped from her mouth. Then she rushed me.

I didn't hesitate. I raised the machete and brought it down on her, splitting the top of her head in two.

Amy's tiny hands kept madly reaching for me, but I yanked the blade out and swung it sideways.

Her head fell from her shoulders and rolled to a stop on the floor. Her dark hair hid her face. Her body began running about the hut, blood shooting from the stump where her head was moments ago. It bumped into the hut's walls and finally fell over and stopped moving.

*****

"You wanna get married?" Stan asked Chad while looking around the church assembly room. "Today of all days?"

Chad sat on a pew while Justin paced before the podium on the dais.

Linda was lying down next to Chad with a pillow under her head. Her glassy eyes open. Mouth still moving in silence.

"I know it's probably stupid, Pastor Phillips," Chad said, making eye contact. "But I'm worried what's gonna happen to our souls after we...you know, after we're no longer here."

As Justin glanced down at Linda, eyes on her belly, Stan nodded in understanding.

Chad grasped Linda's hand. "What happens to the baby if...?"

A tear fell down his cheek, but he quickly wiped his face.

Stan sat on a pew behind Chad and placed a reassuring hand on the young man's shoulder.

"God will look out for your baby."

"Are you sure?" Chad asked, still sad and confused.

"I'm not sure about most things anymore," Stan replied, peering around. "Especially now."

Chad wiped his face and nodded.

"But about that," Stan added, "I'm positive."

"Thank you, Pastor Phillips," Chad said, relieved.

"But as far as getting married," Stan said, shaking his head as he gazed down at Linda. "I'm afraid I couldn't. Especially not like she is right now."

Chad shook his head. "But me and her, we've talked about it. You know, before all this."

Chad looked toward the exit. He swallowed a lump in his throat.

"This is what she wanted. She wanted her baby to have a father after a blessed union in the house of the Lord. It's why we came here. I was gonna do it by myself if I had to."

Stan held out a reassuring palm. "Believe me. I understand, son, and I don't doubt you."

Chad's eyes filled with hope.

"Just not today," Stan added. "Not while she's like this."

Chad held Linda's hand tighter and lifted it to his chest.

"I-I understand, Pastor Phillips. I'm just...I'm scared for us."

Stan nodded and gave Chad another pat on the shoulder, then peered over at Justin, who was now pacing like a madman by the dais.

"You all right, Justin?"

Justin stopped in his tracks and stared at the preacher, then at his brother. Instead of saying what was on his mind, he simply shook his head.

Stan smiled. "Well, if you do end up needing anything, let me know."

Justin nodded and continued pacing.

Stan glanced down and noticed his robe. The sight of it made him chuckle. "It looks like I'm going to need to find some clothes to wear. I'm pretty sure I have something here."

Stan glanced toward the entrance to the room.

"And then I better do something about that front door…before any of those things show up."

Chad lowered his head, looking crestfallen. "I'm really sorry about the door—"

"Relax, Chad," Stan said while standing up. "It's just a door."

Chad nodded as Stan walked away and left the room.

While Justin continued pacing, Chad was still troubled. He glanced toward the exit, then gestured to his brother.

"Would you watch over her for a little bit?"

Justin gazed down at Linda and nodded. "Sure."

"I'll be right back."

Justin watched as Chad leaned over, kissed Linda on the forehead, and followed Stan's path out of the room.

Justin stepped off the dais and sat down beside Linda. He stretched his arm over the pew backing and moved his eyes across her body.

He took a quick peek over his shoulder to make sure the coast was clear, then lowered his arm and hovered his hand inches from her belly.

His eyes shifted to her face, where her eyes were open but staring off into nothing.

He gently touched her belly, his eyes on hers.

When she didn't react, he began to slide his hand toward her right breast and brushed his hand over the top of it. The contact was brief and minimal, but the shudder that went through his body was immense.

He jerked his hand away from her and placed his hands on his lap and glanced back to make sure no one had been watching. But then he remembered.

Someone was watching.

He slowly faced forward, peered up, and saw a large statue of Jesus on the cross hanging above the pulpit.

Fear and shame crossed his face, causing him to look away.

*****

Inside the Duncans' hut, I used a long strand of leftover rope to secure Nora's wrists behind her back. The whole time, she never said a word or moved her gaze while she stared off into the void.

I glanced up as Justin entered the tent. I could tell he was waiting for his vision to adjust before he could make out anything.

I double-checked the knots I had tied. With a firm tug, I felt confident this restraint would keep us safe from her. For a good while, at least.

"What are we gonna do with her?" Justin asked.

Caught off guard, I stood up and peered down at Nora and shook my head. "I don't know yet."

"But we can't trust her. Not after what she did—"

"I know," I interrupted. "But we'll decide that together."

"Who's we?" Justin asked, looking around in a sarcastic manner. "There's only three of us left." His eyes shifted, thinking of Eve, and quickly added, "Adults, I mean."

He gazed down at Nora, who, despite a weird smile forming on her face, seemed oblivious to our conversation.

"I know, Justin, but we'll figure it out."

As he stared down at Nora, his anger rose. "I know what I'd do with her."

"And what's that?"

My gaze fell behind Justin as Linda entered just in time to hear Justin say, "Give me that machete, and we'll find out."

"Find out what?" Linda asked, her eyes darting from us to Nora.

Surprised, Justin spun around to see her. At a loss for words, he stammered.

I walked past him and put him out of his verbal misery. "Let's talk about this outside."

But I saw the look in her eyes as she took in the surroundings. I recognized the look of horror as it dawned upon her face.

I stepped before her to block her view and glanced back at Nora to catch a glimpse at what she was doing.

I got creeped out because Nora was still smiling about something only she knew, which scared the hell out of me.

I nodded at Justin to get Linda out of the hut, only to watch him grab her arm and force her outside.

When I emerged outside, there was barely any light. The rain was now stinging because the wind had gained power. But I did see Linda freeing her arm from Justin's grasp and shoving him away from her.

As he stared back at her with a shocked look on his face, she dismissed him and turned her glare directly at me, a furious look in her eyes.

"What were you two talking about in there?"

I slammed the tip of the machete down into a log, where it held firm, but as I looked at Linda, she took a step back, alarmed.

I raised my hands to let her know I didn't plan to do her any harm, but I guess I was too late. She might have been angry, but now she was trembling.

I took a few steps away from her, hoping that would calm her down. But while that may have worked a little, her anger remained.

I wanted to say something, anything, to defuse the situation, but I didn't know where to begin. I figured I'd just be direct.

"Amy, Lloyd, and Stan are dead."

"Oh my god!" Linda gasped, horrified. Her hands covered her face as she turned toward Justin.

Justin looked down at his feet.

"It was Nora," I said. "When Amy died, Nora...she..."

Now I was at a loss for words.

"Went crazy," Justin added, returning my favor from earlier.

"That's why she's tied up," I stated. "We can't trust her anymore."

What I saw next surprised me.

Linda glared in revulsion at the both of us. I could only imagine what was going on in her head at that moment.

"So now what?" she asked, backing away from us. Like we were the monsters. "Are you gonna kill her?"

I held out my hands again, trying to calm her down. "I don't know any other way."

"There's always a way," Linda replied, furious. She looked over at Justin. "And you're just going along with this?"

Justin looked away in shame, which raised my ire.

We're not the one who killed Stan, I thought. But all that came out was, "What would you have us do?"

"I don't know," Linda said, shaking her head. "Build a jail, keep her tied up. Anything but murder."

"And that's why we're talking now," I said, forgetting her mood and stepping closer to her.

This caused her to step back.

I stopped in place and said as calmly and rationally as I could, "We gotta figure out our next move together."

"Why?" Linda asked, shaking her head again. "It seems to me you two have made up your minds already."

At that, I lost it. Probably not a good move on my part.

"You think this is easy?" I shouted, anger rising in my voice before I could stop it. "I'm just trying to keep all of us safe."

"And who will keep us safe from you?" Linda shouted back. Then she turned to Justin. "Or you?"

"That's bullshit, and you know it," Justin snapped. "You know I'd never hurt you."

"Maybe I don't," she replied, which deeply hurt him. I could see it in his eyes. "Maybe I'm just now finding out the truth about both of you."

Furious, Justin grabbed her by the arm and pointed at the Duncans' hut. "She's a fucking psycho, and she'll kill us all."

"She just lost her child!" Linda yelled while breaking away from his grasp and rubbing her arm. "She's not in her right mind!"

Disgusted, she shook her head at us again. Glaring at me in particular.

"That's no reason to kill her. She's still human, and we don't kill humans. Isn't that what you said once? Or did you forget that?"

That stung me. I didn't have a response.

Linda shook her head at us, at me in particular, then turned and ran away in the direction of her own hut. She disappeared into the night and the sheets of rain.

Justin started to go after her, but I stopped him and held him in place.

"Let her have some space," I said, hoping Justin was listening. "She'll come around."

"Will she?"

Again, I didn't have an answer anyone wanted to hear. So I decided to take care of a necessary task.

"Come on. We have a lot of digging to do."

With the rain pouring down, I turned and walked off toward the beach.

When I glanced back, I saw Justin staring off in the direction Linda had disappeared to. Then he turned and followed me.

*****

In the foyer of the church, Chad had been quietly observing Stan, now wearing a checkered golf shirt and khaki pants as he swept up the shattered glass on the foyer floor near the front door.

Chad wondered how he was going to say what he needed to say.

He found himself glancing out the broken door before clearing his throat.

"Everything's so quiet out there," Chad observed. "No traffic. No birds. No nothing."

"Yeah," Stan replied, nodding in agreement. "It's eerie."

"Uh," Chad said, fidgeting with his hands. "Pastor Phillips?"

"Call me Stan," he replied with a smile and a nod. "Please."

Chad smiled and gazed back down at his hands.

Stan noticed Chad's discomfort and laid his elbow on top of the upright broom handle. "Is there something you need to say?"

"Yeah," Chad said. "I just don't know how."

Stan smiled and replied, "Sometimes it's as easy as just opening your mouth and letting whatever come out."

During a long moment of silence, Stan patiently waited while Chad summoned the courage he needed to say, "I had to kill Linda's father this morning."

Stan rocked back on his heels, stunned.

"Not that it was really him anymore, Pastor Phillips," Chad said, shooting him a look. "Sorry...Stan."

Stan waved it off without saying anything.

"If I hadn't," Chad said, "he woulda killed her."

Stan placed his hand on Chad's shoulder and squeezed. "I'm so sorry, Chad."

"I guess what I wanted to know is, with what's happening out there right now, is it still murder when they're not people anymore and...they're trying to kill you or...someone you love?"

Stan didn't know how to respond. All he could see in his mind were flashes of Eleanor. Crocheting in her favorite chair in their living room. Laughing with their grandchildren. Her body laid out on a metal table at the funeral home. Her undead form chasing after him inside their home.

"Stan?"

Stan came to, still standing in the foyer. He glanced over at Chad, and his mind returned to the moment.

"Sorry, Chad," Stan said. "I was just—"

Chad glanced up and saw a flash of something moving outside.

Before he could shout a warning, the reanimated corpse of Tom Kettle ran through the empty frame of the door. Chad had just enough time to shove Stan out of the way.

As Stan fell, the creature tackled Chad and took him to the floor. Chad had time to scream before the creature clamped its teeth on his right cheek and tore a mouthful of flesh away.

With blood pouring from his face, Chad screamed in agony as he tried to use both forearms to shove the creature away from him.

But it was too strong and resisted him.

It jerked its torso, causing Chad's right hand to slip. It fell onto him with its mouth perilously close to his shoulder. But Chad gave it all he had to keep it from biting him again.

Across the struggle, Stan tried to get back on his feet, but the pain in his lower back was immense, having strained it in the fall. It even hurt him to glance back to see Chad in trouble. Then he forced his way through the pain to get up to his knees.

Chad grunted and pushed the creature away a little more, but it kept lunging its head at his face.

Feeling the strength in his arms begin to ebb, Chad took a deep breath and yelled for his brother.

The creature raised its torso, catching Chad by surprise. He lost his left-hand grip again and tried to correct it, but the creature twisted its head and snapped at his forearm.

Having no choice, Chad managed to move his arm out of the way at the last second and barely avoided the bite. But the creature lunged at Chad again.

Justin ran into the foyer just in time to see the creature clamp its teeth on Chad's right shoulder and tear the flesh away from the bone.

As Chad let out a bloodcurdling scream, a devastated Justin yelled for his brother. But another zombie ran through the doorway.

In a split second, Justin recognized her. Or who she used to be. He couldn't remember her name, but he knew she went to the church and always sat in the front row in her Sunday best. But now she was sprinting toward him, gnashing her teeth, and growling.

Justin fled back into the assembly room with the former church-going parishioner right on his heels.

Stan finally made it to his feet and saw blood gushing from Chad's screaming face and shoulder.

Overwhelmed with tears, Stan peered around the foyer and saw several heavy, gold-plated barrier poles connected by a retractable belt. He hustled over, picked one up off the floor, and ran back over to stand above Chad and the creature.

Stan yelled as he raised the metal pole and brought the base of it down upon the creature's head.

Stunned, it groaned but quickly overcame the hit's effect and lunged back at Chad's face. But this time, Chad's strength was gone.

Before Stan could smash the pole on the creature's head again, it latched onto Chad's neck, twisted its head, and tore away another chunk of flesh.

As blood sprayed from Chad's neck, Stan, in fury, slammed the pole back down on the creature's head with all he had. It slumped lifeless down onto Chad's body.

Stan shoved the still zombie off Chad and knelt beside the young man. The pastor pressed his hand on Chad's neck wound, but the blood continued to pump out between his fingers with every fading heartbeat.

Chad, eyes wide and glassy, kept trying to talk. But as the blood continued to gush out, he became more listless.

Stan was sobbing. "I'm so sorry, Chad. I'm so sorry."

Chad kept his eyes on Stan as he shook his head slowly from side to side and kept mouthing something.

Stan lowered his ear to Chad's mouth and heard his last words.

The preacher froze. His face went slack for a few moments. Lost in his thoughts. But when he came back to the present and gazed down, he saw that the young man's lips had stopped moving, and his mouth had fallen open. His lifeless eyes stared up at the ceiling.

Stan lowered his head to Chad's chest and sobbed even harder than before. All the time repeating how sorry he was.

But then he heard Justin yelling from the assembly room.

Adrenaline enabled Stan to somehow avoid the excruciating pain in his back and eventually rise to his feet. He took a long pained look down at Chad and then ran into the assembly room.

Justin was running toward him with the female zombie on his tail.

"Run!" Justin yelled at Stan.

Stan recognized the creature as Addy Williams, a former faithful parishioner with a very kind, loving soul.

"Haul ass, Stan!"

Like a light bulb going off in his brain, Stan entered fight-or-flight mode and chose the latter.

He turned and fled from the room with Justin a few steps behind. The former Addy Williams gained on them with each step.

The two men ran through the foyer, out the front door, and across the parking lot, but came to an abrupt stop when they saw more zombies heading their way from down the street.

*****

Linda emerged out of the rain holding something in her arms that was wrapped in a blanket. She peered around for signs of the two men, then dashed toward the Duncans' hut.

From the moment she had entered the hut earlier and overheard Adam and Justin's conversation about what they were going to do about Nora, she knew what she had to do. What any mother would do.

Protect another mother who needed her help.

Even though she didn't agree with Nora's motives, horribly misguided as they were, she understood Nora enough to understand why she did what she did. It was something that someone who'd never given birth to a child could ever understand. That no matter what, a mother protected her child.

Linda knew Adam and Justin obviously couldn't see it that way, likely because they never really liked Nora to begin with. So of course they wouldn't try to see things from her point of view. And would refuse to do so even if given the opportunity. Especially when they were angry, as they certainly were now.

She didn't blame them for being angry, but she also knew they shouldn't be making decisions on someone else's fate while being angry, either.

Linda's plan was to spirit Nora away until cooler heads prevailed.

Then when enough time had passed, she'd find Justin and plead with him on Nora's behalf. She knew he would eventually listen to her and see reason. Then together, they'd both go to Adam to try to convince him to give Nora another chance. Or at least change his mind about killing her.

She knew it wouldn't be easy, and he may not agree, but at that point, Linda would have the majority vote. And then Adam would have to agree. Because that's the way it was done on the island. It was what they'd agreed upon when they first got here. Their own small democracy.

After all, Linda owed Nora since it was she who had helped her give birth to Eve. Without Nora, the birth would have had a different outcome. It was Nora who turned her baby around inside her birth canal so she wouldn't breech. No one else knew to do that or knew how to do that. Of all people, it had been Nora.

Linda knew Nora was difficult in every way a person could be difficult. But Nora had told her things she'd never told anyone else. Not even her own husband. That helped Linda to understand her better than anyone else on the island.

As she stepped inside the hut, she knew what she was about to do would infuriate the men, but they'd left her with no choice.

She stood her bundle on the floor, then knelt and unwrapped it. She soon revealed her tired four-year-old daughter, who was grumpy and rubbing the sleep from her hazel-green eyes. Her father's eyes.

"Are you okay, baby?" Linda asked while removing the bed-tangled hair from her daughter's face.

Eve frowned and nodded that she was but was tired and still not happy to be awake at the moment.

"That's a good girl," Linda said, kissing her fussy daughter's forehead. Then, with a warm smile, she peered over at Nora, who seemed to be making eye contact with her.

Linda glanced back at the entrance and pointed.

"I know a place to hide on the other side of the island. We can stay there and hide and wait for everything to blow over."

Nora glanced away, causing Linda to step closer to her.

"I found it last year," Linda added. "No one else knows about it. Not even Justin. Just me and Eve."

Linda glanced back at Eve, who was trying to brush her hair in a small mirror near the Duncans' makeshift bed. Then she turned back to Nora.

"And soon you."

Linda raised up and walked behind Nora and knelt.

"They wanna kill you," she said as she set about loosening the knots Adam had made in the ropes that bound Nora's wrists together. "I won't let that happen. But I need time to convince them otherwise."

Nora turned her head toward Eve, who saw their reflection in the mirror, then smiled and waved.

Nora smiled and said, "Amy?"

Linda looked up. She'd been too busy untying knots to hear her. "What was that?"

Linda waited for a reply, but after another quick glance at her daughter, she went back to untying the knots.

Nora continued to stare at Eve, who was now admiring herself in the small mirror.

Behind Nora, Linda held her tongue between her teeth as she worked the knots. "Almost got it."

Another weird smile slowly formed on Nora's face.

*****

In the church parking lot, Stan and Justin stood still, staring at the oncoming wave of creatures, unsure of their next move.

But they didn't have enough time to think about that because the late Ms. Williams was running up behind them.

Justin saw her and ran away from Stan to draw her away from him.

The move worked. She changed direction and rushed at him.

Justin sidestepped at the very last moment, and she fell and skid across the pavement, tearing layers of flesh in the process. But she immediately sprang to her feet, seemingly unhurt, turned to face them, and snarled.

The side of her head exploded outward before they heard the gunshot.

As her body fell, more shots rang out.

Stan and Justin watched as a large black dually truck careened into the parking lot. It ran over two creatures in the process, then slid to a stop, raising a plume of black smoke from the tires.

Two men standing in the back of the truck reloaded their weapons and proceeded to mow down the rest of the herd. The parking lot pavement was soon covered in blood and shredded limbs, heads, and torsos.

Stan and Justin, mouths open, stared up at their saviors, who peered down at them with nonjudgmental eyes.

The younger man lowered his weapon, while the older one held his high and away. There was a stern-looking bald man behind the wheel of the truck and a wild-eyed woman in the passenger seat.

The older man standing in the back of the truck yelled out, "We're headin' to a private airport to catch a flight outa here!"

The younger man in the back shouted, "If any of y'all wanna tag along, jump in the back with us!"

Stan nodded yes, while Justin glanced back at the church. "We have two more. My brother's hurt."

The older man in the back of the truck removed an earplug from one of his ears.

"Did you say hurt?" he asked. When Justin nodded, the man asked with dread and concern, "Hurt, how?"

Justin looked over at Stan for an update, but all he saw was the downcast, defeated face of the pastor.

Justin shook his head. "No."

"I'm sorry, son," Stan said while reaching out for him.

Justin avoided being touched and backed away from Stan. His tears flowed while he shook his head in disbelief.

Stan said, "I'm afraid he's gone."

"No," Justin snapped, stopping in place. "That's not possible."

Though the others in the truck didn't know who'd been lost, they remained silent out of respect.

But the eyes of the older man in the back of the truck widened, and he put his earplug back in.

As Justin backed away from Stan, blinded by his own tears and sadness, he didn't see the reanimated corpse of his brother emerge out of the church and run toward them.

But Justin did see the two men in the back of the truck aim their weapons at him.

The young man fell to the pavement unconcerned with breaking his own fall, then heard a volley of shots zipping by overhead.

As the former Chad ran, parts of his body were taken apart by the blasts. By the time he was within steps of his brother, he had fallen to the pavement in large pieces.

After the thunderous report of the weapons cleared, Justin raised his head and looked behind him. When he saw what was left of his brother, more tears came, and he laid his head down to cry.

The men in the truck heard noises and turned to see more creatures running toward their location.

"I'm sorry for your loss, gentlemen!" the older man in the back of the truck shouted while reloading his rifle. "But we ain't got all Judgment Day!"

Just then, a piercing female scream rang out from the direction of the church doorway.

Everyone craned their heads around and saw Linda standing outside the church. Her face as pale as milk. Her mouth open in an oval. Her eyes as large as silver dollars as she stared down at what was left of her boyfriend. The father of her unborn child.

"Chad?" she said.

*****

As the rain pounded down, Justin and I were forty yards down the beach from the opening in the tree line that led to our shelters. We were busy using our well-worn island hands as shovels to fill in the fresh graves with sand.

The wet, heavy sand had made it even more difficult, so our grim task was taking quite a while. But we were almost done for the night.

I shouted at Justin in order to be heard over the rain. "We'll find rocks to cover the graves tomorrow!"

Justin, exhausted and overwhelmed on top of being heartbroken, nodded and glanced past me.

As the rain pelted his face, I saw his eyes focus on something in the distance behind me.

I turned as the lightning revealed the shape of someone emerging out of the path to our shelters with a determined gait. They were now treading across the beach toward the water.

"Who is that?" Justin asked.

I couldn't quite tell through the darkness and the rain. I used my hand to shield my eyes from the downpour and could now kind of make out a tall female form a few yards from the water.

"Is that Linda?" I asked.

Somehow, Justin knew it wasn't.

He shot me a horrified glance and took off running. I tried my best to catch up to him, but he was even faster than Lloyd.

As we got closer to the woman on the beach, I could finally make out who it was.

It was Nora, and she never slowed as she walked into the surf.

I knew something horrible had happened. I felt it in the pit of my gut. From the look on Justin's face, I knew he felt it too.

Knowing where he wanted to go and relieving him of any burden for feeling that way, I shouted ahead at him, "Check on Linda!"

Justin didn't respond. I knew all he could think about was Linda, and what Nora might have done. He wasted no time running even further ahead of me in the direction of our shelters.

Despite my heart beating through my chest, the burning in my lungs, and the hitch now forming in my side, I reached the spot on the beach where Nora had entered the water. I stopped in my tracks and stared out.

I saw her waist-deep and still trudging out even further.

I cupped my hands to my mouth and shouted, "Nora!"

I didn't know whether she heard me or not, but she was now in the water up to her shoulders.

I shouted toward her again right before her head went completely under.

After a few moments when Nora didn't return to the surface, I cursed, kicked off my shoes, and ran in after her.

I ran until I was almost waist-deep, and it became too difficult to move my legs. Then I dove under a coming wave.

I held my breath and swam under the water, past the wave before emerging. After taking a gulp of air, I started swimming.

When I reached the point where I thought she went under, I took a deep breath and dove.

I couldn't see more than a few feet in front of my face through the darkness and the silt. When my lungs felt like they were about to burst, I swam for the surface, broke through, and took another deep breath before diving back under again.

I held my breath longer this time. But no matter how desperately I searched or what direction I looked, I couldn't spot Nora.

When I finally emerged from the water having failed to find her, I took in more breaths to calm my burning lungs.

I swiveled my head around and shouted for her, hoping she would hear.

*****

The black dually approached a private airfield located in the county outside the city limits.

Still driving, Lloyd saw up ahead that the double chain-link gates to the airfield were chained and locked. He slowed the truck to a stop and shouted out the window.

"What do you want me to do now?"

Blake, staring ahead and smiling, knelt and shouted back. "Ram it!"

Lloyd shot a worried glance at his wife, who pressed one hand firmly against the dashboard and took hold of the grab handle above her.

Between them sat Linda, whose face was puffy from crying. She stared down at her lap, lost in her own thoughts.

"Hey, girl," Lloyd said to her, trying to get her attention.

Linda looked up and saw the locked gates ahead.

"Hold on to something," Lloyd said.

Linda glanced at Nora, then placed both hands against the dash.

In the back, Adam glanced back at Justin and Stan, who were sitting with their backs against the tailgate.

Adam knelt beside Blake and said, "I'd get low if I were you."

Stan grimaced and lowered himself down while Justin, lost in thought, peered around in confusion.

"Get down!" Adam yelled.

Justin stared ahead as the truck lurched and sped up as it headed toward the gates. He immediately hurled himself to the pickup bed and braced himself.

The truck smashed through the gates, sending one of them hurling back over the truck. The broken chain linking both gates broke in two, sailed up, and cracked the windshield as it flew over.

The vehicle hit a severe dip meant to slow airport drivers, and its wheels left the pavement momentarily. When it came back down, it bounced its passengers up and down like rag dolls.

Lloyd hit his head on the roof of the cab, but his lanky body was so amped up, he didn't feel a thing.

All his concern fell upon his wife, who had placed her hands on her belly and started breathing hard.

"You okay?" Lloyd asked.

Nora kept breathing hard but shifted her eyes toward him and nodded.

Blake tapped the roof of the truck and shouted down at Lloyd to turn left between two groups of facing hangars.

Linda looked over at Nora and down at her belly. "How far along?"

Nora shot her an annoyed look but softened when she saw that Linda was holding her own belly in a protective manner.

"I got one more month to go," Nora told her. "How about you?"

Linda's eyes opened wide in surprise. "How'd you know?"

"Women's intuition," Nora replied, not a trace of warmth on her face.

Linda nodded and rubbed her belly. She thought of Chad in that small moment and did all she could to keep from crying.

"We just found out a couple of weeks ago," Linda said. "And now I don't know what I'm gonna do."

Nora shot her a sidelong glance, then stared ahead. "You do what you have to do to protect that baby."

Linda glanced up at her but saw Nora looking away.

"And if we make it through today in one piece," Nora continued, "you better learn that the only person you can truly depend on is yourself."

Linda looked back through the window at Justin, who was sitting with his back against the tailgate, lost in thought.

Blake pounded on the top of the truck again and yelled, "Stop right here!"

Linda turned her head back around and saw the truck skid to a stop next to a large aircraft hangar. As she peered around more, she realized the airfield looked completely deserted.

Blake jumped down from the truck and landed with a grunt on the pavement.

"Goddamn knees," he muttered as he walked off with a slight hitch in his step.

Adam jumped down after him with ease, followed by Justin, who immediately glanced back at Linda. When Justin nodded at her, Linda smiled in return.

The truck bounced up and down slightly, causing Linda to look back to see Stan crawling over the side of the truck and having some difficulty. But Justin turned and saw him and went to help him.

Linda smiled at Justin's sweetness, and for some reason, she kept staring. She didn't know why, but he seemed so different now. All the time she knew him, he'd just been Chad's little brother to her, but now she could see the resemblance. He was a lesser, more awkward version, though.

This made her miss Chad all the more, and a wave of overwhelming sadness hit her. But she fought it away and wiped her tears while making sure no one else saw them fall.

She looked out the front window at Blake as he wiped his forehead while staring toward the hangar. Then he turned back toward the truck.

"Adam and I are gonna check out this hangar!" he yelled. "The rest of y'all stay back here until we signal for ya!"

"What about me?" Justin asked as Blake removed a single earplug again to hear him better. "I can help."

"Just stay near the truck and keep watch," Blake said. "This'll only take the two of us."

Justin nodded and stared down at his feet.

Blake regarded the people in the cab.

"When we get those doors open, we have to make sure the inside is clear before we wave y'all in, all right?"

"Yeah, I got it," Lloyd replied before looking over at his wife.

As Blake turned away, Nora shot him a distrusting glance.

Lloyd caught her. "What's wrong?"

"Why are we trusting this man?" she asked. "We don't know him." She peered around outside. "We don't know any of these people."

Linda was nervous sitting between them. She didn't know what to do or say, so she just kept quiet while shifting her eyes back to Blake and Adam, then over at Justin standing outside the truck.

"They saved us," Lloyd stated. "What more do you need to know?"

"Exactly where is this man gonna take us in this plane of his anyway?"

"I'm sure somewhere safe."

Nora scoffed. "Don't be naive."

Linda glanced over at Justin, who was staring into the cab at the couple. She guessed he had overheard their conversation, and she wondered what he was thinking at that moment.

But then her attention was taken by the sound of Blake and Adam opening the hangar doors.

*****

Justin ran up to Linda's hut and swung the door open. It began battering back and forth in the gale wind.

The dwelling was made of bamboo and covered in leaves and had been decorated over the past couple of years with Eve's drawings and island-based creations such as shell necklaces and bamboo husk bracelets. Small shells and sand dollars formed mother's and daughter's names on the door.

Once Justin entered, he didn't see either of them, but he called out their names, hoping against hope they were nearby enough to hear him. Then his mind flashed on something terrible, which caused him to shout curses and run out.

He emerged into the rain, which by now was falling sideways thanks to the gusts, and ran toward the Duncans' hut.

Muttering "no" over and over again as he ran, he soon reached the hut and ran inside, yelling their names loud enough to be heard over the storm.

Adam, completely soaked and overwhelmed, ran up to the hut just as Justin reemerged and fell to his knees, pale and sobbing.

Adam knew something terrible was awaiting him inside the hut. He took a few moments to goad himself up and walk past Justin toward it, but Justin grabbed his wrist at the last possible second before he entered.

Adam stared back at Justin, who shook his head. "Don't go in there."

Adam wanted to ask him why, but he already knew.

"I'll take care of them," Justin said. Tears rolling down his face in the rain. "I promised Chad I would."

Adam somberly nodded, and Justin released his arm.

Adam watched as Justin stumbled past him, his legs trembling as if they were made of jelly, and approached the machete stuck into the log.

Justin stared down at it, trying to comprehend why this had happened. Not understanding it at all. He steeled his nerves, grabbed the machete by the handle, and yanked it out with a firm grip.

With grim determination, he strode past Adam and into the hut.

*****

Blake approached the hangar doors with trepidation.

Adam followed close on his heels, removing an earplug while holding on to the AR15. He kept watch while Blake reached into his jacket pocket and pulled out a paper clip.

Adam was taken aback as Blake started picking the master lock.

"Wait a minute," Adam said, then gazed around and lowered his voice. "I thought this was your plane?"

"Well," Blake replied, taking out an earplug and pocketing it while shrugging. "Does anything really belong to anybody anymore?"

Adam didn't know whether to laugh or call him out, so he looked away and shook his head. "I can't believe this."

Blake chuckled to himself. "You'll find there's a method to my madness."

"All I'm seeing right now is the madness."

"It's weird," Blake said, glancing back at him. "With all the bad shit goin' on today, the fact you're upset about a little grand theft plane is really funny."

"Do you even know how to fly a plane?"

Blake laughed and popped the lock open. "I guess we're about to find out, aren't we?"

Adam joined Blake in sliding open the doors. But as light entered the hangar, two undead men in jumpsuits ran from the darkness inside.

Adam panicked and aimed his weapon, but when he pulled the trigger, the shots missed the creatures completely.

One was on Blake immediately, but he managed to hold it off with one arm while reaching for his .357 in his waist holster.

Adam took aim at the other and yanked the trigger. He riddled the running corpse with bullets straight up its body and through the hangar door behind it, but none hit it in the head. It quickly recovered and kept coming for him.

Adam aimed once more and pulled the trigger, but this time the weapon clicked on empty.

"Shit!" Adam shouted, then swung the butt of his weapon.

It made a last-moment connection to the creature's face, causing its head to come open with a sickening splat. The sudden loss of momentum knocked its body backward to the pavement.

In a flash, Justin appeared and finished it off by stomping its head into pulp.

By that time, Blake had cleared his Peacemaker from its holster and shoved the long barrel under the creature's chin that he was fending off.

When he pulled the trigger, the creature's brains flew through the top of its skull, and its body fell forward onto Blake. When he stepped back, this allowed the creature to fall to the pavement face first.

Adam and Blake had just enough time to smile at one another before Linda's piercing scream alerted them to a creature that was running up on Blake from behind.

Adam aimed his weapon, but at the last second, he remembered it was empty.

Blake was too startled to raise his own gun.

They both heard a loud report as a bullet passed through the creature's diseased brain and exploded out the back of its skull, sending its body crashing to the pavement at Blake's feet.

Adam, Blake, and Justin turned toward the truck to see Stan lowering Blake's .270 Winchester.

Justin ran over and started kicking that creature's torso over and over again while cursing and yelling.

While the others stood and watched, Justin kept kicking it. Spittle flew from his lips in rage.

Adam made a move to stop him, but Blake held him back and shook his head.

When Justin finally stopped kicking, he started to cry.

Linda ran past the others and stopped by Justin's side. When he saw her, he hugged her and held her tight while she whispered something in his ear, which seemed to calm him down.

Adam peered around the group, grateful to those who had helped them. But then his gaze found Nora and Lloyd. The latter was partially outside the truck with one foot on the pavement in a noncommittal stance while the former sat in the cab staring down at her lap, talking to the baby within her belly.

A tap on the shoulder caused Adam to turn and see Blake gesturing for him to follow.

Adam glared back at Lloyd and Nora, a disgusted look on his face, then followed after Blake.

Adam soon approached the only plane in the hangar: a white Beechcraft King Air 300, a twin-prop plane capable of holding up to sixteen passengers.

When he didn't see Blake, he stopped and looked around for him but still couldn't find him.

He heard a noise near the back of the hangar and turned to see Blake emerging from a dark office.

"What are you doing?" Adam asked.

Blake raised his hands and jingled a set of keys. "Can't fly without these."

Blake trotted to the plane and went up a ramp leading to an open door.

"Let's hope it has enough fuel," Blake shouted down.

Adam shook his head. "And if it doesn't?"

When Adam didn't get a reply, he looked up at the top of the steps, but Blake was gone.

His eyes shifted over to the cockpit window where he saw Blake checking the instruments.

After a few moments, Adam heard the two engines powering up, and the propellers began to rotate.

Once they were spinning, Adam saw Blake give him a thumbs-up through the window.

Adam turned and ran toward the rest of the group.

"Let's go!" Adam shouted at them. "It's time to get on board!"

As everyone started moving toward the hangar with what little they had on them, Adam grabbed Justin by the arm.

"Stan?" Adam yelled over Justin's shoulder.

Stan was rubbing his lower back when he heard his name being called and turned around.

"You two help me get Blake's gear on the plane."

Stan nodded and joined the other two as they ran toward the truck.

Linda yelled, causing the others to stop to see her pointing toward the airfield.

That's when they saw around a half-dozen zombies running toward their hangar from a long distance away.

Adam shook his head. "Let's hurry!"

After the three men reached the back bed of the truck, they grabbed as many bags and weapons and gear as they could.

Back in the hangar, Lloyd, Nora, and Linda boarded the plane.

While the older couple sat in the front, Linda took a seat as far from them as she could in the back. Then she stared out the window toward the open hangar doors and waited. After a few moments, she started praying.

To her relief, she saw Adam, Stan, and Justin enter the hangar, all carrying bags and weapons, and run toward the plane.

Her eyes went to the doorway just as Adam, followed by Stan, entered. She gazed back out the window in concern as Adam and a grimacing Stan began shoving their bags into the overhead bins.

She heard Justin board the plane and saw his face as Adam and Stan took the bags from him and stowed them away.

Justin kept eye contact with her as he walked toward her and took a seat next to her. They sat and smiled at one another without saying a word.

Blake yelled through the open cockpit door. "Close the main exit door!"

Adam turned and approached the door. After a momentary bit of confusion, he pulled it closed and yanked the handle down to secure it.

"Got it!" Adam yelled over his shoulder.

"All right, everybody!" Blake shouted back again. "Buckle up!"

Adam took a seat in the front and grabbed the seat belt just as the plane lurched and began rolling out of the hangar.

Once the plane emerged fully, Blake turned it enough that the right wing cleared the opposite hangar.

To everyone's immense relief, the plane straightened out and started to pick up speed as it headed toward the runway. But as the passengers looked ahead, they saw that between the plane and the runway were a scattered group of zombies running toward them.

Lloyd appeared in the cockpit doorway and stared ahead. He watched as Blake went out of his way to steer the plane away from the creatures outside and pass them by.

"What are you doing?" Lloyd asked.

"Avoiding contact."

"Why? Just run 'em over. Chop their damn heads off."

"That'll damage the propellers," Blake replied, then shot him a glance. "And then we can't fly."

With the creatures outside now in pursuit, Blake eventually guided the plane to the runway and turned onto it.

"Go back and buckle up!" Blake shouted.

Lloyd stood in place stubbornly, then walked off and sat down next to his wife.

Blake pushed the throttle forward, and the plane began rolling faster and faster.

The last of the passengers put on their seat belts just as the plane's wheels left the ground.

*****

As Justin's eyes adjusted to the darkness, he heard the unmistakable sound of an animal gnawing. Before tears could swell in his eyes, he fought off the sadness and saw the source of the sound.

Linda sat with her back to him. She was hunched over, gnawing on something on the floor. Oblivious to his presence, her head twisted back and forth, and her teeth tore away meat and chewed.

Tears fell as Justin shook his head and stepped closer to her. He raised the machete and started to sob.

Linda's body shifted as she ate, revealing the torn, bloody body of Eve lying dead in a growing pool of blood.

One look at the little girl's corpse broke him.

Justin sobbed out loud, and Linda turned and glared up at him.

Gone from her was all her humanity. Her spark. Yet to Justin, she was still the most beautiful thing he'd ever seen.

The creature rose to its feet and growled at Justin.

"I've always loved you," he said, then swung the blade with all he had in him.

*****

After being in the air for nearly two hours, Blake was sitting in the cockpit staring ahead at the passing clouds. With a satisfied grin, he glanced back to check on everyone in the passenger section.

He found them either engaged in conversation or staring silently out the windows at the brown and green squares of land and bodies of water sweeping past below.

He turned back to stare out the cockpit window just as Adam entered, causing Blake to jump, startled.

"Sorry," Adam said, grinning. "Didn't mean to scare ya."

Blake shook his head. "Just surprised me a little, that's all."

Adam smiled as he slid into the copilot seat. He glanced ahead out the window before asking, "Where are we?"

"We should hit South Padre Island in about ten minutes."

Adam winced. "Did you have to say the word hit?"

Blake started laughing and shook his head.

Adam glanced around, marveling at his surroundings. "I've never been in a cockpit before."

Blake looked over at him. "Is it everything you thought it would be?"

"Most definitely," Adam replied, chuckling.

A red alarm light started blinking and began to buzz. Blake, appearing confident and with no trace of fear, flipped a switch, and the buzzing stopped.

"What's wrong?" Adam asked, sitting forward. The blood leaving his face.

Blake shook his head. "We're low on fuel."

Shocked, Adam spun to face him. "What?"

"The plane wasn't quite full when we took off."

"And you're just now telling me this?"

"I had to make a call."

"But this is our lives."

"Don't worry." Blake turned to him, face devoid of sweat. "I got this."

As Adam watched, Blake pushed more buttons, dials, and switches. Not in a panic but smooth and deliberate.

Adam glanced back to see Lloyd staring into the cockpit. Concern was written on his face as well. The others somehow seemed oblivious and lost in their own thoughts.

Adam nodded back to him, but Lloyd kept staring.

"Look, we can argue about my omission of facts later," Blake said. "But right now, I gotta prepare to land this plane. And even if we're running on fumes by then, I can handle it."

Adam leaned toward him, talking low through gritted teeth. "You're sure?"

"Positive," Blake replied. "Trust me."

Adam shot him a look and shook his head.

"Have I let y'all down yet?" Blake said, smiling.

Adam glanced back at the cabin. He saw Lloyd still staring into the cockpit. A questioning expression on his face.

"How long until we land again?" Adam asked.

Blake checked a few gauges. "About nine minutes. Why?"

Adam gestured toward the others. "I'm gonna tell them to prepare themselves for a possible rough landing."

"Why?" Blake asked, concerned. "You just said you trusted me?"

Adam placed his hand on Blake's shoulder. "I do, but they need to know what's going on."

Blake and Adam kept eye contact until Blake nodded and turned his attention back to the controls.

As Adam walked out of the cockpit, he tried gathering his thoughts. But Lloyd interrupted those when he asked, "What's going on up there?"

Before Adam could answer, Nora shouted, "Lloyd said he heard a noise, and it didn't sound like good news. What was it?"

By this time, the others were invested in the conversation and quickly became nervous and scared.

"All right, everybody, listen up!" Adam shouted, then waited for them to calm down. "We'll be landing shortly. But we might have a problem before then."

"What kinda problem?" Nora asked, rudeness in her voice. She gestured to the cockpit. "Can he land this damn thing or not?"

"You're not helping, Nora," Adam replied, glaring at her.

Nora thought about saying something, but Lloyd grabbed her hand and squeezed it. She glared at her husband's profile.

"We're running low on fuel," Adam said.

Most of them panicked more and stared out the windows toward the engines. Others started shouting questions, hoping to be heard.

"We didn't have to tell you that!" Adam shouted over them. "But we did because you deserve to know."

That caused them to quiet down.

"But don't worry," Adam said. "Blake's got it under control."

He glared at Nora in particular.

"And we have no reason not to trust him. Because if it weren't for him, most of us would probably be dead by now. Or worse."

Some lowered their heads in understanding. Others, like Nora, kept seething.

"I know for damn sure I'd be," Adam said.

As Adam watched, Nora broke eye contact and aimed her glare out her window while Lloyd sighed and closed his eyes.

"Right now, everyone needs to buckle up," Adam said, "and you might wanna remove your seat cushions and put 'em on your lap."

"You mean, crash positions?" Justin asked.

Alarmed, Linda asked, "We're not gonna crash, are we?"

Her panic level rose higher as she peered out her window.

"I'm not gonna lie to you," Adam said, holding his hands out for reassurance. "It could be a rough landing."

"What the hell does that mean?" Lloyd asked while trying to unbuckle his seat belt.

Adam rushed over and placed his hand on Lloyd's shoulder.

"I said, don't worry," Adam told him. "Blake's got this."

Lloyd's face was red, but he didn't say anything.

"It'll be okay," Adam said, staring into his eyes.

He saw Nora roll her eyes as she faced the window. Her mouth forming a straight line.

Adam peered silently around at each of them, but when he saw Stan, a smile came to his face.

"I think we could all use a little faith right about now," Adam said. "Ain't that right, Stan?"

Stan looked up, bewildered. He saw Adam staring at him, then saw everyone else doing the same.

"I heard you were a preacher," Adam asked. "That right?"

"That," Stan said, nodding, "that's right."

"He's a good one too," Justin added from the back.

Stan turned and saw Justin give him a reassuring nod, which did nothing to take away the pained look on his own face.

"How about you lead us in prayer, Stan?" Adam asked.

Stan's mood darkened. Everyone saw it.

"What's wrong?" Adam asked, concerned.

Stan was near tears as he looked up at Adam, then around at the others. "I don't think…"

"What?"

Stan shook his head. "I can't."

"Why?"

Stan wanted to tell Adam the truth right there and then, but he didn't have the guts to tell him or them how he felt about God right then.

So he lied. "I forgot my Bible."

The others became downcast. Their moods were affected as well.

"In all that running around," Stan said, hating himself at the moment, "I forgot to bring it with me."

Adam thought for a moment, then placed a hand on Stan's shoulder.

"But we don't need a Bible, Stan," Adam said. "We have you."

Stan's heart fell as he looked up at Adam, then around at the faces staring at him with newfound hope. With the exception of the Duncans.

Stan decided to fake it. To lie for their own good. It was the least he could do. He managed to smile and nod. Then he peered up at Adam and said, "I'll do my best."

"I have no doubt," Adam replied, smiling back.

As Adam moved back to his seat in the cockpit, he peered back as Stan stayed in his seat and turned toward the others.

"Everyone, bow your heads, please," Stan asked, his voice cracking.

All of them did as Stan asked, except Nora, who was giving him a sideways glare.

As Stan began, Adam turned toward Blake, who winked at him and said, "Good job."

Blake went back to the task at hand.

"Now for the hard part," Blake added, causing Adam to peer over at him.

As Stan's voice rose from the back, Adam turned away from Blake and bowed his own head yet kept his eyes open.

"Our Father, which art in heaven. Hallowed be thy name."

Adam stared ahead and saw nothing but clouds as the group repeated after Stan.

"Our Father, which art in heaven. Hallowed be thy name."

Adam glanced over at Blake to see that his hands were slightly trembling.

"Thy kingdom come. Thy will be done on earth, as it is in heaven."

Blake absentmindedly flexed his right hand and shook it.

"Thy kingdom come. Thy will be done on earth, as it is in heaven."

Adam turned back to see everyone with their heads still bowed while Stan led them.

"Give us this day our daily bread. And forgive us our trespasses."

As Linda and Justin, eyes closed, repeated after Stan, Justin opened his eyes and glanced over at Linda.

"Give us this day our daily bread. And forgive us our trespasses."

Stan shifted in his seat uncomfortably, his voice wavering.

"As we forgive those that trespass against us."

Lloyd kept his eyes closed but only mouthed the words. Not saying them out loud.

"As we forgive those that trespass against us."

Nora kept quiet, only staring out the window.

"And lead us not into temptation, but deliver us from evil."

Blake patted Adam on the shoulder and said, "Hey, look."

"And lead us not into temptation, but deliver us from evil."

Adam turned to Blake, then looked forward. He saw only clouds.

"For thine is the kingdom."

"What am I supposed to be looking at?" Adam asked, confused.

"For thine is the kingdom."

"Were you one of those kids who wanted to know what he got for Christmas before Christmas?" Blake asked.

"The power and the glory."

Adam shook his head and smiled, "All I see is clouds."

"The power and the glory."

"Wait for it," Blake said, smiling larger.

"Forever and ever."

Adam felt his stomach drop as the plane descended below the clouds.

"Forever and ever."

Adam glanced up at the clouds that were now overhead and then saw nothing but blue sky all around.

"Amen."

Adam glanced down even further and finally saw the blue waters of the Gulf of Mexico below.

"Amen," Blake said, along with the rest of the passengers.

Adam patted Blake on the shoulder with a big smile on his face. "Amen."

Adam then turned back to the others.

"I can see the Gulf of Mexico from here."

Excited, they all moved in their seats to stare out the windows.

What they saw brought smiles to their faces.

Stan sat back and wiped his brow. Glad the show and his part in it was over.

Adam shouted, "I told y'all to just have faith."

Those words pierced Stan's heart as those around him started clapping and cheering and whistling. This caused him to fake his own smile.

Adam turned to Blake. "Sorry for doubting."

"Oh, we ain't outa the woods yet, partner," Blake replied.

"What now?" Adam asked, staring out the window.

"I still gotta land, and we ain't gonna make it to the runway."

"What does that mean?"

"It means I gotta improvise, adapt, overcome."

"What?"

"It means we gotta land on something long enough to be a runway."

"Which is?

Blake pointed out the window. "The beach."

Adam shook his head. "Is that safe?"

"It'll have to do."

Adam sat back in his chair, sweat starting to pour, his heart beating fast in his chest.

While Blake checked the instruments, Adam closed his eyes, trying to think of anything else except where he was, and what was happening.

He only opened them when he felt the plane turning and descending at the same time and looked out the cockpit window.

Below was their destination. But to Adam's horror, parts of it were on fire, and the sky above was filled with a thick layer of black smoke, which settled over the island like an umbrella.

Blake pointed out the window. "Run your eyes north along the beach."

"What direction is that?" Adam asked.

"Up."

Adam did as he was told. "What am I looking for?"

"Boats."

As the plane dipped lower, now flying under the smoke, Adam squinted.

"I don't see any boats."

Blake smiled. "Past the beach, in the water."

Adam's eyes looked everywhere. His heart thundering in his chest. On the verge of panic. "I don't see any goddamn boats."

Then right before his eyes, he made several white vessels in the water past the beach.

"Wait!" Adam shouted, smiling. "I see 'em. I see boats."

Blake smiled but lost it quickly when the left engine sputtered, and its propeller wound down to a stop.

Blake quickly shut off the power to the left engine while correcting the plane. He managed to keep it in the air with the lone remaining engine.

"Now comes the hard part," Blake said.

He turned the plane, then straightened it out, keeping it level on the artificial horizon.

Adam saw the beach ahead, and as the plane descended further, it came closer and closer.

That's when the last propeller came to a sudden stop, and the remaining engine sputtered and died, causing the plane to dip dramatically.

This startled the passengers in the back who were already panicking. Some of them began holding each other's hands.

Blake kept the plane in the air while shutting off the power to the last engine.

He deftly balanced out the plane. At the same time, he lowered it in increments.

Adam was afraid to look out the window but couldn't help it.

He watched as the plane glided through a dark cloud of smoke drifting up from below and emerged even closer to the beach.

Blake flipped a switch, and the wheels lowered with a whine and locked in place.

Blake caught Adam's eye and said, "Hold on to your nuts."

Adam turned to the others in the back and yelled, "Get into crash positions!"

He watched as they all lowered their heads to the seat cushions resting on their knees. Then he turned and cupped his balls with both hands, which caused Blake to laugh to beat the band as he kept lowering the plane toward the beach.

That's when Adam realized the only sounds he could now hear were his heart beating in his ears, and the air rushing by outside the craft.

The beach got closer and closer, and Blake's smile got larger, but Adam didn't see any of that.

He had closed his eyes. If he hadn't, he would have seen about a hundred people walking on the beach. But he also would have seen that their motions were no longer human.

Blake raised the plane's altitude. He glanced over at Adam, eyes still closed, who didn't know they had barely cleared a tall building.

Blake kept that secret to himself, then began lowering the plane again.

They were now flying low over the beach and quickly running out of landing room.

Blake yelled to his passengers, "Sorry about this!"

Before the passengers could register what he had said, the plane dropped drastically. The wheels were now low enough to skim the tops of the heads of the zombies below.

As the plane rattled and bucked, Blake lowered the plane further until multiple thudding sounds could be heard coming from the bottom of the plane.

Adam heard the sounds and opened his eyes. When he saw the plane mowing down the herd of zombies in its path along the beach, he let out a high-pitched yell.

The plane's wheels hit the beach surface, causing the nose of the plane to dip. The propellers tore up the sand, sending up a huge cloud before they bent back on themselves.

The left propeller broke off, shearing through the left wing and tearing it from the plane. The wheels broke off, and the plane's belly fell to the earth. It then slid while its nose dug a tunnel in the sand.

The plane came to a stop with parts clicking and clacking as it rested on the ground.

*****

The storm had finally slowed to a drizzle. The moon emerged from the dissipating clouds revealing a beautiful night. The stars were out in full force. The air, tinged with salt, smelled clean.

I had just finished burying Linda and Eve next to the others we'd lost that day.

Completely exhausted down to my soul, I looked down the beach and saw Justin sitting alone, staring out at the water.

Carrying the machete, I took my time walking, but I eventually reached him.

Before I could say anything, he started talking.

"I fell in love with Linda the first time I ever saw her. I was with my friends at the ice-skating rink. But I was too shy to ask her out.

"And the next time I saw her, I was at the mall with Chad, and I had to watch his dumb ass walk right up to her and ask her out right in front of me."

Justin shook his head at the memory.

"At that moment, I knew right away that she liked him. You could just tell. It was love at first sight. I mean, she kept playing with her hair and laughing at all his stupid jokes. All while I was standing right there too.

"But I might as well have been invisible. I mean, they weren't being mean about it or anything. They were just in their own little world. Which is where they were most of the time when they were together. Like no one else existed but them.

"It tore me apart every time I saw 'em together. But I couldn't say anything because she was my brother's girlfriend, and no one would understand why I felt that way about her. I just had to keep my mouth shut about it and never say how I felt out loud.

"What really sucked…I couldn't even hate my brother for it. Because I loved him and wanted him to be happy.

"But the day when everything went to shit, I'd actually sat in church that morning and thought about what it would be like if Chad was gone. Just, you know, imagining what would happen if it was just me and her. That may be in time she'd fall in love with me, you know, after I proved myself to her.

"Then when he died, I blamed myself. Feeling like I was responsible because I'd had those stupid thoughts. And that's why I broke down crying that day. But Linda, she comforted me. She held me close to her, and for a second, it was the best feeling in the world. Touching her. Her touching me. But that was it. That one time. And it lasted just a few minutes. Every day after that, my thoughts about her made me feel a little worse. Like I was betraying Chad. Which I guess I was.

"You know, Linda told me that day that she needed me. That she needed me to look out for her and her baby. That we could all look out for each other from then on and raise her baby together.

"But it didn't happen like I wanted it to. I thought we could end up being a real family. That I could be more than an uncle to Eve and a brother-in-law to Linda. That's what kept me going all these years. That hope.

"But the joke was on me. Even after he died, I still didn't have a chance. Nothing ever happened between Linda and me because she was still in love. Only now she was in love with his memory."

Justin peered up with tears in his eyes.

"How pathetic is that?" he asked, lying down and staring up at the night sky. "I can't even compete with a ghost."

As tiny droplets of rain fell onto his face, he closed his eyes and started to cry.

Not knowing what to say, I stood there in silence a few moments before walking away and leaving him alone with his tortured and regretful thoughts on the beach.

*****

The plane's exit door opened from the inside. Moments later, an inflatable ramp extended out from the bottom of the door and extended down to the beach.

With an AR15 strapped to his shoulder, and a small ammo bag tied around his waist, Adam appeared in the doorway and looked out.

He heard ocean waves hitting the beach and squinted around at the wake of devastation the plane had left behind. The sands were dark with blood and scattered remains and moving body parts here and there.

He shielded his eyes with one hand and surveyed the rest of their surroundings. He saw a few zombies on the beach. Most of whom were having difficulty running on the sand.

He looked straight ahead and saw a parking lot full of zombies behind a long, tall chain-link fence that ran along the length of the beach. Several of the creatures had already gathered at the barrier, trying in vain to get past it but not having any success.

Adam sat down on the edge of the ramp and pushed off. He slid to the bottom and leaped to his feet. He took the weapon into his hands and aimed at a creature lumbering across the sand toward him. He squeezed the trigger and took it down with a short burst.

After surveying the area around him to make sure it was safe, he waved for the next person.

Justin was the next to slide down with a Glock .45 in hand, and a satchel filled with loaded clips strapped around his waist.

While Adam kept watch, Justin got to his feet, looked around, then signaled for the next person.

Linda appeared in the doorway, fear coming out of every pore.

Suitcase in her hand, she peered around and then stared down at Justin. She shook her head. "I don't know if I can do this!"

"You have to!" Justin implored.

"Come on!" Adam shouted, then fired at another oncoming zombie.

As it fell, Adam shouted over his shoulder, "Do it now!"

Linda took a step back, startled at Adam's abrupt haste. She then watched as Justin took down two of those things like he'd been doing it all his life.

Justin turned, nodded up at her, and yelled, "You got this!"

Linda slowly sat down on the edge of the ramp, suitcase in her lap, and took several deep breaths to calm herself. She closed her eyes and slid down, screaming all the way.

Justin was there to lift her up at the bottom and looked her in the eyes. "Now stay behind me."

When she did that, Justin took aim at the nearest zombie. He fired, and the creature fell to the sand.

Stan, armed with the deer rifle, slid down next without a second thought.

Justin fired at an approaching zombie until the clip was empty. He released the clip, letting it drop to the sand, then reached into the ammo satchel and retrieved a loaded one.

He popped it in, racked the weapon, loading a bullet in the chamber, and took aim again. Two pops, and another went down.

With a full trash bag in hand, Lloyd appeared in the doorway and stared out at the undead.

"Come on, Lloyd!" Adam shouted. "Get your ass in gear!"

Lloyd took one more look and started backing away from the door, but suddenly he staggered forward and fell out.

Adam was shocked as he turned and saw Lloyd sliding headfirst down the ramp. He glanced back up and saw Blake standing in the doorway, rifle in hand, grinning down at Lloyd.

When Lloyd reached the bottom, he rolled over, his face red with anger, and glared up at Blake.

"Rub some dirt on it, Lloyd!" Blake shouted. "You'll be okay!"

When Adam realized Blake had shoved Lloyd out of the plane, he couldn't help but laugh at the very thought of it. But a shout of warning from Stan brought him back to the moment. He turned around and took down another lurching zombie with a short burst of gunfire.

Blake saw the snarling, desperate creatures gathered at the fence and flipped them off. Then he jumped onto the ramp and slid down.

Justin was there to lend Blake a hand when he reached the bottom.

The older man used the young man's assistance to get to his feet.

Justin then turned, and his eyes widened as he saw a zombie running up behind Linda.

"Duck!" he yelled at her.

She immediately closed her eyes and fell to her knees as Justin aimed over her and opened fire.

Linda felt something land behind her and spray her with sand.

She opened her eyes and glanced back to find a dead zombie lying face down inches away from her.

Justin helped her back to her feet, and she hid behind him.

Suitcase in hand, Nora appeared in the doorway, showing no fear as she stared out at the chaos below. She lowered herself down to sit on the edge of the ramp and slid down without a second thought.

Whatever had come over her, gone was the panic-stricken woman from just a few hours earlier.

Justin and Linda were there to pull her upright. But instead of thanking them, she turned and glared at her husband, who was still fuming at Blake.

Blake fired into an oncoming creature that was barely able to maintain its balance. The wounded zombie fell onto Blake and grabbed at him.

Blake shoved the creature away, and it fell. He quickly aimed straight down at its head. With one blast, he put it out of its misery.

Lloyd shouted to his wife, face still red with fury, "That damn no-good son of a bitch pushed me off!"

Nora had no time for this. "Oh, quit bein' a pussy!"

Lloyd looked at her in shock as she walked past him while protecting her belly. He glanced at Blake again, cursed, and followed his wife's path.

Adam reloaded and took down two more creatures that were closing in on Lloyd and Nora. The elated looks on their faces were gone as soon as they saw it was him who had saved them. They turned away without saying a word.

Adam watched as Justin and Stan fired in two different directions, while Linda fell in behind them.

Then he saw Blake stumble and fall.

Adam took aim at a snarling creature falling to its knees near Blake and shot it through the neck.

Adam ran over and kicked the creature over onto its back. He aimed down and shot it in the face, then knelt beside Blake.

"You okay, old man?"

Blake smiled up at him. "Just get me to my feet, whippersnapper."

Adam helped Blake up, then sprayed two other creatures.

"Where are the boats?" Adam yelled back at Blake, tired and out of breath.

Blake tilted his chin north.

"You sure?" Adam asked.

When Blake shot him a sarcastic glare, Adam smiled.

"Everybody!" Adam shouted, gesturing ahead up the beach. "Go that way!" He paused to catch his breath. "To the marina!"

"A marina?" Justin asked. Like he'd never heard the word before.

"We gotta steal a boat!" Adam yelled.

Justin immediately got it. His spirits raised, he smiled and nodded, then turned and fired at an advancing zombie.

From that point forward, they worked together to fight their way along the beach toward the distant marina. Those with weapons formed a killing circle, shooting any creature that got close enough.

*****

As Justin stared up at the night sky, the rhythmic waves crashed onto the beach.

Normally, the surf sounds would lull him to sleep, as it had many nights in the past. But tonight, he couldn't drift away. He was thinking of Linda.

Doing so was painful, but he couldn't stop.

Once, during their first few weeks on the island, he had come to visit Linda in her hut while she was pregnant but not showing yet.

He knocked on her door, then opened it and entered without waiting for permission.

"Hey," he said.

Linda had bolted upright on her bed and tried to hide her face from him, but it was too late. He'd seen that she'd been crying, as he knew she did most nights.

Embarrassed and apologetic, he started to back out. "I'm sorry."

But she surprised him when she said, "It's okay."

He stared down at the floor while she wiped her face and nose with the front of her shirt. She was embarrassed and trying to cover it with laughter.

"I could come back later," he said while closing his eyes and shaking his head, regretting his foolishness.

"No, seriously," she replied, trying to smile. "It's okay."

Justin entered, carefully shutting the door behind him. He stood awkwardly in the doorway, nervous, not sure what to do next.

Linda glanced up at him, then patted the spot next to her on the bed, gesturing for him to sit.

"You sure?" he asked, surprised and elated. His mouth dry. His heart beating in his throat and pounding in his ears.

"Unless you think I'm hideous," she replied, a sincere smile on her face that was still red and puffy from crying.

Justin shook his head and approached her. "You're far from hideous."

He carefully sat down next to her like she was a frail, scared animal that he was trying not to spook into running away.

"You're beautiful," he added.

"Sure," she chuckled, shaking her head. "Especially now that I'm pregnant and have snot running everywhere."

"But you are," he replied.

Her head darted toward him, surprised.

When he made eye contact with her, he didn't look away. He looked confident. A new look for him.

As she looked into his eyes, she smiled. She found herself not being able to look away either.

"What?" he asked.

"You," she began, shaking her head and looking away. "You have his eyes."

Justin looked down at his lap. Guilt starting to grow in his conscience.

Linda smiled down at her belly. "I hope my baby has those eyes."

Justin glanced over at her. As he saw her smiling while looking down at her belly, he thought, *There will never be a more perfect time than now.*

Sensing him watching her, Linda turned toward Justin just as a huge grin spread across his face.

When she made eye contact, his heart swelled, and he found himself short of breath. He willed himself to lean forward, and he kissed her.

Her smile immediately left her face, and her eyes widened in shock as her mind registered what was happening.

She shoved him away in anger and stood up from the bed.

"What are you doing?" she asked, wiping her face.

Justin could only shake his head back and forth. He couldn't form words.

"Please leave," she ordered, looking away from him, ashamed and upset.

He stood confused and heartbroken. Tears began to fall down his face as his mouth still tried to say something, but his brain wasn't cooperating.

When she realized he was still standing there, she glared at him and pointed at the door.

"I asked you to leave!" she shouted.

Justin opened his tear-filled eyes on the beach and looked around. As the tears for her loss flowed, he felt truly lost and utterly alone for the first time in a long time.

Even though Linda had never felt for him what he felt for her, she'd at least been there close by the past few years on the island.

But now she was gone for good, and he wasn't sure how he was supposed to go on.

As he covered his face with his arm, he concentrated on the waves and tried to stop thinking. He hoped if he cleared his head that the sounds would work their magic, and he'd finally drift away to sleep.

With the way he felt now, he didn't know if he ever wanted to wake back up.

As he laid there thinking, the waves eventually began to work their magic. Without even realizing, he fell asleep. The snores came soon after, and the dreams continued.

But unbeknownst to him, something stirred under the surface of the water.

*****

When the group made it to the marina entrance, they encountered a closed electronic gate.

As Blake surveyed the group, they all looked dead on their feet, except for Justin, who appeared to have enough energy for all of them.

"Hey, kid?" Blake said, pointing past the fence. "Climb over and open this fence from that guard shack over there."

All eyes went to the tiny building with a window looking out on the parking lot just inside the fence.

Justin saluted with a smile. "Yes, sir."

Everyone chuckled as Justin scaled the fence like a monkey and dropped down to the other side. He ran to the shack, slipped inside, and pressed a series of buttons on a counter.

To his surprise, there was a mechanical rumble as a chain in a track started moving, and the gate began to roll open.

The others were too exhausted to celebrate, but the triumphant looks on their tired faces said it all for them.

Justin gave them a thumbs-up from the shack as, one by one, they entered the marina and made their way to the closest dock.

Without being asked, Justin pressed another button near the last one he touched, and the gate came to a stop midway open.

Justin pressed yet another button, and the gate started rolling closed. Then he ran to rejoin the group.

He caught up with them just as they were passing the harbormaster's shack.

Blake glanced back and saw Justin smiling while walking with Linda. He held up his index finger to the young man and said, "One more favor, por favor."

Blake pointed at the shack.

"Go grab us some keys, please."

Justin smiled, perhaps enjoying breaking and entering a little too much. He ran toward the shack while the rest headed toward a dock.

When Justin reached the door to the shack and tried to open it, he found it locked. He peered around, then used the gun handle to shatter the window on the door. He reached in, unlocked it, and stepped inside.

Meanwhile, Adam was the first to step onto the dock. He found that most of the boat slips were empty, save for a handful of craft. He heard footsteps fast approaching the group from behind and aimed his weapon toward the sounds.

Justin saw the barrel trained on him and stuttered his legs to a stop.

"Whoa! Whoa! Whoa!" Justin yelled, holding up a box of keys. "I found these!"

Blake searched the dock until he found what he was looking for. A forty-eight-foot motor sailer named the *Nightingale*. To him, it was the perfect vessel. It was big enough for all of them, and not only did it have a motor, but it also had sails, which they'd need if it didn't have fuel.

Blake shouted over his shoulder. "Let's see if the keys are in there for the *Nightingale*."

As Justin nodded and began rooting through the box for the key, Linda set down her suitcase and joined him. Both were excited, as if this were a simple scavenger hunt for fun and not their very lives.

Adam heard another noise behind them and glanced back.

A herd of zombies had made it to the marina gate, having probably located them by their scent.

"Shit," Adam said, pointing behind them.

When the others turned to look back, the creatures locked eyes with them and started growling and snarling, as if on cue.

Screams and shouts went up as Blake pointed toward the boat.

"Let's get on board and look for the keys there."

As the group reached the boat, Lloyd helped his wife on board, then got on with their luggage.

Stan climbed aboard after them and gazed around. That's when he noticed the ropes securing the boat to the dock in four different spots; two in the bow, two in the stern.

Linda screamed, drawing everyone's attention to her, fearing the worst. All they saw was her smiling while holding up a lanyard with two keys on a bobber.

"Found 'em!" she yelled.

Printed on the lanyard was "The Nightingale."

Before anyone could rejoice at the find, the sound of metal crashing to the pavement erupted at the entrance.

The group collectively swung their heads around to see the zombies stampeding over the gate after it had fallen.

Linda was the last to turn and spot the oncoming horde running toward them on the dock. She screamed, frozen in place.

Justin wasted no time grabbing the keys from her. He picked up her suitcase, took her by the hand, and yanked her toward the boat.

Standing on the deck near the boat, Adam and Blake stared back and watched as the creatures reached the dock. Many of their paths led them directly into the water, but some managed to stay on the dock on a direct course for the group.

Justin stepped before them and helped Linda aboard the boat, then climbed aboard after her and ran to the helm.

Once there, he set down the luggage and looked all around the steering wheel for an ignition. He began to panic when he couldn't find it.

Linda was soon at his side, joining him in the frantic search.

"Where the hell is it?" Justin screamed.

Before Blake and Adam could climb aboard, Stan stepped before them and pointed at the ropes.

"We gotta untie these, or we aren't going anywhere."

Blake grimaced and jumped on board. He peered back at Adam. "Stan and I'll take the front."

Blake looked around and saw Linda standing outside the helm, watching as Justin searched for the ignition.

He added, "You and her take care of the back."

Adam nodded, then Blake and Stan ran down opposite sides of the boat toward the bow.

Adam jumped on board and yelled for Linda. When she turned, he eyed the cleat on the stern's port side. "Untie that!"

Confused, she watched as Adam began untying the rope from the cleat on the starboard stern side.

Overwhelmed and frozen in place, Linda turned her head and saw the horde on the dock getting closer. Some of the faster ones were shoving others out of their way, knocking them into the water.

"Yeah!" Justin yelled from the pilot's seat.

Linda glanced back and saw that he had found the ignition near the armrest under a folded newspaper.

Working feverishly, Blake managed to untie the rope from his side, then ran over to help Stan, who was just now loosening the rope on his side.

With trembling hands, Justin somehow managed to slide the key into the boat's ignition and turned it.

The motor rumbled to life. Without looking back, he pushed the throttle forward.

Just as Adam untied the rope from his cleat, the boat lurched forward but only turned and slammed into the dock. However, the pads secured to the side of the dock minimized the damage to the vessel.

Nearly everyone on board stumbled and fell where they were.

Adam nearly tipped over the stern into the water below but kept his balance by bracing himself against the stern with his arms.

Linda had scraped her knees on the wooden deck but quickly glanced up and pulled her hair from her face.

At the same time, she and Adam saw that a solitary rope wrapped around the stern port-side cleat was keeping the boat from leaving the dock.

Adam ran over and tried to loosen the rope, but it wouldn't budge. He began kicking at the cleat, trying to knock it loose from the boat, but that didn't work either.

With the creatures closing in, Adam cursed as the rope refused to break.

Near panic, Linda glanced around the boat and saw something reflecting the sun. On closer inspection, she saw something metal tucked inside some netting fastened to the interior side.

Adam saw out of the corner of his eye that the horde was maybe twenty yards away. He yanked on the rope as hard as he could, despite knowing it wasn't going to work but not willing to give up.

A shadow loomed next to him, causing him to glance over at a silhouette. As he blocked his eyes from the sun, he saw Linda holding something above her head.

"Move!" she yelled through gritted teeth.

Adam let go of the rope and stumbled back as his hopes were answered in the form of a machete. Linda brought her arm down with a metal whack. When Adam looked down, the last remaining rope was cut cleanly in two.

The boat lurched forward as if shot out of a cannon. Adam's body slammed against the stern again while Linda fell hard against him, and the machete clanked to the floor. She latched onto him as they both fell back. But at the last second, Blake grabbed Adam by the shirt collar and stopped his progress just enough to keep him from falling overboard.

But Linda wasn't as lucky. Her lower legs hit the stern, and her momentum carried her over headfirst into the water.

Adam yelled and reached for her, but it was too late. She'd already disappeared under the surface. He broke away from a stunned Blake and dove into the water without hesitation.

Justin turned his head around, hoping to see Linda. When he didn't see her behind him or anywhere else on the boat, he panicked.

"Linda!" he shouted. Looking everywhere. Not seeing her. "Linda!"

"She went overboard, you idiot!" Nora yelled back at him from her perch near the doorway of the cabin, down in the hull.

Justin glanced back toward the water near the dock. He saw Linda breaking the surface and taking in whatever air she could. He saw Adam swimming fast in her direction.

Next, he witnessed the zombies running off the dock a few yards behind Linda and plunging into the water in an insane effort to go after their prey. Unlike Linda, they did not come back up.

"Well, the good news is," Blake said to Stan while observing the creatures mindlessly running off the dock like a spooked herd of buffalo running off a cliff in the days of the Wild West. "The bastards can't swim."

Justin spun the steering wheel, and the boat took a sudden left turn, causing everyone on board to lurch to the right. Even though this time no one fell off, judging by the looks on everyone's faces, they were still pissed.

"Watch what you're doing, asshole!" Nora yelled from the stern deck, where she had fallen to her knees.

Justin glanced back and saw Blake giving him a warning glance.

The young man shook his head and calmed himself down enough to negotiate a smoother turn.

He soon brought the vessel back around and headed toward Linda and Adam.

In the water, Adam was exhausted, and the muscles in his arms were burning. He was also coughing due to some saltwater he had accidentally inhaled. But when he heard Linda screaming and thrashing about in the water about thirty yards away, he stopped swimming and raised his head up to see her fighting to keep her head above water.

"Linda!" he yelled, then blew the tingling saltwater sensation out of his nose. "Linda!"

She waved frantically at him, then went back under. When she reemerged in a panic and yelled for him, her mouth was full of seawater.

Adam swung his hands up and used them to break the water's surface and dive under. He emerged, kicking and paddling toward her, taking quick side breaths as he went.

Linda kicked with all her might and tread water with her arms.

Even though she knew Adam was coming for her, that didn't stop her from panicking about going under again. She felt if she did, she would never come back up.

Adam kept swimming, checking on occasion to see if she was still above the surface. But as he watched, she screamed and went under again. His eyes went wide, then he took a deep breath and went under.

Back on the boat, Justin panicked when Linda didn't come back up.

The others were concerned, even Nora, who held her hand over her chest while unknowingly holding her breath.

As the boat approached the spot where Linda submerged, Justin slowed it down. Most of the people on board ran to the port side and searched frantically for signs of life below the water.

Justin pulled the throttle back and shut off the engine. He grabbed a round life preserver and ran to the side to join the search as well.

Stan saw a small ladder with a hook that enabled it to hang from the side of the boat. He ran to grab it.

While everyone stood on the port side, they all heard Adam's voice calling out from the other side, and they ran over to it.

When they looked down, they cheered when they saw Adam holding Linda, who was coughing and gasping for air.

Stan lowered the ladder in place and extended an arm to them.

Despite being fatigued, Adam grabbed onto the ladder, and with his other hand, lifted Linda out of the water enough for Stan and Justin to grab her small frame and pull her onto the deck.

Adam smiled, relaxed, and laid back to rest. As he floated on the water, he looked up at the sky and passing clouds thinking he'd never been more tired.

Blake's smiling face soon appeared over the edge and looked down at him. "Well, don't just lie there getting a suntan. We got a journey to make."

When Blake reached his left hand out toward him, Adam lifted his head out of the water and grabbed hold of the ladder again. With Blake's help, he pulled himself up.

Other hands appeared, and soon Adam found himself lying on his back on the deck, staring up at the group, most of whom had smiling faces.

Justin extended a hand and helped Adam to his feet. With tears in his eyes, he bear-hugged him with all his might.

"Thank you," Justin said, smiling while glancing back at Linda, who also had tears in her eyes as she looked up at Adam.

She ran into him with a little too much force, but he didn't mind. She hugged him tightly and kissed him on the cheek, saying "Thank you" over and over again.

When she finally let him go, Stan patted him on the back and shook his hand.

The crowd parted like the Red Sea to reveal Blake standing near the helm. He smiled and gave Adam a nod and a thumbs-up.

Adam returned a smile of his own and said, "Y'all are making me blush."

As most of them laughed, Justin stepped between Blake and Adam and asked the question that now had to be on everyone's minds.

"Where do we go now?"

Blake smiled and reached inside his jacket pocket. He fished around before pulling out a single folded piece of aged paper. He held it up without revealing the contents and grinned at them.

"You've trusted me so far, right?"

One by one, each of them looked at one another and nodded yes. Even Lloyd and Nora, although not as enthusiastically.

"So trust me a little bit longer, and I'll get us somewhere safe."

He gazed into each of their eyes, saving Adam for last.

"That sound like a plan?" he asked.

Everyone nodded in agreement.

Justin stepped up to him, smiling. "Can I drive?"

The entire group at once shouted, "No!"

They all burst into laughter.

"Come on!" Justin exclaimed, seeming perturbed at first but gradually starting to laugh. "It wasn't that bad, was it?"

"It wasn't good," Blake replied to more laughter.

*****

As Justin slept on the beach, a human head emerged from the surf. But it rose further to reveal shoulders and a torso.

It was Nora. Or what used to be her. Only now she was bloated and covered with seaweed. She was missing pieces of flesh here and there due to run-ins with sharp reefs and hungry fish.

With Justin in her sights, she groaned as she made her approach.

*****

As the boat cut through the water at fifteen knots, Blake kept his eyes on the GPS on the dash. In his left hand was the aged slip of paper he'd been carrying. His other hand, now discolored, rested on the wheel.

Sweat pooled on his forehead, causing him to wipe it with the back of his left hand, but the movement made him grimace in pain.

He glanced around to make sure no one was looking, then he stared down at his right arm. He touched his forearm gingerly with his left hand and slowly rolled up the sleeve. He gently pulled away the fabric that was stuck to a scratch that looked infected.

Blake saw movement out of the corner of his eye and looked over to see Adam staring in horror at his wound, small as it may have been.

Blake shook his head and mumbled something as he pulled the sleeve back down to cover it.

"What happened?" Adam asked, not taking his eyes off the man's arm.

Blake sighed and looked away, as if embarrassed. "It happened on the goddamn beach."

Blake felt like they were being watched and swiveled his head around to catch Lloyd looking away.

Adam lost his temper but kept his voice to a whisper. "Why didn't you say anything?"

"Say what?" Blake replied. "Hey, y'all, I've been scratched. Can I still come aboard?"

"You seriously think we wouldn't have let you?" Adam asked.

"Maybe not you," Blake said, turning and glancing around at the others before peering back at Adam with a grimace.

"Well, maybe I have a little more faith in them than you."

That was when they heard the sound of a bullet being locked and loaded into a rifle chamber.

Adam and Blake turned to see the barrel of the Remington aimed at Blake's head.

Holding the rifle, Lloyd aimed it with a mixture of hatred and fear evident on his face. His wife stood beside him with that defiant smirk of hers. But unlike her husband, she showed no fear.

Blake cocked his head at Adam. "You were saying?"

Adam ignored him and carefully turned to face Lloyd. "Lloyd—"

"He's been bit!" Lloyd interrupted, saying it loud enough for everyone on the boat to hear.

Not surprisingly, the rest of the group reacted in shock.

"He was scratched," Adam replied. "Not bit."

"When did it happen?" Linda asked, sorrow and pity registering in her voice.

"Does it matter?" Nora replied over her shoulder in an abrupt, cold manner.

"It does matter," Adam said, as Nora's eyes shifted to him.

"You know it has to be done," Nora said. "If he turns—"

"Then we'll take care of it," Adam interrupted. "But not while he's alive."

Adam stepped in front of Blake and stared past the barrel into Lloyd's eyes, which kept shifting in their sockets.

"Lloyd, listen to me. If you're gonna shoot him, you're gonna have to shoot me first."

Stan tried to reason. "Lloyd, please back down, and let's talk about this."

"Shut up!" Nora yelled at him. At all of them. "We ain't got a choice here!"

"There's always a choice," Adam said, anger in his tone. He stared into Lloyd's eyes until the older man closed his and turned away.

Adam acted quickly and snatched the rifle from him, then, in anger, he shoved him down to the deck with one arm.

Nora stumbled back in surprise as Adam quickly took aim at her husband's face. She clutched her chest and knelt beside her husband and locked eyes with Adam.

"If you're gonna shoot him," she said, "you better kill me too. 'Cause I don't trust any of y'all with my life. I'd rather be dead."

Lloyd, surprised, wrapped his trembling arms around his wife, never once taking his eyes off the barrel aimed at him.

Adam, his body shaking in rage, placed his finger on the trigger and started to squeeze.

Blake placed a hand on Adam's shoulder. But Adam shrugged it off and stepped forward, moving the barrel closer to Lloyd's face.

"How does it feel, Lloyd?" Adam asked through gritted teeth.

"Please don't," Lloyd said, wet eyes wide, trembling with fear, body dripping with sweat.

"Adam, stop!" Linda said, approaching him from the side. "They're just scared. We all are."

Adam's eyes shifted from her to them and calmed down just enough to see reason. Then he nodded to her, and she exhaled.

"We don't kill each other," Adam said, glaring at Lloyd, then Nora. "You understand? Not while we're human."

Lloyd, relieved, nodded in agreement. Beside him, Nora kept her steely gaze on Adam. Never blinking.

Blake reached up slowly with his left hand and used it to lower the rifle.

Adam nodded, handed the rifle to him, and stalked away to cool off.

*****

I felt more tired that night than I'd ever been in my entire life. Yet I couldn't sleep a wink. Thoughts kept racing through my mind like horses on an out-of-control carousel, and I couldn't stop them.

All I could think was, *What do we do now?*

The answer wasn't coming.

I heard footsteps running outside my hut and rose up in my bed. I listened intently but didn't hear anything else.

"Justin?"

Receiving no answer, I stood up, groaning, my muscles already sore from all the recent exertion, and ventured outside.

I peered around but still didn't see anything due to the darkness. There was barely enough moonlight to see ten feet in front of my face.

"Justin?" I yelled again.

Still no answer.

Even though it was dark, I knew the path to the beach by heart.

I could probably walk it blindfolded. While birds and insects chirped, I kept my eyes on the path before me. I could hear the distant sound of waves getting closer.

When I finally emerged onto the beach, I walked to the point where I'd last seen Justin. But he wasn't there.

Instead, all I found on the white sand was a pool of blood.

*****

As the boat headed further out to sea, Blake glanced down at the GPS, making sure he stayed on course. Then he stared straight ahead again.

By this time, his right hand was cramping up, and he kept having to flex it to relieve the pain. But every time it came back, it was worse than before.

His eyes were drawn to the front deck where Linda and Justin were staring down, watching the front hull of the boat as it smashed through the water. He wondered why they kept pointing down at the surface.

He closed his eyes for a moment and tried to relax his mind. He focused on the wind, which felt good on his skin. He did his best to ignore the pains shooting throughout his body, making him feel like a pin cushion that someone was jamming needles into and twisting them.

He glanced over at the entry to the cabin below deck where he knew Lloyd and Nora were and not by their choice.

Probably stewing and plotting their next move, Blake thought, a wry smirk curling up one side of his mouth. *At least, I would be if I were them.*

Adam and Stan were admiring the wake left behind the boat. But Adam kept glancing back over his shoulder at Blake to check up on him and make sure he was still doing all right.

All Blake had to do was smile and nod back, despite the throbbing pain in his forearm having moved up his arm and into his chest.

Blake stared back down at the GPS, then shifted his eyes to the folded piece of paper lying beside it.

He thought back to the time he was around Adam's age, maybe a little older. Right after he had left the Air Force, which was more their call than his. That's when he'd met the man whose friendship would change the course of his life not once but quite a few times.

Mark Keller had been born to a ranching family in Roswell, New Mexico, in 1942. He'd spent most of his life on that ranch until he enlisted in the Army right out of high school and was soon shipped off to Vietnam.

After surviving his first tour without so much as a scratch, he reenlisted for another and was soon back in the bush, up to his neck in mosquitoes and red dust. Only this time, he wasn't quite as lucky.

One day while on patrol, his unit was ambushed by a hidden Viet Cong unit. Keller's overwhelmed greenhorn first lieutenant called for a mortar strike along a tree line where their attackers were dug in like ticks on a dog. Only the young officer, fresh out of West Point and new to command in the bush, in his haste and confusion, screwed up the coordinates, and their own side ended up raining hellfire down on his own helpless unit.

Any soldier knew the only good thing about mortars besides firing them was you could always hear them coming with their dreaded, all-too-familiar devil's whistle. The bad news was there was nothing you could do about it once you heard it.

When the poor grunt next to Keller exploded in a flash of bloody sinew and splintered bones, many of those tiny projectiles of former body parts entered the right side of Keller's body.

From that point forward, his skin on that entire side was scarred and pockmarked. And for the rest of his life, he would get constant reminders of that day.

First, a small part of his skin would start to hurt. Then, a cyst or a pimple would develop depending upon the size of the projectile. And lastly, Keller's wife, whom he married years after he was honorably discharged, would pop those zits and treat those cysts until the day she up and left him.

Those small tasks she performed were not any of the main reasons why she eventually left him, but it probably contributed somewhat.

After all, once you've sliced open the puss-filled whitehead of someone's cyst, and a piece of tooth or a sliver from a human rib emerged, it was kind of hard to see that person the same way as you did before.

Once his military service was over, instead of returning home to the ranch, which had been expected of him, he joined a fellow returning veteran in New Orleans. There, he was assured that as a decorated war vet, he would get a decent job, get drunk and stoned as much as he wanted, and get laid whenever he was in the mood.

For a while, his war buddy was right.

But after too many nights of drinking, toking, one-night stands, and not enough going to work during the day, he ended his time in the Big Easy and drifted.

Besides being a brawler and drinker wherever he went, he'd been a beer truck driver in St. Louis, a garbage man in Kansas City, and an oilfield worker in West Texas, which was where he met William Blake, who was just starting out as a hand with Keller as his supervisor.

Keller married a West Texas gal, and together they raised a son until a drunk driver erased him from existence one New Year's Eve while he was a senior in high school.

Keller had always relied on beer and pot to make the days more bearable and his wartime nightmares go away. But after his son's death, he devoted himself fully to his vices, and his sleepwalking habit did the rest of the hard work of eroding his marriage.

His wife had always tried to be accepting of this nightly quirk of his, at first. But after he nearly choked her to death one night after she tried waking him up while he was loading a rifle in his sleep, she left him not long after.

He tried cleaning up his act and tried to stop getting drunk, but he never stopped smoking pot. On one of his soberer days, after watching a TV show about deep-sea fishermen, he decided he wanted to give it a try. He sold everything his wife didn't get from him in the divorce and moved to South Padre Island, where he got a job learning the ropes on a deep-sea fishing vessel. The pay was lousy, but the hours spent on the ocean reeling in other people's catch of a lifetime and drinking until he passed out became his life's calling.

After some tort lawyers settled a class-action Agent Orange lawsuit on behalf of him and the surviving members of his old unit, they split the money, and each ended up getting a little over $72,000 for their life-altering pain and suffering. But that was chump change, considering the TCDD, or 2-, 3-, 7-, 8-tetrachlorodibenzo-p-dioxin in Agent Orange, had mutated his DNA on a molecular level.

Instead of using this lump sum to retire, he invested it all in his own previously-owned charter boat.

His remaining years were his happiest. He was his own boss, worked his own hours, and had a woman he saw on a semiregular basis. He even had his own stool at the bar of his favorite beach watering hole.

Life was finally good.

Around the year 1998, he began hearing about a little thing called Y2K. Once he heard the possibility of computers ending the world when the clock struck midnight in the year 2000, he used what money he had left to buy guns, ammo, and all the survival supplies he'd need to hole up somewhere while the world went to hell around him.

Then he remembered something. A snippet of a conversation he had overheard on his boat one night while drinking with a few customers. Now maybe the drunk guy was stupid, or maybe crazy smart, but this guy had said there were unexplored islands out there in the Gulf just waiting for someone to claim them. It was all a matter of getting there first and planting your flag, so to speak.

Starting in the spring of '99, Keller drew a grid over a nautical map of the Gulf and began driving his boat miles out from the Texas mainland, crossing out searched sections as he went.

He'd found a few islands that looked deserted and unclaimed, but upon hitting land, he soon found out he wasn't the first one to set foot on them because some of them were US- or Mexico-government-owned. Since he didn't want to take the chance of anyone coming back to claim them after he did, he marked them off and kept searching for one to call his very own.

He still had a business to run, so when he wasn't searching the Gulf for his doomsday home, he helped get paying passengers too drunk to care that they didn't catch anything worth hanging on their wall at home. But once he had any free time, his search would begin again in grids of Gulf he hadn't charted yet.

He never came close to giving up his search, but he did start to worry once he realized the "end of the world" was less than five months away. But after several more fruitless searches, he finally found what he was looking for—an island with sandy white beaches, coconuts for years, and teams of birds. After staying a few nights to explore it further by day, he'd even found a cave containing a running freshwater source.

He'd finally found his miracle. His very own island. His future home.

After noting its coordinates and charting it on his map, he returned back to civilization, desperate to tell someone his secret.

The problem was, who could he trust? He ended up calling his old friend William Blake from West Texas and invited him down to South Padre. He had something important to tell him.

By the time Blake arrived a week later, whatever good mood Keller was in was gone. One morning, while showering, he'd discovered a painful lump on his neck. He tried putting off going to see a doctor, but after having a cough that didn't go away, he relented and got checked out.

A few days after Blake arrived, Keller got his death sentence.

Throat, lung, and brain cancer courtesy of the ticking time bomb of those Agent Orange chemicals his body was subjected to in the war.

Blake stayed with him at his place and at the hospital during all twelve sessions of chemo.

Keller knew that if the cancer didn't kill him, the cure would. And knowing he'd probably never make it back to his secret island paradise, he reckoned someone deserving should.

That's when he told Blake all about his plan. Once he passed along his information, including how to get there, it was now Blake's plan.

Only Blake didn't act on it. At least, not right away. After Keller died a few days before Y2K came and went, and the world didn't end, Blake went back home to West Texas. Only now, he'd been willed Keller's home with its arsenal of weapons, ammo, and survival supplies.

Having never been a gun nut but being familiar with weapons from his service days, Blake waited about six months before deciding to put those weapons to good use before they rusted.

After firing Keller's weapons at a gun range, Blake was hooked and never looked back. His life was never the same.

Now, here he was, almost two hours into following Keller's course. With the boat's fuel gauge edging close to empty, Blake stared ahead and saw a speck of white on the horizon.

He blinked to make sure he wasn't seeing things, then broke out into a huge smile.

He nodded and said to the sky above, "Better late than never, amigo."

He called back to Adam and Stan and pointed ahead.

As the two men walked toward Blake at the helm and stared forward, large smiles came to their faces.

"That's it?" Adam asked, trying to contain his enthusiasm.

"That's home," Blake replied, grimacing in pain as he opened and closed his right fist once again. A reminder, just in case he'd forgotten his current condition.

Stan ran his hands through what was left of his hair and yelled for joy.

By that time, Justin and Linda noticed land up ahead and began squealing like kids, which they were, in a way.

Stan even went into the cabin below to tell Lloyd and Nora.

Maybe the good news will finally garner a grin from one of them, Blake thought. *Maybe both.*

Adam placed a hand on Blake's shoulder. "You want to be the first onshore?"

"That honor was already taken," Blake replied. "But I'll be happy to be the second."

"Who was the first?" Adam asked.

Blake was about to answer when crippling pain shot through his body. He doubled over, and his right arm inadvertently shoved the throttle forward all the way.

The boat sped up and began slapping hard against the surface of the water, bouncing up and down violently.

Adam went to help Blake to his feet but fell onto him when he, too, lost his balance. Stan tripped on the way out of the cabin and landed on his face, bloodying his nose. Nora and Lloyd were on his heels, cursing and voicing their disapproval of the current state of the ride. Justin and Linda fell to the front deck and held on for dear life to whatever they could grab.

The island was now perilously close. But just as Adam succeeded in pulling Blake's arm off the throttle, the boat came to a violent halt as it hit a large reef below the water.

*****

As I ran back to the shelters, I shouted for Justin but couldn't find him. But I heard something moving in the foliage behind me.

I turned and saw a figure trying to move toward me. But as I looked closer, I saw that it was Nora. Her bloated flesh was a bluish-gray, and salt water leaked from holes and cuts in her body. Her legs were entangled in some creeping vines, and she couldn't get loose.

I glanced around in frustration. I'd just realized I didn't have the machete handy. In my haste to check on Justin, I left it behind in my hut. Before I could even wonder how I could do something that stupid, someone ran up and attacked me from behind.

As I fell to the ground with someone on top of me, I felt teeth tear into my shoulder and warmth as blood spread across my back.

The pain from the bite spread like lightning throughout my entire body. I summoned all the will and strength I had left and rolled out of my attacker's grasp.

When I got to my feet, I saw Justin on the ground, and my heart sank in my chest.

The skin had been torn from the left half of his face leaving behind muscle and bone. His upper and lower jaw were exposed, and his left eye was missing from its socket. That didn't stop him from reaching for me while his tongue hung from his mouth like a thirsty dog.

I kicked him in the face, resulting in a loud crack. That gave me time to look around for something to defend myself with. To my relief, I spied a softball-sized rock a few feet away.

I sprinted for it, palmed it, and picked it up. I ran back over to Justin as he was trying to get back up. I didn't give him the chance. I yelled in anger and brought the rock down on his head.

When his body slumped to the ground, I dropped to my knees.

With tears in my eyes, I raised the rock and brought it down again and again until his head burst open. Then I smashed what was left to make sure he didn't get back up again.

I heard Nora groaning behind me. Though I could barely lift my arms, I stood slowly and faced her. Even though I didn't like her much while she was alive, I didn't take any delight in what I was about to do.

After I turned her head into paste, I fell to my knees. I peered up at the clear night sky and screamed until my voice was a raspy shadow of itself.

*****

The crash opened a long gaping hole in the hull, and the boat began taking on water.

The impact sent Justin flying into the water like he'd been shot out of a cannon. However, once he emerged, even though he was in pain, he yelled out that he was fine.

When Linda finally gained her sense enough to stand, she grabbed a nearby life preserver and jumped in after him.

Adam had hit his head on the helm, which dazed him. But even as blood trickled down his face and neck, he had the wherewithal to hand Stan a life preserver. Then he helped Stan off the boat and into the water where the pastor began to dog-paddle to the shore.

Lloyd and Nora made their own way off the boat and into the water using a large cooler they had found in the cabin as a flotation device.

That left Adam to help Blake, who by this point could barely move, to the shore by himself. He secured him with one arm while treading water with the other that held the machete.

The current was strong, pulling them away from the island. But once they reached the first sandbar, Adam and Blake rested a while to regain their strength before swimming on.

By the time Adam and Blake reached the beach, everyone else was lying on the sand, exhausted, trying to catch their breath. They soon found themselves regarding one another with brief smiles, thankful to still be alive.

Adam asked for Justin's help with Blake, and together they helped him to his feet and walked him over to the tree line. They sat him down with his back against a palm tree with a grand view of the ocean and the fast-sinking boat.

Adam noticed Justin still had the Glock in his waistband.

Out of Blake's eyesight, Adam signaled him and gestured to it.

Justin glanced at Blake, who was busy rubbing his face with his good hand. Then he quietly slipped the gun to Adam, who hid it behind his back, and the younger man walked away toward Linda, who was sitting alone on the beach.

As Adam watched over Blake, the dying man stared out at the horizon with a smile on his face.

"Sorry you weren't second," Adam said, trying to smile along with him.

Blake laughed hard and quickly began to cough. When he pulled his hand away from his mouth, it was covered in specks of blood.

Adam's eyes widened in concern, but Blake waved it off.

"I'm all right," Blake said. "Don't make a fuss."

Blake wiped his mouth with the back of his left hand and watched as the boat sank even further.

"Well, I guess we have no choice but to stay here now," he said. "I hope it all works out."

Adam shook his head, wondering how in the world this man could still be joking at a time like this.

As if reading his mind, Blake asked, "Where's your sense of humor?"

Adam squinted toward the sea-filled horizon where the boat was now gone. "It must've sunk with the boat."

Blake laughed again, then stared at the horizon with him. They stood there like that in silence for quite a while.

"I sure am gonna miss this," Blake said.

"What?" Adam asked, finally smiling. "Our witty repartee?"

"That too," Blake said, then gestured to their surroundings, struggling hard to catch his breath. "But I was talkin' about all this."

Adam tried, but couldn't get caught up in it. It hit him at that moment that he was more overwhelmed by the fact he was somehow still alive.

"Take a look at how beautiful the world is," Blake said while taking labored breaths.

Adam looked along with him but stayed quiet as the man continued talking.

"I wish I'd taken the time to notice this kinda stuff more when things were…normal." Blake chuckled at that last word and shook his head.

Adam nodded and squeezed the gun in his hand.

Blake set his eyes upon Adam and lowered his gaze to his friend's hidden arm.

"Is that a surprise for me back there?" Blake asked. "It's not my birthday."

Adam shook his head but couldn't make eye contact with him. He was too ashamed, so he just stared down at his feet.

Blake said, "I'm not gonna ask you to do that for me."

Adam looked up at him in alarm, as if Blake had read his mind.

"I wouldn't," Blake added.

Adam nodded and revealed the gun. He looked down at it in shame. It felt heavy.

Blake looked down. With a groan of pain, he dug his left hand into his back pocket and pulled out a dark, flat-looking rock. He held it out to Adam and beckoned him with it.

"How about I propose a trade?"

Adam stared at the rock in confusion.

"What is that?" Adam asked.

"Come get it," Blake said, keeping his hand up, "before my arm gives out."

Adam deliberated, then walked over and took the rock from him. As he inspected it, he still didn't grasp its significance.

Blake saw the confusion on Adam's face. "You were never a Boy Scout, were ya?"

Adam stared at him. "Humor me."

"It's a flint rock," Blake stated. "Just hit it with a regular rock, and the sparks will help you start a fire."

A smile formed on Adam's face as his appreciation of the gift grew.

Blake snapped his fingers to get Adam's attention. "Now, are you gonna complete the trade or what?"

Adam came around and glanced down at the gun in his hand.

"Come on," Blake demanded. "Don't be a welcher."

Adam shook his head. The last thing he wanted to do was give Blake the gun, but he knew it had to be done.

"It's all right, man," Blake said, peering up at him. "This ain't on you."

As a tear ran down Adam's cheek, he turned away and held out the gun for him.

With a grunt, Blake took it. He inspected it and laughed. "After all that, I hope this damn thing still works, or this is gonna get awkward real quick."

Adam stared down at the gun. He couldn't look away from it.

"I'm sorry for making you do that yourself," Adam said.

Blake scoffed and let him off the hook. "Don't apologize. Not for this."

Adam glanced away, still ashamed.

Blake grimaced in pain. "You're a good man, Adam. The world needs people like you. Way more than people like me. Always has, always will."

"I'm not so sure about that," Adam said, shaking his head in disbelief. "Especially not now."

"You're a good man," Blake repeated. "You proved that today. A good man doesn't let others do whatever they want. People like you stand up to people like that and protect those that can't."

"But I'm not like you."

"And what is that, exactly?"

"A survivor."

Blake laughed. "Well, evidently, I ain't a good one."

"If it weren't for me, for us, you'd be okay right now. But instead of just looking out for yourself, you saved all of us. And what did you get in return?"

Adam gazed down at Blake's forearm.

"How fair is that?"

"Fair ain't got nothin' to do with it," Blake said, a serious tone in his voice. "Never has, never will. The sooner you learn that, the better off you'll be."

Adam could only nod. He knew Blake was right. "I get it."

"No, you don't," Blake said. "Not yet anyway. But you will… someday."

Blake looked around at the ragtag group of survivors.

"More hard decisions are coming your way," Blake warned. "The next time, what happened to me will happen to someone else. And someone's gonna have to take care of the problem. If not, none of you are gonna make it."

Adam nodded. Then scoffed and smiled.

"What's so funny?" Blake asked, trying to read his face.

"It's not funny, exactly." Adam told him, "But when things were normal, assholes like me made fun of people like you."

Blake was surprised to hear that. He didn't know whether or not to be offended. "What on earth for?"

"We laughed at people like you for being paranoid and preparing yourselves for the end of the world. We thought you guys were nuts."

"Some of us still are," Blake said, smiling.

"Well, I guess the joke's on us 'cause here we are. The world ending all around us. And who's our savior? People like you."

"Well, goddamn," Blake replied. "When you put it like that, I'm a genuine American hero."

Adam heard him rhyme the end of "genuine" with "wine." But instead of it making him laugh, Adam started to tear up.

He fought the feeling because the last thing he wanted to do was cry in front of the man who had come to mean a lot to him in a very short period.

Instead, Adam crinkled up his face and forced a laugh, then put out his left hand.

Blake stared at it, then gazed up at him. "You sure?"

"Thank you," Adam said, "for everything."

Blake nodded and winced in pain as he reached up with his left hand to shake Adam's.

Adam could no longer hold the tears back. As soon as his hand was free, he turned and walked off toward the beach, leaving Blake alone by the tree.

When he got far enough away, Adam wiped his face and glanced back.

He saw Blake gazing out across the water, and to Adam's surprise, the man started laughing.

Adam watched as Blake checked the gun to make sure it was loaded, then looked up at the sky and shouted, "Fuck you very much!"

Adam turned away, knowing that was how he wanted to remember Blake.

Defiant and salty to the end.

*****

I was spent after pulling Justin's body into the hut and laying him next to Nora's body. Because I wasn't honoring what I assumed to be his final wish of being buried next to his beloved Linda, I said a silent prayer for him and asked for his forgiveness.

As far as Nora's soul was concerned, she was on her own.

With one last touch of Justin's hand, I rose up and left the hut.

When I emerged outside, I paused and took a long pained look at all the shelters we had built. Our homes for the past five years.

With tears running down my face, I knelt next to a pile of kindling and dry brush. I banged a rock against the flint, and sparks flew. I blew on the embers until a small flame appeared in the brush and slowly crawled up the kindling. Before long, a small fire was going.

I wrapped a torn rag around a yard-long tree limb and dipped it into the flames. Once the rag was engulfed, I used it to set fire to each of the huts one at a time.

After that, I stood at a distance and watched the flames grow until they consumed most of everything.

After one last look at my home, our homes, I picked up the machete lying on a log and stumbled out to the beach. By this time, my ever-weakening legs felt as if they were made of lead and full of fire.

When I reached the white sand, I dropped to my knees, completely spent, and stared out at the water.

A thought came to me, and it made me smile. It was something my old friend Blake had said once upon a time when he was at his end.

"Take a look at how beautiful the world is," I said, smiling upon hearing Blake's voice in my head.

I did just that. I sat down and gazed up at all that was surrounding me.

I beheld the stars, which looked brighter than I'd ever seen them. I stared out at the water, shimmering and unrelenting. Its waves coming ever closer to me upon each return. I felt the wind cool against my skin.

Then the burning feeling spread into my arms, and I knew I'd better act fast.

But more thoughts flooded into my brain. Once again, I was powerless to stop them.

From a distance, I thought, *this island probably looks like paradise.*

But beauty doesn't guarantee life. And it hides the dark, awful truth. That man needs nature to survive, but nature sure as hell doesn't need man.

Trust me on this. Nature can be a brutal bitch when she wants to be.

I used all the strength I had left to pick up the machete. It took a lot of effort because my hands weren't moving too well at that point. I held it upright with the tip of the blade aiming straight up at the sky, and the bottom of the handle resting on the sand.

I took a long last look around to take in all the beauty, then I centered my forehead over the tip of the machete blade.

After a quick prayer to whoever was still listening, I leaned back and drove my head toward the blade.

*****

With his back to Blake, Adam joined the others on the beach where they had segregated themselves into tiny clusters.

Justin stood near Linda, eyeing her while she stared off into nothing. Lloyd held Nora tight while she, in turn, held her belly. Stan was off by himself, lost in thought.

Faces filled with uncertainty and fear, they stared out at the debris the boat had left behind. While some stared at the horizon, all of them were doing whatever it took not to look behind them.

The crack of a gunshot was heard.

Most of them jumped, startled. Some started to cry.

Adam shook his head, furious. He closed his eyes for a moment and collected his thoughts.

By the time he opened them again, something deep within him had changed. There was a new resolve in his gaze.

I know what I have to do, he thought. *But I don't have the first clue how to do it. Neither does anyone else, but like me, they're gonna have to learn. Even if it's the hard way.*

Because the fact of the matter is, we have to survive.

No matter what the cost.

*****

At dawn, as the rays of light from the sun turned the sky a beautiful yellow-orange, the last remnants of the smoke rose from the island and dissipated.

The waves kept crashing onto the beach, the wind kept blowing, and time refused to stand still.

CONFESSION

It's my turn to hear confessions. My eyes are half-closed as I sit listening to the elderly woman in the adjoining booth giving hers. She is barely visible through the screen that separates us, but that's not the only thing keeping us apart.

As I'm listening to this woman's thoughts of deception and betrayal, my mind keeps wandering away.

At this point in my life, I've probably talked to thousands of parishioners who have sinned both small and large. Since this is a Sunday, that number will go up quite a bit. As I look toward the top of the booth, I ask the man upstairs, "How many more can there possibly be?"

I frown at my question and lower my head. I should be ashamed of myself. I'm starting to lose faith in humanity, even in myself. I've been acting this way for quite a while now, and I have no idea why.

Well, I take that back. I have some idea, but it doesn't make any sense. I shake these thoughts out of my head and turn my attention back to the old woman.

I see the silhouette of her face through the screen. She has dark skin, and her hair is pulled up into a bun that went out of style years ago. She's speaking to me of lust, speaking slowly and carefully, as if I'm a stranger to the subject. It's almost as if she thinks I'm a little kid who needs a sanitized *Sesame Street* explanation for sex.

Somewhat on the subject, I've noticed certain people I've talked to over the years all have a common misconception about priests—that we have no idea what goes on in the "real world." Like we're shut off from what makes everyone who they are, human foibles and all.

That we are perfect—in essence, Christlike.

That couldn't be further from the truth. We are well aware of the things that go on in the "real world," and we're just as human as the next person. For instance, when I speak of events happening in the world, like say, the stock market, I've received some incredulous looks. Looks that say I didn't know priests cared about stuff like that.

I always tell these people that priests are human too. We're not impassive about the ways of the world. We worry about things.

Things like the recession and its effects on everyone, not just the church; the plagues that are still wiping out hundreds of thousands of people every decade or so; the overburdening crime wave that has threatened to run all the good people away from every big city, only to find it has followed them to the small towns and suburbs that were once so peaceful and safe...

Sorry. My thoughts are drifting again. My attention should be fully focused on the old woman. But as I turn my thoughts back to her, I catch nothing but her silence.

I feel a void. Maybe she asked a question and was now waiting for an answer. This is terrible. I hate this feeling. I'm now nervous and ashamed for not paying attention.

To my immense relief, she starts talking again.

Thank you, Heavenly Father.

It would have been extremely embarrassing to say, "Sorry, I wasn't paying attention. Could you repeat that?"

The woman sobs, causing me to turn toward her. I see her wiping her face with a tissue.

"Father, every night before I go to sleep and every morning when I wake up, I find myself having these thoughts about him. He's been my neighbor for over forty years, even when Harold was still alive." She turns to me, holding her hands in prayer. "So why all of a sudden am I just now thinking about him? Oh, I hope these thoughts aren't sinful. I mean, it's not like I've acted on them." She blows her nose. "I just hope these feelings aren't abnormal."

As the woman sobs, I half-smile and say, "No, these feelings are quite normal. And even though these thoughts may be considered sinful, they're entirely human. It's nothing a few good prayers can't fix."

This is entirely the truth. I can feel good about that, at least.

*****

If I seem bored with this particular confession, it's because I'm so used to hearing racier, more passionate ones. Ones so strong in lust and deception that I feel I'm sinning just by listening. It's certainly sinful the thoughts these confessions put into my head. The things they make me think about too often now.

Things like relationships.

What would it be like to have one? Maybe with any one of the women I see every day while walking in the park…

Walking in the park.

There's something that's going out of style. I remember not just ten years ago that a lot of people walked in the park. Now because of the criminal element in the city, the park is as empty as this church.

Maybe it's the neighborhood, so destitute, almost like a mirror of society. It's so hedonistic, especially at night.

Even I won't walk in the park at night, only during the day. By day, it looks so different, almost like it used to. Back in the days when families played together. When lovers held onto one another beneath the trees and lay together in the grass. The artists of all varied types who displayed their work to those who had the fortune—or misfortune, depending on how you looked at it—of crossing their path. Mimes, forever mocking and silent, even getting on a priest's nerves.

I've watched all of them over the years and overheard many of their conversations. It's what I do.

I notice things. I watch people. I see their behavior, though always from a distance. I see and hear every word, from their arguments and their making up afterward to their ways of meeting and getting to know one another.

I love walking up on them while they sit, bragging about their nightly escapades, of their cavorting with one-night lovers, and of their staying up and drinking to excess at all hours of the morning.

Then they notice me and very obviously clam up thinking they look normal. That's when I walk away with a smile.

But at night, I go nowhere near the park. I try to keep from venturing too far from my apartment or the church at night. In this day and age, even priests have a fear of muggers. In the past, maybe priests and criminals had a hidden understanding: I don't turn you in if you leave me alone.

But this is now. No one thinks twice these days about mugging or even killing a priest. These days, criminals are true savages in every sense of the word.

*****

Thinking of the past and how it used to be makes me think of my parents. They died when I was eleven. They were a traveling couple, always off on trips to…everywhere. My father being a pilot made their hobby feasible. One night, their plane crashed en route toward home during a snowstorm. The investigation ruled that ice had formed on the wings of their Cessna, causing it to lose altitude and crash into the Appalachian Mountains.

After their deaths, I was sent to live with my grandmother, a strict Catholic woman, who instilled in me the importance of her religion and of the Bible. I soon grew fond of the Good Book. I loved the characters, the parables, and the moral lessons to be learned. I am probably the only young person to ever willingly read the whole thing cover to cover.

My grandmother helped me understand its meaning. She also helped me understand what it could do for me. And while I learned of faith for my God and love and tolerance for my fellow man, I found the anger of losing my parents was nearly gone. I now knew they were somewhere being taken care of, and that one day I would see them again. And for the first time in my life, I was truly at peace.

At that young age, I'd found my calling. While most young boys were into baseball or girls, I was looking into a career as a priest.

I attended Catholic school, majored in theological studies in college, and soon came to the Bishop Heights Catholic Church to curate under Father Jacob Cates.

Sadly, on the day of my induction fifteen years before, my beloved grandmother died. But on her deathbed, she asked me to give her last rites.

It was a great honor. Something I will never forget.

*****

My thoughts have drifted away from the old woman again. I turn just in time to hear her saying, "Father? Father? Did you hear me?"

I lie. "Yes, of course." I'll pray for forgiveness later.

"Then what should I do?" I can see that her hands are shaking.

Taking a well-practiced shot in the dark, I tell her, "Your husband died ten years ago, and now you find that you have deep feelings for your neighbor, whom you've known for years. You say he's a good man and was a friend of your husband, so I think Harold would approve. And so would he." I look up for added effect, and she follows my gaze toward the top of the booth.

"So, you're saying it's okay to feel the way I do?" I now see that her hands have stopped shaking, and I spot a flash of white on her face. She is smiling.

I say, feeling a little better, "You are still having impure thoughts, so say at least five Hail Marys and two Our Fathers before you go to sleep tonight." I raise my rosary and kiss it, then say the Prayer of Absolution for her.

Afterward, she leans toward the screen and whispers, "Thank you so much, Father."

"May God bless you." I close my eyes, and with my right hand, I give the sign of the cross over my chest.

The woman rises and leaves the booth, opening the door and letting in light from the outside.

After she shuts the door behind her, I sit back and rub my face. I find myself looking up toward the top of the booth again.

"Forgive me, Father. For I wander in my thoughts too much lately."

*****

I've now sat in silence within this booth for what feels like an eternity, but in reality, it's only been half an hour. I spent that time reflecting on myself, my life, and what I've become. I need to get it all sorted out because if I don't, I don't think I can go on.

After all, how can I help others when I'm troubled myself?

Maybe I need a vacation. Well, truthfully, I need a sabbatical. I think it would do me good to get away for a time and get my head on straight.

The more I think about it, the more I'd like to go somewhere where no one knows who I am or what I do. Maybe I'll go to Disney World. Or Disneyland. I've never been to either. Florida this time of year would be nice. The clean air, the warm sun, the rolling ocean, the white beaches, the women…

Sorry, I've been thinking too much about women lately. I've been this way for about six months now. I've been a priest half my life. I should have gotten used to this by now.

But I'm not.

As I look back, I may have been on one date my entire life, and that night ended badly for all concerned. It was a blind date one of my friends had set me up with. Her name was Shirley Delfeeny. She was plain. Not ugly, just plain. She attended my school's sister school across town. We met at a dance chaperoned by her school's nuns.

We danced the whole night, much to the sisters' dismay. And later that night, we slipped away with a few of my friends and their dates. The nuns noticed pretty quickly that we were gone and came looking for us. They found us upstairs in the attic having a make-out session.

Poor Nicholas Larrabee, he was caught on top of his date. They were just kissing, though they probably would have gone a lot further if they hadn't been caught. I remember the sisters hitting him with rulers so hard they left whelps all over his body. He was later expelled.

That lone incident was the extent of my social life.

I got in trouble and was sentenced to mop duty for a month, but I served my time knowing full well that I deserved it.

Looking back on it, the punishment really wasn't that bad. I can laugh about it now.

But now I feel different. I'm starting to feel less and less ashamed of my impure thoughts, and frankly, that scares me. I see women now and I feel…I don't know the word I'm looking for, but I know I want them. I want to touch them. I want to have them. I love their smell, and the way they make you feel when they look at you. And even though I took a vow, I don't feel guilty. I feel…normal.

I haven't yet spoken to Father Cates about my sudden interests.

I guess I always thought they would go away in time, and things would get back to normal—pardon me, to the way they used to be—but they haven't. I'm thinking about women all the time now. Them. The life I yearn for. The things I wish I could do.

Maybe on this vacation, I'll think over my life. Make a decision about my future and go with what's in my heart. Who knows, maybe I'll have a little fun. And if the chance arises, maybe meet someone to talk with, have a relationship with, and…maybe more.

"No offense." I gaze up again.

I guess I'm going through what some call the seven-year itch, an affliction married people get at some point in their relationship with their prospective mates. In my case, my association with the man upstairs. I guess it could also be called a midlife crisis, though I think it's widely overused as an excuse to simply want to feel young and free to make choices again.

What's so bad about that?

I'm not sure if what I'm feeling now is a real psychological malady or an excuse I've drummed up because I've consciously found out I'm too weak to resist temptation. But as I said before, I'm certain that some major restructuring of my life has to occur.

I really can't go about my calling this way. My duties and vows are going in an entirely different direction from where I find myself, if only in thoughts and dreams. So far.

I've always felt the greatest sin a priest could commit was not being honest to those who have put their faith in you to represent them in the eyes of the Lord.

If someone were forgiven by a priest in God's name, would that sin be truly forgiven by God if the priest himself was sinning? Even if only in thought? It's almost too much for me to handle sometimes.

For this reason, I feel like I can't go on doing this. That, and the fact that I fear one day, someday soon, it feels like, I will become absolutely faithless to my work.

I guess that settles it. I need some time away. I'll tell Father Cates after dinner.

At the moment of my revelation, the door to the confession chamber opens. I hear someone stepping in and shutting the door behind them.

It is a man. He clears his throat as he scuffles around. He is breathing heavily like he jogged or ran to get here. I hear the soles of his shoes scraping the floor. I've done enough of these to know they are loafers.

I open the sliding panel, in effect opening myself to him. I see his silhouette through the dark screen. His profile is bathed in darkness, and he is wearing a suit and tie, though it doesn't look like the expensive variety. It looks off-the-rack.

His overcoat extends to his knees. He is looking toward the floor, still breathing heavily. I wait for him to speak. For some, it takes a while. When that happens, after a few moments of silence, I will go first.

Breaking the ice, so to speak.

I lean toward the wall, my elbow on the sill of the panel. I speak softly. "Welcome, my son?"

He acknowledges me by raising his head. His breathing has finally slowed. He opens his mouth to speak, but no words come out.

I straighten my back and speak again. "It's okay. Take your time."

The man exhales. I hear the air leaving his body. He is a tall man, but right now, he seems small, confused, and disordered.

He takes a seat and finally speaks. His voice is low and gravelly, as if he has sand in his throat. "Forgive me, Father, for I have sinned."

I pray for him in my thoughts. "How long has it been since your last confession?"

The man is touching the tips of his fingers together. I still cannot see his face, for he sits in the darkness of the booth. It's almost like he is hiding on purpose. As if he's ashamed.

"It's been a long time, Father." He drawled out the word "long" and seemed to laugh as he said it.

I smile to myself while imagining him smiling as well. "What is it that's troubling you?"

"A lot of things, Father." He shrugs, continuing to look at the floor. "Too many things. So many, I can hear them talking to me at night."

I sit forward. This is getting interesting. "What do you mean when you say you can hear them talking to you at night?"

"Voices," he says. "A lot of voices. I can't drown 'em out sometimes. And they come to me, no matter what I do to silence 'em."

He begins to breathe heavily again. It makes me think of a nameless little boy sitting in a dark room, afraid that he's not alone.

I then say, "And what do these voices tell you?"

The man becomes silent again for a beat. I'm about to repeat the question again when he begins to chuckle. "They tell me to do bad things, Father." He clears his throat. "Really bad things."

"Like what?" I notice that he has his face in a sliver of light. I can see that he is Caucasian, and his eyes are bloodshot. He is an older man, mid-forties, but I cannot quite make out his features.

He suddenly pulls his face out of the light, back into the shadows.

"They tell me to punish the wicked. To show them the way back to the light."

My interest is piqued. He sits silent again. I lean forward. "Who are the wicked?"

The man looks to the floor again. "Them. The women."

"The women?" I ask, shaking my head slowly. "Please explain."

"You know, the women on the streets. The ones who sell themselves. The ones who put their bodies up for hire to anyone with the cash. The ones who come up to your car and ask you if you want a hand job for ten bucks. Sometimes they don't even ask, they just climb in your car."

He sounds disgusted by their behavior, his voice becoming more and more antagonized.

I am starting to get a little worried. As I said before, I keep up with what's happening in the world, especially the city in which I live.

At the moment, the city is dealing with a series of highly publicized murders. The bodies of women of ill-repute—streetwalkers—are being found mutilated. At last count, according to local newscasts and newspapers, the death toll was at eleven. But since these victims are generally people who won't be missed if they happen to disappear, the number could be higher.

Since the victims are prostitutes, most of them drug abusers, it's been found that not too many people care about the cases' outcomes.

All except for the police, that is. They've been on an intensive manhunt to find the suspect since three of the bodies were found and linked to the same killer. They have released information stating they believe the murders are being committed by one man, though they haven't ruled out the possibility of accomplices or copycat crimes.

Surprisingly, prostitutes don't seem to care about a solution to these cases either, despite being the targeted group. I've seen on the news the past several weeks that the prostitutes are still out in large numbers trying to find their customers at all hours of the morning.

When reporters questioned them, they gave sound bites such as, "We have to take care of business" or "We can't afford to stay off the streets just because some maniac out there is hacking up women." Words that don't exactly generate sympathy within the community. I even heard one of them say that her chances of being killed by this maniac were minimal. I believe her exact words were: "There's a lot of us out here. I'd say hundreds on this side of town alone. What makes you think he'll get me? I'm not worried about it."

The victims' bodies have been found all over the east side in alleyways, motel rooms, even dumpsters. But other than that, few details have been released.

One body was found on a park bench, though not in the park I walk in. One limbless corpse was found in a trash can behind a restaurant by a vagrant sifting through it for food.

Her arms were never found.

In another case, a corpse was hidden under a rent-by-the-hour motel bed and wasn't found until three days later. During that time, there must have been half a dozen renters who never even noticed.

That must have struck the killer as pretty funny.

During this time, I've also seen the haggard faces of the detectives investigating these cases on the local nightly news.

I've seen the primary detective so much that I should remember his name. He's a sergeant—that much I know—but his name escapes me at the moment. But anyway, this man can't go anywhere without cameras and microphones in his face asking him why he hasn't cracked the case.

It really bugs me that I can't remember his name. I'm usually very good with them.

Wait a minute… His name is in that song "For He's a Jolly Good Fellow." Either "Fellow" or "Fellows"? Something like that.

The man begins talking again. I snap to attention in order to hear him.

"I try not to listen, but I always end up doing what they tell me anyway. I always do. I've found out it's better not to ignore 'em. They get really angry if you ignore 'em." He wipes his nose with his hand. "I've never been a man to back down from anyone…until they came along."

While trying to get a good look at his face, which I still haven't seen clearly, I notice that I'm sweating. But maybe sweating is too gentle a word.

Perspiration is pouring off me like someone turned on a water faucet over my head. Or like I'm standing in a shower letting the water run over me, though not quite as refreshing. I wipe my forehead with a cloth. "What do these voices tell you to do to these women?"

I can't believe I asked that.

The man looks up, seeming to stay purposely away from the light. "They tell me to show those women that their way is wrong. To get them on the way to where they need to go. The right way. Sort of what you'd call the 'path to salvation.'"

The man laughs again, and a shiver goes through my body.

I've heard of people—deranged, maybe, who knows—who live off the TV. They are the kind of delusional people who take TV images, shows, and personalities seriously, as if the make-believe world were the real one and vice versa.

Like the guy who killed that girl from a TV show decades back. He believed that her character spoke to him through the TV. Therefore, in his mind, they had a relationship. One in which she wanted to be with him.

In reality, she had simply sent an autographed photo to him through her agent in reply to his request. In his mind, she had acknowledged their relationship. When he never heard from her again, he began stalking her. Then, one day, he approached her front door and rang the doorbell. When she opened it, he shot and killed her at point-blank range.

Like him, there are other delusional people who, for instance, watch the news and see a serial killer like Ted Bundy. They become enamored with this psychopath. In the process, they want to be like him. Thus, they become copycat killers or the type of person who calls up the police stations and tells the cops that they are murderers like their infamous heroes. Some even commit murder in the same MO as their idols. Like their heroes before them, these people need to be apprehended before they kill or, in some cases, before they can kill again.

I hope to God that is the case here; that this guy is simply a crackpot or some depressed individual venting out his frustrations that have built up in his mind. I hope I haven't come across the genuine article: the one known to the press as the John.

I try to muffle my heavy breathing. I'm getting really nervous.

What would this guy do if he was indeed the murderer and realized I was onto him?

As I look over toward the screen, I see him staring at me a few inches from it. This startles me. Before I can think about it, he quickly turns away before I can catch a glimpse of him. I curse myself for not paying attention or thinking quickly enough. I could have seen his face. I could have found out who he was.

But wait...how could I have forgotten? What will I do if I find out who he is? Confessions are a private matter between the penitent and the priest. It is information that can never be revealed to any other source but God. To do so would be a grave sin.

This brings an ill feeling to my stomach. I feel dizzy and hot.

My stomach begins to rumble. I place my hand over my mouth, but I continue to listen.

He has been talking, rambling. "These women are vile. They are evil, and they need to be taken care of. They need someone to help them." He pauses. "And I'm the one who's been chosen to do that. I take my mission seriously, and I do it well. So well, in fact, that the police have no idea who I am and have no leads at all in hopes of finding me. And I'm standing right in front of them, out in the open, yet invisible. Do you know how powerful that makes me?"

I sit silently. Not wanting to say anything.

The man moves within the booth. I see that he has sat back again, out of view. His head is tilted back so it rests against the wall.

I can still hear his raspy breathing. He places the pads of his fingers together and rubs them back and forth. He seems nervous and catlike.

I spot something. Something metal. As I stare harder, I see that it's a ring. A class ring. It is engraved with "Syracuse. Class of '98."

The man speaks again. "I know how the police work. They couldn't care less about this case, but they have to pursue it. But their hearts aren't in it because nobody cares if hookers are getting killed. But even if I was killing real people, they still couldn't find me. I don't leave evidence behind. I'm too clean. I know the methods of investigation. I know how they find clues. I'm too perfect. A perfect machine. Running on all cylinders twenty-four hours a day.

"I really know what I'm doing. I've been reading a lot of medical journals...you know, Jack the Ripper did that. I've been reading medical stuff: anatomy, physical science... Did you know"—he sat forward suddenly, his voice rising—"that when you cut off someone's head, it lives on for about four seconds? Sometimes they even say words if you cut just right. But you have to really know what you're doing to accomplish that. And...and"—he sounded like an excited ten-year-old boy—"when you sever a limb, the fingers move like a spasm. Like it has a life of its own."

I am positively ill now.

The man sits back again. The fervor he had built up seems to be dying down now. I hope. He laces his fingers together. "Seeing their lifeblood run out of them is...what's the word?" He sighs. "Exhilarating. Yeah, that's it. Sometimes, I collect their blood in little jars and take them home with me. Then I cover my body with it and lie in the moonlight in my backyard where no one can see me. You know, like camouflage."

I hear him sniffling. I turn to look and see his face lowered with his hands upon it. He seems to be crying. "It's the only way to make them stop. The voices... They shut up when I do it. At least, they're quiet for a while. When I do as I'm told, they leave me alone...but they always come back...always. And I have to go out and do it again...and again...and again...over and over and over.

"But they're never satisfied for long. They always, eventually, want more and more and more."

The man is definitely crying. "I wish they'd leave me alone. I wish they'd go away and bother someone else." He raises his head and speaks slowly, his voice broken up by sobs. "Can you make them go away, Father? Can you make them leave me alone? Can you help me, please?"

I am speechless, unsure of what to say. I want to say something to make him feel better, but at the same time, I don't want to set him off. But here he is asking me for help. I have to say something. May God be with me, I say, "Only you can help yourself, my son. Only you can stop the voices."

The man leans toward the window. His face is once again in the sliver of light. I can almost see him. I can almost see the color of his eyes. He is pleading. "How do I do that, Father? Please tell me."

I purse my lips. "Go to the authorities. Tell them what you've told me. They'll send you somewhere that will make these voices go away and stay away."

"The police?" he whispers. His voice is trembling. He seems to be shaking. "You want me to go to the police? I can't do that. They'll kill me. They won't take any chances of me being set free."

"Not if you turn yourself in and make a deal," I say, backing away to the other side of my side of the booth. "If you do that, they'll help you. I promise."

"How would you know?" His fingers press against the screen separating us. I flinch, and, at once, I know he can see the fear in my eyes. I know this because I can see him for the first time.

And what's scarier, I know him. Or, rather, I know of him.

"Do you know what the police do to people like me? They hurt us. They kill us. And no one knows what's going on. No one ever finds out…never. They make people disappear all the time…and no one knows. Believe me." He looks around, turning his face away. "I can't go to the police. That's…that's out of the question."

"But you need help." My voice is shaky. I am petrified. "And the police can—"

He screams, "No, damn you! Can't you see? I came to you for help. You! But…but you can't help me. I can see that now." His palms and fingers are turning white as he presses them against the screen. His face is twisted and full of anger. "You're no help at all, damn you. No help at all…" His voice trails away. He is mumbling now. "No… help…at…all…no…help…"

I don't know why, and probably never will, but I cautiously reach up and place my hand against his on the other side of the screen. "It's going to be all ri—"

But he quickly yanks his hands away from the screen and falls onto the far wall of the booth, which rocks from the impact.

He stares wide-eyed at me as he slinks to the floor. He furiously wipes his hand on his jacket, as if somehow my germs made it through the screen. He glares at me as he yells, "Get away from me! Get away!"

He sounds crazy and evil. To think this is the last voice his victims hear before they died in horrible, excruciating ways is horrifying.

It saddens me to the bone knowing those people died with that being the last sound they heard.

His voice changes pitch ever so slightly. I now become convinced that more than one person lives in his mind.

It's such a shame too. He asks for help, but at the same time, the others inside him won't allow him to accept it.

He continues on, "You're like all the rest. You think you're better than me. You think you're perfect. You couldn't care less about other people in the world. You're just like everyone else…no different."

I keep silent. Can you blame me? I watch as the man stands and continues breathing heavily. He opens the door to leave but turns back to me and says, "I'm leaving now, but don't follow me. Just leave me alone.

"I'll kill you if you don't mind me."

He steps out and closes the door behind him.

For a split second, I think about stepping out to get a better glimpse of him, just to make sure he is who I thought him to be.

But as my hand touches the latch, I think of what he said and know full well he meant it. I just know that once I step out, he'll be there waiting for me. Waiting to see if I'd be stupid enough to try to follow him. Waiting with a knife or a razor or…God knows what.

After a few seconds, with my mind racing and my body pumping adrenaline, I grab the latch and slowly open it.

It seems to take forever, but I finally crack open the door, letting in light. I peer out through the small crack I made and look around with wild eyes.

I see everything, and at the same time, I see nothing.

I see the church. I see the pews. I see the few parishioners sitting, kneeling, or praying.

I open the door further and step out into the light.

I am now looking over the whole empty congregation. The sweat has stuck to my body due to the heavy cloak I am wearing. I look around to see just the regular handful of worshippers and no one else. A few men are in suits and ties, but none of them are the man I remember seeing and talking to just a minute before.

I feel weak as I walk down the steps from the raised pulpit and take a seat on the front pew. I am a few feet from a lady in black, who acknowledges me with a nod before she goes back to praying.

I must look a mess. My hair is clinging to my sweat-drenched forehead, and I feel trickles of sweat gliding down my body like long, bony fingers. Another chill runs the gamut of my body, and I lower my head to my hands and begin to sob. The tears come slowly at first, but soon they are pouring out.

I feel helpless. I think of going to the police. But what would I say? I can't very well break my oath.

I think of going to Father Cates. But what do I tell him?

I feel lost and totally alone, and worst of all, I don't feel God is with me at the moment. At least, I don't feel any of his comfort right now.

The day I've feared has now come. For now is when I finally realize that my entire life has been wasted. And even worse, there's no direction to go in because I know nothing else.

Oh, God, why me?

Why?

I stare up to the Virgin Mary looking down upon me. It is then that I know what I will do. Tonight, I will go see Father Cates.

Exactly what I'll say is a mystery, but I know I'll get around to telling him that I'm leaving. Where to? I don't know. And I really don't care.

All I know is I have to get away from this place, away from this city, away from these people, and, most importantly, away from this life.

But right now, all I think I have the power to do is sit and cry some more.

*****

As the man in the suit and tie stepped from the church, he looked up into the night sky. Through the fog that was resting at the tops of the skyscrapers, he could barely see the three-quarter moon.

He thought to himself, *At least there'll be no more voices for a while. I gotta couple of more weeks before they return…just like always. Thanks to that young girl in the alley last night. Man, she couldn't have been more than seventeen. She was so nice and pretty, with the most beautiful pouty lips I've ever seen.*

As a matter of fact, he liked her lips so much that he kept them. He was fiddling with them with his left hand at that very moment. They were wrapped in cellophane inside his coat pocket.

He smiled as he rolled them between his fingers and thought back to the night before.

Her blood had been so dark, he thought. *So dark and sweet, not bitter like most of them. Especially as it came out hot after I cut her from her neck down to her sweet spot like a fish.*

He had taken some home in a jar and spread it all over his body.

It tasted so good that he spread it all over his face and lips.

And afterward, as he looked at the moon, he couldn't hear a thing. Though he could see so many things. The voices had faces, and he could see them, but they were quiet. They were just watching him. Quiet. Silent. Not making a sound in the world.

He thought, *Silence. What loveliness. It means everything is going to be okay for a while. And I should enjoy it while it lasts. Because in another couple of weeks, it'll be business as usual.*

As the man stepped off the church steps and onto the sidewalk, a tan Crown Victoria pulled up to the curb in front of him.

The man inside the car was wearing a gray jacket and tan pants.

The police radio in the car was busy spouting off about a body found in the alleyway between Ninth and Lee.

The old fish market, the man outside the car thought. *I know the exact place. I should know because I was just there last night.*

He lowered his head to look into the car at the driver.

The driver craned his neck to look up at him. "They found another one. Let's roll."

The man opened the door and stepped into the car. After settling in, he strapped on his seat belt and grabbed the handset from the radio. He keyed it and said, "Dispatch, this is Car 418. We're on our way."

The dispatch operator cut back, "Hey, Fallows, getting religious on us?"

Fallows looked around incredulously. "Say again."

"Heard you was praying at the old Catholic church."

"Oh, that." Fallows glanced over at his partner, who simply shrugged. "It's nothing." Fallows hung up the handset and glared at his partner. "You got a big mouth, Ryan."

"So sue me," Ryan replied.

Ryan grabbed a police light from the seat, flipped the switch, started the strobe, and reached out the window to stick the magnet end down on the roof of the car. He turned back to look at oncoming traffic and flicked on the siren.

"Did you say a prayer for me in there?"

"Can we drop it?" Fallows asked. He looked out the window toward the church. He scowled and placed his hand back in his left coat pocket, which made him feel better.

As Ryan pulled out into traffic behind a delivery truck, he looked over at his partner and smiled, "Another hooker. Can you believe this bastard?"

Fallows sat stone-faced, still watching the traffic.

Ryan shook his head. "Man, I hope we nail this sick son of a bitch and soon."

Fallows noticed the speedometer inching up toward fifty. He resumed fiddling with the contents of his pocket and added to his partner's statement, "Me too, Ryan."

He peered back up at the moon, ducking behind some tall buildings.

"Then maybe I could get some sleep."

The car soon disappeared into traffic, siren blaring.

CHARLIE

"Ellie!" Carol shouted to her shy, quiet daughter, who was busy playing in a nearby sandpit.

But Ellie, looking precious with her long blonde hair tied up high on her head in a pretty yellow bow that matched her floral sundress, paid her mother no mind.

She was too busy concentrating with every fiber of her four-year-old being on playing with her yellow plastic bucket, a plastic shovel that was almost too big for the bucket, and her imagination.

Ellie's pile of sand may have resembled a crumbling prairie dog mountain to everyone else, but to her, it looked like a castle big and beautiful enough for Elsa, Anna, and all the other Disney princesses to live in happily ever after.

"You've been playing around in that sand all morning," Carol yelled, "so make sure you clean yourself up real good because we're about to have lunch."

The young mother was shouting to be heard over the din of the other children running amok at the campsite like prisoners released on furlough.

"Did you hear me, young lady?"

Carol's voice finally broke through to her daughter, who glanced back and smiled.

"Yes, Mommy."

"I mean it," Carol shouted. "Clean off every grain of sand."

But Ellie was back in her own world again, and all Carol could do was sigh and swat flies away from the mostly-covered food she was setting out on the picnic table.

It was the Fourth of July weekend, and the entire Pratt family was outside a large cabin near a lake in San Marcos, Texas. Overhead and tied by ropes between two tall trees was a large silver Mylar banner with white letters that read: PRATT FAMILY REUNION.

Most of the adult males were busy drinking one too many beers while trash-talking and playing horseshoes far too close to the cabins and their vehicles for Carol's liking. Meanwhile, she was doing all the unfun stuff like preparing lunch and battling flies.

Her sister-in-law, Sheryl, had been standing a few feet away from her the entire time, providing zero assistance. However, she was giving a running commentary on everyone in the family, fueled by what had to be her fourth red plastic cup of vodka and 7 Up.

"Did you hear about Ruthie?" Sheryl asked, trying to whisper but saying it loud enough for most to be able to overhear. "She couldn't make it this year because she's too ill to attend."

"That's what I heard, the poor thing," Carol replied. "That's too bad. I really like her."

"Well, a little birdie told me," Sheryl said, putting her hand up to the side of her face as if telling a secret, yet still being too loud, "she had complications with a little nip and tuck she had. And by that, I mean a full face-lift."

Sheryl laughed and drained her cup, then set about giving herself a refill.

All Carol could do was watch this woman, amazed at her. She never knew if she really liked Sheryl or not. After all, they had nothing in common. Especially not in the looks department.

Sheryl, whose red hair, milky white skin, and large breasts had gotten her plenty of attention since she was twelve, had an outsized personality to match. Carol, on the other hand, while still pleasant-looking, was nowhere near as voluptuous or beautiful.

If their lives were a TV show, Carol would be like Mary Ann to Sheryl's Ginger. So while Sheryl was most red-blooded males' fantasy of what the ideal woman should look like, Carol was the choice for a devoted few.

As for personality, Sheryl could talk to anyone about anything at any given time. Carol, not so much. She was more of a listener, a follower, a fly-on-the-wall, so to speak.

As these thoughts swarmed through her mind while she absent-mindedly swatted flies away from a bowl of German potato salad she'd just laid out, she didn't hear her daughter calling out to her.

"Mommy!"

When Ellie called out to her mother again, Carol didn't hear that either. Her attention was caught between Sheryl rambling on and on about their cousin Ruthie's plastic surgery gone wrong, and the startling sound of a badly thrown horseshoe clanging off a cabin wall.

"Mommy!"

It took Sheryl shutting up for a second for her to finally hear her daughter.

"Mommy!"

"What?" Carol shouted while swatting at a fly that buzzed her face, causing her to almost slap herself.

"Can Charlie eat with us?"

At the very mention of this name, the blood rushed from Carol's face, and her mouth opened wide. Not out of fear, but out of what she was certain was going to happen next.

As Carol's eyes cut toward Sheryl, she saw a question looming on her sister-in-law's lips, and she wasn't looking forward to the conversation that was sure to follow.

"Can he, Mommy?" Ellie asked.

Carol shook her head and closed her eyes. "Sure. Yeah. He can eat with us."

As Sheryl turned her head, contemplating what she was going to say next, Carol felt her heart starting to race.

"Who's Charlie?" Sheryl asked.

Sheryl's hips swung slightly back and forth while a toothy grin grew on her face. She glanced from mother to daughter and back again.

"Has she got a boyfriend?"

Before Carol could answer, Sheryl stepped closer, enough so Carol could smell what she had for breakfast that morning.

"You keepin' secrets from me, Carol?" Sheryl asked, enjoying the moment. "Is your daughter takin' after her aunt in the men department?"

Carol shook her head, wanting desperately for this conversation to come to an end, but knowing it was far from over.

"Already breakin' hearts at…" Sheryl paused and turned to Carol. "How old is your daughter again?"

"She's four," Carol replied, in a tone dry enough to make a man thirsty. "And, no, she doesn't have a boyfriend. Because she's four."

"Honey," Sheryl replied, eyes rolling up to recall her memories, "by the time I was her age, I'd already kissed a dozen boys."

That doesn't surprise me, Carol thought. *Not the least little bit.*

As if reading her mind, Sheryl stepped away. She had a forlorn look on her face, as if something was troubling her.

When Carol saw the hurt look on Sheryl's face that she wasn't hiding nearly as well as she thought she was, it made her feel terrible thinking she was at fault.

At that moment, Carol realized that Sheryl may have had a way of always making her feel uncomfortable, but maybe it wasn't personal.

Carol started to think her perception of Sheryl wasn't based on reality. That maybe anything negative she had felt coming from her sister-in-law was all in her own head. She knew better than anybody that she took things far too personally when that wasn't the other person's intent at all.

That's because Carol knew she was what some people might call uptight and rigid. All her life, various people had told her this in their own way at one time or another. Her parents had. Her friends had. Her ex-boyfriends certainly had, not that there were many of those. Even her husband Don joked with her about it when he wasn't too aggravated by it.

But with Sheryl, Carol thought, *maybe it's just me she rubs the wrong way, and she doesn't even know she's doing it. She does have a strong personality and always has to be the center of attention, but that doesn't make her a bad person. She just is who she is. And maybe I should learn to deal with her better.*

"Charlie is her imaginary friend," Carol blurted out, much to her surprise. Then she took a deep breath and waited for the conversation she was dreading.

But to her disbelief, Sheryl didn't say anything. She took in the information silently as she stared out at Ellie, who was talking to someone at her eye level, as if they were sitting in the sandpit with her.

Carol, nervous, not liking the silence in the air, rambled on.

"I've talked to a few therapists about it, and they all say it's completely normal for a young child to have imaginary friends."

"Really now?" Sheryl asked, giving her a side-eye. A hint of a smirk on her face.

"It's totally normal," Carol replied, in her best parental voice. "And they say she'll grow out of it as soon as she starts going to school and making real friends."

Sheryl turned to her and squinted. "But isn't she already in daycare with real kids now?"

"Yeah, but...," Carol replied, taken aback. It took her a while to find her bearings, but once she did, she began again. "She's just really shy. It takes her a while to warm up to people. But she's getting better."

"Just like her mother," Sheryl said, nodding.

Carol turned and stared at her profile. "What do you mean?"

"Well, don't get mad," Sheryl said, raising her hands in the air and backing away while smiling. "But I've heard every story there is about you."

"Who have you been talking to about me?" Carol asked, a worried look on her face.

"Look," Sheryl replied, placing a hand on her chest and raising her left hand. "It's nothin' personal, it's just...when we first met, I didn't think you liked me."

Carol displayed her best poker face, hoping Sheryl couldn't read it and tell what she was thinking.

"So I asked your mother," Sheryl said while crossing her heart and glancing up at the sky, "May God rest her soul."

Carol appreciated that moment with a sorrowful smile.

"I asked her, why does Carol hate me so much?" Sheryl said. "And she told me you were just shy, so I shouldn't take it personally."

Carol was taken aback but didn't say anything.

"She told me that it takes a while for you to warm up to people," Sheryl said. "That in time, we'd be like sisters, and we'd be laughin' about those first few days when we first met."

Carol looked down at her feet in flip-flops. Ashamed.

Sheryl smirked. "Only here we are, thirteen years later, and we still barely speak."

Carol shook her head and sighed, trying to think of something to say while Sheryl took another long sip from her cup and stared out at Ellie, who was laughing at something her imaginary friend must have said.

Carol thought of something, and a grin broke out on her face. But right before her words could come out, they heard a child scream.

All eyes shot toward the wooden boat dock that extended over the lake about twenty feet. They watched in terror as a screaming child plunged into the water from a great height, resulting in a rather large splash.

Then they saw Sheryl's husband, Jerry, picking up another young child and tossing them high into the air. That child screamed before plunging into the lake with another large splash.

"Jesus!" Sheryl exclaimed, catching her breath. "That scared the livin' shit out of me."

All Carol could do was watch in shock as Jerry picked up another screaming child and threw her high into the air.

"Isn't he being a little rough?"

"Maybe," Sheryl replied, before waving it off. "But look at 'em."

As they watched, as soon as a kid was thrown into the water, they emerged and swam back to the dock and eagerly lined up for another toss.

"They love that roughhousin' shit."

Carol, still concerned, couldn't help but wince as another child screamed as they were thrown in. "I just hope no one gets hurt."

"That's what kids do," Sheryl replied. "They get hurt. It's how they learn. If they do somethin' and it hurts, then they learn not to do it again."

When Sheryl leaned in closer, that was the moment Carol knew—despite what she'd been told all her life—that vodka had a scent. She could smell it on Sheryl's breath as the woman's face was right next to hers, uncomfortably close.

"Except when it comes to sex," Sheryl said, chuckling. "If it hurts, that's how you know you're doin' it right."

As Carol watched, Sheryl chuckled to herself before draining another cup. Then she got a refill with less 7 Up than before.

Carol still had a thought on her mind and decided to clear it out of there before it started bothering her.

"I'm really sorry, Sheryl," Carol said.

This caught Sheryl by surprise. She stopped drinking midsip and stared at Carol, stunned into silence.

"I know I'm not the easiest person to get along with," Carol said. "But I want you to know that even though most things you say are shocking to me, you also make me laugh like nobody else."

A smile broke out on Sheryl's face. "But you never laugh at any of the things I say."

"Trust me," Carol replied, laying a hand on Sheryl's forearm. "I laugh like crazy when I'm alone and think of something you said."

Sheryl's face softened, and she seemed happy to have heard that.

"Hey, look," Sheryl said, "I know I can be a lot sometimes." She rolled her eyes and laughed while adding, "All the time."

Carol laughed along with her.

"But I really do respect you," Sheryl added. "Your little girl is just so precious and so well behaved. I get a little jealous sometimes."

Cheryl's gaze went out to the dock where her two red-haired preteen boys were trying their best to pick up the kids tinier than them and throw them into the water, much like their father.

"Look at my two devil spawn," Sheryl said, pointing at her kids while shaking her head. "I swear to God, they get more like their asshole father every day."

Carol tried to keep from laughing by concentrating on opening a box of plastic utensils.

"I would have divorced his ass years ago," Sheryl said, causing Carol to gasp and stare back at her. But Sheryl was unaware of that as she glared at her husband, who was posing like a strong man on the dock. "But he's so damn good in the sack."

Carol burst out laughing. She couldn't help it.

This caught Sheryl by surprise. A big smile broke out on her face.

"Finally," Sheryl said. "I made you laugh in my presence."

Carol had to lean on the picnic table to catch her breath, but she could not stop chortling.

"You okay there?" Sheryl asked, smiling while rubbing Carol's back. "Don't die on me. Not when you were just startin' to like me."

This made Carol laugh even harder.

Sheryl couldn't help but smile as some of the extended family looked over to see what the commotion was all about.

Sheryl gestured at Carol and said, "She swallowed a fly."

Carol snorted, causing Sheryl to laugh with her.

"A big sucker from the looks of it."

Carol, red in the face, struggled to catch her breath while Sheryl continued to rub her back.

"I..." Carol began.

Sheryl leaned closer. "What, hon?"

"I...," Carol began again, "I can't breathe."

"Here," Sheryl said, offering Carol her red plastic cup. "Drink some of this. It'll help calm you down."

Carol nodded as she took the cup and sniffed it.

"Just drink it," Sheryl ordered. "It won't kill ya."

Carol glanced back at Sheryl, who urged her on, then she took a small sip.

As Carol gagged from the taste, Sheryl took the cup from her.

"The more you drink," Sheryl said, "the more you'll like it."

"Is there any soda in there at all?"

"If I mixed it right, no."

Carol slowly stood upright. Her face flushed red. She was still chuckling, but now it was under control.

As Sheryl took another sip of her drink, Carol smiled. "Can I have another sip?"

Sheryl broke out laughing, nearly doubling over.

Carol laughed with her while Sheryl pointed at her and said, "I'm gonna make an alcoholic outa you yet."

As the women continued to laugh while Sheryl began pouring Carol a red cup of her own, a slightly sunburned, tall, lanky man, wearing a Dallas Cowboys cap to hide the fact he was losing his hair at a rapid pace, walked toward them and held up two bags of ice.

This was Carol's husband, Don.

"It only took forty-five minutes and trips to three different stores," Don said, "but I finally found ice at a real hole in the wall."

"My hero," Carol said as she pointed at two coolers set near the cabin. "Do me a favor, hon, and smash them up and put them in those coolers over there."

"Aye, aye, Cap'n," Don said as he walked off with the ice bags.

As Sheryl turned and handed Carol her own cup, she watched as Don set the ice bags on the ground and opened the coolers. Then she smiled and gestured with her chin at Carol's husband.

"Speakin' of in the sack, how's ole Don in that department?"

Carol immediately blushed.

"Does he fulfill all your needs?"

"Stop it," Carol replied, glancing back at her husband. A wry smile on her lips. "He's a good husband. And a good father."

As a grin formed on Sheryl's face, she leaned in and asked, "But does he make you cum?"

Carol playfully swatted Sheryl's arm as her own face turned red.

Sheryl laughed and said, "I don't mean to put your G-spot on the spot, Carol, but...wonderin' dirty minds want to know."

"I guess," Carol replied, shaking her head, embarrassed.

"There's no guesswork involved," Sheryl said. "You either know or you don't."

Carol shook her head.

"If you're not comfortable talkin' about it," Sheryl stated, "I'll drop it. But this is what women talk about when they get together, sugar. Dick and orgasms."

"Shh," Carol leaned toward Sheryl with a finger to her own lips. "He'll hear you."

Sheryl looked toward Don, who raised a bag of ice and dropped it to the ground, breaking the bag and causing pieces of ice to tumble to the ground.

"Shit!" Don said as he bent to pick them up one at a time and toss them into a cooler.

"If I were you," Sheryl said, still staring at Don, "if he doesn't, there are items you can buy that will do the job instead."

Carol stared at Sheryl in horror.

"Vibrators, girl," Sheryl said. "They're not the devil's work. And they'll keep you from snappin' one day and poisonin' your kids' macaroni and cheese, that I guarantee."

Don closed the coolers and turned to walk back over to his wife, just in time to catch them both in an awkward silence.

As he stared at them, his mind wondered the worst.

"So," Don began, "do I want to know what you two hens are cacklin' about?"

Sheryl took a sip from her cup and glared at him. "About how I stabbed the last man who compared me to a chicken?"

Don got a good chuckle out of that but realized there was no hint of a smile on Sheryl's face. He could also feel the silence between the two women that still hung in the air.

"What's goin' on?" Don asked. "For real. Because you two are making me feel like you were talking about me."

Carol's eyes widened as she looked at Sheryl, who lowered her cup and glanced over at Ellie, still laughing and playing in the sand.

"We weren't talkin' about you, you conceited ass," Sheryl said, pondering her next statement. "But we were talkin' about your daughter."

Carol cast a glance at Sheryl, dreading what was going to come out of her mouth next.

"What about her?" Don asked, a hint of concern in his voice as he glanced from Ellie to his wife. "Did something happen while I was gone?"

"Calm down," Sheryl replied. "Nothin' happened. We were just talkin' about her imaginary friend."

Carol's eyes widened as she glanced at her husband, who looked at her at the same time.

"You told her?" he asked, concerned and surprised.

Carol stammered, not sure what to say. She looked at both of them but couldn't form any words. "I... I don't..."

"Why are you so surprised?" Sheryl asked Don, her eyes narrowing. "Do you not want her to talk about that?"

"What?" Don asked, feeling her judging him. "What are you getting at?"

"I don't know, Don, what am I gettin' at?"

"Are you accusing me of something?"

"I don't know. Am I?"

Don put up his hands and backed away. "Why do I feel like I'm being ambushed?"

"Would you two stop it?" Carol said, catching them both by surprise. Enough to keep them silent for a bit.

Carol took the silence given to her and gathered her thoughts. She gazed out at Ellie, then took a few deep breaths. "We were just talking about Ellie because she asked if Charlie could eat lunch with us."

"And?" Don asked.

"So, I had to explain who Charlie was to Sheryl."

Sheryl glared at Don. "And obviously you have a problem with that?"

"No," Don replied, offended by what she implied. "I'm just surprised, that's all."

"Surprised?" Sheryl asked. "Why?"

"Because," Don glanced at both of them, "you're the last person I thought she'd ever tell about that."

Sheryl aimed her penetrating gaze at Carol. "And why is that?"

Carol, shocked at what her husband had just said, was again at a loss for words.

"Well?" Sheryl asked, impatience in her body language.

"Again, I'm sorry," Carol replied. "Before today, you always made me feel uncomfortable. And I always thought you were doing it on purpose."

"Seriously?" Sheryl asked, surprised, then insulted.

"But that was then," Carol said defensively. "I don't think that way about you anymore."

"So what?" Don gestured at both of them with his hands. "You two are best friends now?"

As he glanced at both of them, his eyes were drawn from the cup in his wife's hand to the cup in Sheryl's.

"And you're drinking buddies too?"

"What's wrong with that?" Sheryl asked. "First, you don't want her talkin' to me about your daughter's make-believe friend, and now you don't want us hangin' out together?"

Don stepped toward Sheryl. "What on earth are you talking about?"

She got in his face, showing no fear. "You know exactly what I'm talkin' about."

"If you're accusing me of something, just come out and say it. Quit being all passive-aggressive with me."

"Okay then, how about I get aggressive-aggressive?"

"Stop it, you two!" Carol shouted and pulled her husband away from her sister-in-law.

As Sheryl and Don glared at one another, Carol stepped between them.

"I mean it. Just stop."

Don stared at the ground while Sheryl stood silent, hand on her hip while one foot tapped the ground.

Carol took another deep breath. "Sheryl, I'm sorry, but that's how I felt about you before today. And I can't apologize enough for not trying to get to know you sooner."

Sheryl closed her eyes and looked down but nodded in understanding.

"And Don doesn't care that I talked to you about Charlie," Carol added.

"Yeah," Don added. "I was just shocked that she told you. She used to worry so much about you finding out and what you'd think about it or what you'd say to everybody."

Carol said, "It's stupid, I know. But that's how I felt."

"Let me get this straight," Sheryl said, carefully choosing her words. "You think I'm this horrible person who would make fun of your daughter for havin' an imaginary friend? And make fun of you because of it?"

"That's not it, exactly," Don said.

Sheryl replied, "Then how is it, exactly?"

"It's exactly that," Carol said. "I thought you would do that."

Sheryl glanced away. Her feelings hurt. She even set her red cup down on the picnic table to gather herself.

"I can't say I'm sorry enough for thinking of you that way," Carol added. "Because now I know different."

Carol placed a hand on Sheryl's shoulder, who looked off at the lake while trying to keep from showing how much she was hurt.

"I'm so sorry, Sheryl. I really am. And I hope someday you'll forgive me."

Sheryl wiped her eyes to keep tears from forming. She shook her head and suddenly smiled.

"You're right," Sheryl said, still dabbing her eyes. "I can be a bitch most of the time. So I don't blame you for thinkin' that way."

As a tear fell down Carol's face, she nodded at Sheryl and moved in to hug her. The hug took Sheryl by surprise, but she accepted it and smiled through her tears.

Don looked on in silence and simply placed a hand on his wife's back.

As the women ended their hug, Sheryl smiled and wiped her face, then raised her cup.

"How about," Sheryl began, "we drink to new beginnings?"

Carol smiled and raised her own cup and tapped Sheryl's with it. "Hear, hear."

With a laugh, both women buried the past and peered out at Ellie.

"So, Don," Sheryl asked, "you're really okay with your daughter's friend?"

"Why wouldn't I be?" Don replied with a shrug. "It's totally normal for a kid to have an imaginary friend. Even the therapists we've talked to said—"

"I know, I know," Sheryl interrupted by waving her hands in front of her. "We talked about that already. It's totally normal and all that jazz."

Don glanced at his wife to see if she was all right with all this, and she looked back at him and nodded.

"I mean, besides," Don said, "I used to have an imaginary friend too."

Sheryl glanced back in surprise. A huge, excited smile broke out on her face. "I think I heard that before."

"From who?" Don replied, then closed his eyes and sighed. "From Jerry, of course."

"What was his name?" Sheryl asked, trying to pluck the answer from thin air.

"It was Harvey," Don replied, embarrassed.

"That's right," Sheryl exclaimed. "Harvey."

"What else did he tell you?" Don asked, anger dwelling in his voice.

He glared at his older brother, who was taking a sip of beer while tossing a horseshoe.

"Just that you and Harvey were thick as thieves. And how you two were always playin' together."

"Anything else?"

"Just that it was weird," Sheryl replied, then cast him a quick glance. "His words, not mine."

"Did he happen to tell you that he used to torture me about it?"

"He said he had a blast makin' fun of you for it."

Don nodded and smiled through his anger. "I'm sure he enjoyed telling you all about that."

"Look," Sheryl said, placing a hand on Don's shoulder. "I know my husband can be a dick—"

Don nodded affirmatively.

"But you shouldn't let what he thinks bother you so much."

"I don't care what he thinks."

"Coulda fooled me."

"What did you say his name was?" Carol asked.

When her husband looked over at her, he seemed confused.

"Your friend?" Carol asked.

"Harvey," Sheryl stated.

"That's right," Carol said. "Harvey."

"Is there something wrong with that?" Don asked.

"No, it's just," Carol said, "you never told me about that."

"Well," he replied, shrugging, "it's not something I like talking about."

"Why not?" Carol asked.

"Because of people like Jerry," Don replied. "And Sheryl here."

He pointed at Sheryl, and she rolled her eyes.

"You know I'm just kiddin'," she said in her defense. "Just havin' a little fun. You're an adult, not a little kid. You can take it."

"Well, my parents weren't kidding when they thought I needed psychiatric help," Don replied, looking wounded.

Sheryl cackled and clammed up just as quickly by placing a well-manicured hand over her mouth. "Sorry."

"But mainly Jerry," Don added. "He was so goddamn cruel. Almost every day, he and his friends would make fun of me and sing songs about it. It was awful."

"But y'all were just kids," Carol said.

Sheryl added, "And Jerry's a real asshole."

Don started to laugh; and the women joined him while they all watched Jerry finish a beer, crumple it, toss it toward a trash barrel, and miss.

"Yes," Don agreed, nodding emphatically. "Yes, he is."

After the laughter died down, Don shook his head.

"Don't tell anyone, please," he said, "and if you do, and it comes back to me, I'll deny it and say very bad things about you both, but..."

"What?" Sheryl asked. "Don't tease us like that."

"Come on, honey," Carol said, hugging him around the waist. "Tell us."

"I don't know why I'm telling y'all this," he said, "and I know I'm going to regret it, but... Harvey was a rabbit."

"Get outa here," Sheryl exclaimed, playfully slapping him.

"I'm being dead serious," he replied.

Carol asked, "Just like in that movie?"

"The one with Jimmy Stewart?" Sheryl added.

Carol asked, "You stole your imaginary friend from a movie?"

"No, no, no," Don said. "Here's the weird part—"

"Oh," Sheryl said in a mocking tone. "There's a weird part?"

"I never saw that movie as a kid. I didn't even know about it until I was a teenager. I just had an imaginary friend who looked like one of those Easter bunnies you see at the mall."

"That's so creepy," Sheryl replied, a perturbed look on her face.

"But it wasn't," Don replied in a defensive tone. "He was just my friend. He was as real to me as the both of you. I remember him vividly."

"That is so weird," Sheryl replied. "At least your daughter sees a make-believe boy. You have to go and conjure up strange men in bunny outfits."

"It wasn't like that," Don said, protesting.

"Carol," Sheryl asked, "would you have married him if you'd known about this?"

Carol did her best to keep from even smiling in front of her husband, but inside, she was fighting to keep from laughing.

"What's so weird about it, Sheryl?" Don asked. "I was three, maybe four."

"A grown man in a bunny suit?" Sheryl asked, a serious tone in her voice. "Are you sure he was imaginary? Are you sure it wasn't the neighborhood pervert, and you're just blockin' that part out?"

"Harvey wasn't a pervert," Don replied, his face getting red. "He was a rabbit."

Sheryl raised her hand and stuck out her little finger and waved with it. "Are you sure he wasn't after your little carrot?"

Carol burst out laughing. She couldn't help it.

As her husband stared at her in shock, she shook her head and kept mouthing she was sorry but couldn't get the words out.

"Et tu, Brute?" Don asked his wife while shaking his head in disappointment.

He took a while to gather his thoughts. He knew he was on the losing side of this battle, but he refused to go down without a fight.

He turned toward Sheryl and lowered his voice.

"Let me set this straight in your adolescent brain, Sheryl."

Sheryl leaned into him with a serious look on her face and batted her eyes at him, which aggravated him even more.

"It wasn't a grown man in a bunny suit," he said, sighing. "It was a tall rabbit who happened to talk like a human."

"Oh, now this is gettin' very interesting," Sheryl said, leaning in closer to him. "What did you two talk about?"

"Lots of stuff."

"But about what in particular?"

"The stuff kids and tall imaginary bunnies liked. Star Wars. Cartoons. Firecrackers. Cookies—"

"Cookies?"

"Yeah. Harvey loved cookies."

"What about carrots?"

Don nodded. "He liked those too, but he really loved cookies."

Sheryl burst out laughing, taking Carol with her for the ride.

Even Don was now starting to smile.

"Every time my mom made cookies," Don said, "I'd get one for me and one for Harvey."

"So what happened to Harvey?" Carol asked. "Did you outgrow him?"

A dark countenance settled on Don's face as he slowly lost his smile. "No."

The women noticed the mood change as everything about Don at that moment grew serious.

"What happened?" Carol asked, taking her husband's hand in concern.

Don glared over at his older brother, who was oblivious to them or their conversation as he slapped a high five with his oldest son while playing horseshoes.

"Jerry ran over Harvey with the lawn mower," Don declared. "On purpose."

The women shared a look of mutual understanding that if they laughed or smiled at that moment, he would never forgive them. But they acknowledged each other with their eyes, and they both knew they were going to laugh about this like crazy later.

Sheryl glanced up at Don and placed her arm on his shoulder.

"What?" Don asked, closing his eyes, expecting her to say something horrible.

"I am seein' a whole new side of you, Don."

"I was a little kid. Give me a break."

Sheryl took her time peering around before asking, "You're not seein' any large bunnies now, are ya?"

Carol did her best to suppress a laugh, but the result was a snort she was too late to cover with her hand.

This cracked Sheryl up, much to Don's further dismay.

"No," Don replied, harsher than he probably intended. "But have a few more drinks, Sheryl, and you'll be seeing pink elephants."

As Don turned and stormed away, the women began laughing as soon as they thought he was out of earshot.

Carol was the first to make herself stop, yet whatever she tried thinking of, she couldn't manage to lose her smile.

Moments later, she checked her wristwatch for the time. Then she started unwrapping the food on the table. Seconds later, she found herself swatting at flies again.

She glanced at Sheryl from the corner of her eyes and asked, "Why do you always give Don such a hard time?"

"Because it's fun," Sheryl said, rolling her eyes. "And Jesus Christ, a giant rabbit? What happened to him as a kid?"

Carol couldn't help but chuckle at that, but one look at her daughter soured the mood.

"I feel terrible," Carol said. "I shouldn't be laughing."

"Why? It's funny."

"What if people make fun of Ellie that way?"

"Oh, it's not the same, and you know it."

"What's not the same?" Carol asked. "They both have...had imaginary friends."

"So?"

"So I don't want people like us making fun of her for it. Or even kids her own age if they ever found out. My heart couldn't take it."

"She's too pretty."

"What?"

"She won't get made fun of because she's too pretty."

"Why do you mean by that?"

Sheryl gestured to her breasts by waving her hands in front of them. "I developed these when I was twelve. I also had the most horrible bangs imaginable courtesy of my mom, who thought bangs were eternally in style."

Carol finished unwrapping all the food and paused to wait for Sheryl to make her point.

"Let's just say the boys didn't care about my hair. I coulda walked in bald. They wouldn't have given a shit."

Carol covered her own smile as Sheryl smiled with her.

"Your daughter is gorgeous. She's gonna be a heartbreaker. No one will ever make fun of her except bitches who are jealous. And even when they do, she won't care because she'll be too busy fightin' the boys away."

"You think?"

"I know," Sheryl said, placing her arm around Carol's shoulder and hugging her from the side.

Carol looked Sheryl in the eyes and smiled.

"You know," Carol said, "I think this is the beginning of a beautiful friendship."

Sheryl smiled and hugged her again, but when they parted, Sheryl started to laugh.

"What?" Carol asked, alarmed.

"Your poor husband."

Both ladies shared another long, stomach-hurting laugh.

Once they composed themselves, Carol announced out loud it was time to eat. But the rest of the family kept doing what they were doing, not even glancing over.

So Sheryl winked at her and shouted loud enough to stop time, "You heard the lady, it's time to eat!"

This time, everyone stopped what they were doing and started walking toward the tables.

Sheryl turned to see Carol walking toward Ellie in the sandpit.

"I thought I told you to get cleaned up, young lady?" Carol asked her daughter, to which Ellie looked up at her, squinting into the sun.

"Can Charlie come with me?"

"To get cleaned up?" Carol asked, disturbed.

Ellie innocently nodded with a smile on her face.

"But isn't he a boy?" Carol asked, feeling icky about asking.

"He needs to clean up too," Ellie said, glancing over at the space where Charlie must have been sitting. "Right, Charlie?"

Then she nodded and turned back to her mother.

"See?"

Carol glanced at the spot where Charlie must have been and shrugged, not knowing what else to do.

"I guess so, but hurry. Everyone's already eating."

"Okay, Mommy," Ellie replied.

Her daughter stood up and brushed some of the sand off her legs and turned back to the sandpit.

"Come on, Charlie!" she said, waving for him to follow her as she turned and ran off toward the cabin.

Sheryl approached Carol and patted her on the back. "At least it's not a rabbit."

Carol shook her head and smiled, despite any reservations she still may have had about doing so.

*****

When Ellie emerged from the cabin, her father saw her from his spot on the picnic table bench and signaled for her to come to him.

As she ran toward her father with a big smile on her face and her arms extended, Carol's heart warmed as her husband picked Ellie up and sat her down beside him.

"I got you a plain, dry hot dog," Don told Ellie while setting her food down before her on a paper plate. "Just as you like it. No mustard. No chili. No cheese. Just plain and dry."

He said all that while looking up at his wife and rolling his eyes.

"Yay!" Ellie yelled, clapping her hands at the special hot dog made just for her. She wasted no time scooping it off her plate and taking a bite.

As she chewed with her mouth open, she smiled up at her mom with her mouth full.

Carol used her hand to mime closing her own mouth to remind her daughter to chew with her mouth closed.

When Ellie obeyed, Carol smiled at her, thinking, *She really is beautiful.*

But seconds later, Carol noticed Ellie had developed a concerned look on her face. Her daughter stared to her right, where there was nothing.

Ellie turned to her father and tugged on his shirt sleeve. When he peered down at her, she beckoned him with her hand to lean down. After he did, she whispered something in his ear, and he glanced up at his wife, eyebrows raised, and shrugged.

Carol mouthed "What?" at him, but he quietly pulled out a paper plate, made another dry hot dog, and handed the plate to his daughter.

They both watched as she took it and carefully set the plate on an empty spot at the end of the table.

"Here you go, Charlie," she said.

As Carol watched, she saw her daughter smile and nod at something before turning back to her dad.

"Charlie says thank you for the hot dog."

Before Don could reply, Jerry looked up from the other end of the table and appeared confused. "Who the hell is Charlie?"

His wife punched him in the shoulder and told him to shut up and eat.

Jerry rubbed his shoulder and muttered, "Why'd you hit me?"

"Because you like it," Sheryl said.

At that, Jerry blushed and smiled at her.

As Carol watched, Sheryl glanced over at her and winked. In turn, Carol mouthed, "Thank you," and grinned at her.

Jerry peered around at the group, and a big, goofy grin broke out on his face. He wiped his mouth with a paper napkin and stood up from the table.

Everyone stopped what they were doing and looked up at him in silence while he took a moment to take a large sip of his beer.

When he reached into one of his pockets to retrieve his cell phone, his impatient wife rolled her eyes.

"What are you doin'?" Sheryl asked.

"I wanna picture of this," he said, gesturing toward the group. "The whole family."

Most of the adults groaned, but the kids all cheered. Even Ellie voiced her approval and clapped her tiny hands.

"It's not often that we all get together," Jerry said. "So I wanted to capture it for, uh…for…" He shook his head, trying to think of something while snapping his fingers. "What's the word I'm looking for?"

"Posterity?" Don shouted out, to which Jerry grinned and pointed at him.

"Ladies and gentlemen, I may have got the looks and personality in our family," Jerry said with pride, "but my little brother here definitely got the brains."

A few of the family laughed. Even Don put on a good show of it. But Carol knew in her gut the remark bothered him. Because everything his big brother did bothered him. She also knew Don would complain about it later when they were alone, as he always did when it came to things his brother said or did.

"Let's take a picture," Jerry said, then held out the phone to Don. "Hey, Don, would you take it?"

As some at the table groaned in protest, and Jerry's sons laughed, Don's face turned beet red as he realized what his brother was asking him to do.

As Ellie glanced around, confused, not knowing what was happening, Carol's heart sank for her husband.

Carol was about to say something when Sheryl slapped her husband on his chest with a flat palm.

"What is wrong with you?" she yelled.

"Ow!" Jerry exclaimed, rubbing his chest. "I was just kiddin'!"

Carol looked over at Don, who was red-faced when he caught her gazing at him with a loving smile.

As they regarded one another with warmth, she mouthed to him, "I love you."

Don grinned shyly and mouthed the words back to her.

"I was gonna take the photo!" Jerry shouted. "Jeez, people, lighten up! Don knows I was just kiddin'!"

Don nodded and smiled that he knew that. But his lying eyes betrayed his face.

Sheryl shouted, "Just take the damn picture and shut up already."

"All right, all right," Jerry said, turning his back to the family.

He raised the camera above his head to get everyone in the frame.

He asked, "Where's Carol?"

He glanced back over his shoulder and saw her.

"Get in the picture, Carol."

Carol blushed and smiled as she approached the picnic table and took an empty spot on the bench opposite her husband and daughter. She composed herself and looked toward Jerry's phone.

"Everybody in the back, lean in," Jerry shouted as he peered up at his phone and steadied it. He pressed the button a few times, and everyone heard the clicks.

He turned to the group with a celebratory smile on his face and said, "Beautiful," and sat back down. He immediately started scrolling through his phone to check out the results of his half-drunken photography skills.

As Carol started to make herself something to eat, Jerry made an audible noise. As she looked over at him, he seemed puzzled while staring at his phone.

"This is so weird," Jerry said, scrolling the photos back and forth with his fingers.

His curious sons stood up and walked behind him to see what had him concerned.

By that time, everyone else at the table was now wondering what was going on.

Don looked back and forth from his wife to his brother. "What's goin' on?"

Jerry glanced up, appearing very confused. His mouth opened and closed, but nothing came out.

"Well?" Sheryl asked.

When Jerry didn't answer her quickly enough, she grabbed the phone from him while he was too shocked and confused to protest.

Sheryl looked at the phone and shook her head.

"What's wrong?" she asked, scrolling through the photos of the family he just took. "What did you see?"

She suddenly stopped scrolling and began staring at the phone. Her intense face inching closer with each passing second.

She glanced toward the end of the table where Don and Ellie were sitting with a shared mystified expression on their faces.

Don held up his hands. "What?"

Sheryl shot Carol a serious look, then stood up and marched over to show them what she had seen.

Carol walked around the table to peer over her husband's shoulder right as Sheryl leaned down to show them the phone's camera screen.

As they all looked, they saw the family smiling and looking up at the camera. But as Carol looked closer, she finally saw what had shaken Jerry to his core, and what was now bringing a crestfallen look to Don's face.

Carol couldn't believe her eyes. She felt like rubbing them to make sure she wasn't seeing things. But a flicker of movement out of the corner of her eyes caused her to peer down.

She saw Ellie getting to her knees on the bench to see what everyone else was gawking at. When her daughter saw the photo on the phone, a huge grin broke out on her face as she pointed at the screen.

"Hey," she said in an excited voice. "It's Charlie."

Carol stared back down at the phone screen again.

In the family photo, standing at the end of the table, smiling up at the camera, was a transparent image of what looked to be a seven- or eight-year-old, blond-haired little boy who was about a foot taller than Ellie. Only the bottom half of him had completely faded away.

His arm rested on Ellie's shoulder as she glanced up at him with a wide grin.

Carol, Don, Sheryl, and the rest of the family watched in amazement as Ellie sat back down, smiled at an empty space before her, and ate what remained of her hot dog.

The adults looked at each other in shock and amazement. But no one could bring themselves to say a word.

HUNTER

A crescent moon hangs low in the sky. From the forest below, rock music is heard.

Four teens sit around a campfire near two tents. They're a duo of lovebirds out having a good time. Drinking, laughing, and sharing a joint.

Suddenly, one of the guys, Lee, hears twigs snapping, and leaves crackling in the distance. His senses on alert, he peers into the dark forest and slowly reaches over and turns down the music on a boom box.

This perturbs Lee's friend Tommy, who glares over at him.

"Hey, man, what are you doin'? I love that song."

"I heard something."

"What? A guy in a hockey mask?"

The girls laugh. They are Dana and Lori. Both are very pretty girl-next-door types.

Lee stands up and walks toward the dark forest and away from the protective light of the fire.

Tommy shakes his head. "I hate to break it to you, man, but those are just movies."

"No, there's something out there."

Tommy blows him off, "Whatever."

"No, dude, I'm serious."

Lori takes a toke. "Hi, serious."

Tommy and Dana crack up.

Lee shushes them. "Will y'all be quiet?"

The others look at one another in silence before cracking up again.

Lori rolls her eyes at Dana. "I think your boyfriend is losin' it."

"I swear I heard something," Lee interjects without looking back.

Tommy takes a toke and smiles. "Maybe it's Bigfoot."

They hear a voice from the darkness around them.

"Or maybe…"

The teens all panic and immediately jump to their feet, gathering in a group for protection.

The voice continues, "It's just an old man who got lost in the forest and saw your fire."

Tommy drops his joint to the ground and crushes it with the heel of his hiking boot.

A tall old man with a craggy, leathery face caused by lots of time spent in the sun and a deep, distinctive voice steps into the light cast by the fire. His smile seems unforced and friendly. He's dressed in a plaid shirt, cargo pants, and hiking boots.

Tommy asks, "Whoa, dude, where'd you come from?"

Blinking fast, Lori places a hand on her chest and shudders, "Oh my god. I thought we were dead."

The old man says, "I've been walkin' out here all day. I was over yonder a ways when I heard your music and saw your fire. To tell ya the truth, you kids are a godsend."

"You got lost?" Lori asks.

"Yeah. Surprised me too. One minute, I knew where I was. The next…" The old man rolls his eyes and shakes his head.

Lee asks, "You, uh, you need something to drink, mister? Water?"

"Call me Ted. And I wouldn't mind at all if you offered me one uh them beers."

Taken aback for a moment, Lee finally collects himself and smiles, "Sure, no problem."

Lee digs into the cooler, brings out a cold beer can dripping with water, and hands it to the old man, then gestures beside Ted to a log.

"Have a seat. I'm Lee. This is Dana. And this is Tommy and Lori."

Ted winks at the group and smiles, showing large yellow teeth.

He opens the beer and guzzles half the can, then lowers it.

He burps and says, "Graci-ass, amigos."

Tommy chuckles at the old man's pronunciation.

Ted takes a seat on the log facing them while the teens sit on the other side, still huddled as a group.

Lee asks, "You hungry, Ted?"

"Famished," Ted replies.

"Well, we got some weenies and some leftover beef stew."

"Oh, I don't wanna put y'all out—"

"It's no problem, really."

"Thanks for the offer, but all I need is this beer and some directions to the nearest road, then I'll be on my way, toot-sweet."

Again, Tommy chuckles.

Ted eyes Tommy for a moment with a dark serious look, then quickly regains his warm smile.

Lee asks, "So what brings you out here, Ted?"

"Well, I've been a traveling man lately…Lee, was it?"

Lee nods.

"I've been takin' my time seein' this great land of ours, Lee. Figured I'd do it while I still had the legs for it."

"What have you been doing? Besides sightseeing?"

"Oh, you know, hitchin' with my thumb, sleepin' under the stars, huntin' for my supper, and goin' wherever the road takes me."

Dana asks, incredulous, "You hunt for your own food?"

"Oh, you know, just whatever I come across that I can still catch."

Tommy asks, "What do you hunt with? 'Cause I don't see anything on ya."

"Well, I got two eyes to see, two ears to hear, two hands to grab, two legs to carry me…and very sharp teeth." Ted snaps his teeth together for effect.

Dana jumps, slightly startled. Embarrassed, she absentmindedly scoots closer to Lee.

Ted notices her discomfort and flashes his warm smile again. "What more does a man need?"

He peers into the fire and starts to chuckle. This leads to a cackle.

The teens regard one another and shrug. They're all starting to get tense.

Ted says, "You know, this fire brings back a lotta memories. Back to when I was a kid, and my dad used to take me campin'."

The teens start to relax again, except for Dana, who still seems afraid.

"Every once in a while, he'd let me bring along a friend or two, and we'd roast hot dogs and marshmallows and such. And my dad, well, he'd let us take a sip of beer every now and then. Not much, mind ya, but enough to make us think we were drunk."

Ted smiles again.

"And right before we went to bed, we'd sit around tellin' scary stories. 'Cause there's nothin' better than sittin' around a campfire with your friends tellin' scary stories."

The teens are quiet. They don't know what to say.

Ted asks, "You wanna hear my favorite scary story?"

The teens look at one another.

Dana shakes her head, but the others smile and nod, much to her disappointment.

Tommy shrugs and says, "Sure. Why not?"

Lee turns to Ted and says, "Go on, Ted. Scare us."

Ted smiles and says, "Well, let's see… One night"—he gazes up at the night sky—"on a night much like this, there were these campers. A lot like you kids. And like you kids, they were havin' a good ole time. Drinkin' beer, listenin' to music…smokin' a little dope."

Ted regards the crushed joint on the ground, then winks at the teens and smiles at them as they all try unsuccessfully to hide their guilt.

"I was young once too, you know."

Tommy chuckles but seems nervous.

Ted goes on. "Anyway, they were young, dumb, in perpetual lust, and had no earthly idea what was comin' for 'em."

Dana gulps.

"Well, into their campsite wanders this stranger. And the teens bein' nice kids and all, well, they welcomed him with open arms. They offered him the warmth of their fire, even a beer or two."

Dana's eyes shift toward her friends. Even Lori starts to look worried. Tommy and Lee, however, are into the story.

"What they didn't know, these kids, was that this man...well, he really wasn't a man at all."

The old man pauses for effect, looking at all their perplexed faces.

On the edge of his seat, Tommy asks, "What was he?"

Ted makes eye contact with all of them one at a time, then slowly grins, "He was a werewolf."

Lee and Tommy look at one another in disbelief and immediately start to laugh. Even Lori and Dana start to smile, relieved at last.

Ted flashes a big grin and continues, "Bet you all didn't see that one comin'?"

Tommy shakes his head and smiles. "No, we sure didn't."

"I bet you kids didn't even know there really was such a thing."

The teens laugh again.

But Ted quickly loses his smile. "Neither did I, once."

The old man's steely glare makes the group go quiet, and the girls get nervous again.

But when he flashes his warm smile, the group relaxes ever so slightly.

"I'll bet all y'all were kids whose parents told ya there were no such things as monsters," Ted says. "I bet when it came bedtime, they even checked under your beds and in your closets just so you'd feel safe enough to go to sleep. But in the back of your minds, you always knew they were lyin'. And guess what?"

He takes turns staring at each member of the group again while they all sit as quiet as church mice.

Ted finally adds, "You were right. There are such things as monsters...especially werewolves. And you happen to be lookin' at one right now. In the flesh."

Ted smiles and gazes up at the sky.

The kids look at one another. They share a similar freaked-out expression, yet somehow Lee remains amused.

"Well, Ted, it's a good thing there's no full moon out tonight. I guess that means we're safe."

"And you'd be wrong, Lee. 'Cause it don't matter what moon is out. All that matters is that it is, even just a sliver. Although, the closer it is to a full moon, the worse the beast's hunger gets…and the less human it remains."

Tommy states, "Ted, I gotta tell ya. You're really good."

Lee adds, "Yeah, man, you really got us goin'."

Ted pats the air with his hands. "Well, hold on, I'm not quite finished talkin' yet. There's more. On nights like tonight, the werewolf is still quite human. And bein' more of a man, it can think. Unlike on a full moon, when it's just a savage, plain and simple. But on nights like this, when it can think, it likes to play with its food a little before it eats it. You know, just to have some fun. Especially since it enjoys the hunt so much, as this particular wolf does."

"Are you sure you didn't get heatstroke today, Ted?" Lee laughs.

Tommy joins him, but the girls stay quiet, too creeped out to laugh.

Ted leans closer to Lee and shoots him a cruel, cold glare. "Shut up, boy."

Lee backs down quickly, taken aback with fear and surprise.

"If I were in your shoes right now, I'd be haulin' some ass," Ted says. "'Cause in a matter of minutes, I'm gonna change into somethin' more comfortable…and then that's your asses."

Lee is concerned. "What's goin' on, Ted? Did we…did we offend you in some way?"

"No, Lee, you and your friends just happen to be in the wrong goddamn place at the most wrong goddamn time."

Ted smiles and lightens up.

At that moment, to the teens' shock and surprise, the old man takes off his boots and socks, rolling up the latter and stuffing them inside the former for safekeeping. Then he nonchalantly starts unbuttoning his shirt, never taking his eyes off the stunned group before him.

Ted says, "Now, never let it be said I'm a total asshole. I do have good news. For some of you, at least. You see, there are four of you. And you could all run in the same direction. But that would just make it easier for me to pick you all off. But if y'all were to run in four different directions, definitely one and maybe two of ya will live to see the dawn. But for two of ya, you won't live that long. Maybe three, if I'm on my game."

The teens can only stare at Ted while shivering in fear as the old man carefully folds and sets his shirt down upon the log he was sitting on, then stands and starts unbuckling his belt and unfastening his pants.

The women are on the verge of tears as the teens all sit there, not knowing what to say or do but stare at the half-naked old man undressing before them. Hoping it's all just a big joke. Waiting for a punchline that will never come.

After removing his pants, Ted folds them neatly and lays them atop his shirt. Afterward, he removes his underwear. Then after folding and setting them down on the carefully constructed garment pile, he stands in sinewy nude glory before them without an ounce of shame.

As the group sizes Ted up with stunned looks on their faces, the old man claps his hands once to make sure he has their complete attention.

Ted points at his face. "Eyes up here, ladies." He pauses and flashes a wicked grin. "And Lee."

Lee immediately looks up and reacts like any faux-confident heterosexual male would when confronted with the fact he was caught staring at another man's manhood. Denial, embarrassment, and immediate blushing regret.

Fortunately for Ted, the rest of the group, much like him, are too terrified to think clearly and react sophomorically like they normally would have.

But Ted laughs heartily. He's enjoying himself immensely, taking in the moment, processing it mentally for later. This is his foreplay before the hunt. He's prolonging it, savoring it.

Ted adds, "So for some of y'all, you have a pretty damn good chance at survival. But you're only gonna have that much if you start runnin' right now."

The teens just sit there regarding one another. When they look back at Ted, he smiles at them. The teens watch in horror as his incisors start to grow, and he begins to groan in pain.

Lee is the first one to his feet. He stares down at Dana and back at Ted, whose body is starting to contort and change. Lee thinks twice and takes off running, leaving the others behind without saying a word.

Dana, in shock that Lee suddenly ran off, screams after him. "Lee!"

Lori gets to her feet. "Run, Dana!"

Dana stares into her eyes. A confused look on her face.

Lori shouts, "Run!"

Dana glances at Ted to see his eyes starting to glow yellow, as if reflecting the flames of the fire.

Ted winks at her, grins, and groans in pain again as his skin starts to stretch and tear.

Tommy shoves Dana and screams at her to run as well.

Dana finally does as she's told, and all three teens flee as fast as their feet will go.

They run in a different direction than Lee.

Ted, his nose and mouth protruding from his face to form a snout, tears rolling from his eyes, raises his gaze to the sliver of moon above. He lets out a human-sounding howl, more like a war cry, that soon evolves into evil laughter.

*****

From a distance, a man wearing hiking boots stops in his tracks. He listens, then starts running toward the beastly sounds.

*****

Ted leans forward, the bones in his back breaking and reforming, rising beneath his flesh, growing larger. Long, sharp claws protrude from the tips of his fingers and toes causing him to scream in agony. His ears shift higher on his head and grow tall and pointy.

Coarse, dark hair begins to grow all over his body.

*****

As Tommy and the two young women run together, Dana falls down and goes into hysterics. Tommy immediately orders Lori to keep running as he turns back toward Dana.

Lori stops in her tracks and stares back at the glow of the campfire in the distance, not knowing what to do.

Tommy turns to see Lori still standing there and runs over toward her, "What are you doin'?"

When Lori doesn't reply, he shakes her by the shoulders. As she starts to come around, he orders her to start running again.

But Lori can't bring herself to move. When Tommy assures her that he'll help Dana, Lori finally does as she's told.

Tommy runs back to Dana and helps her to her feet. But Dana is a basket case. Tears are flowing, and she's inconsolable. Shaking badly and muttering nonsense.

She manages to say clearly, "He left us."

"I know."

"Lee left us."

"I promise to kick his ass later. But right now, we have to go."

As Tommy grunts and pulls her along, Dana begins to run on autopilot. Tommy goads her on, forcing her to move faster.

*****

Now fully formed, the beast lifts its head toward the sky and sniffs the air. It catches a scent, growls, and takes off after its prey.

*****

The man in the distance is still running. Too fast for a normal man. He's in great shape. Not breaking stride. Gaining ground fast.

*****

Lee breaks into a clearing. He looks around. Losing steam.

When he glances back, he loses his balance and falls with a thud, scraping his face along the ground.

"Shit!" he yells in a panic.

He quickly gets back on his feet. He starts running again but now with a slight limp and a hitch in his side, which he's now pressing with one hand.

*****

The beast is at full gallop. Running on all fours, it powers through the woods like a locomotive. Its breath raises plumes of dust from the ground. The earth trembles with each thunderous footfall.

Its large mass snaps low-hanging limbs and branches like toothpicks and sends fallen leaves swirling into the air in its wake.

*****

Lee is slowing. Adrenaline fading. Every breath labored. Eyes wide with fear. There's no confusion on his part. His mind has never been clearer. He knows exactly what is coming for him.

More adrenaline kicks in. A second wind. Lee starts to run faster, ignoring the sharp pain in his side as well as his injured leg.

Tears fall hard and fast as he repeats over and over again, "I don't wanna die."

But in a flash, Lee is taken to the ground with tremendous force. He doesn't even have time to scream.

Towering over its captured prey, the beast lunges its head downward.

It clamps its jaws and rips Lee's head off with a mighty yank and tosses it away. It begins to lap up the jetting blood.

It soon stops drinking, raises its head, and peers around. Blood drips from its snout. It sniffs the air and growls.

Suddenly, something whizzes by the creature's head and hits the ground mere feet from it, raising a plume of dust. The sound of a shot rings out in the distance.

The beast wastes no time taking off. It gathers speed quickly, now in fear, running for its life.

Within seconds, the man in hiking boots stops near Lee's headless body. He kneels down. Searches the ground with purpose. Finally finds what he's looking for.

A spent tranquilizer dart.

The man pockets the dart, and he's off again. Not even a second glance at the body. The man is in single-minded pursuit of the creature.

Nothing else matters.

*****

An old man named Ed drives his noisy, rusty pickup truck down a quiet country road. He's warbling along to an old country tune while taking a pull from a whiskey flask.

*****

As the large, powerful beast smashes its way through a winding path in the woods, the legs of the man in pursuit of it move in a blur.

Impossibly fast and agile for a simple human.

He carries his rifle before him in two hands. His breathing is controlled. Still hot on the beast's trail.

*****

Ed drives on. Takes another tug. Drains his flask.

The feral beast crashes through the tree line on the side of the road. It bounds into the path of the oncoming truck and is briefly illuminated by the oncoming headlights.

Ed's head is tilted back in the cab of his truck, completely unaware of the monstrous sight on the road before him. His eyes are on the flask hanging upside down over his mouth. His thoughts are only on getting the last drop.

In a flash, the creature barrels from the road and smashes through the tree line on the other side.

That's when the man with the rifle emerges from the forest and comes to a stop in the middle of the road, totally oblivious to the headlights that are illuminating him.

The man, the hunter, raises his rifle and aims for the escaping creature. He quickly has the creature in his sights. He blows a breath out slowly and calmly squeezes the trigger.

The creature yelps in pain in the distance as the shot hits its target.

The hunter smiles with satisfaction, then finally notices the glare of the lights enveloping him.

Ed lowers his flask and suddenly sees the man standing in the middle of the road before him. The old man's eyes widen as he yells and slams on the brakes with both feet.

The truck skids. Smoke plumes from the tires.

The hunter yells and braces for the impact.

The truck smashes into him, causing him to soar at least twenty feet down the road.

The front end of the truck is now damaged. The radiator spills steam as hot water pours out under the front of the truck and onto the road. The vehicle ticks and clicks as the engine chortles and dies.

Inside the truck, Ed is lying slumped over the steering wheel. Most of the windows are shattered, and the front of Ed's head is covered in blood, which drips off his nose.

His head moves as he slowly comes to and groans in pain. He slowly raises his head, revealing the ugly, jagged cut on his forehead.

Ed's vision is blurry, and his mind is cloudy, but he manages to clear some of the mental cobwebs and rub the blood from his eyes.

With a sudden gasp, he remembers what just happened.

Muttering curses to himself, he stares ahead and sees the man's crumpled body lying on the road near the edge of his headlight range.

"Oh shit," Ed mutters.

He starts to panic. With a trembling left hand, he reaches for the driver's door handle and immediately groans in pain. He takes a few deep breaths and waits for the throbbing pain on the left side of his chest to subside.

With considerable effort, he moans and slowly raises his left hand to the side of his chest and uses his right one to reach across his body and open the door.

The driver's door creaks open, and cubes of broken glass sprinkle onto the road.

Ed cautiously lowers one leg to the road with a grunt, followed by the other. He places his hands on the door to pull himself upright and slowly steps away from the truck.

With a high degree of painful difficulty, Ed begins making his way toward the body on the road, which isn't moving at all.

Ed begins to silently pray, his lips moving, his eyes darting to the dark sky, hoping against hope that someone up there is listening.

As his long shadow falls over the body, Ed sees that one of the man's legs is at an odd angle from the rest of his body. The sight of it causes the old man to wince in sympathy.

Suddenly, one of the prostrate man's hands moves.

Ed stumbles back in surprise, "Holy shit."

Ed stares at the hand intently, waiting for it to move again, hoping it wasn't a figment of his imagination. A few moments after mentally willing it to move again, his prayers are answered.

Ed asks, relieved, "Hey, buddy, you okay?"

The man opens his eyes, gasps, and sucks air into his lungs.

Ed stumbles back, shocked, but smiling.

The man blinks a few times and shakes his head.

Ed chuckles in relief and immediately grimaces in pain, grabbing his left side.

The hunter looks up at Ed and grits his teeth, "Where the hell did you come from?"

Ed shakes his head softly to keep from hurting himself, "I could ask you the same thing."

The hunter groans as he slowly sits up and looks around. He sees his left leg turned at an impossible angle. Looking less than alarmed, he calmly checks the rest of himself over. He feels pain in his chest and lower extremities.

He scans the road by the wrecked truck and spots his rifle, still in one piece on the pavement before it. He glares at the forest where the creature ran and surveys the area.

Ed notices the man sniffing the air, trying to pick up a scent.

The old man asks, "Do you happen to have one of them portable phones on you? 'Cause you need a doctor."

The man looks at Ed and replies, "You need one more than me."

"You kiddin' me? You were just hit by a truck. Look at your leg. It ain't supposed to be like that."

The man gazes at his broken leg and back up at Ed. "Don't faint."

"What?" Ed asks.

The man grabs his leg, and—with a cringe-worthy snap and a long, loud scream—turns it back the way it should be facing.

Ed stumbles back in shock, "Holy shit! What the—"

"Don't worry. I'll be fine," the man grimaces. "I heal fast."

Ed steps away, not sure what to make of this guy.

"Jesus, how did you…how did you do that?"

The man pushes himself up. Bones are heard shifting, breaking, and resetting as he forces his body to stand.

Ed is beside himself. "My god."

Once the man is back on his feet, he starts limping toward the old man's truck in the distance. The sounds of his bones, cartilage, and tendons repairing themselves while he moves are heard.

Right before Ed's eyes, the man slowly but surely stops limping. He soon picks up his gait. By the time he stops, kneels down, and picks up his rifle, he seems perfectly fine, like nothing ever happened.

Ed closes his eyes and rubs his face. His mind is racing. He can't believe what he's just seen.

The man checks out his rifle to make sure it's still in working condition and peers back at the old man.

"I'll call you an ambulance," the man tells him. "But in the meantime, get back in your truck and stay there until they get here. And no matter what you hear, don't get out until they arrive."

Ed can only shake his head.

The man adds, "Oh, and one more thing…"

Ed waits while the man locks and loads his rifle and glares at him.

"Don't drink and drive."

Ed shakes his head in vehement agreement, "Oh, mister, you ain't gotta worry about that. After what I've seen tonight, I ain't ever drinkin' again."

The man nods, saying, "Good man," then runs off the road and disappears into the forest, following the trail of the creature.

Ed waits a while in open-mouthed confusion and shock before he becomes aware of his surroundings and starts glancing around in all directions. He feels a chill, which causes him to rub his arms. He grimaces from the movement and thinks about what the man told him and shudders.

"Screw this."

He limps as fast as he can toward his truck.

*****

The man, the hunter, strides through the forest, following the trail of broken branches and large animal tracks in the dirt. Something catches his eye and causes him to stop in his tracks.

A path of large animal paw prints has come to an end, where there appear to be signs of a struggle. A little way down from there, the trail picks up again. Only now the tracks are that of a human.

Bare footprints.

The hunter soon emerges over a hill and looks down to an empty ravine below.

There he spots a naked Ted, covered in sweat, dirt, and mud, lying on his back, staring up at the sky as if hypnotized. He is wounded and weak. His breathing is labored. Too sick to move.

As the hunter gets closer, he spots a large tranquilizer dart on the man's side. The area where the dart entered is now covered with pus, and the skin around it is inflamed.

Ted continues to be transfixed by the night sky, but now he's smiling.

The hunter peers up and regards what he's staring at.

It's the crescent moon, which resembles a sleepy eye gazing down at them.

The hunter looks back down to see the wounded man staring directly at him.

"Who are you?" Ted asks.

The hunter replies, "Michael."

Ted gazes back at the moon hanging in the distance above Michael's head and, at once, seems surprised.

"You mind me askin'? 'Cause I'm curious," Ted asks. "How do you hold it back?"

Michael is taken aback.

Ted asks with surprising sincerity, "How do you keep the beast at bay?"

Michael seems ashamed. He looks away and says, "I wanted it that way. It took some time…but I had help."

Ted laughs, "Oh, man. Who'da thunk it? A self-hatin' wolf."

He continues to laugh, then catches his breath.

"You have issues, man. Huntin' down your own kind like this."

Ted sniffs and shakes his head in disgust.

Michael replies coldly, "Someone has to."

"Lemme guess. It's a personal thing with you, right?"

Michael says nothing. But the truth is plainly evident on his face.

The wounded man is not at all apologetic. He seems to enjoy Michael's inner pain immensely.

"Did I happen to kill someone close to you?"

"You did your part."

The wounded man smiles. "Sorry, you'll have to remind me. There've been so many, I've lost track."

Michael grinds his teeth, looks down, and says, "Almost four years ago in New Mexico, there was a sheriff."

Michael pauses and almost smiles, remembering something pleasant. But the almost-smile quickly fades, replaced by a fierce look of hate.

"Sorry. I always forget. He was the chief of police." Michael glares at the wounded man. "That ring a bell?"

"Wait a minute..." Ted thinks back, then chuckles when he remembers. "Yeah. He was out huntin', right?"

"Yeah. And because of you, he ended up like us...and killed a lotta people."

Ted leans his head back and exhales, "Well, what can I say? Shit happens."

Michael's grip tightens on the rifle.

Ted gazes back up at him, "He killed someone you loved, didn't he?"

Michael doesn't answer him.

Ted continues to needle him. "So, was it him that turned you, or was it this...love of your life?"

Michael remains stoic and silent.

The wounded man is enjoying himself immensely, despite the incredible amount of pain he's in. "Now you obviously have a dark debt to settle. And you're not gonna stop till you wipe the whole slate clean. That about right?"

Michael just stands there with a serious poker face.

Ted is starting to lose his enthusiasm. The pain is getting worse, and it's draining his resolve. "Lemme ask you somethin'. What happens when you're done? When you've wiped all of us out? What happens then?"

Michael looks down at the dart in the man's side.

Ted regards the dart, then smiles. "Don't tell me you're plannin' on finishin' yourself off with one of these?"

Michael stays silent.

"Wow. Your self-hate must run pretty damn deep. You're a real piece of work." Ted sniffs the air and registers disgust. "And this is some real foul shit, by the way."

"It's my own personal cocktail, made just for beasts like us."

The dying man chuckles.

Michael nods toward the dart. "As you can tell, it wasn't enough to kill you, but it was plenty enough to knock you down and keep you down until I found you."

Ted nods and says, "And you didn't wanna kill me without me knowing the reason why, did ya? You wanted to look me in the eyes first. Up close and personal-like."

Michael doesn't answer him.

Ted asks, "What was her name? This great love of yours."

Michael doesn't reply right away. Instead, he raises the rifle and aims at the wounded man's torso. "Her name was Jenny."

Ted grins, makes eye contact, and replies, "Pretty name."

Michael fires a tranquilizer dart into Ted's chest.

At once, Ted begins to violently spasm, shake, and scream. White, then red foam begins to pour from his mouth and nose. Blood leaks from his ears and eyes.

With one final bloodcurdling scream, Ted stills and dies. His tortured-looking face is frozen in pain. His lifeless eyes reflect the sliver of moon hanging above.

Michael lowers his rifle. His gaze far away. Thinking of the past.

NOMAD

Several semitrucks with large trailers sat idle, despite their engines running, in the shadows of a dimly lit truck stop diner parking lot.

Large potholes of muddy water peppered the lot like land mines, while a row of mud-covered pickup trucks sat parked near the diner where classic country music—none of that pop-sounding, present-era crap—filtered outside and wafted through the night air.

*****

A mid-forties woman named Lorna checked her reflection in a dingy restroom mirror. The harsh, blinking halogen lights hanging above the sink didn't flatter her aging features, which once upon a time were actually quite something to behold.

She was wearing too much makeup, and her clothes were tight and revealing, leaving nothing to the imagination.

As Lorna hummed along to the tune that was playing on the diner jukebox, she paused and grimaced at the dark circles under her eyes, the blemishes on her cheeks, the way her jowls were beginning to sag, and the wrinkles around her mouth. This moment of doubt, remorse, and stark-faced reality caused her to put on more makeup.

Just then, the restroom door opened, and a pretty young woman in a T-shirt and too-tight blue jeans entered. She immediately cast a disparaging look at Lorna, sizing her up for who she was and what she represented.

Lorna returned the young lady's disapproving look in kind.

As the young woman walked to a stall, Lorna frowned and applied some garish red lipstick.

*****

Lorna exited the restroom and purposefully walked with an extra jiggle in her step past the assorted diner clientele.

Some cast her dirty looks and guffawed as she passed, while most pretended she wasn't even there. Whose actions were worse, she couldn't decide.

Lorna soldiered on with exaggerated confidence, even going so far as to wink at a few of the men who were not so subtly casting her leering sidelong glances.

A particular group of gruff-looking men wearing trucker caps and dirty work boots commented under their breaths about her as she passed their table.

As Lorna sauntered away from them, she pitched her voice to a higher-than-normal volume.

"When you're tired of just lookin' at the best piece of ass in the lower forty-eight, come find out what you're missin'."

The men glanced at one another, surprised and embarrassed at being caught looking. Still, they managed to mumble a few dirty remarks as they turned their heads to ogle her as she walked out.

*****

Outside in the diner parking lot, Lorna was careful to avoid the water-filled potholes in her path.

The clack of her high-heeled shoes eventually came to a stop as she found herself standing near an old road sign marquee that cast a weak glow of light while advertising the diner's daily specials.

With the annoying electric hum of the sign in her ears, Lorna lit a cigarette, took a long drag, and exhaled. She rubbed her arms due to the chill in the air, then turned, high heels clacking once again, and made her way to the side of the restaurant to stand in the shadows.

Once there, she leaned back against the diner wall, smoke encircling her head and rising above her to dissipate into nothingness. She shifted her weight to one leg and propped the high-heeled foot of her other leg against the wall.

From the darkness, she heard the unmistakable sound of boots crunching on gravel.

Her head turned just in time to see a trucker wearing a Dallas Cowboys baseball cap emerging from the darkness. He was coming from the direction of the back of the diner.

As he walked toward her, Lorna's body tingled with fear, but she recovered quickly and gave him her best "come-hither" smile.

"Lookin' for a good time?" she asked.

She took another drag and exhaled the smoke slowly from the corners of her grinning mouth as the trucker walked past her without a word nor a tip of his cap.

Lorna let him go without another comment.

She leaned back against the wall, closed her eyes, and took another long drag. As she exhaled, she opened her eyes and jumped, startled at the sight of a well-dressed, tall, thin man standing in the shadows before her.

After placing a hand on her chest while catching her breath, she belted out some nervous laughter and said, "Whoa! Sorry, honey. Didn't hear ya walk up."

The man, the features of his face obscured by the darkness, replied, "I apologize for scaring you."

Lorna smiled. The strange-sounding lilt of his voice had immediately put her at ease.

"Oh, it's all right. I've had worse scares."

They shared an awkward silence.

Lorna smiled and asked, "So, you just passin' through, or are you lookin' for a quick layover?"

She couldn't help but giggle like a schoolgirl at her choice of words.

The man, however, was unfazed by her flirty banter. "I'm always up for a good time."

Lorna smiled full, showing most of her teeth. "Now that's what I like to hear." She subtly stuck the point of her tongue against the roof of her mouth. "How much of a good time are you up for?"

"You're not shy, are you?" the man asked.

"You want shy, I can be shy." Lorna grinned, stepped away from the wall, and took a couple of slow steps toward him. "For the right price, I can be anything you want."

Nonplussed, the man gestured to the air with his hand.

"Where shall we go?"

"Your ride will do."

"Oh, I'm afraid I came ahead," the man declared. "My ride won't be here for a few hours yet."

Lorna took a deep drag on her cigarette. She crinkled her eyes and pointed with her hand that held her cigarette. "You have a funny way of talkin'. You definitely ain't from around here."

"Where I come from no longer exists," the man replied, then chuckled while he remembered something. "I guess you could call me a man without a country."

"Well, weary traveler, I know a few motels nearby whenever you're ready."

"That won't be necessary. Right here is fine."

Lorna gave him a shocked yet playful glance as she turned and faced the wall while placing her hands on it, as if she were getting arrested. She leaned forward slightly, raising her rear higher into the air, and peered back over her shoulder.

"You're just gonna take me right here? Right up against this wall?"

The man shrugged. "Why not?"

Lorna looked around, surveying the parking lot. Not a soul in sight.

"Well, whatever floats your boat, honey. It's your money—"

When she turned back to face the man, to her sudden shock and surprise, he wasn't there. She looked around in every direction, but there was no sign of him.

Nervous and surprised, Lorna asked the air, "Where'd you go, hon?"

When she didn't receive an answer, she slowly stepped away from the side of the building. As she cautiously backed away from the darkness, she was squinting, trying to peer into it.

"If this is your idea of a joke, I ain't laughin'."

She stepped even further away from the building, turning in half circles, looking for any sign of the mysterious man.

"All right," she exclaimed. "That's enough. I don't like playin' these kinds of games."

She heard a sound in the night air and immediately turned to see a cowboy exiting the diner.

"Hey, you!" Lorna called out to him.

As she began walking in his direction, the oblivious cowboy stopped in his tracks and checked his pockets.

Lorna shouted, "Hey, cowboy!"

Lorna picked up her pace, high heels clacking, still careful to avoid the muddy potholes. But the cowboy hadn't heard her. Instead, he turned and walked back inside.

Lorna's last-second plea of "Hey!" was drowned out by the music emanating from inside the diner when he opened the door.

As the diner door closed, Lorna tripped and fell, landing in one of the potholes with a splash. She immediately pulled herself up to her hands and knees and found herself covered in mud and water.

"Shit! Goddammit!"

She slapped the water in frustration and stood up. But as she tried in vain to clean herself off, she noticed a tear in her pantyhose.

"Son of a bitch!"

She turned toward the truck stop and almost ran into someone standing beside her. She shrieked, then saw it was the well-dressed man from before.

"Jesus Christ!" she said. "What the hell's wrong with you? You scared me half to death."

"I'm sorry, Lorna," the man replied.

Looking down at herself, wiping her dress with her hands, Lorna said, "Look at me. How am I supposed to get work lookin' like somethin' the dog dug up?"

A disturbing thought crossed her face, causing her to look up, suddenly concerned. But all her fear and anger went away as soon as she looked into the man's eyes.

They were dark and penetrating. Seeing through to her very soul.

"How'd you know my name?" Lorna asked. "I never told you."

The man reached out and stroked the side of her face. At his touch, her eyelids fluttered, and a moan escaped her lips. She hadn't been touched tenderly like this in a long time. Not by a man, not by anyone.

"I know a great many things about you, Lorna. Who you are. Where you've been. How you'll die."

As the meaning of the man's last words registered on Lorna's face, she immediately opened her eyes.

"What?" she asked.

In the moonlight, she was just able to make out the man's long, pointy teeth. But before she could react, he lunged toward her.

*****

Lorna's scream pierced the night, then was cut off just as sharply.

Soon, all was silent except for the distant music coming from inside the truck stop and the electric hum of the diner marquee sign.

*****

Accompanied by a chorus of crickets hiding in the tall yellow grass growing wild alongside an interstate road, a very fit, extremely attractive, yet too-serious-looking young woman named Debbie walked backward along the side of the road with her thumb out.

She had on a throwback concert T-shirt, formfitting blue jeans, cowboy boots, and a loose-straw cowboy hat that allowed the sun to shine through it causing tiny suntan spots to form on her nose and cheeks.

Wearing a large backpack, she listened to music through her earbuds.

Upon a closer look, despite her pretty, sun-freckled face, her large eyes suggested something darker within.

This girl had seen and experienced too many bad things in her mere couple of decades on this earth. As evidence, the near-faded bruise of a black eye and an almost-healed split lip.

She glanced behind her and saw no vehicles on the horizon. For a brief moment, her spirit sank and her shoulders deflated. But just as quickly, a determined look returned to her face as she straightened out her posture, threw her shoulders back, and continued walking backward.

She peered over her shoulder again and saw a large green highway sign. She squinted her eyes to make out what it said—Odessa 30 Miles.

She stopped walking and kicked at a small rock. She heard it ping on the road's surface and bounce away and stared in the direction she had come from. That's when she saw a glint of metal in the distance.

She strained her eyes to get a better look and saw that it was a car.

She hooked one thumb in her belt loop and raised the other into the air.

As the car got closer, she could make out that it was a station wagon with a lone occupant.

As it approached, its turn signal came on, and it drove past her, only to pull over onto the shoulder of the road and come to a stop.

Debbie cautiously walked up alongside the car and bent down to look through the passenger window toward the driver. The glare off the window from the sun made that difficult. Until it rolled down.

That's when Debbie saw a casually dressed, pleasant-faced middle-aged man named Dan. As he smiled at her, her eyes quickly shifted down to his bare wedding ring finger.

"Need a ride?" Dan asked.

Debbie shifted her glance back up to his face. *He's kind-looking enough*, she thought, *but I've been fooled by that very thing before. Too many times to count.*

Dan must have sensed her unease, but he smiled it off.

"I apologize in advance for this old mug of mine, but I truly mean you no harm. But if you don't want to get in, I'll understand."

Debbie raised up and glanced in both directions. No sign of another vehicle. She lowered herself to look Dan right in the eyes.

She asked, "You're not a psycho, a sexual deviant, or a religious nut, are you?"

Dan smiled and shook his head. "If I were any of those things, would I tell you?"

As Debbie backed away from the car, regarding him in silence, Dan quickly realized his joke didn't go over well.

"Sorry, bad joke," Dan said, holding up his hands to make the point clear that he was harmless. "I promise that I'm as normal as normal can be."

Debbie squinted and looked once more in both directions. "Well, I'm afraid I don't have much experience with normal."

Dan nodded. "Well, to tell the truth, I always wondered just what the heck normal was anyway."

Debbie straightened up and looked in both directions again.

Who the hell says heck, she thought.

As the young woman stood outside the car, her face out of his view, Dan checked his rearview mirror. There wasn't another vehicle in sight.

Dan regarded her trepidation. "You flatter me with your hesitation. But I don't hold it against you. To tell you the truth, the only reason why I stopped is because of your shirt."

When Debbie leaned down and glared at him through the open window, he gestured to the band logo on her shirt.

"I saw them in concert once. Back in the eighties. One of the best concerts I ever went to. But I do have just one question. Aren't they a little before your time?"

Debbie shrugged. "Good music is good music."

Dan nodded. "Well, look, I promise you, I'm harmless, and my hands will never cross the console."

Debbie peered down at the console and back up at his face.

"Well, just so you know," Debbie said, "I know how to take care of myself."

Dan held up his hands again, as if surrendering. "I consider myself duly warned."

Debbie nodded. "Okay."

She opened the door and started to remove her backpack.

Dan gestured behind him. "You can put that in the back seat."

Keeping a wary eye on Dan, she slipped off the backpack and opened the back door. She quickly shoved the pack in, along with her hat, and closed the door, then opened the passenger door, and got inside.

But after a few moments, Debbie realized the car wasn't going anywhere. She peered over at Dan, a worried look growing upon her face.

She found him staring at her with a pleasant smile.

"Buckle up, please," he said, motioning with his eyes toward her seat belt in case she didn't hear him.

Debbie rolled her eyes and put on her seat belt. After she clicked it in place, Dan glanced back, saw no one coming, and pressed the accelerator.

*****

As Dan's car passed by a sign that read Odessa 21 Miles, Debbie paid it no mind.

Her earbuds were in as she fiddled with her iPod.

Dan had been taking occasional glances at her, wanting to say something but trying to respect her space.

He kept waiting for an opening. A window of time. A moment. But the longer he drove, the more she had retreated into herself. He soon realized the moment he was waiting for may never come. So after a few more side glances, he finally couldn't resist.

He leaned forward to catch her attention and motioned toward his own ears.

Debbie watched him as he repeated his gesture.

As she removed her earbuds, he said, "I'm Dan."

Debbie glared at him, confused.

Dan sighed and said, "And this is the part where you tell me your name."

It finally dawned on Debbie that she was being excessively rude to this man for no reason other than her own personal history of dealing with shitty men. She made the quick decision to ease up on him.

Still, she had to fight her natural inclination in order to be pleasant.

"Debbie," she finally replied.

"Well," Dan said, nodding, "it's nice to finally meet you, Debbie."

Debbie forced a smile and turned her attention back to her iPod.

But Dan wasn't done being sociable yet.

"So, where you from?"

Debbie turned back to Dan, thought it over, then raised her hand and jerked her thumb backward.

Dan smirked. But he pressed on, perhaps knowing what was going to come next.

"And where are you headed?" he asked.

Debbie simply pointed ahead.

Her gesture didn't surprise him, and Dan couldn't help but smile again.

He placed a hand on his chest and continued. "I'm from New Mexico. The Village of Capitan, to be exact."

This caught her attention. A look of genuine interest crossed her face. "You live in a village?"

"No," Dan shook his head and chuckled. "No, it's just a fancy term for a town not big enough to be called a town."

"Sounds tranquil," she replied.

"You mean boring?" Dan added, smiling.

Debbie raised her eyebrows and shrugged. "You said it, not me."

Dan laughed and nodded in agreement.

"Well, I guess you'd be right. Except during hunting and tourist seasons. That's when we get a little overwhelmed with all the big-city folks looking to get away from it all."

They drove on in silence a while before Debbie relented and cut him a little slack.

"So, Dan, what do you do when you're not out picking up young female hitchhikers?"

Dan was pleasantly surprised she was finally engaging him in conversation. Enough to overlook her obviously intended sarcasm.

"I'm an insurance salesman. I'm on my way back from a corporate meeting in Dallas."

Debbie is confused. "Why are you driving? Why not fly?"

Dan immediately shook his head. She had hit a target. "Oh no. Not me. I don't like anything to do with heights. And no way am I ever, ever stepping foot on a plane. Besides, I like driving."

Debbie took that in. In a way, she could understand the appeal of the open road. It was one of the reasons she was here in this car now. Going somewhere she didn't know. Escaping from where she had been. Headed toward freedom and, hopefully, something better.

Escaping from somewhere dark and sad.

"Besides," Dan said, snapping Debbie from her thoughts, "some of my greatest memories were made in cars."

Debbie almost laughed. "Oh, I bet."

Dan feigned being hurt by that remark, perhaps to cover up really being hurt by what this young woman obviously thought of him.

"It's not what you think," Dan said. "When I was a kid, we always drove everywhere. Mom and Dad up front, kids in the back. And I did the same with my wife and kids when they were little."

Debbie threw an alarmed glance toward his bare wedding finger. "You still married?"

Dan paused, immediately becoming a little sad and reflective. "No, she, uh… My Mildred died about three years ago."

Debbie immediately stared out the window looking more than a little upset but trying her best to block any of her own bad memories from coming back.

Dan quickly realized she was upset. "I'm just grateful for the twenty-four years we did have together."

Without looking at him, she asked, "How about your kids?"

This perked Dan up.

"Well, I got a son just out of college and a daughter just starting. What about you?"

Debbie was confused. She cast him a disturbed glance. "What about me?"

"You look about college age."

Debbie calmed down but still didn't respond.

"So?" Dan asked.

Debbie could only smirk. "I tried community college for about a semester. Let's just say it didn't take. So I fell back on waitressing. And that's when I made the latest in my long line of mistakes in the boyfriend department. And now I'm here."

"Do you ever think of going back?" Dan asked.

Debbie became alarmed, incredulous. "To my shit heel of an ex? Hell no!"

"No," Dan chuckled. "College. You ever think of giving it another try?"

Debbie calmed down and shook her head. "I was never good in school. Besides, my daddy always told me I didn't need school because I had common sense. I guess I listened to him too much."

Dan looked straight ahead and calmly said, "Well, you seem like an intelligent young woman. I'm sure if you applied yourself, you could do well in college."

"Yeah, well, I guess I'll never know."

After saying that, Debbie shut herself down. She didn't want to continue this topic of conversation. But somehow Dan, in his infinite maleness, wasn't catching on to the fact this was a forbidden subject to Debbie.

"Look, I don't mean to criticize you or anything—"

"Good," Debbie interrupted. "Let's keep it that way."

"It's just, you seem lost."

Debbie stared ahead, biting her lip. Her face getting redder.

"And if I didn't know any better, I'd say you're running from something rather than going somewhere."

Debbie pointed ahead. "You can let me out up here."

Dan glanced over at her. He seemed shocked and surprised to see the furious look on her face. But he was also smart enough not to argue with her.

As Dan started to pull the car over, he noticed Debbie had already unlatched her seat belt and had her hand on the door handle, ready to spring free.

Before the car even came to a complete stop, she opened the door.

Dan reached over and touched her shoulder. When she yanked herself away from him, he realized he shouldn't have been surprised.

Dan held up his hands again. "Look, I'm sorry. I can't help opening my mouth and giving my two cents, especially when it isn't asked for. I guess that's the dad in me."

Debbie replied, "Yeah, well, dads don't always know best."

Debbie got out and came close to slamming the door, but instead, she softly closed it. She opened the back door, put on her hat, and dragged her backpack out.

As she put her arms through the straps, she heard the driver's door open. She gritted her teeth and turned back to see Dan peering at her from over the top of the car.

Dan asked with a hesitant tone, "Do you, uh, need some money or anything?"

"I'm fine, thanks" was her curt reply.

"I'm sure you are," Dan replied. "But still, if you need a little extra."

Debbie stared down at her boots. She was about to release the floodgates and cry, but the wall she put up within her long ago wouldn't allow it.

Dan saw this and walked around the car to approach her. He stopped a few feet away, continuing to respect her space, and held out some money.

Debbie thought it over for a while, then slowly reached out and took it.

"There's almost a hundred there," Dan said. "Maybe it'll help you get where you're going. And get you there safe."

Debbie could only nod. To do more, she felt, would lead to tears.

Dan continued, "I hope you find what you're looking for. And don't take any crap, especially from people who think they know better."

Debbie nodded again.

"Take care, Debbie. Okay? And again, I'm sorry."

Try as she might, Debbie couldn't make eye contact with him.

Dan nodded and walked back to his car.

As he opened the door, Debbie said, "Thank you," while looking away.

Dan simply nodded, climbed inside his car, and soon drove off.

As Debbie watched the car disappear down the interstate, she noticed the wavy lines of heat rising from the road.

She kicked at a few rocks on the ground, stared up at the cloudy sky, and started walking again.

*****

A sedan pulled into the parking lot of a familiar truck-stop diner. As it came to a stop with a sharp squealing of brakes, the back door opened, and Debbie stepped out, putting on her hat and pulling on her backpack.

She waved at the young daughter of the couple in the front seat and shut the door.

"Thanks for the ride," she said, raising her voice to be heard.

The daughter in the back seat waved excitedly at her as the car drove off.

Debbie adjusted her backpack and stared at the diner. That's when she noticed yellow police tape sectioning off a rather large area of the parking lot near one side of it.

*****

An unseen driver, sitting in the cab of a Peterbilt semitruck, watched Debbie from a distance as she walked toward the diner. He observed her ambling slowly past the police tape, taking in the scene as she did so.

The driver's breathing intensified, and he giggled with excitement.

His hands, with their dirty fingernails, tightened on the steering wheel.

*****

Debbie stepped inside the diner, which was neither clean nor dirty. To her, it was a comfortable in-between that would do for now, because she'd seen a hell of a lot worse. To her slight annoyance, old-time country music greeted her from an old jukebox that still only cost a quarter per song.

She took off her hat and blew strands of hair out of her face as she realized the place was almost empty. She checked her watch and figured she had missed the lunch rush and was a little early for the dinner crowd.

As soon as she approached the diner counter, placed her hat down upon it, and sat on a stool, a fifty-something waitress approached her.

The waitress was wearing a name tag that read: Linda. She had on a blue blouse and pants with a white smock and had dyed her hair a color unknown to nature.

Linda smacked some gum as she talked. "Whatchu wanna drink, hon?"

Debbie leaned back on her stool and replied, "Um, tea with lemon and a glass of water, please."

Linda quickly noticed the trace of a black eye and split lip on Debbie's face but didn't say anything.

"Sweet tea or unsweetened, shug?"

"Unsweet," Debbie replied.

Linda flashed a motherly smile. "Comin' right up."

Debbie watched Linda sashay away, then grabbed a menu from a rack. She opened it and scanned it. But even though she was starving, and food was within the asking, the menu couldn't keep her attention.

She slowly turned her head. Her mind drawn toward the police tape outside.

Linda's voice startled her. "There wasn't any blood."

Debbie quickly turned and saw Linda setting down a glass of tea with lemon along with a glass of water on the counter before her.

"What?" Debbie asked.

"It was the strangest thing," Linda replied. "They found a woman's body, but it had no blood in it."

Debbie held back her shock. "When?"

Linda smacked her gum, all the while staring out the window with a hand on her hip. "Early this mornin'."

"What happened?"

"Hadn't heard yet, but Aaron said...," Linda said, lowering her voice as she leaned down, as if telling a secret. "Aaron's a smokie, but he said she didn't look dead, just pale. And that's because he said the medical examiner said it looked like she didn't have a drop of blood left in her body. He said it was the damnedest thing he ever saw. And it's damn near the worst thing I ever heard. Whatchu orderin', hon?"

Taken aback, Debbie shook her head in disbelief. "What?"

"Whatchu wanna eat?" Linda asked, tapping the top of the menu in Debbie's hands.

"Uh, could I have a hamburger, dry? And a house salad?"

Linda stopped smacking her gum and rolled her eyes.

"Please don't tell me you're watchin' your weight? A skinny little thing like you can't weigh more than a hunnerd pounds soakin' wet."

Debbie was caught off guard. All she could do was shake her head.

Linda smirked. "What do you want on your salad?"

Debbie asked, "Do you have vinaigrette?"

"No one ever orders it, but we got it," Linda replied. "And how do you want that burger?"

*****

Debbie finished eating and checked her watch. The hands read 6:16 p.m.

She reached into her backpack and thumbed through the bills Dan had given her. She retrieved a twenty and laid it on the counter, zipped up the backpack, and stood up to put it on.

As she picked up her hat and started to leave, Linda called out, "What do you think you're doin'?"

Concerned, Debbie turned to face the waitress and defensively pointed at the counter. "I left a twenty."

Linda stared at her as if she was mistaken. "Didn't I tell you your meal was on the house?"

Debbie looked worried and surprised and not sure what to say but "What?"

"Your meal was free," Linda replied, picking up the bill and handing it back to her. "So why are you leavin' money behind?"

Debbie was still unsure what to say or do. "I, uh…are you sure?"

Linda leaned over the counter and said in a low voice, "I'm for you gettin' as far as you can from the son bitch that did that to your face. And any little bit of money counts, you reckon?"

Debbie was at a loss for words. She was embarrassed but thankful.

Linda then handed her a paper bag, which had been unseen by Debbie until then.

"There's two more burgers in there," Linda replied, still holding the bag. "Dry and well done. You just be careful out there."

After a few pensive, ashamed moments, Debbie finally took the bag and muttered, "Thanks."

Linda winked in reply and went back to smacking her gum as she walked off.

Debbie stood there, flabbergasted, before turning and walking out before someone could change their mind about the charity she had just received.

*****

When Debbie stepped outside while putting on her hat, the big rig driver sitting in the parking lot watched while she took one more look at the police tape before walking away.

He peered at her as she walked past his truck, oblivious to his presence. He checked his side mirror to observe her heading toward the access road leading to the highway.

The driver giggled and said, "Almost time. Almost."

*****

Debbie walked on the shoulder of the road. A hint of a smile on her face. Earbuds in. Thumb out. She kicked an empty aluminum can, completely unaware of her surroundings.

In the distance, a semitruck approached and started to slow down. Its brakes hissing and squeaking. It came to a stop after it passed Debbie, who finally noticed it.

As she stood there staring ahead, she saw an arm appear out of the driver's side window. It waved her toward the truck.

Debbie approached it and walked along the passenger side. But before she reached the door, the driver opened it for her. She paused, stepped onto the riser, opened the door wider, and peered in.

Debbie laid eyes on the face of Reggie, a gruff-looking man with greasy hair tucked under a stained trucker's hat and days-old stubble on his face.

He had on dirty glasses with Coke-bottle lenses that made his eyes look huge. His smile revealed brown-coated teeth, and he seemed awfully happy to see her.

Understandably, Debbie thought twice about entering the cab.

"Don't worry, miss," Reggie said. "I may not be much to look at, but I'm as harmless as a fly. Soul to the devil if I'm lyin'."

Debbie set her serious face. The one that meant business. It had always worked in the past, so it was becoming habit.

"Just so you know, if you try anything, I can take care of myself."

Reggie seemed amused rather than insulted. "Oh, you got nothin' to worry about with me, gal. Where ya headed?"

Debbie thought about pointing forward but changed her mind. "West."

"What a coinkydink," Reggie cackled. "So are we."

"We?" Debbie asked, confused.

"Ethel," Reggie replied, patting the steering wheel. "My truck."

Debbie nodded, grinned, and raised her eyebrows.

Reggie sat, looking forward. "Well, if you're gettin' in, c'mon. I gotta be well on my way 'fore nightfall."

Debbie peered around before glancing back at Reggie, who smiled at her again, causing her to look away.

She collected herself and asked, "You're not a psycho, a pervert, or a religious fanatic, are ya?"

Reggie thought about his reply for a moment, then said, "I don't believe I am. Am I?"

In a different voice, he shook his head and said, "Nope."

Then, in his regular voice, he added with a smile, "Didn't think so."

To her surprise, Debbie laughed and thought to hell with it as she climbed into the truck cab, shut the door behind her, and the truck drove away.

*****

As Debbie removed her hat and peered around the cab of the filthy truck, she was momentarily startled when Reggie reached behind her seat, dug around in a cooler, and grabbed a can of Coke.

Relieved, Debbie watched him pop it open and take several large gulps.

His eyes shifted toward her, and he smiled and shook the contents of the near-empty can.

"Wanna soda?" he asked. "There's some more in that cooler behind ya."

Debbie shook her head, smiled, and placed her hat on her lap. "No, thanks."

Reggie shrugged. "Well, if you change your mind."

Debbie watched him finish off the Coke and toss the can over his shoulder and into the back of the cab, where she heard it clink and roll around with other empty cans before settling still.

Debbie gasped when Reggie's open hand appeared next to her.

She darted her head around to see him extending his hand for a greeting.

"Name's Reginald," he said. "But everybody calls me Reggie."

Debbie nodded as she briefly shook his hand.

"The only one ever to call me Reginald was my momma. And only when I did somethin' bad. Which I'm ashamed to say happened quite a bit."

Debbie nodded and replied, "I'm Debbie."

Reggie turned and tipped his cap to her. "Well, pleased to meet ya, Debbie."

Debbie nodded and looked forward.

"So, where ya from?" Reggie asked.

Debbie hesitated a beat before replying, "Shreveport."

"Would that be Texas or Louisiana?"

Debbie closed her eyes, forcing herself not to be sarcastic or mean, but it came out that way anyway. "Would it make a difference?"

Reggie shot her a surprised glare.

At once, Debbie was worried, but Reggie soon started laughing, which, needless to say, surprised the hell out of her.

"Nope," he replied, "I suppose it dudn't."

Debbie watched him laugh some more and repeat her line as he gazed out the window. That was when she noticed the sun was about to set.

As if he read her mind, Reggie said, "This has always been my favorite time a day. Since I was a kid, I always loved a good sunset. And bein' a truck driver allows me to see all kinds of sunsets."

Debbie shrugged, unimpressed. "Aren't they all the same?"

Somehow, this got under Reggie's skin. "What?"

But all Debbie did was dig herself in deeper. "If you've seen one, you've seen 'em all."

"Girl, you couldn't be more wrong," Reggie replied, slapping his steering wheel. "A sunset is like a fingerprint. There's no two alike.

They're all unique. Special. And lemme tell ya, you're in the perfect state to see one. I've been all over this country, and West Texas, by far, has the most beautiful sunsets. By far. Soul to the devil if I'm lyin'."

Debbie smirked, defensive. "All right, I believe you."

But Reggie cast her a sideways glare. "Somehow, girl, I don't believe you do."

Debbie quickly realized she had insulted him, so she changed her tone. "No, really, if you say so, I believe you."

Reggie took a while to calm himself down. Then, almost under his breath, he said, "Girl, what kinda sad life have you led that's kept you from noticin' the common beauties this world has to offer?"

A pained look crossed Debbie's face. "I've been sunset deprived. What can I say?"

This earned her another glare from her driver.

"I'm sorry, what do you want me to say?" she asked with a shrug.

Reggie shook his head. "Well, it's a good thing we met. 'Cause tonight, you're in for a treat. I have it on God's good authority that tonight is gonna have the most spectacular sunset in the history of mankind."

Debbie smirked. "Ooh, aren't I lucky?"

Reggie peered at her over the top of his glasses, which had slid down his nose that was slick with sweat. "I see they grow sarcasm on trees over there in Shreveport?"

Debbie couldn't help but smile.

"Well, little Debbie, you just sit right back and prepare yourself for the spectacle you are about to behold. And trust me, after tonight, your life'll never be the same."

"This better be one helluva sunset."

Reggie replied, "Soul to the—"

Debbie quickly joined him. "Devil if I'm lyin'."

Reggie glared at her over the top of his glasses again, but this time, he shoved them back up higher on the bridge of his nose.

"Girl, you sassin' me?"

Debbie finally laughed, which caused Reggie to smile, though his eyes did not.

"Well, you just wait and see," Reggie said. "Any minute now. It's almost time. Almost time."

*****

As the truck rolled west, true to Reggie's word, a spectacular West Texas sunset occurred. Whether it was the best one of all time, Debbie considered, was still up for debate.

As she watched the sun lower beyond the horizon, Reggie watched her reaction. To him, she seemed genuinely touched at the sight.

"There sure were lots of colors," Debbie said as the day officially became night.

"You just saw the whole spectrum," Reggie replied. "God had his whole paint set out tonight."

"Well, you were right," Debbie said, turning toward him. "It was beautiful."

"You bet your sweet ass it was."

A shocked reaction registered on Debbie's face, but Reggie wasn't watching her to notice. He kept his eyes on the road ahead.

The tiny hairs on Debbie's skin rose, and her mind screamed at her that she could be in danger, but she only sat there, helpless and quiet, waiting for Reggie to do something.

All he did was lick his lips in what could only be called anticipation.

He turned, saw her staring at him, and asked, "You okay?"

Debbie nodded and turned away, hoping the current of fear rolling through her body wasn't noticeable on her face. However, on instinct, her body shifted closer to the door.

Reggie grinned and looked forward. "You feelin' the creepy crawlies up your spine yet?"

Alarmed, Debbie kept her cool. But she ever so slowly maneuvered her right hand toward her back pocket while keeping her eyes on him as he smiled ahead at the road. Her right hand slipped into her back pocket, and her fingers found what she knew was there.

"I know just what you're thinkin'," Reggie said, startling her.

Debbie froze in place. Her face flushing red.

Reggie kept his eyes on the road. "You're a regular Girl Scout. Always prepared."

As she slowly pulled a small knife out of her back pocket, Reggie turned his face toward her, causing her to gasp.

"What was it you said earlier?" he asked. "'I can take care of myself?' Was that it?"

She raised her hand, brandishing the knife before her. It was shaking.

But instead of being surprised or even scared, Reggie cackled like a madman, as if that was the funniest thing he'd ever seen. He began slapping the steering wheel in hysterics.

"Like that's never been done before," he said. "Only I'll spare ya further disappointment. That little pig sticker ain't gonna do you no good. About the only thing that's good for is pissin' me off. And you don't wanna do that. That I guarantee. I could be a good friend to you. See that you go quick and painless. But if you piss me off, I'll make sure you suffer like you've never suffered before."

Without taking her eyes off him, Debbie wrapped her fingers around the door handle and pulled up, but to her horror, the door was locked. Her eyes darted to Reggie, who was leering at her.

"Funny thing about this truck. Even though it hasn't carried kids in a coon's age, we done went and childproofed the locks anyway. I mean, you never know when they're gonna come in handy."

With that, he giggled and pressed a button on his armrest.

She heard her door unlock, but before she could think to pull the handle up, it locked again.

"Sorry! Too slow!" Reggie shouted, laughing to beat the band. "Too stupid and too slow is not a good combination."

Debbie struggled to contain her fear. Breathing slowly and deeply, with a grim look of determination on her face, she looked ahead.

She saw a sign announcing they were just now leaving Monahans.

Debbie tried her best to calm herself before asking, "Could you please let me go?"

"Now what kind of person would I be if I were to let you out all by your lonesome on a night like this? Lord knows what could happen to a pretty little thing like you out there?"

"Please, just let me out," Debbie asked, as a tear rolled down her cheek. "I won't tell anyone about you. I promise."

"Sorry," Reggie replied, shaking his head. "But I just can't do that."

"Why not?"

"'Cause any moment now, he'll be awake," Reggie replied, shifting his eyes toward the back of the cab. "And it'll be time for him to feed. And if I don't have somethin' for him to eat, he might just make a meal out of me. And I would not like that one little bit. No, sirree, Bob."

"You're crazy!" Debbie replied. Those words came out at a higher pitch than normal. Her fear getting the best of her.

Reggie emphatically shook his head like a child refusing to eat his vegetables. "Nope, nope, nope, nope, nope, nope. I'm just a servant. Don't ya get it?"

Reggie sat forward, hunched over the steering wheel with a serious look on his face, hinting with his body language that the conversation was over. But soon enough, he began to smile and hum and cast occasional leering glances at Debbie.

Debbie spent the next few endless moments trying everything in her power not to lose what mental acuity she had left.

Her hand was locked in a death grip on the door handle. So much so, her knuckles had turned white.

She began to silently mouth something to herself over and over again. But Reggie interrupted her quiet mantra.

"I gotta say, he's really gonna like you. And he's gonna be so happy with me."

Debbie couldn't bring herself to look at Reggie or his crazy face. So instead, she kept looking forward.

"You shouldn't be scared, girlie, you should feel honored. I know I was when he chose me all those years ago."

Debbie finally mustered up the courage to ask, "Who's this him you keep talking about?"

This caused Reggie to smile large. "My master. Who you'll meet soon enough."

"And where is this master of yours?"

Reggie glanced behind them. "He should be awake any time now."

Debbie slowly turned and looked back. She saw nothing but a trash-filled sleeping quarter.

Reggie shook his head dramatically again. "Not there, stupid. In the trailer. You think he'd sleep in here? In the open?"

"Who is he, this master of yours?"

"He goes by many names."

"And you're his servant?"

Reggie checked his reflection in a side mirror and stuck out his chin. He looked mighty proud and pleased with himself at that moment. "More like I'm his protector."

As he admired himself, Debbie moved as close to the passenger door as she could.

Reggie shifted his cap on his head and added, "I watch over him while he sleeps."

Debbie was stalling for time but really was curious about the man's cargo.

"What the hell is he that he needs someone like you to watch over him?"

"I'll give you three guesses," Reggie replied, turning to face her. "And the first two don't count."

He began cackling again but immediately stopped when they heard a loud bump coming from the trailer.

Debbie reacted to it. Eyes wide. Then they both heard another bump.

Reggie's eyes widened. Excitement flooding his features. "It's time."

At the same time Reggie saw a dirt road exit up ahead, Debbie saw it as well.

That's when she turned toward Reggie and held up her knife more forcefully.

Reggie erupted in anger. "Now, what in the hell did I just tell you, girlie? Do you not know how to listen? Put that away 'fore you piss me off."

Without a care in the world, Reggie slowed the truck down and turned the wheel.

The truck was soon traveling down the dirt road.

Debbie watched the truck navigate the bumpy, thin road while still holding the knife in her hand before her.

Reggie, tongue clamped in his teeth, checked his side mirror.

The highway was now far off in the distance.

That's when he brought the truck to a stop and shifted the gears to park. The truck hissed, and the engine idled.

In the darkness of the cab, Reggie turned toward her. He saw his own reflection in the blade of her knife.

"This is where you get off. And if I were you, I'd try to make it back to the highway. Because, who knows, you might get lucky and see another car."

Debbie, her heart beating loud in her ears, turned to look out her side mirror. She saw the highway a few miles back.

"But on the other hand," Reggie added, "there might be somebody livin' up ahead. You could maybe hide out somewhere till mornin'. Then when the sun comes up, you could skedaddle. But my money's on you not makin' it very far. It all depends on how sporty he feels."

He turned, pressed a button on his door handle, and unlocked her door.

Debbie immediately grabbed the handle and opened the door, causing the interior light to come on. But for some reason, instead of jumping out, she turned back toward Reggie, who waved and smiled at her.

"You better get goin', girl. Ticktock. Time's a-wastin'."

Debbie glanced at the steering wheel and the gears, then back at Reggie, who grinned.

"What?" Reggie asked. "No last words? All condemned people get their last words."

But Debbie did something unexpected. She smiled at him.

This caught Reggie off guard. But before he could ponder why the hell she was smiling, she jammed the blade of her knife into his right eye.

Reggie squealed like a stuck pig as Debbie maneuvered her body around and jumped out of the truck.

She landed on the ground in a crouch before rising up and running, quickly disappearing into the night.

Reggie, in agony, slowly managed to pull the knife out of his eye. The contents of his eye, along with blood, poured down his face and neck.

All the while, he yelled, "You bitch! You goddamn bitch!"

After pulling the blade free, he grabbed one of the side mirrors and looked into it with his remaining peeper.

"I told you to play nice," Reggie shouted. "I told you. But did you listen? No! You had to go all Lorena Bobbitt on me."

He angrily swung open the door and jumped out.

*****

Reggie held a hand over his wounded eye as he shuffled to the back of the semi-trailer.

"Goddamn bitch. You want sufferin', I'll give you sufferin'. I'll give it to you ten times over. Soul to the devil if I'm lyin'."

He reached the back doors of the trailer and took hold of a lock.

He dialed the combination, yanked it open, pulled the lock free, and opened the latch.

As he swung open the doors, a fog of cold air emerged from the refrigerated trailer like an ancient beast exhaling. After it cleared, he struggled but eventually managed to climb inside.

He ambled past several frozen human bodies hung inside plastic sheets like racks of meat. His breath drifted into the air like smoke as he made his way toward the front of the trailer while putting on gloves he had grabbed from a wooden table.

He reached a metal wall, placed his gloved hands on one end, and slid it open, revealing a small hidden room.

Inside this room sat an expensive-looking, well-built mahogany coffin held in place by a pallet bolted to the metal floor.

Reggie shoved the wall along rollers until it was fully open and stared down at the coffin. He crinkled his face and felt the blood drying. This made him sad and angry.

"The goddamn bitch took my eye, Master. You have to make her pay."

He stepped toward the coffin and opened it.

Inside rested the tall, thin form of his master. A rather pleasant-looking man with a distinguished yet pale face. He had salt-and-pepper hair and long, thin fingers that ended with sharp, talon-like fingernails. He was dressed rather elegantly in a turtleneck, dark slacks, and black loafers.

The man in the coffin opened his eyes.

As soon as he recognized Reggie, the vampire smiled, showing a row of pointed, jagged teeth.

Reggie bowed, as if before royalty. "Good evening, Master. I brought you a gift. She's out there now…waiting."

The master gestured toward Reggie's eye. "Did you underestimate her?"

Reggie tried to hide his embarrassment.

The vampire gazed around and sniffed the air.

"She is near." He smiled.

Reggie added, "But she's defenseless. The stupid bitch left her knife behind."

"But she is resourceful, yes?"

"Lucky, I say. But not much longer. I told her you'd make her suffer for what she did to me."

"And indeed she shall."

The vampire rose from the coffin and stepped out.

Reggie followed a few steps behind his master as he strode through the trailer. When the master reached the end, he took a step into thin air and glided elegantly to the ground.

Reggie jumped clumsily, nearly falling but somehow managed to catch himself before losing his balance completely. When he straightened up, he looked embarrassed.

"My perception's off, Master," Reggie said sheepishly. "This is gonna take me a while to get used to."

The master sniffed the air again, and a concerned look crossed his face.

Just then, they both heard a door slam, and the sound of gears as they shifted awkwardly and loudly. Then the engine revved, and the truck lurched backward.

The master and his caretaker jumped out of the way as the truck rolled past them.

As it backed away, they looked up at the cab of the truck to see Debbie giving them the bird as she went.

When the truck finally reached the highway, she shifted gears awkwardly again, and the truck lurched forward and drove away, engine blaring, smoke belching from its exhaust pipes.

The vampire and his caretaker simply watched as the taillights of the truck eventually disappeared down the highway.

After a few moments of stunned silence, the master asked, "Reggie, where are your keys?"

Reggie, nervous, kept his head down. "I left them in the ignition, Master."

"You think?"

*****

Debbie screamed in jubilation and honked the truck's air horn.

"Up yours, you freaks!" she shouted. "I told you I could take care of myself! Soul to the devil if I'm lyin'!"

She laughed like a crazed loon and honked the air horn again in triumph.

UNSUB

As a bloodred moon glowed in a clear night sky, two men sat inside a black SUV. They were parked in the shadows below trees while facing a dirt road somewhere out in the Middle of Nowhere, USA. Population: You Don't Ever Wanna Visit There.

Their attention was supposed to be focused on the lonely dirt road before them, which they could only see through a night-vision-equipped camera monitor mounted on the dashboard. However, this run-of-the-mill stakeout was the farthest thing from their thoughts at the moment.

The driver—a burly, prematurely bald man and the older of the two by a few years in reality and many years by visage—took a sip of coffee from a thermos cup and, out of the blue, stated, "We missed out, you know."

The passenger, a gangly man with slicked-back hair, mutton-chop sideburns, and the merest wisp of a mustache, who, up to this moment, had been caught up in his own thoughts, glanced over. "Huh?"

"The glory days of our profession have come and gone, amigo."

"What the hell are you talkin' about?"

"The people who did our jobs back in the late last century had it good. Hell, they had targets just about every month. Almost one for every holiday."

The younger man calmly waited for the few-years-older man to make his point.

The driver added, "Whereas nowadays, we're lucky if we get a handful a year."

"And that's a bad thing?"

Paying his barely younger partner no mind, the driver continued, "And the ones we do get pale in comparison to the ones from yesteryear."

"Yesteryear? Is that even a word?"

Ignoring the passenger again, the driver went on with his rant.

"Back then, our forebears had legendary cases. Amazing cases we still talk about and study to this day.

"Cases like the guy in Illinois who cut through a shitload of people to kill his sister.

"Or that burned-up janitor who came back from the dead to take revenge on the parents who murdered him by killing their kids in their dreams.

"Or that family of cannibals in Texas who butchered tourists and served them up as barbecue to their customers."

"I think I heard about that one," the passenger remarked, yawning.

"Or that mutant momma's boy who killed all the visitors who came to that lake where he supposedly drowned as a kid—"

The passenger finally showed interest. "Now, I definitely read about that one. What was the name of that lake?"

"It was Cryst—"

Their two-way radio sparked to life. "Unit 12, do you copy? Over."

The driver quickly picked up the two-way mounted above the console and clicked the transmit button. "Base, this is unit 12. We copy. Over."

"Our satellites confirm a convoy of vehicles filled with potentials approaching your vector. ETA: two minutes. Over."

"Base, we copy. Out."

The driver hung up the two-way, and both of the men waited in silence for a long, tense couple of minutes.

Then they watched as a series of vehicles blasted by them like bats out of hell. Each vehicle filled with hooting and hollering teenagers, ready and raring to party, heading in the direction of a nearby lake.

The driver keyed his two-way again, holding it to his mouth.

"Base, this is unit 12. Potentials have been targeted. We are in pursuit. Over."

"Copy, unit 12. You are ordered to follow the potentials to their destination and observe and report their activities. And also be on the lookout for any potential unsubs. Over."

"Copy, base. Out."

The driver hung up the two-way and started the vehicle. He put the SUV into drive and pulled out onto the dirt road with the vehicle's lights off.

Watching through the night-vision dash monitor, the driver pressed on the gas until the last vehicle in the teen convoy—a topless jeep—came into view about a hundred yards up ahead.

The jeep's taillights glowed white and left long white trails on the monitor.

The driver slowed down and followed the convoy of vehicles from a safe distance.

The SUV trailed the teens to a two-story deluxe cabin near a calm, dark blue lake that perfectly reflected the red moon and the silhouetted tree-lined horizon above it.

The driver parked the SUV a safe-enough distance away with a clear view of the cabin and the campsite around it, then cut off the engine.

After doing a headcount of the teens as they exited their vehicles and gathered their stuff, the men in the SUV followed their orders by settling in and getting comfortable enough to observe whatever was about to happen.

The teens filed into the cabin, turned on the lights, and immediately set about doing the things teens did when they were about to camp in a cabin in the middle of nowhere with no parental guidance.

They started to party pretty quickly as they either had lots of hormones, drugs, alcohol, or a combination of all three inside their bodies or on their person.

The passenger soon remarked, "My money's on less than five minutes."

The driver glanced at his watch and waited for the second hand to near twelve.

"I'll put a twenty on that. Startin' now."

He noted the time on his watch and looked up just in time to see a couple of the teens emerging from the cabin and start walking toward a wooden dock extending out over the lake.

The passenger never took his eyes off the teens as he said, "This is my favorite part of the job. It never gets old. And if it ever does, it either means I'm dead, or I need to be put out of my misery."

As the young couple reached the end of the dock and started to take off their clothes, the passenger cackled and rubbed his palms together while sitting up and leaning forward in his seat.

The driver regarded him with a sneer but quickly peered back at the young woman, who was by then totally nude. The driver's eyes widened slightly, and a leer formed on his lips.

The passenger smiled and shook his head. "Goddamn, look at that tight, little body. And those tits." He then glanced over. "You think they're real?"

The driver's eyes didn't move from the girl's body. "Who cares?"

The passenger cackled again. "Girls sure didn't look like that when I was a teenager. I feel gypped."

The driver added, "Join the resentment club."

The couple dove into the water and began swimming, floating, splashing around, and laughing.

The passenger pulled out a directional microphone and aimed it toward the teens frolicking in the water.

He put in a single earbud and listened in on them but heard only laughing and splashing. Then he turned the mic toward the cabin and smiled at the driver.

Curious, the driver asked, "What are they doin'?"

The passenger listened for a while, then shook his head. "Teenagers may get better looking each year, but they're also gettin' dumber. And their music is getting shittier."

Soon, they noticed the skinny-dipping teens were having sex in the water while the young woman held onto the dock behind her to keep her head above water.

The passenger smiled, "Hello? What's the time, Kemosabe?"

The driver looked at his watch and shook his head with disappointment. "Shit. Less than five."

The passenger put out the palm of his hand. "Pay up, sucka."

The driver handed over a twenty with a hint of good-natured disgust. But as the passenger sniffed the bill and held it up to the moonlight, the driver sneered.

The passenger laughed. "I do love me some free cash."

"If this latest generation had any morals whatsoever, you wouldn't be so happy right now."

"Well, they don't, and I am."

The driver went back to watching the couple bump and grind in the water.

The passenger remembered something. "Oh, this is definitely a case of bad timing, but ain't it about time to check in?"

The driver grimaced and sighed. He lifted the two-way and keyed it. "Unit 12 to base. Over."

"This is base. We copy. Over."

"We're set up fifty yards from the potentials' cabin. A pair has broken off from the others and are currently mid-coitus in the lake, while the others are in the cabin. Over."

The passenger added, "And they're playin' shitty music."

The driver hushed him.

The stern voice on the other end cracked back, "Maintain your vigil, unit 12. Report anything unusual. Over."

"Copy, base. Out."

After the driver hung up the two-way, they sat in silence and watched the teen couple still going at it in the lake.

"Lots of stamina on that one," the passenger observed.

They both heard a beep, and their attention immediately went to the dash monitor.

"Holy shit!" the passenger said, sitting forward, startled. "We got a hit."

They watched as a night-vision enhanced image of a tall, stocky figure walked in the direction of the cabin, stopped, stood for a moment, and changed direction.

Now the visage of the man was walking toward the lake.

The driver looked around and ordered, "Get a bead on the potentials. Can we account for all of 'em?"

The passenger swept the campgrounds with the directional mic.

"Well?" the driver asked, impatient.

The passenger shook his head. "I'm not a hundred percent, but...it seems they're all accounted for."

They kept their eyes on the potential unsub as he approached the dock.

The passenger asked, "What do we know about this unsub so far?"

"Well, all we know is someone's been operating in this locale for three months and is the main suspect in five reported disappearances."

The passenger stared at the night-vision image of the unsub on the monitor, who was now watching the two teens cavorting in the lake from behind some trees near the shore.

The driver lifted and keyed the two-way. "Base, this is unit 12. Over."

"We copy, unit 12. Over."

"We have a possible unsub in sight. Most definitely male. Somewhere between six feet and six two. Two hundred to 220 pounds. Wearing a dark mask and jumper. Over."

"We copy, unit 12. Continue to observe and record the unsub and report back to us if he commits any homicidal activity. If that happens, we have recon on standby a half hour out from your location. Over."

A note of derision came across the driver's face as he eyed the passenger and keyed the two-way. "Understood, base. Out."

The driver slowly hung up the handset and shook his head. "Jesus."

The passenger glanced over and chuckled. "You gonna start up again?"

"How can they expect us to just sit around with our hands up our asses and watch while these kids get killed and simply record it? That's bullshit."

"It's what we signed up for, Cochise. We're civilians, not military."

"Well, there are times when we should be allowed to shoot first and ask questions later."

"In an ideal world, yes, but the last I checked, this world ain't exactly ideal."

"Tell me about it."

They watched as the young couple got out of the water by climbing up a ladder to the dock. The young woman clumsily put on her clothes while making out with the guy at the same time.

When both teens were dressed, they walked off the dock and went back to the cabin where their friends were still partying. The couple kissed one more time before entering the cabin to cheers from their friends.

The observers in the SUV turned to watch as the unsub moved from his hiding place near the lake and walked toward the cabin.

As the passenger observed the suspect, the driver asked, "What kinda mask is that?"

"One of those featureless ones."

"Like a doll's face?"

"Yeah," the passenger replied while pausing to look at the driver. "Kinda unimaginative, if you ask me."

"All I know is it works. It's fuckin' creepy."

"Yeah, if dolls scare you," the passenger replied, amused with himself.

"Don't laugh. One of my TO's first cases back in the eighties was a killer doll."

"A doll? You gotta be shittin' me. How?"

"Don't you ever study any of the old case files?"

"I skim them."

The driver gave him a perplexed look.

The passenger added, "Who's got the time to read all that shit?"

The driver sighed and shook his head. "Anyway, this doll was possessed by the soul of a serial killer who knew some kinda dark voodoo. Anyway, he managed to put his soul into a doll right before he was shot to death by police."

"Seriously? Then what happened?"

"What do ya think? He killed a bunch of people."

"No, I mean, what happened to the doll? Did they ever capture it…or kill it?"

"Well, that's where the story gets weird—"

"Hold on," the passenger interrupted while pointing at the night-vision monitor. "Check him out."

They both watched as the unsub peered through the window of the cabin at the teens inside.

The passenger asked, "I don't see any weapons. You?"

The driver turned toward the passenger, both taking their eyes off the target. "No. But he's probably still in his trollin' stage. If this is our guy, and it for damn sure looks like he is, I bet the house that his weapons are close by."

"But what if he's disorganized? Maybe he's one of those guys who improvises on the spot with whatever's handy."

"That's rare. Most of 'em have a favorite implement or two."

"But it's been known to happen. Like with that lake guy we were talkin' about earlier."

"Yeah, but again, he's the exception. Most of 'em have a preference. Knives, machetes… The one guy with the freaky knife glove."

The passenger added, "And chainsaws. Don't forget about chainsaws."

"Who could forget that?"

"Wait a minute."

"What?"

"Where'd he go?"

They both looked at the cabin through the monitor.

The driver was upset. "Weren't you watchin' him?"

"Weren't you?"

They glared at one another and said, "Shit," in unison.

After a frantic search of the perimeter from their view inside the SUV, the passenger asked, "You see him?"

"No."

"Well, he couldn't have gotten far."

The driver was perplexed. He couldn't believe he just heard what he heard. "How many of these cases have you been on?"

The passenger shrugged.

The driver's temper flared. "Well, if you have, you'd know these guys have a way of covering huge distances in no time flat. One minute, they're way behind you. The next, they're right in front of you. That's Advance Team 101. How do you not know that?"

"What are we supposed to do then?"

The driver grabbed the two-way but didn't key it. Instead, he paused and said, "We call in and report that we lost him."

The passenger reacted as if he'd been spit on. His face turned red. "And get written up? Bullshit. I'm not gettin' written up. You know what happens to advance teams who get written up, they get their pay docked…or worse."

"So what are you suggestin'?"

"That we go find him on our own."

"Are you out of your cotton pickin' mind? You heard our orders—"

"Man, fuck our orders. I ain't losin' my job just because I took my eyes off this nutcase for five goddamn seconds."

"So instead, you wanna lose your job by disobeying direct orders?"

"How are we gonna lose our jobs if they don't even know we didn't follow orders?"

"They always know. All they'd have to do is check the goddamn footage."

"Holy shit! That's genius. Rewind the footage."

"What?"

"The footage. Rewind it."

"Oh shit. You're right. Why didn't I think of that?"

The driver rewound the footage to a point, then played it back.

They watched as the unsub peered in at the teens through the cabin window, then he slowly gazed around and walked around the other side of the cabin.

The driver looked toward the cabin. "Dammit! He could be anywhere."

"What do we do now? Call in and report that we lost him or save our jobs by findin' him?"

The driver couldn't decide. Not in the limited time frame he had.

The passenger continued, "Because I'll go with whatever you decide. Though I think I've made my point abundantly clear that tellin' base we lost him is the dumbest fuckin' idea of dumb fuckin' ideas."

The driver shook his head. "All right, but this decision ain't all on me. This is on both of us. And you're not gonna throw me under the bus come report time neither just because I'm in charge here."

The passenger raised his arms in a surrender gesture and patted the air with the palms of his hands. "I would never do that. You're my partner. I'll always have your back."

"Goddammit. I can't believe I'm saying this, but…let's go find the son of a bitch. But only find him. Once we spot him, we pull back and report in."

"You think I wanna face down this sick bastard? Pullin' back sounds good to me."

"Actually, it sounds like a bunch of bullshit, but outa the two shit-sandwich options we got on the menu, this one might taste a little less shitty."

"Then let's roll, partner."

They stepped out of the SUV, walked to the back of it, and opened the hatch.

They snapped open a metal case and pulled out two handheld night-vision camcorders. Next, they retrieved handguns and popped in the ammunition clips.

As they started to turn away, they paused, regarded one another, and pocketed a couple more ammunition clips, just in case.

They holstered their weapons and silently shut the hatch.

The driver took a few short breaths to calm his nerves. "Okay, as I see it, we got two choices. And like I said, both of 'em are pretty shitty, but they're all we got.

"The first choice is we split up and search on our own. We'll be more vulnerable that way, but we'll be able to cover more ground in a shorter amount of time. And since time is of the essence here, that's important to remember.

"However, if we search for the unsub together, we'll be able to watch each other's backs, which is also very important, but the downside to that is the search'll take longer, and we won't be able to cover as much ground. So I'm gonna leave the final decision up to you as to what you think we should do."

The passenger shook his head. It's clear by the expression on his face that he hated this entire situation. "I say we split up and cover more ground, though I'm not too fond of that option. But like you said, time is of the essence here, and we ain't got diddly squat when it comes to time, especially when it comes to savin' our fuckin' jobs."

"All right. So we'll maintain radio silence until one of us spots the unsub. And whoever spots him first will send his GPS signal to the other, so that he can get there ASAP. Sound like a plan?"

"Sounds like bullshit, but what other choice do we got?"

"Then let's move out."

They started to walk away from one another, but the driver turned back and called out in a harsh, whispering voice, "Hey!"

The passenger turned to face him.

"Be careful out there. And watch your six."

The passenger nodded and turned away to walk off.

Once the passenger got far enough away from the driver, he muttered, "Be careful out there? Who says that shit?"

The driver stealthily moved within the shadows and used the trees to shield his silhouette.

Using his camcorder, he scanned the area. He found no sign of life anywhere, except inside the cabin that was filled with the partying teens.

He moved to another tree, where he paused and scanned the area before him. He spotted nothing at first, then picked up a moving image in the distance and soon realized it was his partner and relaxed.

He watched as his partner propped himself against the side of a neighboring cabin to the occupied one and scanned the area before him.

To the driver's chagrin, his partner scanned in his direction, then paused as he got a bead on him.

The driver raised a middle finger into the air and muttered, "It's me, dumbass."

The passenger returned the gesture in kind.

The driver shook his head and smirked, but it quickly faded once he caught another moving image walking up behind his partner.

As the driver's eyes widened, he shouted, "He's right behind you!"

But before his partner could react, the driver witnessed the unsub ram a long, polelike object through his partner's upper body.

The driver screamed out for his partner, but it was too late.

As the unsub lifted his partner off the ground with the pole, blood sprayed from his torso like a geyser.

The driver dropped his camcorder to the ground. He pulled his handgun from his side holster, racked it to chamber a bullet, thumbed off the safety, and took aim.

It was then that he realized he was too far away for a clear shot.

"Shit," he said.

The driver ran off toward the unsub.

*****

Almost forty-five minutes later, a recon military squad arrived at the campgrounds.

As they moved swiftly and cautiously through the pitch-black area toward their objective, their square-jawed, no-nonsense squad leader, with the aid of his night-vision goggles, spotted an object lying on the ground a few yards away.

He motioned with a closed fist for his squad to stop moving.

Once they followed his orders, the squad leader—a sergeant—moved toward the object and knelt before it.

He finally realized what it was.

The sergeant glanced around at his squad. "It's a camcorder. It belongs to our civilian advance team."

He picked it up and examined it.

"Its power's drained, but it still looks to be in working condition." He handed it off to a fellow soldier.

"Get that powered up, Private. I wanna see that footage."

"Yes, Sergeant," replied the soldier, who took the camcorder and ran off.

The sergeant hand signaled for his men to move forward and to keep an eye out. He followed the point man toward the cabin that had been occupied by the partying teens less than an hour before.

The location was now dark and quiet.

The sergeant rested his weapon and held up two fingers on each hand. Then four of his soldiers converged on all entry points to the cabin, a pair of men for each door. These men stopped before the doors and held their positions.

The sergeant waited a few seconds before shouting, "Go!" into his headset.

The soldiers kicked open the cabin doors and swarmed inside like locusts. The others maintained their positions outside and waited in silence while the soldiers inside the cabin secured the location.

Over the headset, the sergeant heard the sounds of doors being busted in and the shuffling of boots on wooden floors followed by several shouts.

"Jesus Christ!"

"What the fuck!"

"Look at all the fuckin' blood!"

The sergeant shouted over them, "Cut the chatter and secure the location."

"But, Sergeant, it's a bloodbath in here."

"Man up, Private, and tell me what you see."

"Bodies, Sergeant. Lots of 'em."

"Anyone still alive?"

"It doesn't look like it, Sergeant."

"Is the cabin cleared?"

"The cabin's secure, Sergeant."

"Okay. Maintain your positions. We'll be there shortly."

The sergeant turned to the rest of his men and shouted, "Conroy?"

"Yes, Sergeant?"

"Call in to command. Tell 'em what we got here."

"Yes, Sergeant," Conroy replied, pausing in place a few moments before asking, "What do we have here, Sergeant?"

"A massacre."

Conroy blinked rapidly and nodded. "Yes, Sergeant."

The sergeant motioned to another soldier, "Jeffries, you're with me."

"Yes, Sergeant."

"The rest of you, fan out. Look for any sign of life. And be careful. The unsub may still be in the area."

"What are the standing orders, Sergeant?"

"Anything that poses a threat, take it out."

"Yes, Sergeant."

As the other troops headed out, the sergeant and Jeffries jogged toward the cabin in question.

As they approached, a soldier emerged from the doorway of the cabin, bent over, and puked on the ground.

The sergeant reached him, pulled him up, and glared at him.

When the sergeant spotted tears flowing down the young soldier's face, his compassion came through as he asked, "You all right, Jenkins?"

Jenkins took a few deep breaths and, through his tears, answered, "I don't know, Sergeant."

The sergeant nodded and started to go inside the cabin, but the young soldier stopped him. "I'm sorry, Sergeant. It's just that…"

"What, soldier?"

"I served two tours in Afghanistan. And I've never seen anything like what I just saw in there."

The sergeant nodded, placed a firm hand on the young man's shoulder, then entered the cabin.

*****

The smell hit him first. Not of the bodies, because they hadn't had time to decompose yet, but of the blood. It was an overwhelming combination of copper, which is similar to the smell of a penny, and shit, which had by that time permeated every square inch of the cabin.

The sergeant held a hand over his nose and mouth and gasped as he surveyed the carnage.

Blood and entrails were everywhere. Thick and clumpy on the floor and splashed upon the walls.

There was a body of a teenage male in the main room of the cabin. His head partially severed. A knife had been shoved down his throat, the hilt protruding from his mouth. His lower torso had been cut open, and his intestines had been yanked out.

A decapitated female's body was laid out on the stairs. Her severed head, with its eyes open, and its mouth forming a silent scream, was propped up on the banister to face whoever entered the room.

A soldier stumbled down the stairs and somehow managed to catch himself before he tripped over the headless body.

One look at the soldier's face told the sergeant all he needed to know about what had happened upstairs.

Still, despite already knowing the answer, the sergeant asked his next question anyway. "Any survivors?"

The soldier's head shook. "No, Sergeant."

To the rest of the squad, the sergeant asked, "Any sign of the advance team?"

"No, Sergeant," the soldiers answered.

One went further and replied, "At least, not that we can recognize."

The sergeant activated his headset. "Everyone outside, report in. What have we got?"

"Nothing, Sergeant."

"Same here, Sergeant."

"The whole place looks deserted."

The sergeant replied, "All right, maintain your positions. Call out if you see anything."

A chorus of, "Yes, Sergeant!" rang out.

The sergeant peered around in shock, but he maintained a stoic visage for his men to see and be comforted by. "Give me a dead count, and then we'll regroup outside to wait for forensics. But be careful not to destroy any more of the evidence."

"All there is is evidence, Sergeant."

"Stow it, Private."

"Sorry, Sergeant."

The sergeant eyeballed the private, who regretted what he said.

But before the private could say anything, the sergeant turned and exited the cabin.

*****

Upon stepping out, the sergeant took in several deep breaths of fresh air and rubbed his face.

He would never admit it, but he had felt his breakfast trying to come up on him. But instead of risking embarrassment in front of his men, he stepped outside to reign in his emotions in the hopes of settling his stomach.

While he gathered his thoughts, a private ran up to him, arm outstretched, holding an iPad. "Here's that footage, Sergeant."

The sergeant reached out, took the iPad, and pressed the Play button on the screen.

As the footage started, he saw the view from the car as the advance team watched the country road.

The sergeant used his finger to scroll through the footage and pressed the Play button again.

He and a few of his men who had gathered around him watched as the passenger agent was impaled by the unsub in the distance, then the camcorder was dropped to the ground.

When the image finally settled, they watched from a severe slanted angle as the footage showed the driver agent running toward the unsub and his partner.

The driver agent stopped before the unsub just as he dropped the slumped body of the passenger to the ground, where he laid lifeless.

The driver had the drop on the unsub, and the soldiers around the iPad watched as he motioned with his handgun for the unsub to get on the ground.

When the unsub refused to follow orders, the driver unloaded his weapon into the unsub, who fell backward to the ground.

The driver agent quickly approached the unsub's body and kicked it. Then he turned his back to the unsub's body and checked on his partner.

The private watching the footage over the sergeant's shoulder shook his head and groaned, "Bad move."

The sergeant glared at the private before turning back to the footage.

They watched as the unsub sat up and regarded the back of the driver, who was still checking on his partner.

The unsub rose to his feet and slowly approached the driver. He reached out, grabbed the driver by the head, and violently twisted his head around.

The squad watching the footage winced in horror but kept watching.

When the unsub let go, the driver's body fell to the ground like a sack of potatoes.

After that, the unsub stood there looking down at the advance team's bodies, almost as if he were admiring his handiwork.

Then he turned and regarded the cabin, where activity was going on inside. He approached it, paused at the door, and stood there.

The sergeant waited a while, then finger-scrolled through the footage.

During the sped-up footage, the unsub stayed in that one spot wavering back and forth. Then, a few moments after the cabin's interior lights went out, he finally opened the cabin's back door.

The sergeant pressed the Play button and watched as the unsub stepped inside the dark cabin and closed the door behind him.

The sergeant scrolled through the footage, then stopped, backed it up a little and started it again.

He watched as the back door of the cabin opened, and the unsub stepped from it. He walked toward the lifeless bodies of the advance team still on the ground. He grabbed a leg from each one, dragged them past the cabin, and out of frame.

The sergeant scrolled through the rest of the footage but saw nothing else of interest.

He handed the iPad back to the private and said, "Get that to tech support. I want every second of that footage analyzed."

"Yes, Sergeant."

As the private ran off, the sergeant noticed the sun starting to rise along the horizon. He took a moment to appreciate its beauty and immediately got back into command mode.

"Conroy?"

The radio officer snapped to attention. "Yes, Sergeant?"

"Call in to command. Tell 'em we have a priority 1 situation. We need a cover story to throw off the local authorities and the media. We also need to set up roadblocks within a twenty-mile radius. No, make that thirty. No one gets in or out."

"Yes, Sergeant."

As Conroy made the call, the sergeant stared out over the lake and heard the call of an unseen loon in the distance.

The sergeant closed his eyes for a moment and mumbled to himself, "It's gonna be one of those days."

He turned back and started yelling out more orders to his men, who snapped to attention and set about following them.

UNDER THE INFLUENCE

There's beautiful, and then there's sexy.

Beauty is all on the surface. It is an aesthetic that can be achieved by almost anyone who has enough time, money, patience, and desire to accomplish such an endeavor. In other words, it is a commodity that can be bought, faked, made, or sold.

Sexy, on the other hand, is a trait you either have naturally, or you don't. It's hard to define and even harder to explain. It just is. It exists somewhere between what is visible on the surface and a particular state of mind.

Contrary to popular belief, you don't have to be beautiful to be sexy. Frida Kahlo was by no means anyone's idea of a classic beauty, but one could lose count of all the lovers she had under her spell.

The same goes for Cleopatra. Despite the fact that everyone pictures Elizabeth Taylor when they think of this ancient queen of Egypt, she lived, in fact, far from the land of the beautiful. But what she lacked in appearance, she made up for by having tremendous sex appeal, a vibe she exuded that was enough to bewitch both Caesar himself as well as his general, Mark Antony.

Then there is a select class of women who fit both of those aforementioned categories to a T.

This type of woman isn't impossible to find. Most of the time, they aren't unattainable to the average schlub. Sometimes, they go out of their way to make it incredibly easy. The problem is when you find one, most of the time, you end up wishing you had never met her at all. Because no matter how good they make you feel when they're at your side, on your arm, or in your bed, women like these have a way of making you do things you would normally never do.

They cause you to step outside yourself and helplessly watch as the stranger walking around in your skin does really crazy things… horrible things…fatal things. You can scream at the top of your lungs all you want at the being that was once you, but it will fall upon deaf ears. You can do nothing but helplessly watch as this empty doppelganger commits acts that will alter the course of your life forever. You clearly see the path of the road it is following all the way to its final dark destination, and there's absolutely nothing you can do to stop it.

All it takes for you to step over that too-thin, invisible line between crazy and normal is for this beautiful, sexy temptress to whisper sweet nothings in your ear while running her fingers through your hair. To seal the deal beyond a shadow of a doubt, she'll follow that up with a teasing, soft, wet wisp of a kiss across your neck that promises more to come later if you make her happy. And make her happy, you will, because in your lust-filled mind, you have no choice in the matter. You have to keep her happy.

You're so hard for her you can't think straight. All your boiling blood flows to the little head that's been in charge since she first entered the picture. But unfortunately for you, the little guy has no conscience. It can't see the big picture, only what is right in front of it. It doesn't know right from wrong, and it acts only on pure instinct. All it knows is its insatiable need to be happy and content in the now, at that moment.

But the satisfaction only lasts a little while, and pretty soon, usually the length of time it takes to smoke a cigarette, the mad cycle starts all over again. It compels you forward as if your limbs are moving by remote control. Common sense is no longer a factor in your decision-making. The reality bus left the station a long time ago, and it doesn't look like it's coming back anytime soon.

Before you know it, you have a gun in your hand, and it's pointed at the head of someone who is standing between you and her. And even if they really aren't in the way, you don't care because what matters is you think they're in the way. There's no time for reason in times like these. The next thing you know, your body grows cold as you bleed to death from a bullet wound to the gut while you're slumped in the driver's seat of a beautiful muscle car you've loved the idea of since you were a kid. The car that came into your possession at the exact same time as she did.

But you're not thinking of coincidences. How one thing is not possible without the other. All you're thinking about is her. The woman who's still at your side.

While you are dying, all you care about is that she's still there whispering sweet promises in your ear while running her fingers through your hair and brushing her lips across the sensitive skin of your neck while making promises you know you won't live long enough for her to keep.

Despite the fact your life will soon be over, and she's the one responsible, you still love the fact she's with you, even if the whole time you're wishing you two had never met.

Then it all begins to slip away. As the world slowly, ever so slowly, fades to black, your skin is on fire at her touch. You want nothing more than to have more time with her.

You shudder as you feel her hot breath on your ear as she whispers ever so sweetly, with an undercurrent of sheer malice you recognized was there the whole time but simply chose to ignore—"I'll miss you when you're gone, baby."

And just like that, you're over.

*****

But before the end, let's go back. Not the beginning. Not even the middle. None of that stuff is important. How he and she met, and how they got from point A to point B to point C isn't relevant.

The only thing that matters is a particular moment in time. The beginning of the end.

*****

The sleek red 1967 Mustang GT500 Shelby convertible with its ragtop down is a thing of beauty. It glows under the outdoor lights of the convenience store parking lot, calling attention to itself without even trying. The big-block V-8 purrs impressively, like a giant jungle cat waiting patiently to pounce on its prey.

Even more impressive than the car is the young woman in the passenger seat. A statuesque beauty with the body of Aphrodite and the face of Helen of Troy. She says her name is Crystal. Now, whether this is her true name or another in a long series of lies isn't important; what matters is she is there. Her bright eyes sparkle even when she is tired. Her lips are red, full, and moist, even without lipstick. The entrance to her mouth is capable of keeping deadly secrets, making empty promises, and giving indescribable pleasure. Her long raven locks frame her face perfectly, never a strand out of place and aching to be pulled and yanked in moments of sheer ecstasy.

The best thing that could be said about the guy behind the wheel is that he is with her. The kind of guy you pass on the street and never look at twice, if you even notice him at all. Not ugly, not handsome, just there. There's a word for men like him: *milquetoast*.

He's like a ghost passing through his own life, never one to stand out in a crowd, never one to be a part of any crowd. The fact he is in this parking lot, in this car, next to a woman like this is a shocking surprise.

Especially to himself.

His name is Nick, which is the coolest thing about him. Until today, he has led a very uneventful existence. Maybe at one point in time, he had big dreams of what he wanted to do with his life, but not in a very long time has he thought about where he ended up.

Never one to examine his choices and his place in the world, Nick simply existed, sleepwalking through his days, barely noticing the passing of time, living like a supporting character in a movie of his own life with the first and last reel missing.

But here he is. With Crystal. Her tongue licking his earlobe, causing the hair on his neck and arms to rise. Her right hand massaging him through the crotch of his jeans. He feels the slight pain and discomfort of his manhood swollen at an awkward angle beneath the denim.

As her mouth passes over the side of his face, her breath is hot against his skin, echoing within his ear. He hears a slight giggle as she moves across his face, tongue gently sliding as it goes, then her lips meet his. He opens his eyes to see her looking into his.

She giggles again. "Havin' fun, baby?"

Her lips move down his chin, settle on his neck. Her hand still massaging his crotch. The pain down there becoming more prominent.

"Oh yeah."

"I want you so bad."

"Me too."

"You want you so bad?" She giggles again.

"No," he replies, "I want you really bad."

"You have me."

Nick closes his eyes. He thinks to himself, *I could die right here and now with no complaints, Lord.*

"Penny for your thoughts, baby."

He opens his eyes and stares into hers. "I was thinking of you. How happy I am you're with me. More than happy. Ecstatic."

"How sweet."

She kisses him on the lips again, flicking her tongue into his mouth, flirting with his. When she finally pulls away, a line of spittle hangs between them that reflects the lights of the store. She grins and goes back to kissing him, raising her hand that was on his crotch and running it through his hair.

Nick takes the opportunity to reposition himself both in the seat and within his pants. Then his hands begin roaming freely about her body, paying extra attention to her breasts beneath her blouse.

"I love it when you touch me, baby," she coos.

"I love touching you."

She kisses down his face again, moving to his neck. As she does, Nick half-opens his eyes and happens to gaze into the convenience store.

That's when he spots a young man, wearing a smock, standing behind the counter, looking out at them through the window.

Suddenly self-conscious, Nick shifts ever so slightly.

Crystal feels this and raises her face to his. "What's wrong, baby?"

Nick motions with his chin toward the cashier. "We got an audience."

Crystal turns and looks back at the cashier. She licks her lips and winks at him while flashing a perfect smile. "I think he wants to join us."

"Too bad for him."

"I don't know, he's kinda cute."

Nick glares up at her. "This here is just about me and you."

Crystal looks back at Nick with a surprised look on her face.

"Ooh, so forceful." She kisses him. "That turned me on."

Nick raises his hands and holds her face. "This is just me and you. No one else."

She starts to kiss him again, but Nick stops her and stares into her eyes.

"I need you to say it, Crystal."

"No one else, baby," she says with a smirk. "Just us."

This time, Nick kisses her much more forcefully than he has been. And with lots more passion than he has shown thus far.

"Man," Crystal exhales. She playfully fans her face with her hand. "I should flirt with other men more often."

Nick's face reddens as he glares at the cashier, who is still staring at them from his position behind the counter. He moves in to kiss Crystal from her neck all the way down to her cleavage.

Crystal moans with pleasure, face toward the night sky, all the while running her hands through his hair.

She opens her eyes, looks down at him, and asks, "Do you want me, baby?"

"Yes," he replies. His voice is muffled against her skin.

"How much?"

"Bad."

"Prove it."

He stops kissing her. He slowly moves his head back and looks up at her. A quizzical look upon his face.

He asks, "What?"

"Prove how much you want me."

"What do you mean?"

"You say you want me. Now I want you to prove it."

He smiles, figures it's a game. "How?"

She gazes back at the cashier, who's no longer staring but taking brief glances at them.

She looks back at Nick and beams, "You know what I want, baby."

Nick glances at the cashier and slowly loses his smile. He's confused until she turns and looks back at the cashier, still taking sneaky glances.

Nick asks, "Him?"

"Yeah, baby." She turns and kisses him again. "Him."

Nick stares past her toward the cashier again. He watches as the young man shoots them another quick look. This time, they make eye contact.

The cashier smiles at him and shakes his head, highly entertained by the show they're putting on.

Nick looks up at Crystal again. "I don't understand."

A cold look crosses her face.

To his growing consternation, she crawls off the console where she was sitting and parks herself in the passenger seat to inspect her long, cherry-red fingernails.

A concerned look crosses Nick's face. "What's wrong?"

"You know," Crystal replies. She flips down the visor and checks her makeup and hair. Using her pinkie nail to wipe away a little smear of lipstick, she smiles at what she sees.

"No, I don't," Nick says. "What do you mean?"

Crystal raises the visor back to its original position and stares ahead at the cashier. "Look at him lookin' at me. He's been doing that ever since we got here."

Nick glares at the cashier again. "Yeah. What about it?"

"There's no doubt in my mind that he wants me."

"What are you getting at, Crystal?"

"Nothing." She grins at Nick. "Just, I think he's cute. Maybe we should invite him along on our little ride."

Nick's face reddens as he stares intently at the cashier.

"Of course, you'll both have to take turns sharing me, but I think we can work it out."

Nick's knuckles turn white as they grip the steering wheel. His voice goes down an octave. "Why are you doin' this?"

"Doin' what, baby?"

"Getting me mad."

"'Cause that's what I do, baby. I need excitement. And if I can't get it from you, I'll find it somewhere else."

Nick turns toward her. He sees her staring at the cashier. She runs her tongue along her upper lip and smiles in that guy's direction.

Nick glances toward the cashier to see him talking on the phone while taking occasional glances at them.

Nick glares at Crystal. "There ain't gonna be no one else but me. Especially not him."

Crystal smiles at him. "Then do something about it."

"What do you want me to do?" Nick asks. "Tell me and quit playing games."

Crystal grins and leans forward in the seat. Her hand reaches out to the glove compartment and opens it.

To Nick's surprise and escalating unease, resting inside the tiny compartment is a shiny, nickel-plated gun. A .38 snub-nosed revolver.

Nick's mouth is agape. "Where the hell did that come from?"

"It's always been there, baby. Waiting for you."

Nick glances at the cashier, Crystal, and the gun.

Crystal continues, "If you want me, baby, you either learn to share me with your competition or get rid of it."

Nick glares at the gun, then back up at the cashier, who's hanging up the phone and staring out at them again.

"What's it gonna be, baby?" Crystal asks. "The three of us...or just you and me?"

Nick thinks it over, gets angrier.

Crystal runs her hand across the steel of the gun.

Before Nick knows it, the gun is in his hand. He feels the cold steel against the flesh of his palm. It's heavier than it looks, but it feels good. Like it was made for his grip.

Nick leans toward Crystal. "It's just you and me, baby. No one else."

Crystal smirks, a glint in her eyes. "Then prove it."

Nick gives her a kiss and turns to open the door. He gets out and shuts the door while holding the gun behind his back, out of view of the cashier.

He glances back at Crystal and smiles at her.

"I'll be right back."

She gives him a flirty air kiss. "I'll miss you when you're gone, baby."

Nick grins and walks toward the sliding doors of the convenience store. They open for him, and he strides inside.

*****

The store smells of Pine-Sol and bleach. The music over the speakers is the elevator variety. A golden oldie rock song stripped of all its soul and beauty.

As a determined Nick steps up to the counter, gun still hidden behind his back, he reads the guy's name tag: Kenny.

The look on Nick's face is one of anger and nervousness.

Kenny stands against the wall of cigarettes behind the counter.

It's easy to see that the sight of Nick unnerves him, but he tries to do his job.

Kenny asks, his voice cracking, "May I help you?"

Nick stares out at Crystal sitting in the Mustang. She smiles at him and blows him another kiss. Red in the face, Nick turns his attention back to Kenny.

"You like what you see out there?"

Kenny takes a moment, unsure of what to say. "Pardon?"

"I asked you a simple question," Nick replies. "Do you like what you see?"

Kenny looks out the window toward Crystal and the car.

He shrugs. "Yeah, sure."

Nick leans over the counter menacingly, "Yeah, sure, what?"

Kenny's really nervous now. Beads of sweat are breaking out on his upper lip. "She's a real beauty."

Nick is really upset now. To the point he's almost shaking. But he calms himself down enough to ask, "And you'd like nothing more than to have her, right?"

Kenny raises his hands to hip level, patting the air in front of him.

"Dude, can I… May I help you with something?"

Nick glances back out the sliding glass doors at Crystal and quickly raises the gun in his hand.

When Kenny sees the gun, he backs up hard into the cigarette wall. Packs fall to the floor. Immediately, he cowers, shielding his face with his arms.

"Please, dude, don't shoot." Kenny's eyes are closed. "Just take what you want."

"I want what's mine." Nick points at Crystal. "And she's mine, you hear? All mine. Not yours."

Kenny, still not looking at Nick, nods. "Sure. Yeah. Whatever you say. She's yours. I don't want her."

Nick pulls back the hammer with his thumb.

Kenny hears the click and starts to sob.

"Please don't shoot me. Jesus Christ. Take whatever you want, but please don't shoot me."

Nick walks all the way up to the counter and aims the barrel of the pistol a few feet from Kenny's head.

Kenny can't help but start to cry. He refuses to look at the gun and cowers from it.

Nick says, "What I want is her."

"Dude, please. Don't shoot me."

Nick looks around. He notices the cash register for the first time. He motions toward it with the gun.

"Put the money in the register in a bag." Nick aims the gun at Kenny's head again. "All of it."

Kenny nods in compliance and steps toward the register and pushes a button to open it. All the while, he refuses to make eye contact with the madman.

When the cash drawer pops out, Kenny reaches beneath the counter and pulls out a plastic bag.

Nick raises his voice, "Hurry. Quick."

"All right, all right." Kenny begins putting the money in the bag. "Just please don't shoot me."

Nick steps away from the counter and peers outside. He sees Crystal still sitting in the passenger seat of the Mustang. She's checking her nails again.

Nick turns his attention back to Kenny, who puts the last of the money into the bag.

Nick approaches the counter, aiming the gun at Kenny again.

"Hurry and gimme the money," Nick demands.

Kenny hands him the bag. "Take it, take it. Just don't shoot."

Nick, holding the bag by its plastic handles, backs away to the doors, which open automatically. He stares between Crystal and Kenny, who still has his hands up in the air.

Nick approaches Kenny, who still refuses to make eye contact with him.

"Hey," Nick says. "Look at me."

Kenny shakes his head and stares at the floor.

Nick gets angry. "Look at me!"

Slowly, Kenny raises his gaze to make eye contact with Nick.

"She's all mine," Nick states.

Kenny can only nod at Nick's madness.

Then Nick pulls the trigger.

The bullet enters the center of Kenny's chest. Blood splatters on the wall of cigarettes behind him.

A look of dumbfounded surprise crosses Kenny's face as he looks down at the smoking bullet hole.

When he glances back up at Nick, another bullet goes through his upper lip. Blood spatters the cigarette packs behind him as he falls to the floor.

Nick sees the droplets of blood everywhere. At first, he is petrified. But a grin breaks out on his face, and he runs from the store.

He approaches the Mustang and opens the driver's door. He quickly gets in and hands Crystal the bag of money.

Nick asks, "What did you think of that?"

Crystal smirks. "I knew you could do it, baby."

"Now it's just me that you want, right?"

"Yeah, baby, just you."

He puts the Mustang in reverse and peels out. The V-8 roars like a dragon, echoing in the night. Smoke rises from the tires as the car stops, turns, and shoots through the parking lot and out onto the street.

*****

As the Mustang flies through the city streets, Crystal raises herself up and perches herself on top of the seat. Her hair flaps and swirls in the wind as she screams at the top of her lungs.

"Faster, baby, go faster!"

Nick presses the accelerator, and the speedometer goes past seventy on its way to eighty.

"Faster, baby!" Crystal yells.

Eighty-five. Ninety. Ninety-five.

Nick hollers in celebration as the needle passes a hundred.

Crystal screams and holds her arms up in the air like she's on a rollercoaster.

They pass right by a police car sitting in a business parking lot.

It wastes no time setting off in pursuit.

Nick mashes the gas pedal as the needle approaches one hundred and ten. He hears the sirens before he sees the red and blue swirling lights. A worried look crosses his face.

Crystal, on the other hand, looks back and smiles.

"Step on the gas, baby! They're no match for you!"

With the police car gaining, Nick presses the accelerator some more. He's soon got the car up to one hundred and twenty.

Crystal yells again, "Nick is the man!"

Nick smiles up at her as she lets the wind whip her hair around.

Nick yells up at her, "You're so fuckin' beautiful!"

She yells back, "So are you, baby!"

Nick is all smiles until the engine sputters. His eyes dart to the fuel gauge. It's on empty.

"Shit," Nick says.

He glances in the rearview to see the police car gaining.

The speedometer starts to fall. Falling under a hundred. Approaching ninety.

Crystal feels the loss of speed and looks down at Nick.

"What's wrong, baby?"

"We're out of gas."

"Shit, baby."

"I know. I'm sorry."

Crystal looks like a sad little girl as she lowers herself down into the seat. She uses her fingers to remove stray strands of hair from her face.

Nick senses her disappointment. "I should've checked. I'm sorry."

"What are we gonna do now, baby?"

"The only thing we can do. We gotta stop."

"And then what?"

He grins at her. "We surprise 'em."

Suddenly, Crystal smiles again. "You know how I love surprises, baby."

"I know," he replies. "And this is gonna be the biggest one yet."

"What are you gonna do?"

"If I told you, baby, it wouldn't be a surprise, now would it?"

Crystal smiles and leans over. She kisses him passionately on the lips. When she pulls away, a smile grows on her face as she looks him in the eyes. "I love you, baby."

"I love you more."

Crystal is on pins and needles, excited as Nick brings the dying Mustang to a stop on the side of the road. He turns off the car and turns toward her.

The police car skids to a stop about thirty feet behind them. Within seconds, the two policemen open their doors and step out. Using their doors as shields, they aim their guns toward the Mustang.

The first officer on the driver's side yells at them, "All right! Now slowly, very slowly, open the door and step out of the car with your hands up!"

The second officer shouts, "Slowly, like he said!"

Nick stares at Crystal as he shoves the gun in the back waistband of his pants.

He smiles. "You ready?"

A big smile crosses her face. "I'm always ready, baby."

Nick opens the door, raises his hands, and steps out.

The first cop yells again, "Slowly!"

Nick steps away from the vehicle, hands still raised.

The first cop steps out from behind the squad car door and approaches him, gun raised. "Get down on your knees! Now!"

Nick looks back at Crystal. He grins.

Crystal smiles. "I'll miss you when you're gone, baby."

Nick turns and faces the cops.

The first cop yells again, "Get down on your knees, goddammit! Now!"

Nick glances at both cops. An evil smile forms upon his face as he drops his arms and reaches for the gun in his waistband.

Before the cops can react, Nick raises the gun and aims at the first cop.

The first cop's eyes widen as he sees the barrel.

The second cop yells, "Gun!"

Nick aims center mass at the first cop and fires.

The first cop slumps to the ground.

The second cop pulls the trigger on his sidearm.

The bullet hits Nick in the gut near his waist. The shot turns his body. But he recovers in time to get off another shot.

Nick's bullet shatters the passenger door window.

The second officer somehow ducks out of the way and regains his balance.

Nick takes aim again and pulls the trigger.

His next shot zips past the second cop's head.

The second cop gets off another shot. It hits Nick in the leg.

Nick screams in agony and falls to his knees.

In extreme pain, Nick grimaces and aims his weapon again. He fires.

The bullet hits the second cop in the neck.

The cop grabs his neck as blood oozes through his fingers. He gargles and gasps as blood fills his throat. He tries to take another wet breath but to no avail. His eyes are wide-open as he falls face forward to the ground.

Nick, lying in a pool of blood, begins to scream in pain, "Fuck! Fuck! Fuck! Fuck! Fuck!"

He checks his leg. He sees the steam rising from his wound.

"Damn!" he yells. "This fuckin' hurts!"

He grits his teeth and cranes his neck to look over at the Mustang. He can't see Crystal from his vantage point.

"Crystal?"

No response.

"Crystal? Come here."

Still no response.

"Crystal!"

When he still gets no response, a crease appears on his forehead.

Now worried, he turns his body over and crawls to the car in spite of the agonizing pain it causes him.

It takes a while, but he finally reaches it and pulls himself up to look into it.

There, he sees Crystal sitting in the passenger seat, checking her hair for split ends.

"Crystal?"

She doesn't even look at him. "Yeah, baby."

"Didn't you hear me calling you?"

"What, baby?"

"I've been shot."

"I'm sorry, baby."

"Help me. Please."

"Help you with what?"

"Help me get into the car."

"Can't you do it? I don't wanna get any blood on me."

"Crystal, what the…would you please help me?"

Crystal sighs. She finally looks over at him. "I can't. Some things you have to do for yourself."

She goes back to checking over her hair.

Nick shakes his head in disbelief. He reaches up with considerable effort and grabs the top of the steering wheel. He pulls with all his might, using his good leg to get some sense of balance. He slowly manages to drag himself into an awkward position on the driver's seat.

As he reclines, one leg still outside the car, he catches his breath.

Crystal glances over. "I knew you could do it, baby."

"Yeah," Nick replies, out of breath. Getting in the car took a lot out of him.

When she leans over and kisses him on the lips, he smiles and reaches up to touch her face. That's when he sees the blood on his hand.

He looks down at his waist and sees all the blood covering his shirt and pants. "Oh, fuck."

She asks, "How you feelin', baby?"

"Not good."

He tries to catch his breath, but it's getting harder and harder. His feet and hands are starting to tingle.

"I think I'm dying."

He looks up at her to see her smiling down at him.

He adds, "I feel cold."

"That's what happens when you bleed out."

A worried expression crosses Nick's face as he asks, "Don't you even care?"

"Of course I care, baby," she says while kissing him again, then leans down to whisper in his ear. "But what can I do about it?"

Nick can't believe what he's hearing.

She adds, "You're dying."

"Jesus. Why are you acting like this?"

"It's my nature. You expect me to change for you?"

"Who are you?"

"I'm sure the answer's in the back of your mind. You've just chosen to ignore it until now."

"What the...what are you talking about?"

"Come on. You're not stupid. Figure it out. I know you can do it if you try."

A tear falls down his cheek.

Crystal quickly leans down and licks the tear from his face and closes her eyes. "Um. Yummy."

"You're not..."

"Yeah, baby."

"You don't love me."

"Of course I love you, baby."

"No, you don't. You can't love."

"You tryin' to hurt my feelings, baby."

"You can't hurt what's not there."

She laughs while stroking his face.

She says, "Despite what you believe, I really do love you. Just like I love all mankind. Flaws and all."

She kisses him on his forehead. On the nose. On both cheeks. Then full on the lips.

"You're the devil," he says.

Crystal smiles. "There. I knew you'd figure it out eventually. I had faith in you."

"Why me?"

"Why not you?"

He looks up at her as she smiles again.

"I chose you, Nick, because I knew you were capable. I knew if I pushed the right buttons, you'd fulfill all my expectations and then some."

Nick looks away. He can't believe what he's hearing. He coughs and feels something on his chin and wipes it away. He sees fresh, dark blood on his hand and fingers.

Crystal adds, "But that doesn't make you special. Guys like you are a dime a dozen. Willing to sell your soul for any pretty girl in a nice car who'll give you the time of day."

He coughs again. More blood.

Crystal leans down and kisses him again. She comes up with blood on her lips, which she licks at with her tongue.

She continues, "I gotta ask, though. In the end, after all the things you've done, looking back, was it worth it?"

Nick glances back at her. He smiles at her. "No."

She puffs out her lower lip, trying to look sad.

Nick adds, "But you were."

She raises her eyebrows in surprise.

Nick says, "Where I'm going, will I ever see you again?"

She smiles and looks up into the air.

He asks, "I mean it. Will I ever see you again?"

"You never know where I'll pop up."

Nick laughs and coughs again. Even more blood comes up. Some of it gets on Crystal's blouse.

"Shit. I told you not to get blood on me."

Nick starts laughing.

"Stop laughing. It's not funny."

She looks down at him, into his eyes, and finds herself smiling again.

"Just so you know, of all the dime-a-dozen guys I've met, I've had the most fun with you."

"You mean that or are you lying?"

She smiles and kisses him. When she looks at him again, his eyes are closed. She smiles, leans down, and whispers in his ear. "I'll miss you when you're gone."

A smile forms on his lips, then fades as he passes.

Crystal lays his head back onto the seat. She brushes hair from his forehead and turns away. She opens the door and steps out. She takes another look at him and walks away.

As she does, she disappears. A few seconds later, the door shuts by itself.

*****

In a cluttered office, three detectives in white shirts and ties are gathered around a computer monitor. As they watch a surveillance video taken at a convenience store, they see Nick, plain as day, entering the store and talking to the cashier.

The first detective, seated in front of the computer, says, "So here he is talking to the cashier. He looks aggravated."

They watch as Nick shoots the cashier and leaves the store.

The second detective looks down and shakes his head.

The third detective says, "I've seen this. What's the something new you were talking about?"

"Right here," the first detective replies. "Watch this."

He clicks a mouse a few times, and now they see footage from outside the convenience store.

They see Nick sitting alone in the Mustang having an animated conversation with himself.

The first detective says, "He was out there a good ten minutes before he worked up the nerve to enter the store."

The other detectives watch as Nick kisses someone who isn't there.

The second detective says, "This guy was out of his fuckin' mind."

"In the footage from the squad car, he was talking to himself the whole time," the first replies.

The second detective observes with a shrug, "He was crazier than a shithouse rat."

The first detective says, "But that's not all. Strange as it may seem, similar murders are happening across the country with the same MO. In all the cases, young men, acting alone, are going on crime sprees and committing murders. And the majority of these seemingly unrelated cases end with their deaths, whether by their own hand or cops. The people may change, but I think it's all connected somehow."

The third detective asks, "How?"

The first clicks the mouse a few more times. "I don't know yet, but check this out."

As they watch the monitor, they see the back of Nick's Mustang from the squad car dash camera. Suddenly, the passenger door opens by itself.

The first detective looks back, excited at what he has discovered. "You see that?"

The second detective shakes his head.

"Wind probably blew it open," the third replies.

The first nods. "Okay. Then explain this."

The passenger door closes. Again, by itself.

The first points at the monitor and looks back at the other two. "You're telling me the door opened and closed by itself?"

The other detectives are at a loss for words.

"What are the chances of that happening?" the first asks.

The second laughs. "What do you want us to do?"

"Yeah," the third joins him. "You wanna make a case against the invisible man?"

"I got your wanted poster," the second adds while holding up a blank sheet of paper.

As the other two chuckle at themselves, the first stands, exasperated with his closed-minded colleagues.

"Come on. You saw for yourself. There was something there, something we can't see, but it's there."

The second stands up to leave. "I think you've been sitting in front of that computer too long."

The third follows him. "Yeah, maybe the gamma rays are finally getting to ya."

The first pleads, "Guys, I know it sounds crazy, but it's right there. It's all on the footage."

"I got some fives to catch up on." The second waves him off.

"And I got doughnuts to eat."

"Guys, come on."

"Maybe you should call, like, the X-Files or something," the third chuckles.

The other detective laughs. "Or maybe you should take a vacation. Get some fresh air. It'll do ya some good."

"I heard the Bermuda Triangle is a good place to go this time of year."

Both of them laugh as they exit the room.

"I'm telling ya, there's something here," the first detective yells after them. "I haven't figured it out yet, but it's here."

After a few moments of pacing while in deep thought, he sits down and starts scrolling through the footage again. He sees Nick talking to himself in the car. Kissing something or someone that isn't there.

"It'll happen again," he says. "And it'll keep on happening until someone stops it."

With no one there to listen, the first detective shakes his head, sighs, and sits back in his chair, never taking his eyes off the monitor.

*****

As Randall Horn steps from the bar and stumbles his way across the parking lot, he checks his pockets clumsily for his keys.

Randall's not quite a looker, but he's not ugly either.

He sees two women walking toward him. So he sucks in his gut and saunters past them as they head toward the bar. He turns and leers at them as they walk past. He admires their too-tight jeans that show off the nice shapes of their asses.

"Shake it but don't break it, ladies."

One of the women casually looks back. An irritated look on her face. "Fuck off."

Randall stares after them, mouth agape, then shrugs it off, turns, and walks toward his car.

As he does, he sees the woman we know as Crystal standing before him.

It's obvious by the look on his face that she's the most beautiful woman he's ever seen. And her butt is parked on the fender of his dream car—a light blue 1963 Corvette.

To say he is taken aback at the sight before him is an understatement.

"Jesus," he says. He runs his hands through his hair, totally amazed at what he sees.

"Not quite," she replies. "My name's Veronica."

"I love your car."

"Thanks," she says, raising her eyebrows. "You want it?"

He stumbles back slightly, blinking his eyes in disbelief. "I'm sorry. I've had a few drinks tonight. Did you ask me if I wanted it?"

"Yeah."

"What's goin' on here?" Randall looks around. "Am I on TV? One of them practical joke shows?"

"Nope." She holds out her hands like a model on a game show. "This is all too real."

"Seriously? No foolin'?"

"No foolin'."

"You're just gonna give me your car? Just like that?"

"Well, not just like that. You have to give me something in return."

"What's that?"

"Your soul."

He stares at her, not sure what to say. Then he breaks out laughing.

She steps away from the car, swinging the key chain on her index finger. "If you give me your soul, not only will you get the car, but you get me as well."

He points at her. "What do you mean, I get you?"

"If you give me your soul, I'll do whatever you want me to do. And I mean anything."

"Anything?"

"Anything."

He smiles at her and nods. "This car and you? For my soul?"

"That's it. Simple as that."

"Has anyone ever told you you're a crazy bitch?"

"Have we got a deal?"

"If that's all it takes to have you, you got it."

"Is that your final answer?"

He laughs again. "I love this. Yeah, that's my final answer."

"Good."

She tosses him the keys. He catches them and stares at her.

"What do you wanna do first?" she asks. "Drive the car or drive me?"

"Holy shit."

He walks toward the car and into her arms. She lays a kiss on him that rocks his world. When she pulls away, he smiles.

"Wow. You're the most beautiful woman I've ever seen."

"Thank you, baby."

He opens the passenger door for her. She gets in, and he closes it afterward. As he walks around to the driver's side, he gives out a rebel yell.

To the skies, he yells, "This is awesome!"

He opens the door, gets in, puts the keys in the ignition, and starts the car. He revs the engine and looks over at the girl he knows as Veronica.

"Veronica?"

"Yes, baby."

"I'm gonna do things to you you've never heard of."

"I'm looking forward to it, baby."

He looks around, then looks down at his crotch. "You mind if we start now?"

"Sure, baby. Whatever you want, it's yours."

He unzips his pants and glances at her.

She smiles and shifts herself in the seat. She leans over the console and takes him with her mouth.

Randall leans his head back. His eyes are almost in the back of his head.

He says, "Oh god. Whatever I did to deserve this, thank you."

The Corvette drives off, raising dust as it goes.

Randall shouts another rebel yell as the car's taillights disappear around a corner, its engine echoing in the night air.

THE NIGHT CREW

A gas-guzzling dinosaur of a car slowly rumbled across a deserted parking lot. With a squealing of brakes, it came to a stop before a ten-foot ivory-colored concrete wall that enclosed the cemetery.

Swirling winds whipped at fallen leaves as well as the untrimmed oak trees lining the inside of the cemetery wall. Large metal letters hanging upon a decorative, squeaky iron gate read Forest Lawn Cemetery.

The driver of the car was eighteen-year-old Neil Prescott, a fresh-faced, nervous, shy young man, who, on this night, had an overwhelmed look about him.

After he turned off his car, he waited inside while it died a slow, chortling death. He glanced at his watch and saw that it was three minutes till midnight.

He got out of his car and shut the door behind him. He shuffled toward the gate. Once he reached it, he paused in his tracks and peered through the bars.

He saw a long, paved road that led straight into darkness. He also made out a branch from the main road that appeared to lead toward the graveyard, while yet another branch came to a stop at an uninviting, nondescript small building with yellow light cascading through its windows.

The wind blew Neil's hair around, which annoyed him to no end. He tried in vain to put it back in place but had no such luck. It was like his hair was caught in a whirlwind.

Neil realized, with some hint of irony, that the small building seemed to house the only sign of life inside the gates. He shouted,

"Hello!" in its direction with the hopes of being heard above the howling winds.

After getting no sign of a reply, Neil, impatient, checked his watch again. The hands read two minutes till midnight.

Still early, he thought.

Neil cupped his hands around his mouth and shouted again. "Is anybody there? Hello!"

A sudden whir of machinery startled him, causing him to jump back. A gate began rolling open upon a metal track on the ground, the source of the grating noise.

After the gate finished opening, Neil stepped through and looked around. As he did, an eerie thought occurred to him. He realized that no light from the outside world was getting inside these walls.

But before he could ponder this more, the sound of the gate rumbling again brought him back to the moment.

While the gate closed, Neil turned his attention toward the little building, which now had its front door ajar letting out a sliver of yellow light.

Neil regarded this image for a while, mulling something over in his head before finally deciding to walk toward it.

He eventually made it to the doorway and stepped inside at almost exactly the stroke of midnight.

*****

As Neil stepped inside, he tried again to run his hand through his windblown hair to put it back in place. But it felt like a carpet full of static electricity that stuck to his hands. This sullied his mood because he preferred things to be in their place. And when they weren't, it made him off-kilter.

In the dingy room before him were two wooden desks. One was cluttered with papers, Styrofoam cups, candy wrappers, and empty boxes of takeout. The other was completely bare, with the exception of a thin layer of dust.

A row of filing cabinets aligned one wall, and opposite that there was a small kitchen area that contained a sink, a minifridge, a microwave, and a coffee maker. All these appliances ranged from being well used or on their last legs.

A toilet flushed, and the restroom door opened. From a cloud of smoke emerged a large, grizzled, grumpy-looking mid-fifties-looking man with a cigarette dangling from his lips. He had huge shoulders, a big gut, unkempt hair, and a few days' growth of stubble.

The man was wearing overalls that were more dirty than clean and a torn, dingy white T-shirt. The only thing that looked new or clean on him was his heavy work boots.

Upon seeing Neil for the first time, the man merely glared at him with a knowing smirk. It was almost as if he didn't believe the young man was really there.

Neil immediately and perhaps much too eagerly put out his hand to greet him.

"You must be Mr. Cole."

Mr. Cole did nothing but stare at Neil's extended hand before reaching inside his shirt pocket in order to retrieve a metal liquor flask. He unscrewed the cap and took a long pull from it. And he did all this without removing the cigarette from the corner of his mouth.

"At least you're on time," Mr. Cole said. He sounded like he had gravel in his throat.

As Mr. Cole took another healthy tug on his flask, Neil, still taken aback by the sight of him, couldn't help but flash a look of immediate disapproval.

With a disbelieving tone, Neil asked, "You are Mr. Cole, right?"

Mr. Cole peered around. "Who else would I be?"

Neil forced a smile. "I'm Neil Prescott."

Rather than be impressed, Mr. Cole stood in place and lazily gestured toward the room he had just emerged from.

"Shitter's in there." He pointed at the empty desk before Neil. "There's your desk." Then he motioned toward the kitchen area. "And here's the kitchen."

While standing there, Mr. Cole poured the last bit of coffee from the pot into a Styrofoam cup and motioned his chin toward the empty desk.

"Have a seat. I imagine you're exhausted from the tour."

Neil walked over toward the dusty desk and ran a fingertip across the surface. After peering at his finger, he quickly wiped it off on his pants.

"Want some coffee?" Mr. Cole asked.

"Yeah. That'd be great."

"Then you'll have to make some."

Neil shook his head in annoyance as Mr. Cole walked past him and sat down at his messy desk. The man opened his flask, poured more liquor into his cup, and took a hearty sip.

Mr. Cole smiled and pointed at his cup, "Now that's some damn good coffee."

Neil waited a few beats in silence before opening his mouth. "On the phone, they were kinda vague about what I was supposed to do here."

"What'd they say?"

"That I'd be a caretaker."

"They say anything else?"

Neil shook his head.

Mr. Cole grunted what could be mistaken for a laugh. "That's pretty goddamn vague."

Neil added, "They also said you'd answer any questions I had in person."

Mr. Cole shrugged and said, "Ask away."

Neil raised an eyebrow. "What will I do here, exactly?"

"It's simple, really." Mr. Cole settled into his chair, twiddling his fingers. "We keep things in their place."

Neil shook his head, confused. "What does that mean? Do we protect the place from vandals or something?"

Mr. Cole bobbed his head as he thought things over. "Every so often. Mainly around Halloween."

"What do we do when that happens?"

"We call the police. Let them handle it."

"We don't handle something like that ourselves?"

Mr. Cole shook his head and grimaced.

"So," Neil added, "what kind of stuff do we handle ourselves?"

Mr. Cole deliberated a while before rising from his chair and saying, "I guess there's only one way for ya to find out, and that's to show ya."

*****

Mr. Cole and Neil stood before a freshly filled-in grave, looking like the same-sex version of the old farmer couple in the famous *American Gothic* painting—with the exception of Neil holding a shovel rather than a pitchfork.

As Neil glanced around, he spotted a backhoe parked a few feet from them.

By this point, the wind had died down, but Neil's breath came out like steam from a train while Mr. Cole took long drags on a fresh cigarette.

Neil threw some curious glances at his supervisor before finally speaking, "I'm thinking now's a good time for you to fill me in."

"What do you wanna know?"

"Well, for starters, why am I standing near a grave holding a shovel?"

Mr. Cole pulled up his shirt and showed Neil a .38 revolver tucked into the waistband of his pants. "You registered to carry a gun?"

An alarmed Neil replied, "No."

"That's why you have the shovel," Mr. Cole replied, as if that answered everything.

Neil brandished the shovel before him. "But what am I gonna do with it? 'Cause I didn't sign up to be a gravedigger—"

"It's backup," Mr. Cole interrupted.

"Backup for what?"

"In case the gun don't work."

Goose bumps on Neil's flesh rose at that remark. "And why do we need a gun?"

Mr. Cole sighed and let down his guard a little. "Do you know anything about this land we're standing on?"

"Other than it's full of dead people?"

Mr. Cole quickly became aggravated. "I'm talkin' about its history, smart-ass?"

Neil shook his head. "No. What about it?"

Mr. Cole gazed up and around. "This land once belonged to the Comanche Indians, who considered it sacred. Their holy land. It's where they came to die."

Neil shivered and glanced around.

Mr. Cole continued, "When white folk took their land from 'em and relocated 'em all those years ago, the Comanche put a curse on it."

Neil couldn't help but flash a knowing smile.

"And now, all these years later, the curse is still going strong."

Neil didn't say anything. Instead, he started chuckling. Low at first, but it soon evolved into full-blown laughter.

Mr. Cole got angrier and even more confused. "Something I say strike you as funny?"

"Only all of it," Neil replied.

"But it's true, kid."

Neil nodded. "Okay, sure."

Deeply offended, Mr. Cole delivered a serious tone. "What? You don't believe me?"

Recognizing the foul mood of his supervisor, Neil stopped grinning long enough to nod.

"Look, I get it," Neil said. "This is what you do. You have fun punking the new guy. You know, show him a gun and tell him some spook stories and freak him out. Have a good laugh with the boys on the day shift. I get it."

Mr. Cole simply replied, "I'm not jokin'."

Neil nodded again. "Okay, I'll bite. What's supposed to happen next?"

Mr. Cole shook his head in annoyance and disbelief and gestured toward the freshly dug grave.

"You shouldn't have to wait long. It should be any minute now."

"Okay," Neil replied, grinning like the cat that ate the canary. "I'm ready. Show me what you got."

They continued standing next to each other for several minutes, with Neil smiling like an idiot, while a somber Mr. Cole kept his eyes glued to the grave.

As time passed, Neil's smile began to fade, replaced by irritation.

He began to glance back and forth from the grave to Mr. Cole, who was a study in focus.

Neil waited a few more moments before saying, "So—"

"Shhh!" Mr. Cole immediately shut him down.

"What's happening?" Neil asked.

"Shut up!"

Seeing no hint of humor in Mr. Cole's order, Neil held up his hands and patted the air. "Okay, I get it. I'm shutting up."

Mr. Cole gave Neil a sideways glance, as well as a sneer before turning his attention back to the grave.

A few minutes later, Neil watched in slight amusement as Mr. Cole knelt down near the grave to stare more closely at the dirt.

The young man wondered just how far this strange man he had just met was willing to go in order to prank him.

But just as Neil was about to say something, the dirt on top of the grave began to move.

Mr. Cole quickly stood up and cocked the hammer back on the .38, gesturing Neil back with his other arm. "You might wanna step back."

Neil, still amused, but less so than he was a few seconds before, kept his eyes on the dirt where it had previously moved.

That's where he saw a small hole appear.

Just like the hole growing before him being created by something under the grave's surface, Neil's eyes got bigger.

Neil jumped back, startled, as a dirty, pale hand with shredded fingernails erupted from the ground.

As Neil watched in complete befuddlement, the hand clawed at the dirt around it.

The ground next to the hand started to rise and fall, as if it was breathing. Then another hand emerged.

Neil's knees gave out, causing him to lose his balance and stumble back. After he landed on his butt, he yelled, "Son of a bitch!"

The hands clawed at the hole, making it even wider. Then, to Neil's absolute horror, the top of a human head appeared. Its hair was wiry in appearance and covered in dirt.

Mr. Cole glanced down at Neil. "Hey, college boy. Say hello to Mr. Adams."

In wide-eyed shock, Neil slowly rose to his feet, keeping his gaze glued to the corpse's head rising from the grave. His eyes then shifted to the tombstone with the engraving:

JAMES FRANKLIN ADAMS

1942–

BELOVED HUSBAND AND FATHER

When Neil saw Mr. Adams's face, dried up, eyes open, mouth sealed, the corpse moaning from somewhere deep inside itself, the young man dropped his shovel and backed away, panic-stricken.

When Mr. Cole saw the shovel on the ground, he pointed at it. "Pick it up!"

Neil could only watch as one of the dead man's shoulders appeared, followed quickly by the other.

Mr. Cole snapped his fingers in front of Neil's face and shouted, "I said, pick it up!"

Neil immediately looked from the corpse to the shovel. With shaking hands, he moved ever so slowly and finally did what he had twice been told.

Neil peered up to see Mr. Adams using his arms to push himself free of his grave. Soon, he cleared it and stood before them in all his recently buried glory.

Mr. Adams, wearing a dirt-covered blue suit-and-pants ensemble with black wingtip shoes, glanced around. He was not very steady on his feet and appeared very confused.

Mr. Cole shook his head, sadly. "Poor things. They don't know what's goin' on, really. It's almost like bein' born, I guess."

Mr. Adams set his gaze on Mr. Cole. Then his eyes shifted toward Neil standing off behind him.

Neil finally found his voice, though it was extremely meek.

"Shoot it."

Mr. Cole looked confused. "You say somethin'?"

Neil's voice was more audible now. "Shoot it."

"Did you say shoot it?"

"Yes. Please."

"You sure I'm not pullin' your leg?"

Neil finally mustered everything within him and shouted, "Shoot the goddamn thing!"

Mr. Cole smiled, savoring the moment. "You sure you don't wanna take a few swings at it with the shovel first?"

"Shoot it!" Neil shouted, even louder than before.

With a satisfied smirk, Mr. Cole aimed the gun and pulled the trigger until it was empty.

Neil watched in horror as dust and pieces of skull and skin flew from Mr. Adams's head.

When the smoke cleared, Mr. Adams was somehow still standing.

Neil screamed as Mr. Adams grabbed his head, teetered, and fell to his knees. Neil only stopped screaming when Mr. Adams fell facedown with a heavy, wet plop.

As both men watched, they observed that Mr. Adams was officially no longer moving.

After a few seconds, Neil finally caught his senses. His eyes shifted toward Mr. Cole. "Is he dead?"

"He always was," Mr. Cole replied.

As Mr. Cole reached down and grabbed Mr. Adams by the shoulders and dragged him from the top of his grave, Neil looked around, still scared out of his wits. "Are there gonna be more?"

Mr. Cole shook his head. "Not tonight. His was the only burial today."

The older man stopped dragging Mr. Adams's corpse and wiped his hands off on his pants.

"They only rise once, kid."

Neil still couldn't believe what he had just witnessed. "Jesus Christ. Do people who bury their loved ones here know this happens?"

"Of course not," Mr. Cole replied as if it were the dumbest thing he'd ever heard. "It's a company secret."

He pointed at Neil and lowered his voice an octave.

"One that you'll keep, regardless of whether or not you keep workin' here."

Neil was too flabbergasted to do anything but nod.

"Besides, if our customers ever found out, there'd be such a stink that this place would close and no tellin' what would happen down the line. The county might bulldoze this whole place over and build a hospital or a school or something. And we can't have that, can we?"

Neil nodded in agreement.

Mr. Cole regarded the overwhelmed young man, whose face was drained of all its color. "You okay, kid?"

Neil exploded in righteous anger. "No! I just saw a fucking zombie rise out of its own grave! I'm pretty fucking far from okay!"

Mr. Cole smiled and said, "I meant to say, are you gonna be okay bein' alone here while I work the backhoe so we can rebury him?"

Neil ran his shaking hands through his hair. The static electricity from the contact and his wild eyes made him look like a mad scientist.

Neil pointed at the corpse. "He's not...he's through moving, right?"

"Yeah. He's done."

After Neil assured his boss that he'd be all right, Mr. Cole walked off toward the backhoe.

Neil took a moment to reflect, then slowly sat down on the ground and buried his face in his hands.

*****

As Neil sat ashen faced at his desk, Mr. Cole soon walked by and set a Styrofoam cup of coffee down before him.

Neil watched as Mr. Cole sat down at his own desk and poured liquor into his coffee before asking, "How come no one told me?"

Mr. Cole thought it over, then replied, "Would you have taken the job if we did?"

Neil shook his head.

"Well, there ya go." Mr. Cole took a sip.

Neil asked, "How long have you been doin' this?"

Mr. Cole thought a long time before answering. "Twenty-nine years next May."

"And how many guys have come before me?"

Mr. Cole grimaced. "Too many to count."

They both sat quietly for a long while, then Neil broke the silence again.

"Why do you do it?"

Mr. Cole simply shrugged. He was too tired to do anything else. "Someone's got to."

Neil picked up his coffee cup. His hands still shaking. He eyed Mr. Cole's flask and pointed at it.

"You mind?"

Mr. Cole smirked and tossed the flask over to him.

Neil caught it with some difficulty and eventually poured some of its contents into his coffee. He screwed the lid back on when he was done and tossed it back to Mr. Cole, who snagged it effortlessly with one hand.

Neil hesitantly tasted the coffee and raised his eyebrows approvingly.

After a few seconds, he took an even bigger sip, smiled, and said, "Now that's some damn good coffee."

Mr. Cole laughed heartily. And soon, Neil joined him.

A VAMPIRE WALKS INTO A BAR

As I made my way along a rain-soaked downtown street, I remember noticing with undeniable pleasure what a clean-smelling night it was.

Rain had a way of doing that. Making things fresh.

I always loved the smell of rain, along with the sweet smell of a lawn after it's been freshly mowed. Or the delicious smells of a pancake-and-bacon breakfast. Or the intoxicating scent of perfume on a nervous young woman out on a date with a man she fancies.

I was on my way to Leonard's Tavern in this nostalgic state, not thinking about much else, when I picked up a scent that didn't belong. It was a scent barely strong enough to notice most times but enough that night to stop me in my tracks.

My senses on alert, I glanced around slowly from my spot on the sidewalk. I could now smell the unmistakable human aroma of desperation and nervousness in the air.

If I were still a human being, I wouldn't hesitate to pay heed to the tiny shivers within warning me that I was in personal danger.

And thus, being mortal, I would listen to those senses and get the hell out of there. But since I was no longer human, all it amounted to was my acknowledgment that someone—maybe one person, possibly more—was out there, watching and waiting, biding their time, waiting for their moment.

I did not know at the time who or what was out there, but I did know that I didn't like it. Not one little bit. I much preferred being the one hiding in the shadows, having the clear advantage, doing the watching.

Still, if I've learned anything in my past four decades of immortality, it was to never underestimate anything.

With as much subtlety as I could muster, I glanced around while taking the last few puffs off my cigarette. I exhaled deeply before dropping the nasty, habit-forming thing to the pavement, where I crushed it with the sole of my boot. After that, I walked on with a purposeful gait, suggesting to any unseen, prying eyes that it was best not to mess with the likes of me.

I approached the entrance to the tavern, but as my hand grasped the door handle, I paused yet again. Not from the smell of danger, but due to the muted music coming from inside that brought a smile to my face. It was "Little Red Riding Hood" by Sam the Sham and the Pharaohs. Immediately upon hearing this, I was taken back to the day I had first heard it.

I was a pleasant-faced, plump teenager wearing my prized Davy Crockett coonskin hat to my first boy/girl party. At the time, I had no idea girls looked down on frontier wear, especially if said frontiersman was slightly overweight. But I soon learned my lesson and stashed the hat behind a couch, retiring it for good.

It was a little while later, as we were sitting around playing some lame card game, that the hostess of our little get-together, Susan Blakely, brought the room to life with her record player. I had been ignoring her initial music offerings of "Sugar Shack" by Jimmy Gilmer and the Fireballs and other songs I'd heard a billion times before when "Riding Hood" came on.

To say it caught me by surprise was an understatement.

It rocked my little world.

I skimped and saved every bit of my allowance for the next few months until I could afford to go down to the record store on my own and buy it. Then I proceeded to play that record until the grooves wore out.

It's amazing how quickly music can stir up long-forgotten memories like that. Up until that moment, I hadn't thought about being that young in years. It seemed like a lifetime ago. Then again, maybe it had been. That was back in the days when I looked upon the world with fresh eyes and a naive outlook. Back in the days when I could feel the sun's warmth on my skin without worry. Back in the days when I was still alive.

With the passing concern of being spied upon now firmly in the back of my mind, I opened the door and stepped inside.

Leonard's was a cozy, candlelit place where demons, spirits, and the like went to relax and enjoy a quiet evening among others deemed unnatural to the normal world. In here, we were free from judging, fearful mortal eyes and our own, at times, savage impulses.

Compulsions that serve to guide us, motivate us and, most importantly, sustain us.

That isn't to say humans weren't allowed in Leonard's. On the contrary. Most nights, quite a few could be found in here. Some knew exactly what they were stepping into when they came here. We called them Potentials. They had one foot in the mortal world, while the other was firmly planted in the desire to be just like us—immortal, powerful, feared.

Sometimes, though rarely, we granted the most deserving their wish. The rest of the time, the humans kept on hoping and dreaming, wishing to be something other than what they were, despite knowing deep down that day would never come.

Then there were the rest of them. The human beings who were convinced that they were the center of the world. The top of the food chain, so to speak. We went on letting them think that way, because why not let them think that way? What was the harm to either side?

It was this deluded human belief system that had worked in our favor for such a long, long time.

What's that old saying? Why fix it if it ain't broke?

Anyway, when the blissfully ignorant humans dropped by Leonard's, convinced that this was more of the same old, same old, we welcomed them. The whole time, keeping our true natures and, if necessary, our appearances secret, for if the truth ever got out about Leonard's base clientele, let's just say the world wouldn't be ready for it. But that knowledge wouldn't keep the humans from trying to get rid of us because that's what humans do. It's in their nature. If they don't understand something, they kill it or, at least, lock it away somewhere where it could be studied and subjugated at will.

Leonard's was run, appropriately enough, by the steady hoof of its namesake. In his true form, Leonard was a demon, who from the waist up looked like a goat with three horns atop his head. He also had a goat's beard, whiskers, and ears. In addition, he had a penetrating set of inflamed, furious eyes. This stood in contrast with his personality; for most of the time, Leonard was laid-back and reserved, willing to sit back silently and observe all the goings-on around him.

But when the situation called for it, this fearsome entity, with his deep, booming voice and immense strength, was a demon to be reckoned with and feared. To say that no one in the know caused trouble at Leonard's place was an understatement.

But to those humans with not one iota of this "other" world, Leonard looked like an ordinary black man—an immense black man—but ordinary just the same. To these people, Leonard's nature reeked of melancholy and anger. They immediately sensed that this was a man who did not suffer fools gladly and was not one to be messed with. So they usually tried their very best to get on his good side, not knowing how near impossible a feat like that was.

I went there quite a lot, so I should know.

It's funny to me, and this never got old, but every once in a while, one of those humans made Leonard smile.

I didn't say laugh. Leonard never laughed. I said smile.

It was sort of like what happens when a pet entertains its owner by doing something amusing or foolish.

In Leonard's case, it usually happened when one of these mortals got drunk enough to begin making bold proclamations of their success in life or whatnot, or when one of them droned on and on about their unfulfilling life while drowning their disappointments in alcohol. When that happened, when you could see the corners of Leonard's mouth moving upward, for a very brief moment, you could also see a flicker of fire in his dark eyes. And if you're anything like me, at those times, you can catch the unmistakable scent of sulfur.

Those were the moments when you knew it was going to be a good night at Leonard's.

From the outside, the place looked like a small dive.

Dive in the worst sense of the word.

It was tucked into the shadows of a neighborhood long gone to seed. Without a sign telling you it was there, you'd hardly notice it if you were just passing by on the outside unless you already knew it was there. But once you stepped inside, it seemed much larger and gave off a strange yet pleasant vibe, as if you had walked through a time warp and gone back to a simpler, more innocent time—if there had ever really been such an era.

As you came in, a loud, colorful jukebox greeted you on the right. It played no music that had been released past the year 1990.

Leonard hated country, rap, and what would pass for current top forty, so none of it was allowed in the machine. He preferred late '50s or early '60s rock and roll, a time he thought all good music, or entertainment for that matter, began and ended. It was only after several years of complaints from his female and vampiric waitstaff that he relented and finally added some new wave from the early MTV days to its playlist.

All the walls were black and red, each covered with a series of large-framed posters featuring Elvis, Bogie, James Dean, and Marilyn Monroe hanging out together, doing various things, still looking the way they did when they were in the prime of their lives.

The long bar Leonard stood behind was made of solid, dark oak. It had stools before it, but very few were ever used. That's the way Leonard liked it. He needed his space.

On this night, however, one of them was being used, but I'll get back to him later.

There were many four-seat tables in the open, while comfy booths lined the walls. All the tables were covered with red cloth and large candles, which, with the exception of a series of muted lights over the bar and pool tables, were the only sources of light.

On this particular night, on the shiny black floor, there was a yellow sign that read "Wet Floor, Watch Your Step" near the path leading to the restrooms. Whether this was evidence of something sinister happening earlier that night or something as simple as a spilled drink or flooded restroom, I'll leave that to your imagination.

As I looked around, there weren't many beings there at the moment, but that would soon change. It was much too early for most of us.

Like almost every night before, there were only two waitresses slinging drinks. They were the pale, tall, stunning, dark-haired twin vampire sisters Eva and Ava.

Wild and carefree Eva was wearing a slinky, sexy red number showing lots of cleavage, while the more careful and proper Ava was dressed head to toe in an elegantly long, formfitting black dress.

Wild, hard-partying Eva—a long story of my own for another time—gave me a pearly-toothed smile and a wink as she headed from the bar toward a dark booth in the corner.

There sat three black-suit-and-tie-wearing demons with gaunt faces and small horns that protruded from their hairless heads. Their long, spindly arms ended in talon-like fingers.

This well-dressed demonic trio were all trickster demons.

Thankfully, they were paying none of us any mind as they were deep into a disturbing, laugh-filled yet quiet conversation that I had absolutely no interest in eavesdropping upon.

I found out a long time ago that it was best not to engage in conversation with any trickster demon you happen to meet, for they love to talk. Their favorite topic of conversation being themselves and all the horrible, clever things they did.

For your future consideration, once you get one started, they'll never shut up or leave you alone until you kill them. Trust me on that one. And don't say I never warned you.

Shy, when compared to her sister, Ava stood near the jukebox contemplating a selection, then pumped a quarter into the machine.

Only one, you say? What can I say? It was an old jukebox.

Ava pressed the appropriate buttons, and I soon heard the opening drum riff of the Go-Go's new wave classic, "We Got the Beat."

I watched with a pleasant smile on my face while the sisters danced, slinging their arms wildly and moving their legs and bodies to the beat.

I noticed from the outskirts of my vision that Leonard gave them both a disapproving shake of his horned head and a snort before resuming his wiping down of the bar. Leonard was and always will be a stickler for cleanliness.

A slightly transparent specter sat at a small table in the back near the restrooms keeping quietly to himself. Most people called entities like him a restless spirit, but he appeared quite the opposite at that moment. He was nursing his drink and staring into the empty space before him. He seemed to have a lot on his mind, and everyone was being nice enough to give him plenty of room.

But getting back to the story at hand, there was one patron there who had my curiosity piqued above all the others.

It was the guy sitting at the bar. His unmistakable scent enabled me to recognize what he was right away. But I'm quite sure he had smelled me long before I even set foot in the place.

I thought twice before making a move, then I took a stool one removed from him and sat at the bar.

I smiled at Leonard with the warmest smile my cold face could muster and said, "I'll have my usual, please."

Leonard looked at me as if we'd never met before. I made sure I grinned only after he looked away. That was his personality. He proceeded to make my drink without saying a word. He merely grunted.

I slowly turned my attention to the tense, moody-looking gentleman sitting closest to me. He was tapping the ashes of his cigarette into an ornate ashtray.

I set my gaze forward, pretending to watch Leonard prepare my drink, but I was really looking into the mirror behind the bar at the guy next to me. I couldn't see my own reflection, of course, but I saw him staring into the mirror as if he could see mine.

I darted my eyes away from the mirror, and finally, after a few moments, I glanced over in his direction.

As I looked closer, I noticed a nasty-looking long, old scar running down the left side of his face. It started just below his cheek and ended somewhere below his neckline.

He was wearing a dark leather jacket with a button-up shirt underneath, blue jeans, and brown work boots. I also picked up the faint smell of Brut from when he had last shaved, which appeared to be a few days before.

If he had been wearing a cowboy hat, I would have likened him to the Marlboro Man. But unless that classic corporate character sprouted hair and fangs and ran on all fours while howling at the full moon, I would have been way off.

I must've been lost in my thoughts because all of a sudden, I realized he had turned toward me.

"You got a problem?" he asked.

His eyes were stern and dark green. They seemed to burn right through me, much like his reflected gaze did a short while before.

His voice sounded weary and tired, as if he'd had enough of whatever he'd gone through but still appeared willing and ready to fight, if necessary.

I told you before that I hardly ever get scared, but just then, if for only a moment, I was taken aback. I decided to tread lightly.

I lost my grin and said, "Sorry, I couldn't help but notice the humorous situation we have here."

"What humorous situation?" he asked, not seeing any humor at all.

He took a heavy drag on his cigarette and blew it out through his nose. The smoke enveloped his head like a cloud before eventually rising and disappearing. He still clearly wasn't seeing this situation the same humorous way that I did.

"You know, a vampire and werewolf walk into a bar," I replied. The smart-ass smile returned to my face. "You gotta admit, that's pretty funny."

"Depends," he said. He stubbed out his cigarette and turned his body toward me. "Do they get along?"

Suddenly, Leonard set my drink before me, causing my attention to completely shift toward it. I know I'm going to sound like an alcoholic or a drug addict, but so be it. Let's call a duck a duck. At that moment, all else faded away. I was, and still am, a slave to my thirst. I am helpless in its sweet yet heartless embrace. And on this night, it was just the right temperature and the perfect color. A dark, rich red.

It was hog's blood, which was sort of similar to a human's. It's nowhere near as good, but it's suitable enough to get you by. It's kind of like wanting ice cream but finding only yogurt in your fridge.

Yet despite the siren's call beckoning before me, I somehow managed to pull myself back to the situation at hand.

That was when I realized Leonard was still leaning over the bar, peering back and forth at both of us.

He asked, "There a problem here?"

I picked up another tinge of sulfur in the air.

Glancing between them both, I gave them my best Eddie Haskell smile. It's the same one I used to give my mother all the time while I was growing up. It was the same one that almost always worked.

I was quite the little charmer when I had to be.

"No problem here, Leonard," I retorted. "Trust me. The last thing I wanna do is fight a werewolf."

I meant that. I'd done it before. It took way too long for the fight to end, and even though I was the only survivor, I actually think I ended up worse for the wear.

A side note—here's a lesson you kids out there really need to learn. Despite the fact well-fed vampires heal really fast, fighting a lycanthrope is never worth it. Just apologize, run away, and live to drink another day. Consider that another important supernatural lesson to be learned.

Now back to the story.

When Leonard was satisfied with my answer, he turned his menacing glare on the Marlboro Wolfman. "And you?"

For a second, I thought Wolfie wasn't going to back down. It was something in the way he hunched his back ever so slightly. I could imagine the fur rising. It was also the way he perched himself on the balls of his feet on the floor. But good and welcome common sense must've raised its hackles in his mind because all too quickly he relaxed. He calmly reached into his jacket pocket and slid another cigarette from its pack, and all sense of danger passed. He shook his head no at Leonard, who was satisfied enough to walk away to the other end of the bar, where Eva was waiting to place another order.

While Leonard poured the drinks, he paid no more attention to us, but I had noticed Eva staring at my lupine pal with an unmistakable glare of intense hatred.

You've heard the phrase, if looks could kill? Well, that applied to the situation here. You see, for many centuries, well before recorded history, as I was once told by a being older than me, vampires and werewolves have never gotten along. Whether it was a difference of philosophy or a deep-rooted prejudice (who knows how these things start?), for some primal reason, there's a lot of bad blood (pardon the pun) between our species. It doesn't matter if you were born into your supernatural team or were turned later, one of our most basic instincts was to dislike the other side.

But I have always been a pragmatist. Unless someone wronged me personally, I held nothing against anyone. Sure, I've told my share of "How many werewolves does it take to screw in a light bulb?" jokes. But when it comes down to it, I didn't and still don't dislike them as a species. I'd gotten into a row with one, as I had previously mentioned, but that was over a beautiful female siren who ended up really not being worth all that trouble. But like I said, that particular beast actually did something to me personally. This new guy, he was just minding his own business, sitting in a bar.

I turned as Wolfie glanced in my direction again, but it quickly dawned on me that he was glaring past me.

I turned around to see Eva still giving him the stink eye.

To his credit, he didn't back down. He simply smiled at her.

In turn, she curled her lip at him before walking away from the bar.

Round 1 to the wolf.

I tried my best to defuse the tense situation. "I know, generally speaking, our two sides don't really get along, but I'm not like all the others."

"Really now?" he replied, with a smirk on his face.

As I added, "I don't have anything against skin shedders personally." I immediately realized my racial slight and regretted it just as quickly. One gets so used to saying certain words or phrases in select company that you stop bothering to think about it, even in front of strangers. I felt bad.

But before I could apologize, he surprised me by starting to laugh. I braced myself for the physical attack I was positive was going to come next, but before I knew it, he had gone and loosened up on me.

"I haven't heard that one in a while," he said.

I took a slug of my drink, savoring the taste. "I have a million more."

"I have a few myself."

"Really?"

"Oh yeah," he replied. "Let's see…shit sucker."

I countered with, "Fleabait."

"Fangers."

"Leg humpers."

"Veiners."

"Hairballs."

"Wannabes."

"Fuzzy wuzzies."

"Vampers."

Pretty soon, we found ourselves laughing pretty loud. Loud enough that the other patrons were now watching us.

"Anyway," I changed the subject. "The name's Connor." I extended my hand, which he shook.

"Michael."

"So how long have you been howling at the moon, Michael?"

He thought a while. "Four and a half years this February. How long have you been a sun runner?"

I smiled at that. "A few decades."

Michael tapped the tip of his cigarette on the bar before placing the filter between his lips and lighting it.

"That's a bad habit you got there," I said.

"That's the least of my bad habits."

I asked, "What's your story in a nutshell?"

"Sure you wanna hear it?" he asked.

"I wouldn't have asked if I didn't."

He looked away for a moment. I saw a quick trace of regret on his face, but he launched into his story anyway.

"It happened on a hunting trip. It was on me before I knew it. For some reason, it left me alive but pretty chewed up. I healed really fast, which freaked the doctors out, and before I knew it, people I knew started disappearing, only to be found a few days later torn to pieces. I left town before any more people I cared about got killed… or worse. Been on the road ever since."

I gestured toward his jacket pocket. "You mind if I bum one?"

"Why?" he asked, glaring up at me, trying to figure me out. "I can smell cigarettes on you."

"But there's nothing better on earth than a free cigarette," I replied.

"What about dirty habits?" he asked while reaching into his jacket for a cig while grinning from ear to ear. He handed it to me.

"I got a few of those myself," I replied, a smile on my face.

"What's your story, Connor?" Michael asked.

He downed his shot of bourbon and signaled Leonard for another.

I sighed. "It's hard to put my story in a nutshell."

"I got time," he replied.

I lit my cancer stick and launched into my own past.

"For me, it was a girl I met my sophomore year in college, right about the time Ole Tricky Dick left office on his own accord." After a large puff, I went on. "One night, a few buddies and I went to this major party house off campus that we kept hearing about. We'd heard it was the hookup spot. That if you went there, you were bound to get lucky.

"Well, we were young, eager, and horny as hell, so we went and tuned in, turned on, and dropped out. It was the times, what can I say? Then, out of the blue, standing right before me was a hippie goddess on high heels. She had raven hair and ruby lips, and to this day, she's still the most beautiful thing I've ever seen. And once I looked into her eyes, I was a goner. She stole my heart right then and there.

"The next thing I know we're making out, feeling each other up on a couch, and I'm thinking to myself, I'm the luckiest son of a bitch in the world.

"Before I know it, we're leaving the house together, sweet and sordid promises of a wild night of sex floating in the air. Only, as we're walking, she gets this devilish look on her face. She smiles, grabs me by the lapel of my jacket, and literally pulls me into a dark alley…willingly, I might add."

Michael chuckled as he downed another shot of bourbon.

"I'm not boring you, am I?" I asked.

"No," he replied. "Seriously, go on."

"So there we were," I continued. "We're in the alley, in the shadows, and I'm hard as a rock. I mean, I was hard enough to cut diamonds." Another guffaw from my audience of one. "When, from out of nowhere, her face changes. It goes from human to nonhuman like that." I snapped my fingers. "And before I knew it, before I could even scream or piss my pants, that came later, she's latched her teeth onto my neck, and she's drinking me like there's no tomorrow."

I took another drag. Exhaled. "I don't remember much after that, other than I woke up in the alley covered in blood and saw that the sun was about to come up. Let me tell you, until the first time you see smoke rising from your flesh, you don't know what running fast really means."

"So," Michael said, "both of our lives changed dramatically overnight."

I tilted my head. I was reflective for a few moments. "Sometimes, not often, but sometimes, I find myself wishing I would have stayed in the sun that day. But then I quickly remember how much I like myself and laugh it off." I smiled, then took another sip of my drink.

It was getting lukewarm, so I finished it off.

"Did you ever find her again?" Michael asked.

"My raven-haired beauty?" I replied.

Michael nodded affirmatively.

"No. What would be the point? She'd probably just end up being a real bitch anyway."

Michael laughed again. I joined him. I was feeling good. The hog's blood had hit my system just right, and I was feeling a slight buzz.

After a few seconds of silence, I peered around. A few more beings had arrived that I hadn't seen enter.

There was a young-looking vampire couple sitting in a booth. They were obviously in love with one another, holding hands while staring into each other's eyes.

They were sharing a warm glass of blood with two straws, all the while doing that annoying baby talk to each other.

I decided to dub them Joanie and Chachi.

Another being—a short, bulbous, ghoulish-looking, green-skinned demon—plodded its way to the restroom. I was only curious enough to see which door it would enter, and when it went through the one marked His, I turned my attention back to Michael.

"What brought you to this place?" I asked.

"I, uh, sniffed it out," he said. He glanced around the place, locking his gaze on Eva. "First, I sat at a table, but let's just say I wasn't getting any service."

We both sat and watched Eva for a while. With a body like that, it was easy to see why she was such an effective hunter. But right now, she was busy cleaning the table where the trickster demons had been sitting. She looked rather disgusted about something they had done.

"Some vampires are old-fashioned," I said. "Too set in their ways."

I noticed him grin. Then he said, "That reminds me. Do you watch movies?"

"Sometimes. When I'm really bored."

"Well, there's this one called *Underworld*," he stated.

I interjected, "Is that the one with Kevin Costner?" Again, I was being somewhat of a smart-ass.

"No. That's *Waterworld*," he corrected me. He never even picked up on my humor. Oh well. "The one I'm referring to is about vampires versus werewolves."

I raised my eyebrows. I'd seen it. The main vampire chick was hot.

"Any good?" I asked.

"No, like all vampires, it sucked," he replied, making me chuckle. "But in it, a vampire gal and a werewolf guy meet and fall in love, much to the dislike of their respective kinds."

"So it's sorta like Romeo and Juliet?" I asked. Pretty cleverly, I might add.

"Sorta," he replied.

I was getting slightly irked that he wasn't recognizing me for my wry intellect and overall great sense of humor.

"What happens?" I asked.

"She ends up betraying her own kind in order to be with him."

"Interesting," I said and sort of meant it. I only watched that movie to see the main girl get naked. But since she didn't, I pretty much erased the movie out of my mind. Then it occurred to me to have a little more fun with the guy.

I said, "I think the last movie I saw was *Interview with the Vampire*."

Michael shook his head vehemently as he put out yet another cigarette. "Don't even get me started on that one. Tom Cruise?" He rolled his eyes. "Please. A Scientologist who's a bloodsucker. If it wasn't so ironic, it'd be laughable."

"I don't get out to the movies much," I said. "It's hard to be around that many humans." I looked around the bar. "It's kinda like an alcoholic working in a bar or a fat guy going to an all-you-can-eat buffet. Why put yourself through it?"

"To be close to your food supply?" Michael joked.

I was about to retort when I saw the smile disappear from his face.

He quickly turned and faced the entrance to the bar, and I heard a low grumble coming from his throat as his eyes started to glow yellow.

Right then, the doors splintered open with terrific force.

By now, everyone in the bar was watching as three people, two men and a woman, entered.

The two men had their shotguns raised while the woman brandished a handgun. The trio smelled of B.O., booze, and drugs, heavy on the former, and they had the wild-eyed look of those on the edge of reason. Needless to say, they looked as if they meant business.

In any other bar, it would have been a very effective entrance.

The key words here are "any," "other," and "bar."

"Get down on the floor now!" their leader yelled. He had a rough face, very leathery. A lot like old Robert Redford. But only the Sundance Kid could get away with a look like that. Also in this guy's disfavor, he had big pockmarks all over his face from the teen acne that had gone wild during his obviously misspent youth.

It was then that I remembered the feeling I had before entering the bar earlier that night. It wasn't me they had been watching. They had been casing the whole joint. That was why I hadn't felt any sense of personal danger.

The other man was younger than Redford Jr. but more gaunt and sickly looking. At the time, I thought he had features that made him resemble a hawk. He had weird, beady, stern-looking eyes that darted everywhere they looked as if he couldn't control them. He had a crook in his nose that made it seem like a beak. And the divot, or whatever the hell that thing is called in the middle of the upper lip, was really prominent. It was much later when I finally realized whom Hawk-boy reminded me of.

There was an entertaining, yet stupid B movie that came out a few decades ago called *The Beastmaster*. Now, I don't remember the actor's name, but he was also in *V*, a TV show that came out about the same time that was about Earth being invaded by human-eating lizard aliens. This particular actor, whose name I can't remember, was the hero in both of those, and he always struck me as being very weird looking. Well, whatever his name was, I think I found his long-lost son.

Anyway, I'm referring to this weird-looking guy as Hawk-boy because that's what I've always called him when I tell this story, so I'll continue to refer to him that way; even though I've established he looked more like the Beastmaster.

Now that I got that out of the way, the entire time this holdup took place, Hawk-boy was covered in a sheen of sweat so thick, he was constantly wiping it from his face. He showed proof of his rage when, in his haste, he shot into the ceiling with a thunderous boom, thinking somehow he was putting an exclamation on his associate's point.

As the bits and pieces of plaster rained down upon them, I pinpointed this as the exact moment they finally realized their planned entrance had not had the desired effect.

All of us, the bar's regulars (the very word makes me laugh), had not moved at all from our previous places. Most of us were sharing a look of mild amusement at what had transpired. It was almost like we were watching a very entertaining reality show. We wanted to see what would happen next. And who would be the one to do it.

I was putting imaginary money on the ones who weren't human.

"Do y'all wanna get killed?" Redford Jr. asked. "Then do what I said! Get down on the floor!"

I've always been proud of myself for having the particular talent of saying the right thing at just the right time. A well-timed joke can alleviate any tension-filled moment. So it goes without saying, even though I'm saying it, that I felt the time was right to say this to our guests: "Man, you people picked the wrong place."

Leonard, angry because of what Hawk-boy did to his ceiling, glared at the young man who did the damage. The demon's eyes had a furious glow about them. "You're gonna pay for that."

The most strung out of this human Mod Squad, the woman, stepped forward. While once upon a long-ass time ago this woman may have been a beauty, years of drug and alcohol abuse had taken their toll, leaving behind a husk of a woman who'd been ridden hard and put up wet. The veins on her forehead and neck were as prominent as lines on a road map. Most sadly comical of all, her eyes were open so wide, they were literally bulging from their sockets.

To this woman, in her agitated state—jonesing, I've heard it called—Leonard looked like a big, unarmed black guy who was being an obstacle along her path to get what she wanted. She screwed up her courage and aimed her pistol directly at Leonard's face.

"Does it look like we're kidding?" she yelled.

To her surprise, Leonard didn't flinch. Instead, he licked his lips in what could only be called anticipation.

I watched as Michael raised his hands, as if he was about to speak, but Hawk-boy rushed over toward him and slammed the butt of his weapon into Michael's gut. Werewolf or not, it must have hurt, because the blow sent Michael to his knees, gasping for air.

Redford Jr. nodded, and Bug-Eyes produced a plastic garbage bag from her jacket pocket and began to open it.

Redford Jr. reasserted his pseudo-dominance over the room.

"We want the money in the register, and anything of value y'all have on you! Put it all in the bag! Do that, and no one else gets hurt!"

I couldn't help but smile. But Redford Jr. saw me. He wasted no time in walking forward and putting his shotgun right under my chin.

"What's so funny, pretty boy?" he asked.

"You really have no idea where you are, do you?" I replied.

Bug-Eyes was by my side in seconds, slamming the side of her gun against my head. I actually winced from the pain.

"Shut up before you get your head blown off, asshole!"

She had screamed into my ear, which actually hurt more than the impact of the gun.

I felt the side of my head, then looked at my blood-covered fingers.

She had opened me up pretty good. It was amazing what a little adrenaline and drug combo did for someone's strength.

Redford Jr. yelled again, "Put all your valuables in the bag! Don't make me tell y'all again!"

Bug-Eyes walked over to the young couple at the table. But when she held out the bag for them to drop their possessions into it, the young couple merely smiled back at her, revealing their sharp, pointy teeth, and waved their fingers.

Suddenly nervous, Bug-Eyes' head looked like it was on a swivel. She had hardly paid attention to the patrons before now, but as she shifted her protruding eyes from one table to another, a look of creeping horror dawned upon her face.

"These aren't people," she said. It was under her breath, barely audible, but not to me. But then she let out a bloodcurdling, high-pitched scream, which everyone in the place did hear.

Redford Jr. turned in a panic to see what was going on. He saw her running to his side. She immediately latched onto his arm and buried her face into his chest, muffling her panicked sobs.

"What the hell's wrong with you?" Redford Jr. asked, getting angry.

In between sobs, she screamed, "These aren't people!"

"What?" Redford Jr. asked. Now he was angry.

Michael raised his hands to speak again, like some little kid in school. This time, he wasn't punished for it. Instead, Redford Jr. nodded his permission.

Michael straightened himself up and laughed, "She's saying we aren't exactly human."

Redford Jr. looked from hysterical Bug-Eyes hiding her crying face in his coat back to Michael. Now Redford Jr. was starting to appear uneasy. "What the hell does that mean?"

"Just what I said," Michael replied. "Look around. See for yourself."

Redford Jr. did just that. He looked from Michael, to me, then over to Leonard. And that was when it dawned on him.

I could tell just by looking into his eyes.

He had finally seen Leonard the way we all saw him, in all his horned glory.

At that very moment, urine spread across the crotch of Redford Jr.'s pants and ran down his leg leaving a trail. He stumbled back into a table. That's when he saw the young vampire couple behind him.

Joanie and Chachi smiled, baring their sharp fangs. Their features became sinister and animal-like.

Redford Jr. yelled in horror. He tore himself away from his woman, leaving her defenseless. He tried to back away from everyone, but instead he clumsily fell and landed hard on the floor.

Bug-Eyes merely screamed and stood in place, covering her eyes. Maybe she thought by doing this, we would all disappear.

Hawk-boy had his shotgun held out before him. He was moving in quick arcs and circles, trying to keep anyone, or anything, from sneaking up on him.

That was when the restroom door in the back opened. We all turned our heads at the same time and saw the short green demon standing near the restroom. Its mouth was hanging open in surprise because it had walked out of the restroom, not having any idea this was all taking place.

This was a pretty funny moment, if you ask me.

Now fully panicked, Redford Jr. got to his feet. That's when he saw the morose spirit sitting at the table a few feet from where the green demon was standing.

The spirit waved at him. He had a crooked smile upon his face.

Even he was having a good time with this.

Redford Jr. screamed loudly and started running for the door, but he was quickly met by the twin vampire waitresses. They were smiling and giggling, clearly in their element. They both shook an index finger back and forth, as if to suggest to Redford Jr. he wouldn't be going any further.

"Jesus Christ," Redford Jr. said.

Michael stepped forward, trying to be the reasonable man. But before he could speak, Hawk-boy fired his shotgun into Michael's chest.

The force of it blew Michael's body against the bar. He slumped lifeless to the floor, eyes open wide, blood spreading in a pool below him.

Bug-Eyes began screaming again. This was already too much for her to take, and now, I'm afraid, she had totally lost it. Her screaming went from being entertaining, in a macabre sort of way, to just plain annoying. That was when I made my move.

As Bug-Eyes screamed and ran about like a chicken with its head cut off, I ran over to her, grabbed her by the head, and twisted it around. The sound of the bones in her neck breaking was mercifully quick yet loud. There was only silence as her body fell like a sack of potatoes to the floor, landing in an awkward position. The front of her body laid flat upon the floor while her open-mouthed head with her bug eyes faced the ceiling.

Redford Jr. was immediately swarmed by Eva and Ava, who took him to the floor and began feasting on him. He managed to scream a good, long while, but eventually the sounds drifted away.

Don't ask me to explain how, but during the melee, Hawk-boy almost managed to escape out the door. Unfortunately for him, he was caught at the last second by our young vampire couple.

Joanie and Chachi had just enough time to throw the screaming man down upon a table when Leonard's voice thundered across the bar.

"No! He's mine!" Leonard said. "Bring him to me!"

Joanie and Chachi did what they were told. Did they have a choice? They carried Hawk-boy, still screaming, over to the bar and laid him forcefully atop it.

There, they held him down as Leonard towered over him. I smelled a foul stench coming from the man—and it wasn't urine.

I watched in particular glee as Leonard reached under the bar and came up with a steel spigot. He connected it to a long plastic tube. He wasted no time as he jammed the spigot into Hawk-boy's carotid artery.

We all watched hungrily as the man's lifeblood ran through the tube to an awaiting empty keg. It was similar to siphoning gas from a car by using a rubber garden hose.

The unfortunate man screamed until there was hardly any life left in him, which took quite a while. Afterward, Leonard pressed and squeezed the man's body, cracking and breaking many bones in the process, all in an effort to force out every last drop of blood.

It was like he was wringing out a wet rag.

As this was going on, I saw a sight I thought I'd never see. I watched as Eva—dried blood upon her face, neck, and clothes—helped Michael off the floor.

As Michael stood up, he winced in pain, all the time rubbing the area on his chest where he'd been shot. The physical wound had already healed, to the point where it looked like it had never even been there, but the sensation remained. His pellet-shredded, blood-soaked jacket and shirt were now the only physical proof he had ever been shot.

I asked him, "You all right?"

"No," Michael replied, shaking his head in irritation as he fingered his shredded jacket. He was truly disappointed. "This was my favorite jacket."

He sighed but soon noticed Eva standing near him. He appeared pleasantly surprised when she gave him a smile, revealing fresh blood upon her teeth.

Michael surveyed the aftermath. As he reached inside his jacket, he let out an audible groan. He took out a ruined cigarette pack and shook his head in disappointment.

I quickly offered him one of mine.

"Thanks for the free one," he said.

As I lit his cigarette for him, he raised his eyebrows in a funny way.

"What'd I miss?" he asked.

We shared another good laugh.

Leonard shouted over all of us, "Who wants some fresh blood on tap? On the house!"

Cheers went up all around the bar, and I could almost swear that I heard Leonard laugh.

Don't hold me to that. I said almost.

Anyway, as we bellied up to the bar, I noticed Michael was still fiddling with his jacket.

"You can always buy a new one," I stated.

"But I really liked this one."

I could only smile as I patted him on the back.

When our glasses were full—ours with blood and Michael's with bourbon—we all made a toast to the night, to the bar, to old friends, and to new.

Later on, I made my leave. I would like to say I'd had my fill of fun and drink, but that wasn't the case. I'd always had a problem being around too much happiness. It made me nervous. Even when I was human, whenever things were going well, I was the one waiting for the other shoe to drop. Waiting for sorrow or misery to kick down the door and make its presence felt. But tonight, I had merely gotten bored watching Michael and Eva dance to the same damn Cyndi

Lauper song over and over again. "Time After Time" will forever be ingrained in my memory banks until the day I decide to snuff myself out. But considering how much I really like the pleasure of my own company, hopefully that will be a long time from now.

As I left, humming that damn song, content enough with my life as it was and the friends I had made, I thought to myself, *It was a good night at Leonard's.*

I SUSPECT

April 20

I'm starting to think that my new next-door neighbor is not what he seems.

Why do I think this?

Maybe it has something to do with the fact that sometimes when I'm up in the middle of the night, I see him standing naked in his backyard staring up at the moon. And not just any run-of-the mill nights, mind you. Nights with full moons.

He's been doing this for the past few months—since February of this year, as I recall.

You may ask, why am I just bringing this up now near the end of April?

Well, it's very simple.

My curiosity began to unfold on April 7.

You see, on the morning of that day, while reading the local paper, I came across an interesting article in the local section. A section I rarely read due to my being a sports and comics man. Yet somehow, I managed to spot it.

It was a small article, but the story it told was huge.

It had to do with a woman's body that had been found in a vacant field on the west side of town.

The article explained how the corpse of the unidentified woman was found by an old man walking around collecting aluminum cans.

The lot where her body was found is notorious for being a nightly hangout for kids to drink and get laid without the worry of being hassled by cops.

It's also a virtual gold mine in beer cans for collectors the following mornings. I guess this old man knew that, and that's why he went there. Only while collecting his aluminum mother lode, he found far more than he bargained for.

When questioned, he told the police that when he came across the body, he immediately called the authorities. The police, in all their infinite wisdom, were positive the woman had met with foul play.

They admitted to the press that they had no leads and no suspects at that time but planned a full-scale investigation.

Anyway, the related article I found and read yesterday appeared to continue that story. The county coroner had identified the woman through her dental records.

She was Nicole Tanner, twenty-six, of Odessa. She had been reported missing on the morning of April 5. Her friends told the police that she had left for work in her car the night before and that no one had seen her since.

She worked at one of the local nightclubs as a waitress but had failed to make it there. Her car was found a few blocks from the club a couple of days later, but there was no trace of her nor her belongings anywhere near it.

The reason I'm bringing this case up is because the night she disappeared also happened to be the night of a full moon.

I found this out when I checked my calendar with the lunar dates printed on it. And I did that because of my neighbor. You see, I have a feeling he has something to do with the murders. After all, who else stands naked in their backyard and stares at the full moon?

And on the very same night that a woman had been murdered?

You may be thinking that I have an overactive imagination, and you very well may be correct, but I honestly feel it in my gut that I'm right about this.

You may also ask what kind of guy watches his neighbor while he stands naked in his backyard staring up at the full moon?

To that, I say this: I've been having trouble sleeping lately.

Insomnia runs in my family. The doctors can't do anything for me. And believe me, I've tried everything. Every cure imaginable. From warm milk—yuck!—to honey and coffee.

I've come to the conclusion that I might as well face it—a good night's sleep is just not in the cards for me.

But I'm rambling again. Back to my neighbor.

I live alone in my modest two-story house on Oleander Street.

My wife left me a few months ago for another man. It still hurts, but I'm finding ways to move on. My friends try to set me up on dates every now and then, but they never really work out.

It's too soon, I think.

Maybe my divorce has something to do with my not sleeping well. Not only is my ex wanting to get alimony from me—and she's the one who cheated on me!—but she also took my sleep with her.

Sorry.

I should stop talking about her because talking about her makes me angry. It's still a fresh wound. But I promise from here on out, I'll try my best to stop.

Though do keep in mind, no one's perfect.

Anyway, late at night, while I'm wide awake, I sometimes walk around my house, especially when there's nothing good on TV.

Hint: all the time!

Well, on the full moon night of February 4 (lunar calendar, remember?), I was drinking warm milk (yuck!) and looking out my bedroom window when I happened to see my new neighbor doing his naked thing.

Needless to say, it caught my attention. And to avoid being seen, I hid in the shadows behind my curtain. And from my hiding spot, I saw him just standing there, naked as a jaybird, staring up at the full moon.

The next month on March 5, the same thing. Another naked night with a full moon.

And the last time I saw him doing it was on April 4.

Anyway, as soon as I read the article about this dead woman found on April 7, and the follow-up article yesterday giving her identity, I decided I'm going to go look up old newspaper articles on the internet. Maybe I'll find more articles on dead women surfacing in other abandoned areas around town. Dead women that, so far, no one else has connected.

Maybe, just maybe, I'll reveal the pattern of a serial killer. Maybe my naked, moon-loving next-door neighbor is that serial killer. You never know.

Be writing again tomorrow.

See ya!

*****

April 21

I did as I said I was going to do. I did some internet sleuthing and turned up some pretty bizarre stuff.

In the February 9 online edition of the local paper, I came across an article similar to the one I found a few days ago. It read that the police had found another woman's mutilated body stuffed inside a fifty-gallon drum at an abandoned oil-drilling site. It also said they had no leads and no suspects.

Big surprise there.

I went through a few more of the online editions and found an even smaller article.

That one said the county coroner had identified the dead woman as twenty-one-year-old Melinda Fox, a stripper at a local topless club. She'd been missing since she failed to show up for work on the night of February 4.

On my calendar, I can see that night was a night with, you guessed it, a full moon. And, again, this happened to be a night my neighbor did his nude thing.

With a lot of adrenaline, I kept searching. My eyes were really tired, but I had to go through with it.

On March 6, another body was found floating facedown in our local pond called Buffalo Wallow. The authorities didn't release any more information other than to say it was a suspected prostitute.

I skimmed further.

On March 19, another article. This woman had been identified as Maria Carrubio, thirty-two, suspected prostitute and drug addict.

She had last been seen on the morning of March 4. The night before, she had been arrested by undercover vice cops for prostitution. She was released the following morning and was never seen again.

According to my trusty lunar calendar, the night of the full moon was March 5. Well within that time frame.

I'm hot now. I've found new energy. I've linked three bodies together to the same killer. At least, I think I have. If so, I'm the only one who has. The police haven't, that's for sure.

Then again, maybe they have and just aren't announcing to the public that a serial killer is in our midst. Maybe because it might start a citywide panic. Maybe keeping it quiet is the smart thing to do. Maybe I'm wrong about the intelligence level of the local boys in blue.

But even if they do have knowledge of a local serial killer, I still know something they don't. I believe very strongly that my neighbor has something to do with all this.

I think I'll spend tomorrow getting some information on him.

Even if that means snooping around his house when he leaves for work.

Yeah, I know. It sounds dangerous and crazy, but I feel like it's my civic duty.

May God be with me.

*****

April 22

Well, I did it!

It's now 8:00 p.m. I did something tonight, and I don't know how I should be feeling right now. Needless to say, I was right about my next-door neighbor.

He's definitely *the* guy!

His name is Greg Hanley. A weird name for a serial killer, now that I think about it. He lives there alone and works at a big accounting firm downtown, so he's gone most of the day.

This morning, I called in sick to work. They didn't care. They don't like me much anyway. They hate anyone smarter than them.

I watched and waited for my neighbor to leave. He drives a dark blue Lexus, which is a nice car if you can afford it.

I can't. Not on my salary. Working where I work doesn't link you with the Trumps and the other billionaires of the world.

I sipped my coffee and waited. He finally came out of his house in his charcoal three-piece suit and looked around warily. Like he'd been doing something he shouldn't have been doing. He then got into his car and took off.

I decided to wait another couple of hours just to make sure he was really gone. Then, around eleven, I got dressed in blue jeans and a nice T-shirt and stepped out the back door. As I did so, I slipped on a pair of surgical gloves I had bought a long time ago.

I looked over his fence and into his backyard. I didn't see any dogs, so I scaled it. No sooner was I in his yard than I realized what I was really doing—breaking and entering. The thought hit me like an anvil, like in one of those old cartoons I watched as a kid. But I didn't feel guilty. As a matter of fact, I felt good. Breaking the law was kind of fun.

I was now officially a criminal. But I felt absolutely no remorse at all.

I wonder if that's how old Greg feels after killing someone.

I walked through his yard toward his sliding-glass doors.

I tried to open them, but they were locked. I learned a trick or two as a young man about sneaking into my house after curfew. I opened my wallet, pulled out my credit card, and used it to jiggle the lever inside the jamb of one of the doors. After a few seconds, I was inside.

His house was very neat and orderly, the same as mine. He had very nice furniture and some paintings I recognized. They had to be prints; there was no way they were originals. If they were, that would mean this guy's a millionaire. Then again, that would explain the Lexus.

And it may only be amazing to me, but his white shag carpet was pristine. Not a single spot on it. That made me guess that he never brought his victims there. Murder might mess up the place.

By looking around his house, it was easy to realize he's a neat freak, just like me. Everything had some kind of pattern to it. The towels in his bathroom were the same color and uniformly hung on the towel rack. His kitchen and bathrooms were spotless. I could even smell potpourri.

Now I ask you: what sane guy has potpourri in his house if he lives by himself? And talk about weird. Even his CD collection was in alphabetical order, for Pete's sake.

I was even more amazed by his bedroom. The bed was covered with high-thread-count satin sheets. His closet was filled with expensive suits and clothing, and its door was beset with a full-length mirror. He even had a shoe rack that would make Kim Kardashian proud.

This guy was certainly vain.

I looked through the closet first, somehow figuring he'd left some kind of evidence in there. I found nothing.

Then I moved to his bed. I searched under it but found nothing.

I moved toward his dresser drawer. And I should've known in advance that what I was looking for was there. After all, it's where I'd keep whatever evidence I wanted to hide.

He had his in an old wooden cigar box.

As I picked it up, I took notice of my trembling hands. It wasn't nervousness making them shake, like one would think in a situation like that. It was an excitement I could barely contain.

Even so, I didn't open the box right away. Instead, I laid it upon the bed and stared at it for a long moment or two. Though it beckoned me, calling on me countless times to open it, I stood my ground. But the longer I stood there, taking in the sight of that box, another voice started calling to me. An unmistakable voice. One I'd heard quite a few times in my life.

It was my fear.

I'd never faced my fears, really. So I didn't know them very well.

In some ways, that's a good thing, but in some cases, it's bad. Like that very moment.

I mean, no scaredy-cat would ever break into a maniac's house to snoop around. Maybe because of that reasoning, scared people lived longer lives.

But I digress.

Now, I've always been a very realistic guy who found a reason for everything. Even as a kid, I was never afraid of the dark. I knew it was exactly the same as it was in the daytime. There were no monsters hiding under the bed or in the closet. There was only me and whatever room I was in.

However, I know that monsters exist. But my monsters were very human. I didn't believe in ghouls, goblins, or vampires. No. No way. My monster was my dad. He drank a lot and sometimes when he got angry…

Well, you probably don't want to hear about that. Nor do I want to rehash it. I was there. I went through it. And I really don't want to talk about it. It's all in the past.

Where was I? Oh yeah.

I was staring at the cigar box. Strangely enough, it looked exactly like the cigar boxes my dad used to get his cigars from. It was a stained-wood pine box with a wood etching of three men, who all looked like Ben Franklin.

I used to sit and stare at my dad's cigar box for hours. I'd add voices to the pictures of the men dressed in patriotic American forefather suits.

I talked to myself a lot back then. Basically, it's what I'm doing now. Except I'm writing it all down in this journal. That doesn't make me crazy, does it? LOL!

I didn't think so.

Anyway, I eventually opened the box. And you know what I found? Well, of course not. I haven't told you yet. You must think I'm a silly goose. Well, without further ado, here's what I found—a human finger.

No doubt about it, I found a human finger. A lady's finger, to be precise. All slender and moist and chopped off at the second knuckle.

A dark patch of blood had coalesced at the stump, and it lay wrapped within a gauze pad.

I threw up when I saw it, though I somehow managed to make it to his pristine toilet before I did. Thank God!

If I had thrown up anywhere else, especially on his perfect white shag carpet, he would have known someone was there. And in his sick, demented mind, he would have reasoned it was a nosy neighbor.

And somewhere in his dark thoughts, he'd know it was me.

You know why I think that? I'll tell you why.

One night, on one of those naked full moon escapades of his, while I was looking out at him standing in his yard, for some reason, he turned and looked up at my bedroom window.

At the time, I wasn't even bothering to hide myself behind my curtain, as I had usually done. I guess I'd gotten pretty comfortable spying on him.

Well, anyway, he had turned and looked up at my window, and I backed up as quickly as I could into the shadows of my room. But something in me told me he saw me. And that something was my fear.

As I said, I've never been scared a lot in my life, but this guy... this guy really scared me. And I guess it's because of my fear that I did what I did.

By finding out all I could about him and getting enough evidence on him to turn him in, I can get rid of him. And by sending him away to prison, or, by God, to the electric chair, I'll get rid of my fear.

After throwing up into his toilet, I went back over and wrapped the severed finger back inside its gauze-hiding place. I then closed the cigar box because I didn't like the feeling it gave me. I couldn't stand looking at that thing any longer, so I swept the box up carefully into my hands and placed it back where I found it.

I tried to put it back exactly where it had been, but maybe it was off by a few millimeters because I was in a hurry. I hope he doesn't notice.

I then went back and checked the toilet. I found some leftover splotches of my vomit, and I quickly cleaned it up with some toilet paper, threw the refuse in, and flushed the toilet again.

Convinced I had not left any evidence of myself behind, I started to leave. I definitely felt I had enough evidence to turn him in.

I thought at the time that a discreet phone call made from a pay phone on the other side of town would be enough cause for them to search my dear neighbor's house. I'd disguise my voice and tell them to look in the dresser drawer for a cigar box. In it, they'd find what they were looking for. And when they'd ask me for a name, I'd simply hang up. That would be enough cause for them to search my dear neighbor's house, I think.

But my plan revealed a sudden hitch. That's because I heard the sound of an engine idling in the driveway.

His driveway.

I ran to his bedroom window and peeked through his Venetian blinds. Panic ripped through me like I'd never felt before. Not even when my dad… Well, let's just say that never in my life had I been so scared and out of control.

There in the driveway was Mr. Hanley. He wasn't wearing his jacket; he had it wrapped over his arm. He stepped out of his Lexus and walked around to the passenger door. He opened it and a rather shapely female leg stepped out onto the cement of the driveway.

My eyes bulged, and I backed away from the window and started pacing like a nervous Nellie. I remember saying to myself, "Oh my goodness, another victim. You have to do something." But I also knew that I couldn't.

I heard the couple approaching the front door, and I heard him unlocking it and opening it. I quickly ran into his closet, but there was nowhere to hide in there because it was too lighted and spacious.

Then I remembered.

When I was little and had to hide from my dad, I used to hide under my bed. He could never find me there. I was too good at hiding.

Too good at blending into the dark.

I still am.

I climbed underneath the bed and closed my eyes, that way he couldn't see the whites of my eyes if he happened to look there.

I heard them enter, heard the woman's laugh, heard him talking, and then I heard him say out loud, "What the hell? I thought I closed that."

I then remembered that I had left a sliding glass door open.

An idiotic, stupid thing to do. But then again, breaking into a serial killer's house looking for evidence of his crimes is a stupid thing to do.

I felt so foolish at that moment, and that made my vomit rise up in my throat. I felt the rancid acid entering my mouth, but somehow I held it in and refused to let it out even though it was burning my throat. I swallowed the putrid stuff, closed my eyes, laid my head on the floor, and tried to calm myself down and concentrate on not coughing.

That's when I heard footsteps coming up the stairs. I tried to freeze myself in place, but the muscles in my back and thighs began to quiver, jump, and shake.

Then I heard him entering the room.

Against my better judgment, I opened my eyes and saw him from the shins down as he stood still and looked around. I heard him say, "Maybe I did leave it open." But I guess just to make sure, he began to search the room.

I saw the backs of his shoes as he entered his closet and looked around. I then heard him start to hum as he moved toward his dresser.

I closed my eyes and prayed that he wouldn't look in the drawer or under the bed, and that's when God saved me.

Or rather, the woman did.

She spoke from the entrance to the bedroom. "There's no one here but us chickens."

She laughed, and he laughed with her.

I saw her remove her bright-red high-heeled shoes. The kind that turned me on like nobody's business. I saw him cross the room toward her, and their feet faced one another. They must have been kissing because her left foot began to rub the inside of his right calf.

He moaned that it "felt good" and for her to "go a little higher."

She giggled as they walked over toward the bed.

The bed sagged as both of them laid atop it. The middle part of the bed touched my face as I heard them rustling above me.

I saw a red blouse as it cascaded to the floor, followed quickly by a bra. His white shirt then floated down on top of her clothes, and her panties quickly joined them. Their breathing became raspier as the mattress began to rock up and down, at times pushing my head down with it. Their moans began to get louder as their motion became faster.

She began to say words that I won't repeat here, but suffice it to say, my mother should have been right there to wash her mouth out with soap.

My mother had names for women like this. She called them "dirty women."

I remember once when Momma caught fourteen-year-old me in my room with a girl two years younger named Beth. She was a sweet little blonde who one day took off her clothes and told me to get naked on top of her. She instructed me on what to do next, and before I knew it, I was inside her. I did my business really quick—too quick—but not fast enough for my mom not to catch us.

The sight of our naked, cavorting young bodies unleashed Mother's mighty wrath. I soon felt a broomstick on my back and head as she began beating the tar out of both of us, all the while yelling, "You dirty children! Dirty children! The devil's work is what you're doing! Dirty children! Dirty children go to hell."

I remember her nearly chasing Beth all the way back to her home with that broomstick. And when she got back to our home, she used the broomstick on me again.

Needless to say, when my dad got home, she told him what I had done. And then he did his business to me too…but I really don't want to talk about that.

Anyway, somehow, while I was waiting for my neighbor to finish his business with the woman in his bedroom, I managed to fall asleep under his bed. I didn't plan on it. It just happened.

So when I snapped awake sometime later, I panicked and looked around.

I quickly realized I wasn't hearing anything. And all I could tell by looking around at the darkened room was that the sun was going down outside. I listened a little while longer, and when I was sure no one was in the room, I slid out from under the bed.

My arms and legs had fallen asleep, so it was rough going trying to slide out, but I finally managed. And I quietly and eventually raised myself up and looked around.

I was right. There was no one else in the bedroom.

I stood up, and after a good minute of getting the circulation flowing again, I walked out of the bedroom. I hesitated at the foot of the stairs and looked around at the living room below. I walked back into the bedroom and peered through the window blinds. What I saw made me sigh happily.

His Lexus was gone.

As I looked around the bedroom, I noticed there wasn't any blood. So I assumed he hadn't killed her there.

Something else I should have remembered then, but somehow didn't, was the fact he only killed people on nights with full moons.

And the next full moon was a little more than two weeks away.

But at that moment, I was simply eager to get out of that house.

Before I did, though, I thought of something else. I gasped and ran over to the dresser. I remember thinking at the time: What if he found the cigar box? But my fears abated when I found that the cigar box was still in the drawer.

I didn't want to, but I opened it up and hesitantly felt the gauze pad.

Yep, the finger was still there.

I gathered my wits and ran from that house as fast as I could ever remember running before. Even from my dad. Somehow, despite my haste, I remembered to shut the sliding glass door behind me as I left.

I soon scaled his fence in record time and found myself in the safety of my own home. I quickly got my car keys, left my house, and got into my car, which is a gold VW Beetle. I'd had it for close to ten years, and it was still in good condition.

I rode across town and parked at a 7-Eleven. I got out, ran up to the phone booth, and placed that 911 call. I even remembered to disguise my voice. I tried to sound like McGruff the Crime Dog.

Taking my bite out of crime, so to speak.

Maybe the cops got my joke.

Anyway, after that, I went to work to keep up appearances and waited patiently for certain events to happen. But that was a couple of hours ago.

Since then, what seems like the entire police department and all the local news crews have been swarming Mr. Hanley's house.

I watched one forensic specialist exit the house with a package wrapped in a plastic baggy. It was the cigar box. The one with Ms. Carrubio's finger in it.

Now the more astute of you might be asking yourself how I knew whose finger it was. Well, I'll tell you, you silly geese. I should know it was her finger because I'm the one who cut the damn thing off. I did it after I gutted her open like the dirty, little whore she was. She was doing the devil's work, and she needed to be stopped.

But I don't want to talk about her right now. Because it's my journal, and I'll write what I want to. Lol!

Anyway, here I am next door to my house at the crime scene. Asking neighbors questions. My neighbors, obviously. Because that's what detectives do. They ask questions.

Surprised? Well, I'm not one to usually toot my own horn, but considering how successfully my plan just turned out, I deserve to boast.

As my fellow officers, techs, and I canvassed my neighbor's house for more evidence, I kept waiting for someone worth their salt to dig up more incriminating evidence in my neighbor's backyard.

Something I saw to previously over the past few nights.

I guess I must have forgotten to write that part down too. I'm just full of secrets, aren't I?

And while I'm now being truthful, I also planted my dad's cigar box in Mr. Hanley's drawer.

Oops! My bad. I hope you forgive me for lying to you.

You see, I know that lying is the devil's work too, but I'm sure God will forgive me for it. After all, I am doing my mission for him.

I'll be moving in a couple of days. I think it's for the best. I put in my notice at work and will be transferred to another police department in another state soon.

Where, you might ask?

Sorry. That's a secret. I have to protect myself, you know.

Anyway, the reasons why I'm moving should be obvious. It won't do me much good to continue doing what I'm doing so close to where all this went down.

Besides, I'm already tired of the news crews and my fellow coworkers' questions.

"How does it make you feel knowing that an alleged serial killer lived next door to you? Right under your nose the whole time?"

Some detective you are, Detective Fallows, they're probably thinking with plenty of derision and a few scoffs.

"Did you ever see anything out of the ordinary over there, Detective?"

Obviously not, they'd think. *It's why Hanley went undetected so long.*

But that's okay if they think that way about me. Because the joke is really on them, isn't it?

Those arrogant, stupid dirty birds. Talk about dense.

But I'll put up with the false conjecture. I'll fall upon my own sword, so to speak. Self-preservation is way more important than ego.

It's something I can live with.

I also have to fight the urge to tell them all about the times I saw my neighbor naked in his backyard, staring up at the full moon, but that would be another lie.

It was me doing that.

And what a man does in the privacy of his own backyard should stay private.

Well, I'm gonna go now. I'm really tired, and I've had a very busy day. I think I'll take a vacation from writing for a while. I have to save all my energy for my upcoming move and job transfer. Both have to happen well before the next full moon.

I can't wait to pick out a good candidate. One who's truly worthy.

One who would never expect what's coming for her.

They never do.

It will all come as a sweet, sudden vicious surprise.

Well, I'd better get some sleep. Good night. Talk to ya soon!

*****

May 5

Tonight was almost perfect. Too good to be true. She came to me so easily. Taking her was like taking candy from a baby—only she was a dirty baby. Dirty! Dirty! Dirty! But I cleaned her just like Daddy. Daddy's little boy, he called me. I stopped her from doing the devil's work. Mommy would be so proud.

This hotel room is okay. It'll have to do until I find a house. That is the only place I can really do my work. Here, you have to be careful no one sees you. In a house, no one cares. You can make all the noise you want, but like I said, it'll do for now.

I will stop writing now. I have to go talk to the man on the moon. He's my friend! He likes talking to me, and I like talking to him even though he doesn't wear clothes. All the people on the moon don't wear clothes, so I don't wear clothes. He likes me better that way. And you know what? I like myself better that way too. I'll say hello to him for you. What? Oh, you silly geese, of course, he likes you. He likes everyone. And soon, I'll show all of you just how much. But you'll have to wait until later. Right now, he only talks to me.

Bye-bye for now!

GHOST HUNT

I can't believe I'm doing this, Scott thought.

One moment, he was on campus in Lubbock in a cramped dorm room that smelled like worn socks and ramen. The next, he was back in his hometown two hours away and freezing his balls off.

It was a shade past one in the morning in Creed, a small town off the beaten path southwest of the petroleum-rich cities of Midland and Odessa in West Texas, which were already off the beaten path to begin with.

A bitter October wind cut through his jacket as if it were made of crepe paper. Shivering, Scott stomped his feet and opened and closed a glove-free fist a few times to get the circulation to his extremities going. His other hand cradled a camcorder high and tight against his chest.

He shook his head and cursed at himself for being where he was.

Back in the dorm room, he'd been studying and doing his best not to think about his roommate, Ty, and Ty's best-bro buddy, Jimmy.

They'd spent the past few hours giving him the silent treatment. This was no different from most of the past week when he might as well have been invisible on his side of the room.

Ty and Jimmy were drinking beer and watching *Ghost Adventures*, a paranormal reality series about a gang of bros who travel across America investigating haunted places. Every time one of the guys on the show said "bro" or "dude," Ty and Jimmy drank, so they were well on their way to getting pretty hammered.

Ty was eighteen years old and invincible. He had a cocksure, devil-may-care attitude that made him exciting to be around most of the time. He was one of those guys always willing and ready to have fun. If there was a party going on, an activity taking place, or a game being played, chances are Ty was there.

But as Scott soon learned, being around Ty for extended periods of time grew tiring.

When Ty wasn't fun, he was moody and distant. Normal Ty never shut up, while moody Ty hardly ever spoke. The majority of the time, he was easygoing and affable. The other times, not so much.

Despite all that, Ty wasn't what one would call an asshole. One on one, he was capable of being a good friend. A good listener. Good at giving advice. Good at not being completely annoying.

Jimmy, on the other hand, was a year older than Ty and Scott and was currently repeating his freshman year at a different college than his last one. He was, to put it mildly, too much. No matter the occasion, you could always count on Jimmy to wear out his welcome fast.

Such as the day Scott first met him.

Scott had spent another boring hour in English 101. He had returned to the dorm hall yawning and considering a nap. But as he reached the top of the stairs to his dorm floor, he was met with loud music and chatter coming from the end of the hall.

Scott slowed his walk and stared straight ahead. A sense of dread rose within him as he saw a too-familiar open door at the end of the hall. Once he saw a few students streaming in and out of the room, he could no longer deny to himself that it was his and Ty's.

Reflux reached the back of his throat. His heart began jackhammering in his chest. Blood rushed to his face, and sweat began to form on his forehead. All he could think about was how much he dreaded entering rooms full of strangers. There was nothing he disliked more. The way people would look at him, judge him, and see right through him. He knew it was ridiculous, but he couldn't help but feel that in moments like that, everyone knew all his inner thoughts and feelings.

As he neared the room, he wiped his brow and summoned up what internal strength he could muster. He slinked into his own room carrying his books before him like a weak shield. He glanced around, and to his immediate relief, he found Ty.

His roommate was hanging out with a handful of other guys in a beer-chugging contest. A goading, chanting coed crowd cheered when Ty won that round and crushed the can against the side of his head and roared like a lion.

Scott's eyes darted toward his side of the room. There were people he didn't know sitting on his bed, and lo and behold, they were going through his things.

Scott's face turned beet red. His anger level rose. He hustled over and slammed a drawer shut, just in time to keep a nosy coed from seeing his boxers.

The pretty but vacant-faced coed acted as if he had nearly assaulted her and walked away from him in a huff.

A frustrated Scott made eye contact with Ty, who seemed ecstatic to see him.

"You made it!" Ty yelled from less than six feet away.

He was either too drunk to care about Scott's state of mind, or he didn't care. Probably a mixture of both.

Scott tried everything to calm himself down at that moment, but it was no use. "What the hell is going on?"

That's when Scott first came face-to-face with Jimmy. And from that point forward, Jimmy took special delight in rubbing Scott the wrong way.

"It's a party, bro," Jimmy replied. "What does it look like?"

Scott instantly did not like him, not the least little bit. However, he was intimidated because Jimmy outmuscled him by a good twenty pounds. Yet despite this, for one of the few times in his life, Scott squared shoulders with someone.

"I live here," Scott declared. "Who the fuck are you?"

Jimmy, unfazed, squared up right back.

Scott had just enough time to regret his decision to confront Jimmy before Ty slipped between them. Whether he knew there was about to be a one-sided fight or not, Ty instantly put things at ease.

"Jimmy," Ty said, squeezing Jimmy's shoulder. "This is my roommate, Scott."

Jimmy glanced at Scott from head to foot. He had a smarmy look on his face that said everything for him, despite the words that came out of his mouth. "No harm, no foul, bro."

Jimmy extended his hand while keeping his beady eyes locked on Scott's.

Scott peered from Ty's drunk, grinning face to Jimmy, who was barely hiding his disdain. Not wanting to be a dreaded party pooper and bad roommate, he reluctantly shook hands.

"No problem," Scott replied.

Ty laughed and clapped both of them on the back.

"Now that we're all friends, let's drink."

As Jimmy and Ty whooped and slapped high fives, Scott gave a look of protest that was immediately dismissed by a Ty-offered beer.

"C'mon," Ty said with a wide, perfect smile. "One beer won't kill ya."

Scott smirked, his anxiety somewhat forgotten, and finally took the beer. He watched as Ty and Jimmy both opened one of their own and counted down from three.

Before he knew it, Scott was chugging, and the rest of the party was a distant blur.

Upon reflection, Scott reasoned that day hadn't been all that bad. He did end up having fun. But one thing he did know for sure from that day—he did not care at all for Jimmy.

And the feeling, he soon learned, was mutual.

Yet Ty, whether he knew or cared about his two friends' disdain for each other or not, corralled them all together as if they were the next coming of the Three Musketeers. From the beginning of the semester, the trio did almost everything together. With Ty as their ringleader, most of those nights were fun and exciting, despite a lot of side-eyeing and insults between Scott and Jimmy while Ty wasn't paying attention.

But now it was a week before Halloween, and Scott, no matter how much he liked Ty, had seen a drastic change in his roommate.

While Scott could blame Jimmy for the dark shift in his personality, that was letting Ty off easy. Truth be told, Ty was becoming meaner and even less responsible than he already had been all on his own.

Where they once were a trio, the past couple of weeks saw the group downgraded to a duo, with poor Scott on the outside looking in. This was something that bothered him more than he'd care to admit.

But now, a reckless comment made in desperation had brought them to where they were tonight. Freezing in the cold while standing in an overgrown, weed-filled front yard before the Mahoney house.

With its asymmetrical shape and steep, pointed roof that made it look like a medieval tower, the rundown two-story Gothic-style Victorian structure loomed before the trio like the stuff of nightmares.

The reckless comment in question happened while Ty and Jimmy were watching the paranormal show. And it was all because Scott couldn't keep his mind on studying. No matter how hard he tried to hunker down and comprehend what he was reading, he couldn't stop thinking about how tired he was of being shunned by his roommate.

While tapping his pen against the pages, he glanced over his shoulder at them. He saw them laughing and drinking and having a good time despite him, and his jealousy got the best of him.

At the same time, something that had been said on the TV show caught his ear. He heard the lead ghost bro say that the paranormal team was about to investigate one of the most haunted places in America. And before Scott could stop himself, he had opened his envious mouth.

"I know a haunted place," he said. Not in a boastful way. Just very matter-of-fact.

"What are you talkin' about?" Jimmy asked.

Scott finally had their attention. It felt good. "I said, I know a haunted place."

Ty grinned at Scott. "For real?"

"For real," Scott replied while trying not to blink.

"You're fulla shit," Jimmy said, shaking his head and turning back to the TV.

But to his chagrin, Scott had Ty's full attention.

"Where?" Ty asked as Jimmy glanced at him, confused.

"My hometown," Scott replied.

"No bullshit?"

"No bullshit."

Jimmy couldn't believe what he was hearing. "It's total bullshit."

Scott turned around in his chair to fully face them. "It's the honest-to-God truth."

Ty asked, "How do you know it's haunted?"

"I mean," Scott replied. "I don't know myself—"

"Of course he doesn't," Jimmy interrupted. "I told ya. It's bullshit."

Scott continued, "But I do know a guy whose uncle went in there on a dare back when he was in high school."

"And let me guess," Jimmy interrupted again, "he saw a scary ghost." Only he pronounced scary like a little kid with a lisp.

In a confident manner, Scott replied, "He saw a woman in a red dress."

"Who was she?" Ty asked, now on the edge of his seat.

Scott shrugged and shook his head. "All my friend told me was his uncle said one second she was there, and the next, she was gone."

"Was she hot?" Jimmy asked, before breaking into a hearty laugh.

Scott did his best to ignore him. He kept eye contact with Ty.

"I'm just telling you what I heard."

Ty asked, "Do you really believe it's haunted?"

"Like I said, I don't know for sure," Scott replied before smiling. "But why don't we find out?"

When a huge grin broke out on Ty's face, Scott immediately regretted saying anything. He knew what was going to happen before his heart sped up, and his poor stomach began churning.

"Tell me everything you know about it," Ty said.

*****

Much to his dread, Scott peered up at the house, dreading what he might see staring back from its windows. What he noticed were broken windows caused by hundreds of rocks thrown at the house over the decades, whether from dares, hatred, or fear—or all three.

He also saw paint coming off the walls in large strips.

A cold wind picked up, causing a loose drainpipe on the side of the house to begin vibrating and humming, adding to the spooky ambience.

"You guys ready?" Ty asked, his voice breaking through Scott's thoughts like lightning.

"Hell yeah!" Jimmy replied. "Let's do this shit!"

As Jimmy peered through the windows into the inky darkness within, Ty approached Scott and talked low. "How about you?"

Scott tried his best to swallow his fear and failed.

Ty, sensing his friend's discomfort, squeezed his shoulder. "It'll be all right."

Scott nodded, feeling slightly better. But once his eyes took in the Mahoney house again, looking like a macabre dollhouse out of an insane little girl's dream, stomach acid rose into his throat.

Thankfully, Ty had turned away before Scott swallowed and coughed to clear his throat.

Unfortunately, Jimmy saw it all registered on his face.

"What a chickenshit," Jimmy said before laughing and turning back to peer through the windows of the house again.

Ty walked over and stopped before the steps leading up to the one-story front porch before turning around to face Scott.

"Okay, dude," Ty said. "I'll start out here and say some cool shit. Then I'll back up onto the porch toward the door while saying some more shit. And all you gotta do is keep as much of the house in the shot while centered on me as you can. I want this thing to dwarf me. And I want it to scare the shit outa whoever's watching."

"I don't think you'll have a problem with that," Scott replied under his breath.

"What do I do?" Jimmy asked, walking toward Ty while grabbing his crotch. "Stand here with my dick out?"

Ty smiled. "I don't think Scott's camcorder has a microscopic lens, so don't worry, dude."

"Burn!" Scott exclaimed, laughing.

Jimmy glared at Scott with a grimace, causing Scott to stifle his grin and look back down at his camcorder.

Jimmy's sneer turned into a fake smile for Ty's benefit, then he laughed off his friend's joke.

As Scott turned on the camcorder and checked the audio levels, he opened the viewscreen and aimed it at Ty and Jimmy.

While Ty was checking out the Mahoney house, lost in thought, Jimmy glared at the lens and flipped Scott the bird.

All Scott could do was shake his head and mumble under his breath.

"What'd you say?" Jimmy asked, anger flaring as he stepped toward him.

Ty, snapping out of his thoughts, stepped between the two and held Jimmy back.

"Hey, cool it," Ty barked, warding him away from Scott with a hand on his chest.

Jimmy started to walk off but abruptly turned toward Ty. "What are we even doing here?"

He pointed at Scott while facing Ty.

"You know we're wasting our time, right? This place isn't even haunted, so we're not gonna see shit."

"It's all in good fun, bro," Ty replied, now with both hands upon Jimmy's shoulders.

"Fun? You call this fun? Freezing our balls off in the middle of Hicksville, USA? This is fun to you?"

Scott, tired of Jimmy and his shit, shouted out, "You didn't have to come!"

"Hey, fuck you, man!" Jimmy shouted back, pointing at Scott while trying to get past Ty.

Alarmed, Scott stepped back.

But once again, he was relieved when Ty stopped Jimmy in his tracks.

"Scott's right," Ty told Jimmy, holding his palm against Jimmy's chest. "You didn't have to come."

Jimmy pouted. Not making eye contact.

To Scott, Jimmy looked like he was about to cry. But to his surprise, Jimmy quickly put on a smile that betrayed the hurt that was evident in his eyes.

"What?" Jimmy replied, his obvious fake smile growing larger, locking eyes with Ty. "And let you have all the fun?"

At that, Ty smiled. The two friends engaged in a bro handshake, clasping hands and bumping chests and forearms.

Scott could only shake his head as Jimmy turned and ran onto the porch of the house. But when Ty turned and winked at him, Scott couldn't help but smile and give him a thumbs-up.

Ty grinned and raised his arms like a showman. "Are we ready to shoot this bitch?"

As Scott raised the camera toward Ty, now standing before the porch, Jimmy ran toward the camera and put his face right up to it.

His breath fogged the lens. "I'm ready, bro! Eye of the tiger, baby!"

Scott cursed and lowered the camera to look right into it. "I told you not to touch the lens."

Jimmy mocked him by repeating what he just said as he walked off.

Scott took a square of cloth from his pocket to wipe off the lens.

"Dude," Jimmy said, "you treat that thing like it's your girlfriend or something."

Ignoring him, Scott checked the lens once more for any sign of a smudge. Then he pocketed the cloth and aimed the camcorder at Ty, who waited patiently by the porch.

Jimmy whined, "Is your precious lens clean?"

Scott didn't answer. Just aimed.

"All right," Ty said, "let's do this before someone calls the cops."

"I've been ready," Jimmy replied.

"And you." Ty gestured at Scott. "You ready?"

Off Scott's nod, Ty smiled.

"'Cause I'm depending on you to film all this. And that means going inside."

Scott glanced up at the house again, and his anxiety started to rise.

"So, can you?" Ty asked.

Scott broke out of his trance and nodded. "I said I would, and I will."

"Okay," Ty replied. "It's showtime."

Jimmy turned to the house and shouted at it, "You hear that? We're comin' for you, Mahoney! Get ready to show us something!"

"Keep it down, dude," Ty said, shushing him.

Scott raised his voice at Jimmy. "Are you sure it's wise to piss off whatever's in there?"

"Fuck 'em," Jimmy replied. "They're dead."

Scott shook his head, not liking how things were going.

Jimmy shook his head at Scott. "Why did we bring you along again?"

"'Cause it's my camcorder."

"Ladies," Ty interrupted. "Let's shoot."

Scott raised the camcorder again. He centered Ty at the bottom of the frame and nodded toward him.

Ty rubbed his hands together and peered back at the house. He turned to face the lens and lowered his voice an octave.

"In every town, there's a house with a dark history. One that's reputed to be haunted. And in this sleepy little town of Creed, Texas, that place is the Mahoney house."

Scott stood silent. He was impressed watching as his friend turned and walked up the steps to the porch like an actual reality-show host. He was a natural.

"Almost thirty years ago, a man named Roger Mahoney built this house for his bride, Ann. They intended to raise a family and live the rest of their lives here."

Scott stepped closer with the camcorder as Ty looked around at the front door and the busted windows to the side of it.

"But life never turns out like we plan. Roger and Ann never had children. And over the years, what was once a happy relationship turned bitter and angry."

Ty stopped before a broken window and looked back.

"Neighbors said that Ann was a nag and a shrew. That she ran roughshod over Roger and made his life a living hell. That is, until the night he snapped." Ty snapped his fingers for effect. "In this very house with an ax, Roger killed his wife while she slept in her bed."

Scott walked up the porch, filming as he went, and aimed the camera through a broken window inside the house, where it was too dark to see anything.

"The number of times Roger struck his wife that night seems to grow with each telling, but let us all agree that, in the end, Ann was as dead as Scott's sex life."

Jimmy guffawed off camera while Scott made eye contact with Ty, who couldn't help but burst out laughing.

"Sorry, dude," Ty said, chuckling. "I couldn't help it."

As both of them laughed, Scott nodded and stopped the recording.

"Very funny," Scott replied, then, under his breath, muttered, "Assholes."

This only made the other two laugh harder.

Finally, Ty stopped chuckling and beckoned Scott to start recording again.

Scott did as he was asked, but it took a few moments for Ty and Jimmy to stop giggling before they could finally record.

"But the story's not finished yet," Ty said, shaking his head. "Oh, no. Not by a long shot. After chopping up his wife, Roger tied a rope around a closet doorknob and threw the rope over the top of the door. Then he placed the noose around his neck, lowered himself to the floor, and strangled himself."

"Now that takes dedication," Jimmy interrupted.

"Think of that," Ty added, ignoring his friend. "As Roger Mahoney was strangling himself, the whole time he could have simply stood up in order to save his own life. But he didn't. Instead, he went through with the act and killed himself."

Ty walked toward the door and stopped before it.

"When the police finally arrived a few days later, they found a note taped to this door." Ty turned and touched the door. "The note said one thing and one thing only."

Ty put his face close to the lens.

"She wouldn't shut up."

Jimmy laughed again. "Whoa! That's awesome."

"In the end," Ty continued. "All Roger Mahoney wanted was a little peace and quiet."

Once again, Jimmy shoved his face before the lens. "Hey, ladies, give me a piece, and I'll be quiet."

As Jimmy laughed, Ty motioned to Scott. "We can edit out what he just said, right?"

"I think so," Scott replied. "Maybe."

"Let's do that again," Ty said, shooting Jimmy an angry glance, "without the interruption."

Scott saw Jimmy's smile fade as Ty approached the door again and stood before it.

"When you're ready," Ty said to Scott.

Scott aimed the camcorder again.

Ty counted himself down, then said, "When the police finally arrived a few days later, they found a note taped to this door."

Ty touched the door.

"The note said one thing and one thing only."

Ty put his face close to the lens.

"She wouldn't shut up."

Ty waited a few seconds before smiling. Then he turned to open the door but found it was locked.

"Shit!" Ty said.

Scott looked around the porch and pointed. "Go through the window and unlock it from the inside."

"Me?" Ty asked.

"Yeah."

As Scott and Ty stared at one another, neither one of them moving, Jimmy walked toward the broken window beside the door.

Jimmy said, "Since none of you pussies will do it."

Jimmy slipped through the window opening and disappeared into the darkness.

To Scott, it was like the house had swallowed him whole.

A few seconds later, after a few clicks, the door creaked open, and Jimmy stepped onto the threshold.

"Ta-da!" Jimmy shouted, then bowed like he was getting applause.

*****

A short time later, the camera was on Ty as he stood near the front door, which was now closed.

"Over the decades, other families have moved into the old Mahoney house. But none of them have ever stayed very long. And for the past decade, no matter how much the current owners of the property have lowered the price, the house has remained empty."

Scott panned the camera away from Ty on the porch to begin filming the neighborhood before circling back to Ty.

"To the other people who live in this neighborhood, this house is an eyesore. An albatross that lowers their property values. A place they'd love nothing more than to see torn down."

Ty opened the door and let the door squeak open by itself.

"But to some, this house is bloody, spooky history. And tonight, we're going inside so that we can see with our own eyes what this house is all about."

Ty began backing into the house, slowly disappearing into the darkness.

"And you lucky viewers out there are coming along with us. If you dare."

Jimmy followed Ty in, leaving Scott alone with his camcorder on the porch.

Scott looked around, his feet before the threshold, gathering his courage. With a deep breath, he entered, keeping the camcorder rolling.

All he could see through the viewscreen was darkness. He fiddled with the camcorder and turned on an external light. Now he could see a radius of about ten feet before him. Outside the zone of light was pure blackness. He took a few more deep breaths and walked further into the house.

As the camcorder panned the empty room, he saw walls filled with cobwebs and the floor covered in trash and dead leaves. A thick layer of dust covered everything else.

"Scott! Over here!" Ty yelled.

Scott spun the camcorder around and located Ty, who was standing in front of a dilapidated staircase.

"The death room has to be up there," Ty said, gesturing behind him.

Ty turned and ascended the creaky stairs, being careful to avoid loose-looking steps as he went.

Scott heard a noise on his left and panned the room in that direction to find Jimmy standing in an empty, dirty kitchen.

Jimmy noticed the camcorder was on him and grimaced while making a show of reaching into his pants pocket. He pulled out his cell phone, pressed a few buttons, turned on his phone's harsh light, and pressed the record button.

"You're not the only one who can film shit," Jimmy said, aiming his phone at Scott. "Say action, douchebag."

"Congratulations," Scott replied, shielding his eyes and turning away. "Your parents must be proud."

Jimmy flipped him the bird with his free hand.

Scott aimed his camcorder up the stairs. After taking a few deep breaths to calm his nerves, he slowly scaled them until he could see Ty's silhouette at the top as he entered a dark hallway.

Scott began to climb faster, nearly losing his balance as a step loosened and creaked under his weight. He raised his leg off the loose board, stepped onto the stair above it, and used the dusty banister to pull himself up with his free hand.

When he finally reached the top of the stairs, he aimed his camcorder light down the hall. He managed to catch a glimpse of Ty disappearing into a room.

"Shit," Scott said, hesitating a few moments before walking down the hall.

When he reached the room Ty had entered, he braced himself. After another deep, hesitant breath, he went in.

*****

Alone back in the kitchen, Jimmy aimed his cell phone at himself.

"The only thing scary about this place is how much of a shithole it is. I mean, look at this shit."

He panned away from himself and around the living room and back into the kitchen. Everything within the small radius of light was dirty and grimy.

He switched the phone's video camera back on himself.

"I mean, it's not scary, it's just disgusting."

He glanced around and shook his head.

"We definitely aren't gonna get to be the next *Ghost Adventures* in this place."

He heard a creak beside him, causing him to gasp and turn toward it quickly.

"What the fuck was that?"

Breathing heavily, his shaky hands made it difficult to see what was there on the viewscreen.

"Hey, guys!" Jimmy shouted, getting more and more nervous. "I heard something!"

Stepping from the kitchen, Jimmy aimed his cell phone light up the stairs. From his vantage point, he couldn't see the top of them.

"Guys! If that was you, that shit ain't funny!"

He could hear nothing in reply.

"If that was you, you're the biggest assholes I know! You hear me?"

Still no reply.

Jimmy spun the cell phone around again. He could still only see a few feet in front of him. His breathing was getting quicker and heavier. The footage was even shakier than before.

"I swear to God if one of you guys jumps out and scares me, I'm gonna beat the livin' shit outa both of—"

As he spun the camera around, he came across the swollen, dead face of a decrepit old man with wild hair and white eyes.

Jimmy screamed and ran for his life from the house, down the porch, and across the yard, huffing, puffing, yelling, and swearing as he went.

*****

In a freezing, empty room with thick dust on the wooden floor, Scott found Ty standing near a broken window.

Scott took a step toward him, which caused a creak.

Alarmed, Ty spun his head around toward the doorway, where Scott was standing, filming him.

He let out a relieved sigh. "You scared the shit outa me."

"Sorry," Scott replied, walking forward.

But as Scott aimed the camcorder at Ty, his roommate got excited and pointed outside.

"Holy shit! Look!"

Scott ran over and filmed out the window.

The lens took a while to focus, but when it did, it showed Jimmy running away from the house and jumping over the fence at the edge of the yard.

"What the hell!" Scott said, almost laughing.

They watched as Jimmy, hands on his knees, stopped on the street to catch his breath.

Scott aimed the camcorder at Ty as he took out his cell phone and made a call. Scott panned toward Jimmy as he answered his ringing phone.

"What happened?" Ty asked.

The camcorder caught an out-of-breath Jimmy making big gestures as he yelled into his phone.

"Quit yelling and slow down," Ty said. "I can't understand a word you're saying."

Scott leaned toward Ty to hear what Jimmy was saying over the phone but couldn't quite make it out. Ty looked into the camcorder and shrugged at him.

"This is crazy," Ty said to the lens, "but he said he saw a face."

Ty turned to look back out the window at Jimmy in the distance. "What are you talking about, dude? What face?"

Jimmy's filtered, screaming voice was still barely understandable to Scott.

"Whoa, dude, calm down," Ty said. "Did you record it?"

Ty glanced back up at the camcorder lens.

"Calm down, man, and take a few deep breaths."

Jimmy's filtered screaming voice got louder as Ty shook his head and held out the phone to the lens.

"You goddamn calm down, asshole!" Jimmy yelled. "I saw a dead fucking face!"

Ty put the phone back to his ear. "Jimmy, calm down and relax. You're okay."

Ty paused and waited.

"Are you relaxed?"

Off Ty's nod, Scott aimed the camcorder back on Jimmy outside and noticed that Jimmy seemed calmer. His gestures not as big as before. Scott panned back to Ty.

"Take a look at the footage you got," Ty said, "and see if you caught it."

Ty nodded and gave the lens an exasperated look.

"Then bring it here and let us look at it."

Ty rubbed his forehead. His anger level rising.

"Okay. Then stay out there and be a pussy while the real men do the investigating."

Ty ended the call and looked up, past the lens at Jimmy.

"He's lost it," Ty said while gazing around the room. He took a deep breath, then stared into the lens. "I'm gonna go check out that footage. You okay in here?"

"What?"

"Don't tell me you're wimpin' out on me too?"

"No. I just—"

"What?"

Scott took a few more deep breaths before replying, "I'll be okay."

"We'll see," Ty said, not believing him.

As Ty turned and walked out of the room, the camcorder followed him. When he reached the doorway, he turned back to point at Scott.

"No matter what happens, you keep filming. But if I shout, you come running. You hear me?"

"Yeah."

"Okay," Ty said before tapping on the door frame and walking out of view down the hallway.

Scott spun the camcorder around and focused on Jimmy, who was still standing at the edge of the yard, staring back at the house.

Against his better nature, even though he himself was on edge, Scott waved.

*****

From the road, Jimmy saw Scott waving at him from a second-floor window.

"What the fuck are you waving at?" Jimmy asked, raising a middle finger at him.

He watched as Scott turned his back to the window and walked into the dark.

Jimmy raised his cell phone and saw that it was still recording.

He aimed it at the house and panned the length of it. He couldn't see anything inside the rest of it but darkness. But as he panned back up to the window Scott had just been standing in, a gray female figure in a red dress was there looking out at him.

"Shit!" Jimmy exclaimed, lowering his phone, shocked to see nothing in the window with his own eyes.

He immediately raised the phone back up to see the woman in red turning and walking away.

Not knowing what to do, Jimmy cursed and started yelling. "Hey! Something's in there! Look behind you!"

There was now nothing beyond the window but darkness.

"Shit!" Jimmy yelled.

He turned in circles on the street, then made up his mind and ran toward the house. He was soon breathing heavily as he scaled the porch and rushed inside.

As soon as he entered, he ran right into Ty, causing both of them to scream.

"Jesus, dude!" Ty yelled.

"I saw something in the room with Scott!"

"What?"

"It looked like a woman!"

"The fuck!"

Ty wasted no time running back up the creaky stairs and down the upstairs hallway while Jimmy followed.

"Was she young?" Ty asked when they reached the room. "Old?"

"Old and gray," Jimmy replied. "Wearing a red dress."

Shocked, Ty stopped in his tracks and stared at Jimmy. "You're shitting me."

Jimmy could only shake his head.

Ty turned toward the room. "Put on your light and film this."

"What?"

"You heard me. Do it!"

Jimmy raised his phone. His hands still trembling. He turned on the light and aimed it at Ty, who shielded his eyes.

"Not at me. In front of me."

As the light left Ty's face, he followed it into the room with Jimmy close on his heels.

"Scott!" Ty whispered. "Where are you?"

Suddenly, Ty froze in place, looking down.

"What?" Jimmy asked, sensing something was wrong.

"Look," Ty said, pointing down at the floor.

Jimmy aimed the light down in the direction Ty was pointing and saw a dark pool of what looked to be blood on the floor.

Jimmy asked, "Is that…?"

Ty knelt down to investigate closer.

"Is that what I think it is?" Jimmy asked.

Ty turned his head and gazed along the floor until he pointed to his right. "Look."

Jimmy's phone aimed where Ty pointed, and he made out a smeared blood trail that led to Scott's camcorder lying upside down on the floor.

"Holy shit!" Jimmy said as Ty walked over and picked up the camcorder.

As Ty inspected it, he saw that the red light was still on the viewscreen.

"It's still recording," Ty said.

They heard a creak from outside the room, causing them both to gasp.

Jimmy panned the cell phone light around the room again. Then stopped on Ty.

"You heard that too, right?" Ty asked.

Jimmy nodded. Eyes wide with fear.

"Film this," Ty said, holding the camcorder for Jimmy to record.

Jimmy aimed his phone at it just as Ty ended the recording session.

He switched the camcorder over to video playback, and a blue screen appeared on the viewfinder.

Ty hit the Play button and saw shaky footage of what he inadvertently shot while picking up the camcorder. He pressed Rewind, and they both watched as the footage whirred backward for a few seconds. He pressed Stop, then Play, and they both watched Scott's footage of Jimmy out in the yard through the bedroom window.

The footage panned away from the window and swept the room.

As Scott walked toward the doorway, there was a growl off camera, and a vicious-sounding hit was delivered.

Ty and Jimmy reacted, shocked, as the camcorder dropped to the floor, accompanied by the sound of Scott falling hard soon after.

The camcorder rocked back and forth while upside down.

As the camcorder settled, Scott could be seen lying on the floor before it. With blood streaming from his head, his eyes fluttered open, and he stared into the lens in a daze.

Scott opened his mouth to speak, but something dragged him out of frame. His fingernails scraping across the floor as he went.

Ty almost dropped the camcorder but somehow managed to hold onto it. "Holy shit!"

"What happened?"

"It took him."

"What took him?"

Ty shook his head and glanced around the room. He didn't know what to do.

"What do we do?" Jimmy asked.

Ty's mouth opened and closed, but nothing came out.

"Ty, what do we do?"

Ty stared at the viewscreen with eyes open wide. Still too shocked to say anything.

Jimmy, tired of waiting, grabbed Ty by the arm. "Let's get the fuck outa here."

Ty could only nod as Jimmy led him out of the room and down the hall. But he soon came out of his terror trance.

"Wait!" Ty said. "Where are we going?"

Jimmy, walking fast, didn't reply as he led them down the stairs toward the living room.

"Dude, wait!" Ty said. "We can't leave Scott."

"We gotta get outa here," Jimmy replied.

As they reached the bottom of the stairs, Ty looked across the living room and saw the open doorway. He pulled back on Jimmy's grip in an effort to slow both of them down.

"We can't leave Scott!" Ty said.

Jimmy stopped in his tracks, turned, and grabbed Ty by his shirt, pulling him close.

"Scott's dead," Jimmy said with wild eyes. "And we will be too if we don't get the fuck outa here."

As Jimmy turned toward the front door, it slammed shut on its own.

Ty screamed and witnessed Jimmy spinning around to face him with a horrified look on his face.

Before Jimmy could say anything, his body was hurled through the air and slammed into the ceiling with tremendous force. Then the forces of the house began repeatedly smashing him into the floor and ceiling like a bouncing ping-pong ball, shattering his bones until he resembled a rag doll.

A loud, monstrous roar followed that reverberated throughout the house.

Ty screamed and fell backward just as Jimmy's body crashed to the floor a final time with a sickening splat.

The camcorder flew from Ty's grasp, clanked to the floor, and slid to a stop near the stair landing.

Ty rolled over and spotted the camcorder near the stairs. His hands pawed the floor until he gained enough traction to slowly pull himself toward it.

When the device was finally within reach, his fingers fumbled with it a few times before he managed to grab it, pick it up, and press Record.

Ty's sobbing, frightened face soon filled the viewscreen.

"I'm so sorry," he said into the lens while tears streamed down his trembling face. "We shouldn't have come here."

Monstrous, earth-shaking footsteps began to pound overhead.

Ty's eyes darted up and followed the sounds of the steps as they stomped across the ceiling in the direction of the stairs. Each powerful step caused dirt and dust to rain down to the floor.

On the camcorder viewscreen, Ty's eyes widened in shock at the sight of what was standing at the top of the stairs that only he could see. His face turned pale, and his body shook as whatever monstrous sight he saw roared down at him, causing him to panic.

As it began stomping down the stairs, Ty tried to scoot away. But his body wasn't responding to his brain's commands.

Before long, the unseen creature towered over him.

"No! Please, don't!" Ty yelled, eyes insane with fear. "I'm sorry! Please!"

There was another terrible roar as a blast of putrid, hot breath hit his face. Then it dragged him out of frame on the viewscreen as Ty screamed and dropped the camcorder, which spun to a stop while aimed at the dust-covered floor.

The unseen beast roared again, cutting off Ty's bloodcurdling scream. Then all was silent.

The camcorder kept recording.

FIRST GIRL

Imagine a terrified young woman as she runs away from something or someone. She keeps glancing back over her shoulder and screaming as loud as she can while running for her very life.

It will soon be revealed to you, the movie viewer or the book reader, that she's running from a masked man who's dressed all in black and carrying a large knife.

This guy, just in case the creepy mask and big-ass knife didn't give it away, is the Killer with a capital K. And surprise—he's trying to kill the terrified, fleeing young woman.

The confused young woman runs haphazardly, taking quick peeks over her shoulder at the masked man in an effort to see where he is.

Now you'd think at a time like this, she would just concentrate on trying to get away by running as fast as humanly possible. But for some reason, she keeps glancing back, which not only slows her down, but causes her to keep slipping, tripping, and falling.

As for the masked man, he simply glides effortlessly across the ground right on her heels, smooth and methodical.

In addition, the Killer somehow only has to walk in order to keep up with her, which isn't really that hard when she keeps looking back, which causes her to slip, trip, and fall.

When she hits the ground, she looks back, sees the masked man getting closer, and tries desperately to get back on her feet.

But instead, the masked man dives on her and knocks her back to the ground.

She tries to fight back the best she can, but he's too strong.

He also ignores her swinging arms and grabs her by the throat.

Now you might be thinking, this does not look good for the young woman, and you'd be right.

The masked man squeezes her throat, which causes her to stop trying to hit him and forces her to resort to trying to pry his fingers loose so that she can breathe.

The lack of oxygen makes her face go red and her eyes bulge as she stares up at the masked man while he raises his knife.

This is the point where the poor girl starts shaking her head, begging with her eyes for him to stop.

He raises the knife above his head and holds it there. His eyes study her for a moment as she tries to speak, to beg him for her life.

But in the end, it's all for naught on her part because, right then and there, the masked man brings the knife down, and he watches heartlessly as life slowly leaves the young woman's eyes.

Her hands fall lifeless. She takes her last breath. Her body is soon still.

The Killer studies her face carefully, then, almost as if he truly cares about her, he slowly removes a few stray strands of hair from her face.

Then he rises to tower over her, studies her some more, and walks away.

Pretty brutal, huh?

Well, that's the short sad life of the first character, usually a female referred to as the First Girl, who gets killed at the beginning of a book or a film, usually in the prologue or right before the opening credits.

While this character may not seem important in the overall scheme of things, she actually is.

You see, the First Girl's murder is the death that sets the tone for the rest of the story. And if that murderous act does its job, you're intrigued enough to keep reading or watching. If not, the rest of the movie or book is pretty much screwed from the get-go.

As for the First Girl, her part may be over pretty quickly, but that doesn't mean her job is finished.

No, far from it.

You see, every time the film gets watched or the book gets read, she has to die all over again.

She'll be running for her life from a man dressed all in black as he's carrying a large knife.

She'll run haphazardly, using the same clumsy methods of trying to get away, making the same mistakes.

Meanwhile, the masked man will glide effortlessly across the ground right on her heels, smooth and methodical.

She'll look back one final time, then trip and fall.

Once she hits the ground, she'll look up and see the masked man getting closer.

She'll try in vain to get back up on her feet, but the masked man will dive on her and knock her back to the ground.

She'll fight back the best she can, but he'll be too strong for her.

He'll ignore her swinging arms and grab her by the throat and start to squeeze.

She'll stop hitting him and resort to trying to pry his fingers loose so she can breathe.

Her face will go red, and her eyes will bulge as she stares up at him.

He'll slowly raise the knife, and she'll start shaking her head, begging with her eyes for him to stop.

Once the knife is above his head, he'll hold it there.

His eyes will study her face for a moment as she tries to speak. To beg him for her life.

Then he'll bring the knife down.

The Killer will watch as life slowly leaves her eyes.

Her hands will fall lifeless, and she'll take her last breath.

And when her body is still, he'll carefully remove a stray strand of hair from her face.

He'll rise, stand over her, admire his gruesome handiwork, then walk away, leaving her lifeless body behind like refuse.

So the next time you watch a slasher film or read a good thriller, instead of rooting for the villain or relishing another sweet yet gruesome kill, all I'll ask you to do is feel a little bit sorry for the poor First Girl, who has to get killed at the very beginning of the story just for the sake of entertainment over and over and over and over again—ad infinitum.

It's a tough, dirty, thankless job, yet someone has to do it. And in this case, that person is the extremely unlucky, overlooked, doomed to repeatedly die for your entertainment First Girl.

And she'll see you the next time she sees you, because she's not going anywhere.

She'll be right there at the very beginning, waiting for her time to die, setting the tone for all that follows.

NIGHT OF THE LIVING

Brian "the Brain" Whitaker was once a brilliant student destined for bigger and better world-changing things. But in order for him to have achieved that bigger, better future life, Brian first had to experience the trial-by-fire known as public high school, which was, for frail young men like Brian, a cruel and unforgiving institution where the meek were at the mercy of the strong.

As the class valedictorian, a low-ranking post among the mindless, muscle-bound cretins and the cruel, pretty, vapid femmes if there ever was one, steadfast, noble Brian had to summon his strength on a daily basis to make his way through a gauntlet of jock jerks knocking his books out of his hands while he was on the stairs, giving him bruised shoulders in the hallways, and embarrassing him with the occasional atomic wedgie in the locker room.

His gallant shame was rewarded with a billowy cloud that contained the added bonus of a silver lining. For he had the great fortune of being the advanced student assigned to tutor the beautiful and luminous Peggy Carson, who was on the verge of flunking Algebra II and losing her title of head cheerleader in the process.

Like most beautiful people who get whatever they want from society, mainly due to their looks, Peggy suffered from extremely low self-esteem. This was due to an overly critical mother named Barbara, herself a former beauty queen who married for all the wrong reasons—love, attraction, and devotion—instead of the correct superficial ones, which would have led to a life of comfort, status, and wealth.

Adding to Peggy's grief, she had to cope with her mother's venomous anger toward her late husband, Charles, an extremely handsome and much-too-carefree young stud in his prime, who unfortunately became a bloated, alcoholic, miserable shadow of his former Adonis self in middle age.

To Peggy's knowledge, her father was a one-time alpha male superjock until an unfortunate twist of fate occurred at the knee during a high school football playoff game. After barely graduating in the bottom tier of his class, Charles—Chuck to his buddies—soon became a full-time member of his uncle's building construction crew.

Unknown to Peggy and her mother, her father, while driving home from work, especially on Friday nights during autumn, would pass by the multimillion-dollar local football stadium and clumsily wipe away the tears that would come in waves and were sometimes powerful enough to cause him to pull over in order to get a hold of himself.

Over time, this daily drive became easier for him. His days of standing in the stadium spotlight, bathing in the cheers of the worshipping crowd, soon became just another garden-variety distant memory.

But every once in a while, an overwhelming sadness would envelop him in its dark shroud, and a cold, awful tap on the shoulder by his subconscious would remind him that he had peaked much too early in his life. And though he didn't know it at those times, this negative feeling became the root cause of his overwhelming later-in-life depression.

While on the job, Chuck, the former champion party keg binge drinker, began his habit of consuming several beers a day, often at lofty heights. Some ten-odd years later, according to his fellow coworkers who had witnessed his death on a fateful, windy spring morning, the father of a beautiful preteen daughter and the henpecked husband of a malicious shrew did not trip or stumble or fall from the top of a tall structure. Rather, they swear he took off his hard hat, laid it down gently at his feet, then stepped off the edge of a steel beam as if he were diving into a pool of water.

From that point forward, Peggy carried all her sadness deep within her so well that no one ever really noticed. Truthfully, few ever dared to look beyond her surface, for if they did, they would have seen the cracks of self-doubt and lines of misery etched upon her face like a canvas.

Yet despite the dark cloud of gloom that constantly hung over her, Peggy had the power of a thousand suns in her smile. Her overwhelming beauty was equally blinding and all-consuming. Her eyes—bright, green, wide, deep, and probing—saw things few would ever visually process on their best day. And it was with these eyes that she and she alone noticed the real Brian. Not Brian the Meek or Brian the Brain or Brian the Bully Bait. She noticed the witty Brian. The funny Brian. The kind-of-cute Brian.

The only thing Peggy failed to see when it came to Brian was how much she loved him, long before it even occurred to her that she did.

To Brian's credit, he always saw Peggy like no one else had. That may have been because he knew sadness all too well, for he experienced it every day in some way, fashion, or form. So right away, at first sight, long before she even knew he existed, he recognized her pain, sensed her loneliness, and knew what she longed for, which was someone who would look past the pretty veneer and see the reality that was her—insecure, sad, vulnerable, imperfect—and love her anyway.

Like most star-crossed romances, these two young adults were strangers at first since both ran in completely different social circles—Brian with the rest of the dweebs and Peggy with the popular people—but with each passing tutoring session, they slowly became close yet extremely secretive friends. For as nice as Peggy really was, she still desired to be well-liked and admired by her peers, even if it was only on the surface level. She knew all too well that if word got out that she was dating below her social level, it would be akin to her committing social suicide and would probably make Brian an endangered species on the verge of extinction once the alpha jock gods were alerted to his foolish mistake of flying too close to the sun.

After a period long past the point of Peggy actually needing Brian's tutoring services anymore, but still needing that cover to shield their relationship from the prying eyes of the public, the couple had their first kiss.

Once their lips touched, with a tiny amount of saliva shared between them, but not too much, along with the tiny hairs on their bodies standing on end, Peggy knew Brian was the one.

But their burgeoning relationship didn't sit well with her spying, jaded, ever-observant mother. To the faded beauty queen's critical eye, Brian came from the wrong side of the tracks, meaning his parents didn't make enough money or know the right people, and his ill-fitting clothes were either hand-me-downs or were bought in discount stores and retail outlets.

Even though her mother forbade her from seeing Brian, that didn't stop Peggy from sneaking out of the house once her mother fell asleep in her easy chair with too much booze in her system and a lit cigarette between her fingers.

Upon escaping the stifling confines of her home, Peggy would make her way to a carefully planned rendezvous with Brian, who would always be waiting anxiously to greet her with a single flower, each time of a different variety.

On one glorious night, with a bloodred hunter's moon hanging in the night sky like an angry eye, they met in a park. While there, they snuck through a gaping hole in a chain-link fence in order to skinny-dip in the cool, mostly clean, chlorine-filled waters of a community swimming pool.

Then they made love, and both climaxed with the intensity of a supernova. Their flesh set on fire with each touch, whether glancing or firm.

Afterward, they lay together on a towel upon the cool cement near the pool and stared up at the stars. It was there that each made their silent wish on the brightest one. He hoped they would always be together while she asked to always be as loved as she felt at that moment.

Within weeks, a slip of the tongue by someone Peggy considered a close female friend led to her relationship with Brian becoming school-wide knowledge.

Needless to say, this angered and shamed the petty and cruel local superjock, Johnny Hearst, who had called dibs on Peggy on the third day of seventh grade and forever sealed her lucky fate, as far as he was concerned.

His invisible mark upon her ensured a wide berth for her in the hallways, free from being hit on by every available red-blooded male enraptured by her beauty from that point forward.

The fact this didn't sit well with Peggy didn't matter. What Johnny wanted, Johnny always got. It was as simple as that.

Johnny, like all the alpha superjocks before him, was self-predestined to become an All-American linebacker at a major college powerhouse, who would somehow manage to scrape by with the minimum passing GPA and was destined to one day sign a professional NFL contract, guaranteeing him a huge signing bonus that would allow him to keep a pretty but clueless trophy wife like Peggy in the lap of luxury, while he slept with every available woman he could get his large, powerful mitts on.

Though his clumsy pleas and shameful attempts to win Peggy's affection fell flat before her, it didn't matter to someone like Johnny.

He knew he would eventually win her over because good things come to those who wait. In the meantime, he could have whomever he wanted free from the guilt of commitment.

But once Johnny learned about Peggy's relationship with Brian, all the longing and lust for his chosen one turned to hate, pure and simple.

He still wanted her, that didn't change, but to him, she was now broken, useless, and used. Worst of all, he deemed her undeserving of his kindness. From that point forward, he swore to break her completely, as if she were a wild stallion that needed to be tamed.

He swore he'd turn her into a pariah and bring her high-and-mighty attitude crashing to the ground to the level of a bottom-feeder, where losers and castoffs and outcasts were banished.

As for Brian, Johnny had special plans for him. The very next night, the reigning alpha jock swore on a twelve-pack of beer in the presence of his loyal but fearful friends that Brian the Brain, also known to him as Half-wit Whitaker, would get everything that was coming to him for daring to open Johnny's crackerjack prize before he did.

But all that happened the night all hell literally broke loose.

In an event that would be known years later by the survivors as the Uprising, the recently departed began walking the earth, and just like in the movies, they had an insatiable appetite for human flesh.

And the plans of man, both big and small, grudges and dreams alike, became a distant memory.

*****

Five Years Later

Brian stood in place on the red dirt in a grassless vacant lot, gazing through milky-white eyes at the chain-link fence that separated the quarantine zone—in which he stood—from the outside world.

To this day, surviving family and friends of loved ones lost all those years ago continued to lay a moat of flowers and bouquets against the fence, on this, the date of the Uprising anniversary. All despite the fact some of the people considered lost and long gone were still up and walking around inside the quarantine zone.

Drool leaked from the corners of Brian's mouth. His face, with skin of a dull grayish hue, was covered in cracks, lesions, and abrasions.

A low, anguished moan escaped his chapped, bluish lips as he craned his neck, vertebrae cracking and popping, to stare up at the cloudless, birdless brown sky.

He stood in place transfixed, as if under a spell, even as another walking corpse bumped into him while making its own path.

Brian kept his gaze on the dead-looking sky, ignoring the other shambler who momentarily stopped to stare at him, as if wanting a confrontation or perhaps even wanting to connect.

But after a few silent moments between them, the other undead being turned away and ambled off.

That's when Brian peered down from the sky and noticed that member of his brethren approaching the fence.

Brian slowly raised his left arm, the one that still moved without too much difficulty. With a dirty palm facing out, he groaned in the other's direction.

The other zombie stopped in his tracks and slowly turned, teetering on his feet for balance, and gazed back. His face was gaunt and decayed. One eye was missing, leaving a hollow, dark space, while the other eye was solid white with yellow pus leaking from the corners.

In life, this decomposing being's name had been David, a hard-working corporate-tax lawyer, a loving father of three, and a devoted husband. He was a man whose career may not have been exciting or a hot topic of conversation at parties; but it was consistent and lucrative. Most importantly, it afforded him all the time in the world with his daughters, an adorable pair of eight-year-old twins and a precious newborn baby.

When David did work, he was so completely focused on his tasks that he was ignorant of the world around him. So on the first day of the Uprising, he was completely unaware of all the news reports and internet ramblings concerning the apocalyptic events starting to happen around the world. And even if he had known, it's doubtful he would have thought he'd ever find himself in any kind of danger; therefore, it was equal parts arrogance and obtuseness that led him to his fate.

The biter came out of nowhere while David walked through a dimly lit parking garage toward his newly leased Lexus. Luckily for him, he had his metal coffee thermos with him, which allowed him to knock down his attacker long enough for him to get in his car and escape. What he didn't know at the time was how close he had come to being killed and eaten. He had mistaken his attack as a random attempted mugging by a crazy person who happened to take a bite out of him. But instead of going to the hospital—which, in hindsight, wouldn't have done him any good anyway considering how fast the virus destroyed living cells—he used his wounded arm to steer his car home despite immediately feeling waves of stomach-churning nausea.

All the while, he kept his free hand pressed against the gaping wound on his forearm, trying to staunch the bleeding that would not stop no matter how much pressure he applied. At the same time, crazy thoughts whirled through his mind, as if his brain had been hacked and chaotic mental transmissions were being uploaded and streamed against his will. The jumbled images and thoughts that flashed before him threatened to strip away his sanity, so much so that he started cackling like a loon. His laughter was low at first, almost guttural, but soon he was wailing to beat the band.

That's when he knew he had lost his mind because what kind of sane man thinks it's hilarious that a chunk of his own flesh was inside a crazy man's stomach?

Before he turned later that night, David had become extremely ill. Sick as a dog was the expression. The fever came on suddenly and only got worse. With his devoted and caring stay-at-home wife trying her best to keep his temperature down while at the same time trying to get through the busy phone circuits to an overwhelmed emergency service, she could only watch helplessly and in a fair bit of shock as her husband regurgitated everything he had consumed recently, and when that wasn't enough, he heaved up bits of his stomach lining and disgusting, blood-covered black bile.

It had been the most pain he had ever endured in his life by a wide margin. Despite the presence of his loved ones, the pain was so excruciating that he prayed and wished for the sweet release of death.

Soon, he got his wish and expired, alone on the floor of the bathroom near the toilet. Unfortunately for his family, he rose a little over a half hour later.

Now, standing a few feet from the quarantine fence, David stared back at the zombie named Brian and remembered what it was like to cry. Only he couldn't. His tear ducts no longer worked.

Like that night years before, David prayed for death to embrace him, to swallow him whole, to take away everything and leave nothing behind. Though his brain no longer functioned the way it used to when he was a living, breathing human being, he still had memories.

The synapses could be cruel that way.

He remembered eating pieces of his wife and children over the course of a few days after he turned. He'd been unable to stop himself because the compulsion to feed was much too great. It was also the moment he realized that feeding on human flesh was the only thing that stopped the pain of his all-consuming hunger, which could only be described as a constant all-over body ache that got worse the longer his system went without nourishment.

But he still had emotions. He still loved and longed for his family. Even while savoring each bite, tearing off each chunk, and swallowing each piece, he shed tears for them.

In the days following, he still thought about them, trying his best to remember their faces as they had been and not the stripped carcasses he had left behind.

From that point, their visages haunted him, blamed him, screamed at him, hated him. But the guilt couldn't compete with the hunger. And an insatiable monster, his undead appetite was—never satisfied, always yearning, constantly driving him forward, much like a shark cruising through the depths of the cold, unforgiving ocean searching for its next hapless meal.

As David stood near the fence in that barren field, gazing back at the other shambler he didn't know or had even met until the moment he had tried to stop him, to warn him not to go any further, he chose to ignore him. Because he had decided today was truly the end. He had made up his mind. He couldn't go on anymore.

Brian could do nothing but stand in place and watch while David turned away from him and limped toward the quarantine fence.

Upon reaching it, David slipped through a large enough opening with very little difficulty. Without looking back, he marched into the forbidden zone where the humans dwelled.

Though Brian couldn't see his face, David walked with his head held high, and his rotten teeth bared in a content, lipless smile.

The last thing that entered David's brain before the sniper bullet shattered his skull was of the last Christmas he and his family had spent together.

It had been a perfect day. It had snowed the night before, bestowing upon them a white Christmas to remember. The weather had stayed cool enough to keep the snow on the ground well into the next day.

As David watched from the front porch with a steaming cup of coffee held in his right hand, his giggling twins pelted each other with slushy snowballs. To make the moment complete, his pregnant wife stepped beside him and took his free hand in hers. Without a word spoken between them for the next few minutes, they watched their children play.

David peered down at his wife's protruding belly, the baby due any day now, and then leaned over slightly, careful so as not to spill his coffee, and whispered ever so softly, "I can't wait to meet you."

Brian witnessed David's head explode in a red, pulpy mist, chunks of brain and skull splattering in each direction.

At the sound of the distant rifle's report that quickly followed, a dog in the distance started barking. It was soon joined by another.

David's body kept walking, driven by something more than will, until it finally stumbled and fell forward to the ground, bringing up a cloud of red dust that swirled about the corpse before rising and dissipating into nothingness.

Brian stood there. Eyes now closed. Arms spread beside him. Ready and waiting for what came next.

But nothing happened.

No more shots were fired. No one came out to inspect the near-headless body. It just lay there. The last of what the shambler formerly known as David had ever been, now gone. Never to rise again.

Brian stood there a few more moments thinking about taking that same last walk. Something he found himself doing more and more with each passing day. Hence why he was standing where he was now, contemplating taking that stroll into the blackness of a final death.

But there was still something holding him in place, something that always kept him from ending it all. What that something was, was this very day.

It was time again for his annual journey. Only unlike David, Brian meant to return to the quarantine zone, which meant he had to prepare, which meant he had to be smart.

Smarter than the average zombie, at least.

As was just demonstrated moments before, Brian knew that to walk out of the quarantine zone during the day was tantamount to suicide. And while it was still very dangerous to slip through the fence and travel to where the humans lived at night, at least the darkness afforded him a slightly better chance to slip through the shadowed streets unnoticed.

After all, he'd done it before.

Much like David doing whatever it took to end it all, Brian would do the same to see Peggy again. The woman he once loved.

The woman he still loved.

Or he was going to die trying.

For real this time.

*****

After night had fallen, Brian patiently bided his time, waiting in the shadows for the right moment to make his move. He kept his eyes on the dwellings that seemed to be abandoned on the other side of the vacant lot. But he knew all too well that there was at least one itchy-trigger-fingered man with a rifle hidden within those dilapidated structures waiting for an opportunity to let off some pent-up steam.

Brian heard the distant sound of a rock song blaring loudly over stereo speakers, accompanied by the revving of a powerful engine. A few moments later, the many lights of a single vehicle crested a small hill in the road and grew larger and more blinding as they got closer.

Brian watched as a white dually pickup truck pulled up next to the fence and skid across the loose dirt before coming to a complete stop. Mounted all over it were swamp lights aiming in every direction, illuminating everything around it within a hundred feet. A cloud of dust enveloped the truck, then blew in the general direction of the dwellings.

Two men climbed out of the cab and surveyed the scene beyond the fence. Other rowdy drunken men riding in the back of the truck, with rifles slung over their shoulders and holstered guns strapped to their bodies, soon jumped out to join them.

To Brian, standing just outside the reach of the vehicle's powerful lights, these men smelled of sweat, body odor, dirt, and liquor.

He could also smell the tangy scent of copper in the blood flowing through their veins, a sensation so powerful it was like the ringing of a dinner bell. This feeling was so overwhelming it immediately began its assault on his senses, forcing him to think of one thing and one thing only.

Feeding.

But Brian forced himself to look away and tried to think of something else to occupy his mind's desire. He was unsuccessful at first, but an image finally managed to break free of all the clutter of basic animal urges and float to the surface.

He could now see Peggy's face. More luminous than any moon. More beautiful than the prettiest flower. More intoxicating than any alcoholic beverage. But her face soon rippled and faded away as Brian heard the men start singing along to the tune coming over the truck's speakers, while the rest were calling out to the residents behind the fence, shouting things like "It's dinnertime!" and "Come out and play!"

A couple of the men stooped down in the back of the truck and rose back up with their arms full of bloody meat that smelled strongly of decay. These men grunted as they swung and tossed the spoiled meat just outside the opening in the fence.

Brian glanced at the spoiled meat on the ground just a few feet outside the quarantine zone and winced as the sharp pains in his head intensified. But he endured the agony and opened his eyes and watched as the ravenous hordes of his kind slowly began to emerge from the shadows of the buildings and the stranded vehicles, drawn in by the scent of the offerings before them.

Powerless to resist their urges, they ignored everything else, especially common sense, willing to do whatever it took to stop their own pain. Those who could walk, no matter how barely, took full advantage of their remaining skill and outpaced those who could only crawl or drag their bodies across the ground.

The humans hollered encouragement to those beings whom they wanted to reach the prize first. Brian could even hear two of the men discussing the exchanging of prized goods and possessions with one another over the outcome.

When the first of the shamblers made it through the fence opening, approached the spoiled meat, and dropped to his knees to begin feeding, the humans celebrated by giving the spoils to the one of their own who correctly picked the winner.

By that time, more undead had cleared the fence opening. They reached the near-rotten offerings and dropped to their knees in order to consume their share.

That's when the men who arrived in the truck grew silent.

Watching the undead beings outside the fence eat, the collective looks upon the men's faces began to change. Whatever good humor they previously displayed was now gone, slowly replaced by seething hate and anger, as if these undead beings were the very ones who had wronged them at one time or another.

Brian could smell the unmistakable, sweet-tinged scent of the men's adrenaline levels rising and knew what was soon to come.

That meant it was almost time. The moment he had been waiting for.

Keeping to the shadows, he made his move.

Walking with his back to the brightly lit scene at the fence, Brian didn't look back, even when he heard the first rifle shot. He heard a groan as a body slumped to the ground accompanied by a sickening splat.

Before he knew it, a volley of shots rang out. The distant pops filling the air like a bundle of lit firecrackers on the Fourth of July.

But Brian trudged on, making his way across the empty field, away from the carnage taking place, staying within the confines of the darkness. He occasionally glanced back at the dark dwellings across the field hoping upon hope that the snipers' eyes within were currently trained on the massacre taking place behind him.

It seemed to take forever, but Brian finally saw a brief flash of moonlight upon metal before him. But before he could relax or celebrate, the shooting suddenly stopped.

Brian quickly came to a halt. He wanted desperately to turn around to see what was happening behind him but willed himself not to. He stood there for several moments, not sure what to do, afraid any movement at all would catch someone's attention.

But soon, acting against every basic survival instinct deep within him to stay and remain safe in the quarantine zone and give up his foolish quest, he slowly put one foot in front of the other and soon found himself walking again. Knowing it was too late to turn back now, he closed his eyes, raised his arms, and stretched out his hands before him, hoping to find purchase.

Finally, to his immense relief, his fingers looped around thin wires of cold metal, and he stopped and opened his eyes. He beheld a chain-link fence looming before him. Rather than celebrate the moment, Brian began gazing around, turning his head in both directions before finding what he was looking for.

On many occasions in the past, starving wild dogs foraging for food would dig their way under the fence line, often to their own detriment at the hands and teeth of the starving undead creatures inside it. But these poor, unfortunate, neglected animals were too desperate for nourishment to pay their typical strong sense of danger any heed.

Thanks to them and their unwilling sacrifice, Brian made his way toward one of these shallow holes under the fence line and knelt to lie facedown beside it while cartilage and tendons, beset by rigor mortis, cracked and popped their usual form of resistance.

He slowly rolled over onto his back in the hole and reached backward over his head to pull up the bottom of the fence just high enough to slip his head under it. Digging in with his heels, he pushed himself under the opening, past his neck. He shoved the fence further upward, gaining enough clearance for the bulk of his chest to pass through and under.

Once he made it that far, he released his grip on the fence and lowered his hands to his side with his palms flat on the ground. He began using his elbows to raise his torso up and began to wiggle and scoot his body out the rest of the way.

Only once did the fence manage to snag him, but within seconds, he pulled himself free and was soon standing on the other side of it.

Then, and only then, did he look back at the humans' handiwork.

While his brethren's bodies littered the ground, the smiling men celebrated by taking selfies with the corpses and drinking liquor from bottles and beer from cans. A few blew off steam by yelling at the sky, cursing at whoever above that was still in charge of the mess below.

Brian turned away from the fence and stood still. He knew if a shot were to come, it would be at this moment. Of course, he wouldn't hear it, but it would happen, nonetheless.

He closed his eyes and thought of Peggy, figuring that was as good a last thought as any to have. But after a few seconds, he realized there would be no shot. Not for the moment, at least.

Once certain he had still not been seen, he began walking again, away from the fence, remaining careful enough to stay within the shadows while not looking back.

*****

Brian slowly made his way through a quiet, still neighborhood, which to him was a forbidden zone.

He could hear muffled voices within the homes along his route. Most of those coming from shows on television or songs through stereo speakers. But a few were people speaking about the mundane things people talked about within the confines of their own private, protective walls.

He paused on the sidewalk outside a home where the curtains were open like an invitation he was helpless to refuse.

Inside, he could see a middle-aged woman pacing nervously in her living room, smoking a cigarette, and rubbing her face in worry.

She seemed to stop and stare right out her window at him, causing him to move behind a nearby hedge to hide.

But he needn't have bothered. She couldn't see out, he suddenly remembered. From the inside, the only thing one could see through a window inside a lighted room on a darkened night was your own reflection. But he stayed behind the hedge watching her, not willing to take any chance on being spotted. Not on a night as important as this.

The settings in his brain were on fire and engorging his appetite. But he withstood the hunger pangs and ignored his inhuman nature. He waited until the woman continued pacing before lumbering on, crossing through yards to avoid the yellow overhead beams shining down on the sidewalks like prison searchlights.

*****

Brian heard the little girl before he saw her. Terrified, he tried to remain still so he wouldn't be spotted. But it was too late.

A little girl playing in her front yard had already seen him and stopped jumping during a round of hopscotch. She was now staring at him in wide-eyed wonder. Then, without a trace of fear or hesitation, the little girl looked him up and down. After what seemed an eternity to him, a large smile broke out across her tiny face.

She gave him the tiniest of friendly waves. Before he knew it, he had returned the gesture. That's when she took a step toward him, causing him to step back.

Afraid of what he might do, Brian held up his arms, dirty palms facing her, and shook his head.

The little girl paused. For the first time, she seemed concerned. But just as quickly, her smile returned.

Brian kept his hands up and backed away from her, but while the little girl stood still, she kept her piercing gaze and wide smile upon him.

He watched her from the corners of his bloodshot eyes until he got to where he assumed was a safe distance, then he angled his body away from her, took his eyes off her, and continued on his journey.

But that's when he heard the soft, rustling sound of small feet running up behind him on the grass, yelling the word "Mister!" over and over again in order to catch his attention.

Brian stopped and took quite some time to turn as quickly as he could. Once that journey was complete, he saw the little girl standing before him, looking up at him with that same warm and innocent smile.

"My name is Sally," she said. "What's yours?"

Brian retreated from her, emphatically waving her away. He closed his eyes, trying to suppress his savage impulses. He tried to speak the words he could remember somewhere deep within the recesses of his brain, but phonetic words were too difficult for him to form, so all the sound he could muster was a deep, guttural groan.

This took the little girl aback. Her smile finally leaving her face.

That sparked something within him. Realizing the only way to get away from her and get her away from him was to do one of the few humanlike things he was fully capable of.

He set his eyes, glared down upon her, and let loose with a savage growl.

Tears shot from the little girl's eyes as she screamed, turned, and fled in the opposite direction.

At once, Brian realized his shortsighted mistake, for a few porch lights immediately came to life in the vicinity. Not wasting any time regretting his decision, Brian turned and began moving as fast as he could shuffle, hoping to get as far away from the area as quickly as possible.

Another light came on behind him, and he heard a door open.

Then, what must have been the little girl's mother asked her daughter, "What are you doing outside?" When the little girl replied, "I saw a man," and followed that up with, "He scared me," Brian stepped behind a tree and hid there a while, hoping its trunk was large enough to conceal his body.

"What man?" the mother asked.

"He went that way," the little girl replied, surely pointing in his direction.

Brian slowly began moving again, away from the tree and across the yards, trying his best not to make a sound. He sped up his gait but was still moving slow, yet somehow through the grace of whatever higher power that was helping him, he managed to evade the reach of the porch lights and stay within the safety of the darkness.

To his dread, he soon noticed every porch light was now coming on along the neighborhood street, and people were beginning to emerge from their homes, obviously frightened, but more eager and curious to find out what was happening.

Still, luck was on Brian's side. The neighbors were looking in the direction opposite of where he was now walking.

He eventually managed to reach a street corner where he felt safe enough to stop and glance back. The neighborhood street was now filled with people who were gesturing in his general direction.

But by some miracle, Brian was still within the shadows and managed to avoid their detection.

Rather than risk his luck any further, Brian started walking again, down the adjoining street, and soon disappeared around the corner.

*****

Nearly ten minutes after Brian left the street, the large white dually with the swamp lights and blaring loud rock music drove down it and parked before a few of the neighbors who were still outside.

The occupants of the truck turned the music down for a few moments to have a conversation with them. After some of the neighbors pointed in the direction their suspect must have fled, the driver revved the truck's engine, the music went back up to a deafening level, and the vehicle drove off in pursuit.

*****

Brian peered up at the street sign looming before him, trying to dredge the depths of his memory for the answer he was seeking. But try as he might, the memory just wasn't coming to him.

He resorted to looking down the streets in his vicinity, at all the similar houses in their rows, hoping to see something, anything at all familiar. But this street resembled all the other streets he'd seen that night.

Frustrated, he stared up at the sky and closed his eyes, thinking if he didn't try so hard, maybe the answer he sought would come to him. But with the ticking clock in his brain telling him to hurry before he was spotted and that he was staying in one place far longer than he should, he thought about giving up and heading back.

But at that very moment of doubt, he suddenly remembered something. He lifted his head to the wind and checked for scents.

Turning this way and that, he tried to locate a particular one. To his amazement, he soon found it.

Somehow, his faulty memory and undead instincts combined to bring him to the right street, after all. Before he knew it, and much to his delight, he found himself standing before a quaint little house among other quaint little houses.

Peggy's home looked the same as what he could remember of it.

The yard's grass was a little overgrown, and the house needed a new coat of paint, which, much to his delight, showed the lack of a man's touch. There were two large trees on opposite ends of the yard whose canopy of leaves shielded those standing below from the sun. There was a large window looking into a modest living room, its curtains partially open, as if beckoning him to come and take a look and see what was going on. And built right in front of the house was a tiny brick-walled garden that was blooming with all varieties of flowers, each with their own unique scent, which combined into a mighty superscent he had tracked once he remembered to sniff for it.

A memory hit him like a sugar rush, and it made him feel like smiling; even though the muscles on his face and his dry, cracked lips kept him from doing so on the outside. He slowly closed his eyes and let the recollection come to him.

He remembered how much Peggy had dearly loved flowers. How he had listened to her during one of their very first study sessions, before they took a turn for the romantic, when she had made an offhanded comment about it.

From that day forward, he had made it a point to always have a flower for her when they'd meet up for one of their clandestine dates. Due to his youth and overeagerness, he took it a step further by always having a different one for her in order to go through the process of elimination to discover which one was her absolute favorite.

On the only night they had ever made love, he'd met her in the park near the pool and presented her with a purple lily. He'd given her roses, daisies, tulips, and even an orchid, but none made her eyes light up like that lily had. Why, he never knew. He never had a chance to ask because the world had gone to hell the very next night when he'd been bitten, and he never saw her again with human eyes.

In the handful of years since, on that day's anniversary, he made this dangerous annual journey just to be near her again. To peek through her window and hope for a mere glimpse of her, no matter how fleeting. He'd been lucky once while spying on her to hear her voice while she was talking on the phone in another room. But so far, to his regret, he hadn't been able to see her again, but hearing her voice that time had been enough for him to gather the strength to return to the quarantine zone and wait another year to try again.

Looking left to right to make sure there were no prying eyes along the block watching him, he approached the window, where a flicker of light beamed out through a small curtain opening from the living room inside. As he got closer, he peered in to see a television screen playing an old black-and-white movie. Brian found himself trying to remember the name of it but couldn't quite recall. Yet deep within, he knew that he must have seen it once upon a time because he had been a movie lover in his all-too-brief life and made it a point to see every film he could.

His feet hit something solid, causing him to peer down. The front of his shoe was up against the tiny brick-walled barrier that had been laid around the garden below the window. He realized there was no way to get closer to the window without stepping over the brick barrier and into the garden itself, but he would never dream of doing that and ruining any of the carefully attended flowers.

As he looked down at them, something caught his eye. Among the variety of flowers growing in the small garden, featured prominently were, of all things, purple lilies.

Before he could ponder the sight of them any further, he heard Peggy's voice. His senses, excited and overwhelmed, caused him to rise back up and peer through the curtain opening just as her shadow loomed on a wall near the living room leading from a hallway. If his heart had still been beating, it would have fluttered the moment Peggy entered the living room, looking as beautiful as he remembered despite having more worry lines on her face.

She walked toward the TV and manually shut it off. Then she turned and approached an easy chair, where someone was reclining.

Brian realized he hadn't even noticed someone had been lying back in the chair watching the TV with their legs wrapped in a blanket while propped up on a footrest. But he watched as Peggy leaned down over that person and gently removed a lit cigarette from between their fingers.

Brian extended his body a bit further until he could finally see the reclining person's face and realized it was Peggy's mother who was slumbering. Her mouth was open as she slightly snored while her glasses sat slightly askew on her face.

He heard a bit of sadness in Peggy's voice as she sighed and said, "Mom, I asked you to quit smoking in the house."

Brian watched as Peggy regarded her mother with a paternal shake of her head and lowered herself enough to put out the cigarette in an ashtray on an end table near her mother's chair. When she rose back up, she closed her eyes and rubbed her temples.

Brian looked away. Seeing Peggy sad hurt him in a way he never expected. He found himself wishing there was something he could do to cheer her up. Then as he stared down at her flower garden, a thought of what just might occurred to him.

That's when he heard another voice from somewhere else inside the house. He peered back inside just as Peggy asked over her shoulder, "What is it, baby?"

As Brian watched, a little girl entered the living room while rubbing her eyes with both hands. Her hair was tangled by sleep, her face was red and puffy from crying, and she didn't appear to be in too good of a mood.

Brian stared in amazement at the both of them, stunned and silent. Deep in the recesses of his brain, he knew Peggy must have moved on without him. She had to, and he didn't blame her. But the sight of the little girl hurt him, nonetheless. It was proof to him that life went on, and the past was quickly forgotten by most, no matter how much others didn't want it to.

*****

"What's wrong, sweetie?" Peggy asked, chuckling while she knelt before her four-year-old daughter, Beth, and marveled at the wild mane of hair that made her minidoppelganger resemble a tiny, sleepy, moody lion.

As Peggy tried to tame her daughter's hair in what she soon realized was a losing effort, Beth shook her head and whined while rubbing the sleep from her eyes.

"I had a nightmare."

"Oh, I'm so sorry, baby," Peggy said, a devilish smile forming on her face. "But there's one thing that will make the nightmares go away."

Before Beth could react, Peggy said, "Mommy's kisses," and began kissing her daughter repeatedly all over her face.

All Beth could do in return was twist her head back and forth in a futile effort to evade the kissing assault. But Mommy kept at it until she surrendered and erupted into full-blown laughter.

Suddenly, Peggy's mother groaned and shifted in her chair, causing mother and daughter to quieten themselves immediately. Both of their mouths formed o's as they stared at one another with wide eyes while their faces trembled due to the exertion of trying to keep from laughing out loud.

When Peggy's mother didn't make any further noise or movement, Peggy slowly craned her neck around to look behind her and saw that her mother was still fast asleep. But when she turned back around to face her daughter, her eyes were crossed, and she was making a duck face.

At the sight of this, Beth started laughing again. But the moment was interrupted by the sounds of loud rock music, and a truck engine that grew louder the closer it got to the house.

Peggy and Beth both turned to look through the opening of the living room curtain just as it filled with blinding lights.

While shielding her eyes, Peggy, alarmed, turned to Beth and told her, "Go to your bedroom and lock the door."

But as Peggy placed a hand around her daughter's waist to guide her in the direction of her bedroom, she could feel Beth trembling with fear while not taking her eyes off the window.

Peggy carefully shook her daughter by the waist, getting her attention. "Did you hear me?"

Beth was on the verge of tears, which broke her heart.

Peggy pulled her close and said, "Everything's okay. Just go to your room and lock the door."

Beth nodded into her mother's chest but still wasn't moving.

Peggy pulled away from her daughter and said, "Go to your room, baby, and don't answer it for anyone but me or Grandma. Understand?"

Peggy nodded, and Beth did so in return.

"Now go," Peggy ordered.

Peggy watched as Beth stared toward the window again before turning and leaving the room, but not before glancing back at her.

Peggy put on her best-smiling face and said, "Everything's okay, baby. Just do what Mommy says."

Beth nodded and wiped away a tear brimming in her eye, then did as she was told.

Peggy waited until she heard her daughter's bedroom door click shut before the smile left her face, and she rose up to face the window.

"What's going on?" her mother asked, still half asleep in her chair.

"It's okay, Mom," Peggy told her. "Stay inside."

Peggy glared at the window with a look of anger and determination.

"I'll take care of this."

*****

Peggy stepped from the house while averting her eyes from the harsh glare of the lights coming from the white truck, now parked halfway in her yard. As she walked away from her front door, it slowly and softly shut behind her as she approached the vehicle.

One by one, she noticed her neighbors peering out their windows and looking through partially open doors, yet keeping themselves inside, unwilling to confront the neighborhood visitors.

Peggy stopped before the truck and yelled loud enough to be heard over the rock music blaring from its front cab. When the truck's occupants failed to respond, she yelled at them again. But when she didn't receive a response for the third time, she became furious and kicked the front bumper. When that too didn't lead to a reply, she kicked it again, much harder.

The music lowered, and the driver's door opened. An angry, red-faced, out-of-shape man wearing a Texas Rangers baseball cap, an orange hunting vest over an ill-fitting T-shirt bearing a US flag design, and jeans that hung way too low over his waist stepped out onto the street and pointed at her.

"Hey, lady, quit kickin' my truck!"

"Then get it off my property!" Peggy yelled back.

As the driver walked around to the front of his vehicle, he inspected the front of it very closely for damage. "I swear to God if you so much as put a dent in my—"

"You ain't gonna do shit!" Peggy shouted. "Now back this piece of crap off my yard and get the hell outa here!"

The driver raised up and turned toward her. "Who do you think you're talkin' to, lady?"

"The asshole who scared the hell out of my daughter when this goddamn truck pulled into our yard."

As the driver stepped toward her, Peggy held her ground.

"We're out here riskin' our lives every night, protectin' you from undead fucks," he said while pointing a fat finger at her face. "And this is how you talk to us?"

"No one asked you to do it!" Peggy replied. "You boys just like going around shooting things and getting drunk and being assholes."

The driver stepped toward her with an angry look in his eyes. It was enough to cause a look of concern in Peggy's own. But she still stood firm.

"I've had enough of your mouth, lady," he said, his right hand forming a fist at his side.

Her eyes shifted to a silhouette of a man sitting on the passenger side of the truck, then back to the sweaty driver, who was conflicted while debating his next move. But Peggy showed him no fear.

"Go on," she told him. "Take a swing, asshole."

The driver, caught between backing down in front of his friends or going through with what was on his mind, decided there was no backing down. He took a step toward her and raised his fist just as a shot rang out from the direction of the truck.

This startled Peggy and the driver, who both peered up at the silhouette of a man holding a rifle while standing up in the truck bed.

"You're not layin' a hand on her," the man with the rifle said before lowering the tailgate and jumping down to the street.

As he strutted toward them, the man's face was lit up by the streetlights, and Peggy drew back in surprise. She was caught speechless at the sight of Johnny Hearst, who, despite gaining some weight and losing some of his hair, still hadn't changed much from when he was in high school.

"Hey, Carl," Johnny said to the driver, "why don't you do as the lady said and back your truck off her yard?"

Carl, fuming, stared over at Johnny's profile, not liking what he'd just heard, especially in front of the woman.

But as Peggy watched, a smile broke out on Johnny's face, and he kept eye contact with her.

"You got a problem with that, Carl?" Johnny asked.

It took a few moments, but Carl backed down. With one last disapproving glance at Peggy, he marched back to his truck and climbed inside, then did as he was told.

But after the truck backed off the yard and reparked in the street, the radio volume went back up.

Johnny kept smiling as he looked Peggy up and down and nodded in approval.

"I swear you get more beautiful every day!" he shouted to be heard over the music.

Peggy refused to make eye contact, looking at anything else but him. She rolled her eyes and asked, "Why are you here, Johnny!"

Taken aback, Johnny lost his smile and peered around.

"We had a shambler sighting about six blocks over!" Johnny replied while glancing back over his shoulder at the truck. "So I just wanted to swing by and make sure you and Beth were okay!"

Peggy finally made eye contact with him. It was a look of hatred. "You don't say her name!"

Johnny stepped back in surprise at the venomous glare on her face.

Peggy raised her voice. "You hear me?"

Johnny cleared his throat and glared around. "It still doesn't change the fact that I'm lookin' out for you…and your family!"

"We can do just fine without you!" Peggy replied.

She glared at those in the truck and pointed at them.

"That goes for all of you!"

Johnny stared down at the ground and shook his head. "All I'm doin' is lookin' out for you, Peggy! Like I always have!"

Peggy backed away from him. An overwhelmed look forming on her face.

"Are you serious?" she asked, shaking her head in disbelief. "All you ever did was make my life a living hell!"

"How could you say that to me?" he asked, staring at her in disbelief of his own. "All I ever did was love you!"

"The only person you ever loved was yourself!"

Johnny shook his head again, unsure of what to say.

"Love isn't treating someone like property!" Peggy said. "Love is selfless! Love is kind! Love is…something you're not capable of!"

Johnny seemed to be on the verge of tears, but after lowering his head, his face suddenly changed, and he glared up at her. Gone was any sense of sadness, regret, or warmth.

"Did the love of your life show you all that?" Johnny asked with a wide smile. He faked peering around and acted surprised when he didn't see anyone else close by. "So where is he now? 'Cause I don't see him!"

As a tear fell down her cheek, Peggy grimaced at him. "Get back in your truck and leave!"

As Johnny backed away from her, he laughed. "One of these days, Peggy, you're gonna regret this!"

Peggy stared back at him in silence as another man extended his arm to help him step up onto the back of the truck.

Johnny walked across the bed toward the cab and smiled back at her. "And you're gonna wish you hadn't said the things you said tonight!"

He knocked on the roof of the cab, and the engine revved. The truck spun its back tires and left a plume of putrid smoke behind as it took off down the street. The rock music soon faded with it.

Peggy stood on her lawn, staring at the glow of the truck's taillights as it drove farther away. Then she noticed her curious neighbors still looking at her from the safety of their own homes.

Peggy shook her head, raised her arm, and extended a middle finger. She directed it at all the people in their houses along the block, making sure they all knew who it was intended for, before turning and walking along the sidewalk toward her front door.

When she reached it, she saw something lying on the welcome mat. She knelt and looked closer, then reached out and picked it up.

It was a purple lily.

A smile came to her face as she stared at it in wonder. Then, just as quickly, a troubling thought wiped out her smile.

*****

As Brian ambled down a dark alley with a hurried, lurching gait, he felt a sense of contentment wash over him. He had finally seen Peggy once more. But as images of her drifted through his mind, he kicked a metal can lying on the ground, which was loud enough to cause a dog nearby to start barking.

Other dogs soon joined that one, just as Brian saw a gray SUV pass by the alley on the intersecting street ahead and heard its brakes squealing as it skidded to a stop.

When he saw the glow from the SUV's reverse lights growing on the street as it backed up, he shuffled toward a dumpster a few yards away and lowered himself behind it just as the vehicle came into view.

He heard the SUV roll to a stop, a door open, and someone running around the vehicle while whisper-calling his name.

Not believing his ears, Brian was tempted to take a peek over the top of the dumpster, but he willed himself not to move. But the next time he heard his name being shouted, he recognized the voice.

Her voice.

It was Peggy.

Brian slowly raised up behind the dumpster and saw her standing at the alley entrance. She saw him and stepped forward, but when he stood up enough for her to see him fully, she stopped in her tracks and lost her smile.

His heart sank as he stepped out from behind the dumpster and saw the color drain from her face while she stepped back in fear, putting her arms up to shield herself.

He stood still as tears fell down her face while she placed a hand on the trunk of her car to hold herself up. She covered her face with her other hand and sobbed.

Brian stood quiet and still in the alley. He could smell her from where he was. But while it caused immense pain to flare throughout his body, he never once thought about harming her, as the mere sight of him was hurting her right now.

When Peggy finally managed to look up at him, he held up his palms toward her and shook his head while taking a few steps back.

She surprised herself by taking a step toward him, only to watch him back away further. A hint of a smile came to her face, and the fear in her eyes started to recede.

She raised her palms to him and asked, "You're not going to hurt me?"

Brian stepped forward a little, wanting more than anything to go to her, but he held back and simply shook his head.

Peggy smiled and asked, "You can understand me?"

Brian nodded in reply.

Peggy's smile grew wider, then she remembered something and started searching her pockets in haste.

While Brian watched her, she removed her hand from her jacket pocket and raised it to show him the purple lily he had left on her welcome mat.

"Did you leave this for me?" she asked, her eyes filling with tears.

Brian nodded, and she started crying. Then she laughed through her tears and wiped them away.

"Just like all the other flowers these past few years?"

Brian nodded again, and she broke out into full-blown laughter.

"I knew it," she said, kicking the ground and pumping her fists. "I knew it was you."

Brian wanted to walk toward her but didn't move.

"I just never knew why you didn't come to me," she added, looking him up and down. "But now I do."

Brian didn't know what to do, so he just stared at her and remained quiet.

"All this time, and I didn't even know," she said, wiping her face in disbelief.

They heard the loud rock music before the rumbling engine.

Panic set in as they both looked up and saw the sky lighting up a few neighborhoods over.

Peggy looked back at Brian and waved for him to come to her.

At first, he didn't move until she motioned for him again.

"Come on," she said, an urgent tone in her voice.

He slowly started walking toward her car as she ran and grabbed the keys from the ignition. She turned and flicked through the keys on the ring as she trotted back toward the trunk.

There, she stopped and glanced back over her shoulder to see if the lights from the truck were getting closer or farther away and couldn't tell.

With shaky hands, she somehow managed to pop the trunk open. But she shrieked when she turned and saw Brian standing only a few yards away.

When he didn't move toward her, she relaxed and apologized and tried to calm down. She soon realized, after he stepped into the light and she could now see him fully, that even though his body was decayed and covered in lesions and boils, she could still see and feel him in there, somewhere.

The rock music grew louder behind them, and she snapped out of her funk and pointed toward the trunk.

"Get in!" she said.

Brian glanced from her to the trunk, then back toward the neighborhood where the truck was driving.

"Get in, Brian," she said. "So I can get you somewhere safe."

Brian looked back at the trunk and understood. She knew he didn't want to hurt her, but that trust only went so far. He didn't blame her. She had too much to live for.

"Please, Brian, we haven't got much time."

As he stared into her eyes, she pleaded with them.

"Please," she said.

She reached out and touched his hand, causing him to step back on reflex, which frightened her and caused her to jerk her hand away as well. But one look into his eyes again caused her to reach back and slowly place her hand on his again.

"Let me do this for you," she said, "and our daughter."

Brian stumbled back, stunned at the knowledge. His mind swimming in emotion. He opened his mouth to say something, but only a groan emerged.

Peggy nodded, tears in her eyes. "Her name is Beth, and you'd be so proud of her."

Brian nodded that he was. He struggled to raise his other hand but finally managed to hold her hand with both of his.

He could feel her trembling with fear. Her eyes darting back and forth from his hands to his face in case he made any sudden moves. He also felt the pangs of hunger, making his insides feel like an exposed nerve in a tooth. But he willed those feelings away and started walking toward the trunk.

She backed away to a safe distance as he stepped before the trunk and tried to lift his leg to get inside. When he couldn't, Peggy heard the music getting louder and decided to help him.

She aided him in lifting his leg high enough to get it inside the trunk and watched as he bent low enough to crawl inside. She then helped him lift his other leg off the ground and into the trunk.

As she peered down at him in the trunk with one arm behind him and his legs at awkward angles from the rest of his body, she winced and said, "I'm sorry," before shutting the trunk and enclosing him in darkness.

*****

When Peggy opened the trunk again, Brian was still in the same awkward position, staring up at her as if he were a helpless turtle lying on its shell, not able to turn over.

It took a while, but she eventually helped him out of the trunk, and that's the moment he realized he was just outside the fence of the quarantine zone.

But as he gazed into her eyes, a bullet hit his right shoulder and exited out his back, followed by a loud report.

As Brian fell, he turned and saw that Peggy had stumbled back in shock and fell to the ground with blood spatter on her face. His blood.

He reached out to her in a hopeless effort to hold her and keep her safe, but she was too far away.

While Peggy turned to him, another bullet pierced his chest and knocked him flat to the ground, raising dust below. She screamed and scrambled on her hands and knees toward him to throw her body across his in order to shield him.

She rolled over while covering him and held up her hands in surrender while screaming, "No!"

After the echo of her voice sounded in the air, no more shots came. In the moments of silence that followed, she rose up and helped him off the ground.

"Get inside the fence!" she shouted, while Brian stared back at her in shock. "Go!"

While helping Brian move toward the opening in the fence, she used her body to shield him. Another bullet hit the ground at her feet, causing her to jump, startled, but she quickly realized it was just a way to get her to run and leave Brian unprotected.

"You think that's gonna scare me?" she shouted toward the buildings.

As Brian made it to the opening in the fence and slipped inside, Peggy glanced back and saw that Brian was now standing inside the quarantine zone, while the other undead emerged out of the shadows behind him, drawn by the gunfire and her presence.

She grinned at Brian, and he raised his hand to give her a slight wave when they both heard a truck engine coming around a corner, its lights flooding the area.

The truck pulled to a stop behind Peggy's car, and the men within it and in the back stared down at her. But at the sight of the shamblers approaching the fence like a slow-moving, undead army, they drew their weapons and aimed.

Peggy backed toward the opening and raised her arms.

"They're in the quarantine zone," she declared. "They're safe as long as they're inside."

The men in the truck kept their weapons aimed at the undead beings while Johnny jumped over the side of the truck, where he effortlessly landed and approached Peggy.

"The hell are you doin' here?" he asked before seeing the blood on her face and clothes. A worried look crossed his face, and he reached for her. "Have you been shot?"

"No," she replied, slapping his hand away. "I'm fine."

He grimaced at the stinging sensation in his hand that hurt far less than his pride. "Then answer my question. What are you doing here?"

As she stood there, trying to come up with a reason, she glanced back at Brian, who was moments away from being joined by the other undead at the fence.

Johnny followed her gaze and saw the shambler, who was standing there staring back at him.

"What the fuck?" Johnny said, raising his rifle and aiming it at Brian. "What are you lookin' at, asshole?"

As Brian remained stoic, staring him down, it soon dawned on Johnny who it was.

"Holy shit," Johnny said, cackling in disbelief. "It's you."

Peggy stepped beside Johnny. "Leave him alone."

"Who?" Johnny replied, not taking his eyes off Brian. "Your old boyfriend?"

"He's safe inside," Peggy replied. "You can't touch him."

Johnny leaned toward her and smiled. "Who's gonna stop me?"

As he turned back to Brian, he closed one eye, lined up his sights, placed his finger on the trigger, and squeezed. But Peggy jumped on his back, and the shot went wild.

The other men in the truck heard the shot and opened fire on the undead approaching them from inside the fence.

As bullets fired all around Brian, Peggy screamed for him to run.

Brian wanted desperately to go to her to help her, but a bullet hit him in the leg, and another went through his chest, causing him to back away. He turned and started walking toward the darkness beyond the truck lights.

He soon passed his fellow undead, who were drawn past him toward the humans like moths to a flame. Most were taking bullets to their bodies but still kept trudging forward on mindless autopilot, drawn by the scent of human flesh, and the blood pumping beneath.

Only those who suffered direct shots to the head fell lifeless to the ground.

*****

Peggy clung onto Johnny's back like a professional bronco rider as he tried his best to get her off him. In anger, she raked her fingernails across his eyes, trying to inflict as much damage as she could.

Johnny screamed in agony, but at the same time, his adrenaline spiked. It gave him enough strength to lean over, and the momentum flipped her to the ground, where she landed roughly on her back.

His face was bleeding, and he could barely see through the blood and the damage she had done to his eyes. But in his fury, he could see well enough to aim his rifle down at her.

When she saw the look in his eyes and his finger on the trigger, she raised her hands in front of her face and slammed her eyes shut.

But when nothing happened, she slowly opened her eyes and stared up at him.

With blood dripping from his face, he glared down at her with his finger squeezing the trigger, but not with enough pressure to fire.

Peggy stopped shaking, lowered her hands, and glared up at him.

Johnny shook his head, tears mixing with the blood on his face.

One of his team shouted, "Hey, man! Look out!"

Johnny glanced over toward the fence. Even with his vision obscured, he saw that a shambler had reached the opening and was about to climb through.

Johnny aimed at its head and fired.

As a dark mist shot out of the back of the creature's head, its head snapped back, and its body fell to the ground.

Johnny took aim at another close to the fence and fired again, taking it down.

With a glance back at Peggy, still on the ground, Johnny sneered. "I hope you said goodbye to your boyfriend."

Peggy's eyes widened as Johnny turned back toward the fence, took aim at another creature, fired, then ran inside the quarantine zone.

Peggy rolled over on her side and screamed, "Look out, Brian! He's coming!"

That's when she saw more undead beings reaching the fence. In their bloodlust, they battled each other to get through the opening.

She stood up, ran to her car, got inside, and locked herself in.

*****

Johnny ran through the quarantine zone toward the darkness, taking aim at any shambler that got too close, all the while yelling various forms of, "Oh, Brian! I'm coming to get you!"

When he reached the darkness, he came to a stop and began peering around as best he could. The lack of light and the damage to his eyes made it near impossible for him to see anything, so he tried being as quiet as possible so he could listen for any sounds around him.

The only ones he could hear were the distant pops of gunfire, his own loud breathing, and his footsteps as he nervously shuffled in place on the dirt.

He wiped his eyes to clear away some of the blood. But as he glanced toward the lights of the truck, it caused a strobe effect that made it seem as if he were looking through a kaleidoscope.

"Fucking bitch," he muttered, blinking rapidly to clear his vision before hearing movement to his left, causing him to open fire in that direction with a short burst.

When he didn't hear any further sound from that direction, he turned and was grabbed by the arm. As Johnny screamed, Brian bit down on his forearm.

Johnny managed to rip his arm away from Brian's mouth and swung the butt of his rifle at him. The stock connected with Brian's chest and knocked him to the ground. Johnny swung his rifle around and aimed down at Brian, who was now staring up at him.

When he saw Brian lying there, helpless, he couldn't help but start laughing.

"Brian the Brain," Johnny said, enjoying the moment. "You ain't so smart now, are ya?"

Johnny squinted and tried to take as good a look as he could. Amazed and repulsed by what he saw.

"How does it feel to be dead?" Johnny asked.

All Brian could do was stare up at him with hate in his milky white eyes.

"What's a matter? Cat got your tongue?"

Johnny started laughing again. He couldn't help himself. But the smile soon left his face as he stepped even closer. He placed the barrel a few inches from Brian's face and sneered down at him.

"Just know," Johnny said, "that one of these days, Peggy's gonna be mine. She's not gonna have a choice. 'Cause I always get what I want. Always."

Lying prostrate and disadvantaged, Brian grimaced, feeling the rage rising within. But he was frustrated at not being able to do anything about it.

"I'll be sure to give her your goodbyes."

Just as Johnny was about to squeeze the trigger, an undead being emerged out of the darkness and snapped at his face.

Johnny screamed and stumbled away before the being could bite him. Once he found his balance, he took aim and fired. But as that creature fell, more of them appeared out of the darkness, surging toward him from nearly every direction.

Johnny saw how many were closing in and considered taking them all out. But there were way too many of them, and deep down he knew it wasn't worth taking that chance. Having no choice, he turned and ran toward the lights of the vehicle beyond the fence as fast as he could, stumbling and barely able to maintain his balance as he did.

When he reached the fence, he pulled himself through and was greeted by his team with slaps on the back and laughter.

"Did you get 'em?" a large bearded man wearing full-body camouflage named Bobby asked, giddy and hyped up on adrenaline as he rubbed his sweaty palms together.

Johnny stared across at Peggy's car as the door opened, and she stepped out and glared at him.

"Yeah," Johnny nodded. "I got him real good."

He took no satisfaction in watching as Peggy's face crumbled before him, and she began fighting back tears. But he covered his feelings with a forced smile and glanced away before she could tell he felt lost.

"Come on, guys," Bobby said. "Let's get outa here before the cops get here."

Johnny wanted desperately to talk to Peggy, to say something, anything, but found he didn't have the guts to face her. All he could do now was follow after the others.

"Hey, what the hell is that?" Carl asked.

Johnny returned to the moment, after being lost in his own head, to find the other men standing before him like a wall. Gone was any hint of a smile or friendliness. Instead, they were glaring at him with alarm and fear.

Johnny stared back at them in confusion. "What?"

"That?" Bobby pointed at Johnny's arm. "On your arm."

As Johnny looked down, he suddenly realized he'd been bitten.

At that moment, he remembered who did it, and the anger within him began to swell.

"Did you get bit?" Carl asked.

"Whoa, guys," Johnny said, raising his hands in the air and backing away. "I just cut myself on the fence, that's all."

"I don't know, man," Bobby said, squinting to take a better look while shaking his head. "That looks like a bite to me."

"Hey, come on," Johnny replied, concern rising in his voice. "If I told you it's a scratch from a fence, it's a scratch from a fence."

Bobby said, "Then let us see for ourselves."

"Yeah," another guy named Steve agreed. He was a skinny guy with a childish face and nervous, twitchy eyes, looking much too young for his age and far too unstable to be trusted with a weapon.

Bobby stepped forward. With a menacing tone, he said, "Take off your jacket."

"Are you kidding me?" Johnny asked, peering at them. He hoped his best smile would put them at ease, and they could move on as if nothing happened.

Bobby's hand moved to hover over a SIG Sauer in a leg holster. "I ain't kiddin'."

As Johnny watched, one by one, his friends' hands reached for their weapons.

Realizing he had no choice but to do what they said, fear came through in his voice.

"Hey, come on, guys," he said. "It's me. I started this group. Without me, none of you would have had the balls to do any of it."

"I'm gonna ask you one more time," Bobby said. "Take off your goddamn jacket."

Johnny, breathing heavily, trembling, knew that if he did as they asked, he was a dead man. So, with his mind gears turning, he nodded his head in agreement and smiled.

"Okay, I'll do it," Johnny said, shaking his head. "But just know there are consequences to your actions."

As Johnny began taking his jacket off, he saw Bobby relax and glance away for a split second. Like a cobra, Johnny struck, swinging with all his might and clocking him in the face, stunning him and knocking him back into the arms of two of the others.

Before the group could react, Johnny turned and ran. But as he saw Peggy standing outside her car, something clicked in his brain.

Now knowing what he had to do, knowing it was insane and unforgivable, he changed course and ran toward her.

As Johnny's team members aimed their weapons, Johnny was fixated on Peggy while reaching for the Ruger in his shoulder holster.

He yanked it out and aimed it at her while yelling her name, thinking if he couldn't have her, no one would.

Peggy saw him rushing toward her and had a moment of disbelief, which slowed her actions. But once she saw the look in his eyes, one of anguish and desperation, she knew what was coming.

She tried to turn away and shield herself with her hands, knowing it wouldn't do any good, but it was all she could think to do.

That's when a bullet fired from the direction of one of the nearly abandoned buildings entered Johnny's left eye and exited the back of his head, along with some of his brain and skull. His lifeless body hit the ground and skidded to a stop near Peggy's feet, and all she could do was stare down in shock.

As the other members of Johnny's team scuttled like cockroaches to hide behind their truck, the sniper waited a few seconds, then took another shot and blew out one of its swamp lights, followed by another shot that took out a headlight.

The remainder of the team obeyed the message the sniper was sending by scrambling to get into the truck.

However, Carl stayed hidden and shouted over the hood, "Stop shooting my truck!"

His team began yelling at him to get in, but Carl was too scared to move out into the open. But the pressure of the name-calling got to him, forcing him to throw his rifle down, raise his arms, and run around the front of the truck, taking a glance at the broken headlight as he ran by.

He climbed into the truck, started it up, and shifted the gears. The truck raised a cloud of dust as it tore away from the area and disappeared into the night.

Peggy raised her arms, glanced back at the building, and shouted, "Thank you!" before hearing something move from inside the fence.

She turned and gasped as she saw Brian emerging out of the darkness and stopping behind the barrier. He gazed out at her and tried to smile but still wasn't succeeding at it.

Peggy sighed in relief. "I thought you were dead." Then, after realizing what she said, she shrugged. "You know what I mean."

She approached the fence and stood before him as he raised his better arm and clasped the fence with his hand. She reached out, hesitant, and touched it.

Brian closed his eyes and took this feeling in, hoping it would stay in his memories above all the others he had of her.

When he opened them, she smiled and said, "How about next year, I come see you."

*****

Brian stood in the quarantine zone staring up at the sky. It was another spring day. Not too hot and not too cold.

As the wind carried past him, he caught a scent in the air. He gazed down and looked for the source. He found himself staring past the fence to where a few people were gathered.

He saw a family laying down a bouquet of flowers near the fence line for a missing loved one. Soon afterward, they lowered their heads and began praying.

The sound of tires crunching on gravel drew his attention away from them, and he glanced over just as a gray SUV came to a stop.

The driver's door opened, and Peggy stepped out wearing a pretty purple dress, matching shoes, and a sunhat. She waved at him and walked to the back passenger door and opened it. She knelt out of sight for a few moments, then raised back up and began walking around the back of the car.

When she came back into full view, Brian saw that she was holding hands with Beth, who was wearing a pretty little dress and hat of her own, while hiding her free hand behind her back.

Mother and daughter approached the fence line and stood before it. Peggy glanced down at Beth and knelt beside her. She whispered something into her daughter's ear, and the little girl peered up at Brian with a nervous grin on her face.

All Brian could think to do was raise his arm and give Beth a tiny wave, but he didn't dare step any closer. The last thing he wanted to do was scare her.

While Peggy watched with tears in her eyes, Beth smiled and raised her hand.

There, held delicately in her grasp, was a purple lily.

A present for her father.

ACKNOWLEDGMENTS

I cannot express enough thanks and appreciation to my family for their continued support and encouragement. They mean the world to me. Without them, this book would not have been possible.

In particular, I want to thank Bridget Hollowell, my oldest niece and most faithful reader. She's usually the first person to read anything I write and always gives me her honest opinion. It means the world to me to know that she's in my corner.

I want to give my sincerest thanks to my friends: Rusty Edwards for spending a lot of his free time creating his magnificent illustrations; Billy Pon for his guidance and invaluable help along the way; Chet Cooper, Corey Aven, Robert Capen, and Michael Shields for always being there; Ryan Clapp for being the truest kind of friend you could ask for; and Bill Oberst Jr. for his time and recommendation.

Special shout-outs to Ashley Cox for her invaluable proofreading skills, and the peace of mind that instills inside an author's mind, and Nicole Reefer of Page Publishing for her help and guidance along the way.

Finally, to my mom, Vera Verene, and my grandparents, C. L. and Zoe. I know you are all no longer with us in person but will always be with us in spirit. I hope I've made you all proud, and I look forward to the time when we see each other again. Hopefully, we'll have some great stories to tell one another.

Aaron Ray Ballard
March 2021

ABOUT THE AUTHOR

Born and raised in West Texas in 1969, Aaron Ray Ballard spent a little over two decades in the mad, mad world of advertising and has been working at a TV news station since 2014, telling other people's stories by making commercials and PSAs for their businesses and nonprofits. But ever since he was captivated by his very first episode of *The Twilight Zone* as an impressionable kid, he's wanted to be a storyteller, whether it's writing short stories, screenplays, or making films, much like his literary heroes—Stephen King, Rod Serling, and Richard Matheson. This is his first book.

He is single, has no children, and writes horror fiction in his spare time, so something is obviously wrong with him.

CPSIA information can be obtained
at www.ICGtesting.com
Printed in the USA
LVHW100819181122
733278LV00009B/202